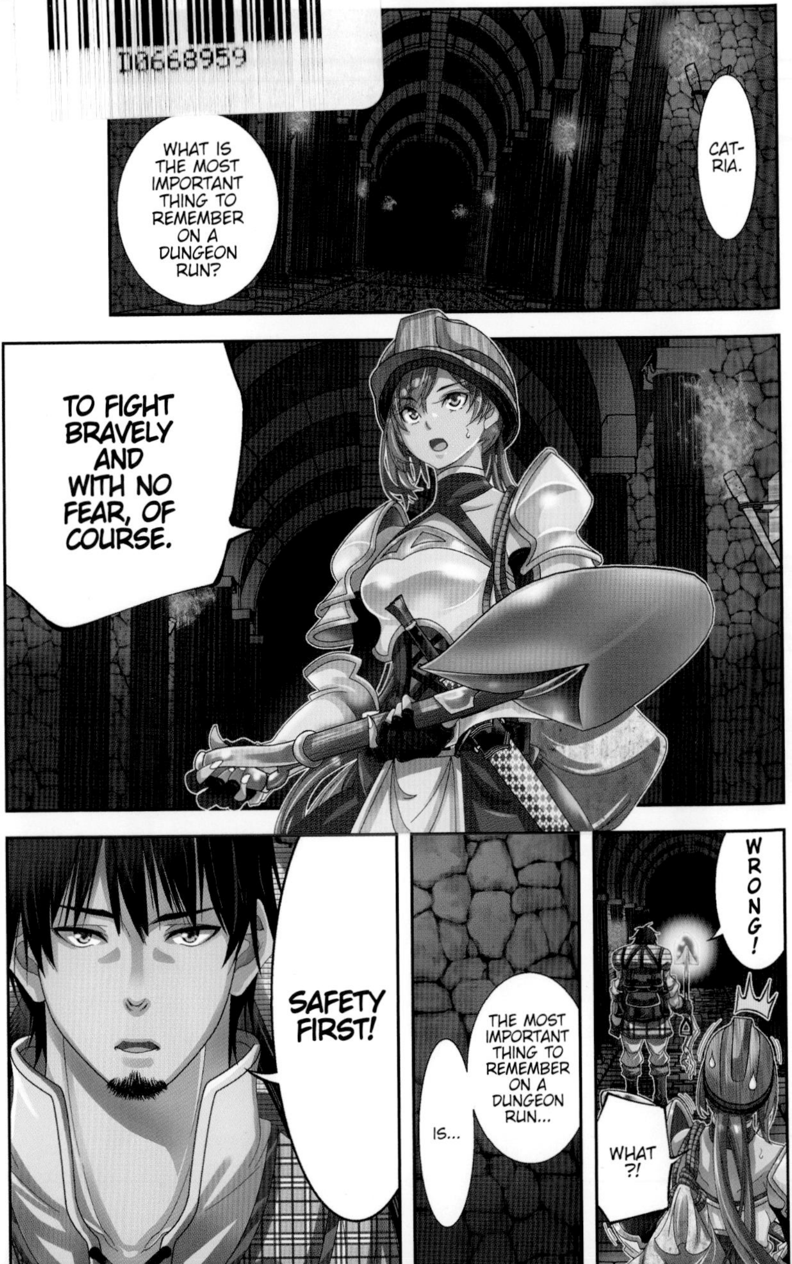
CAT-RIA.
WHAT IS THE MOST IMPORTANT THING TO REMEMBER ON A DUNGEON RUN?
TO FIGHT BRAVELY AND WITH NO FEAR, OF COURSE.
WRONG!
WHAT ?!
THE MOST IMPORTANT THING TO REMEMBER ON A DUNGEON RUN...
IS...
SAFETY FIRST!

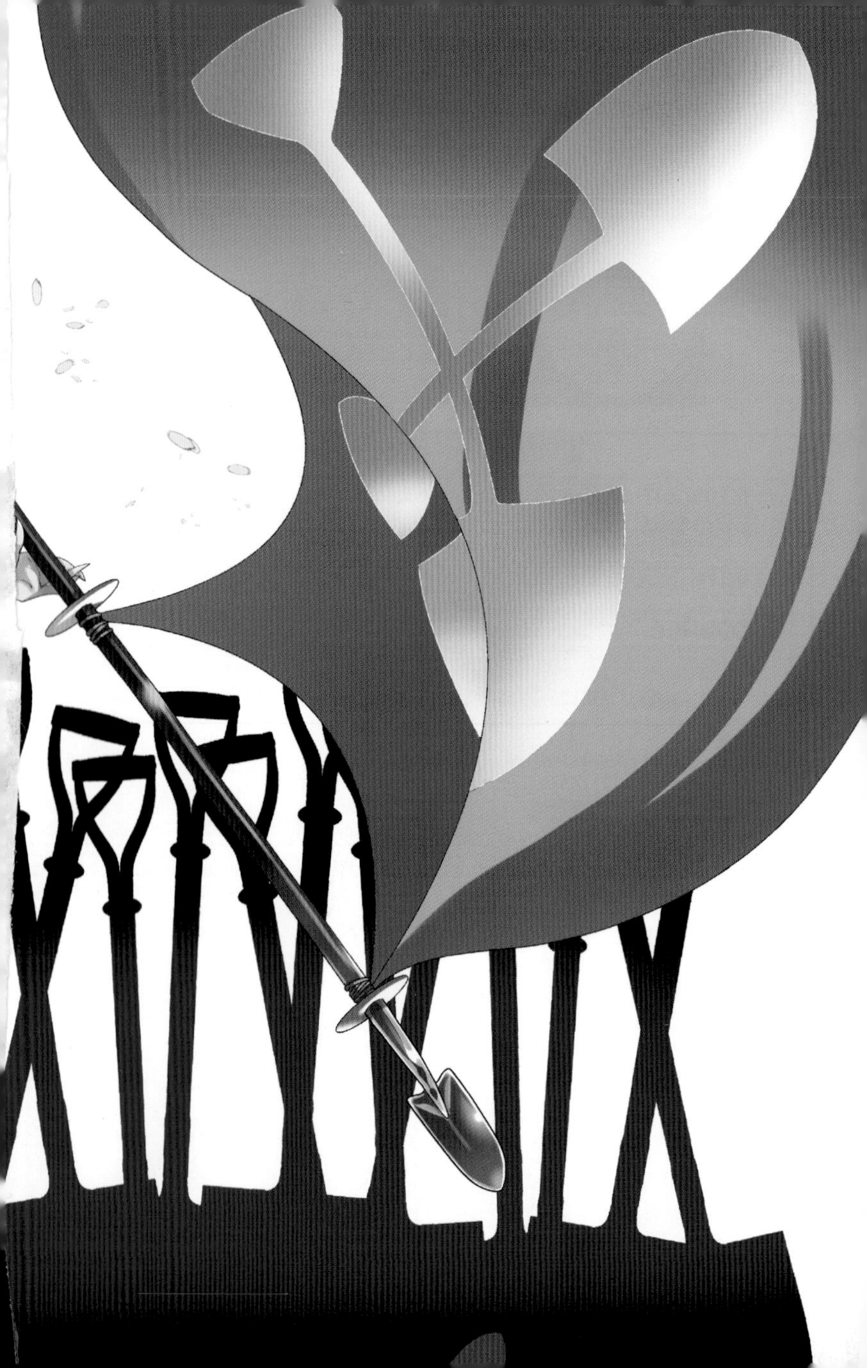

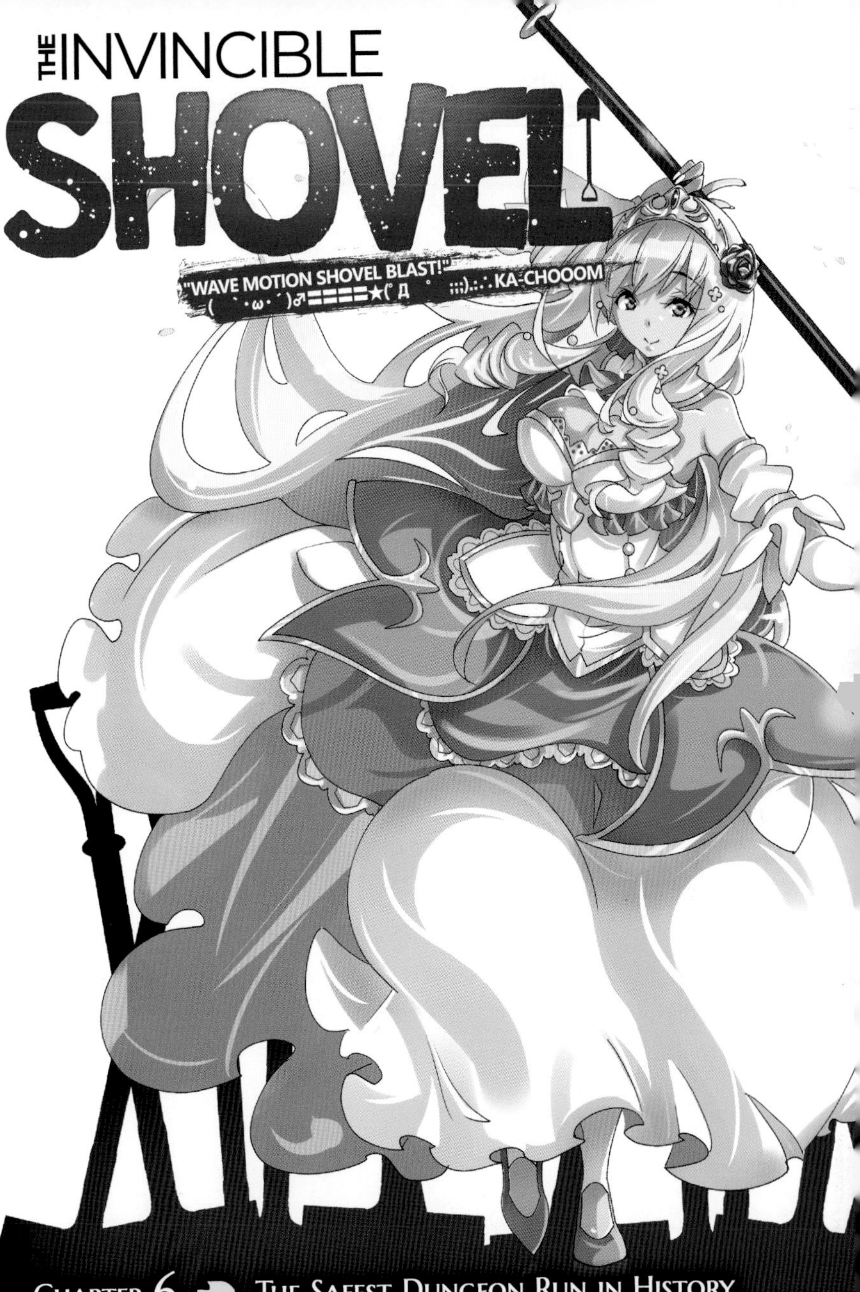
THE INVINCIBLE SHOVEL
"WAVE MOTION SHOVEL BLAST!"
=(　`･ω･´)♂=====★(ﾟД ﾟ ;;;).:∴.KA-CHOOOM

Chapter 6 ➔ The Safest Dungeon Run in History

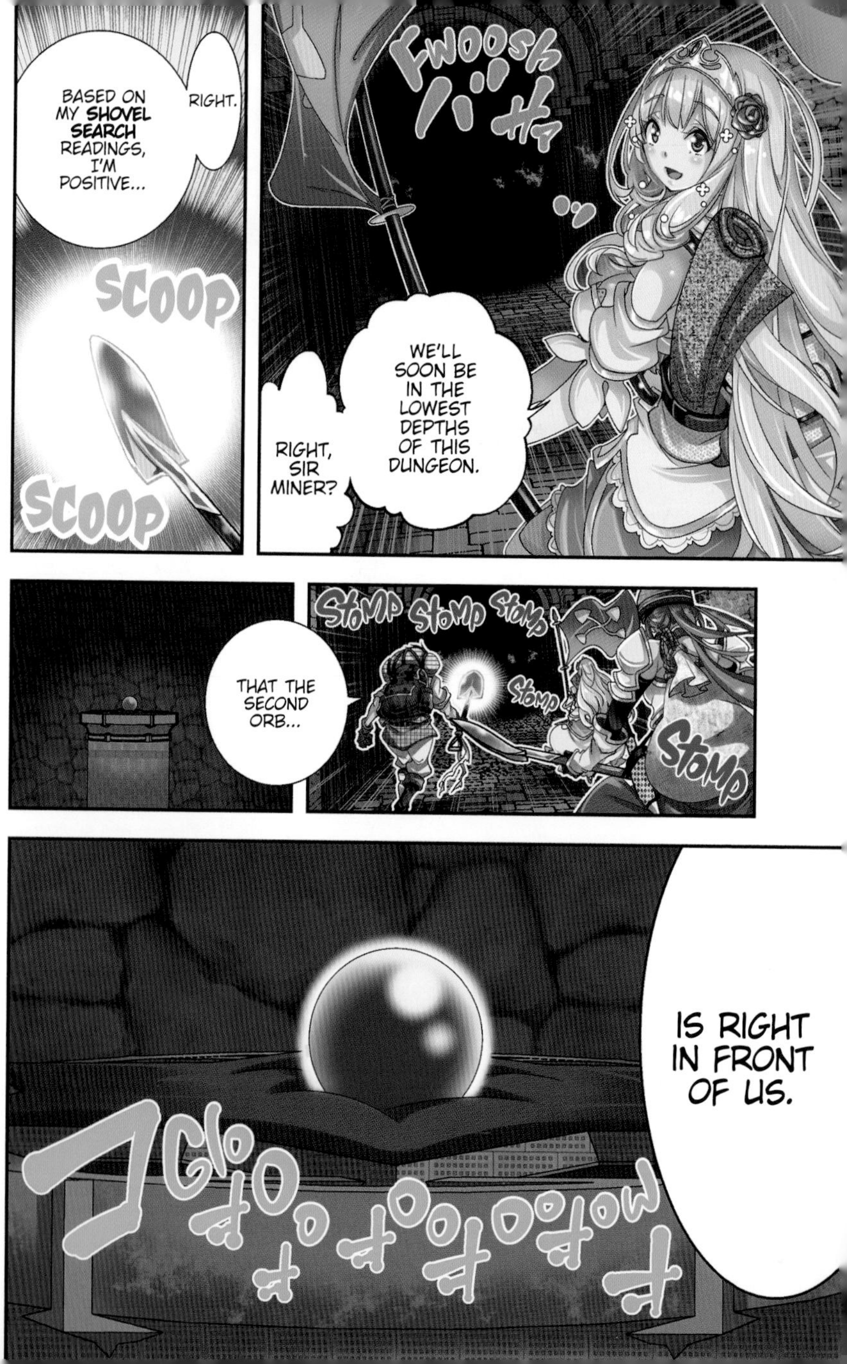

FWOOSH
WE'LL SOON BE IN THE LOWEST DEPTHS OF THIS DUNGEON.
RIGHT, SIR MINER?
RIGHT.
BASED ON MY **SHOVEL SEARCH** READINGS, I'M POSITIVE...
SCOOP
SCOOP
STOMP STOMP STOMP
THAT THE SECOND ORB...
STOMP
STOMP
IS RIGHT IN FRONT OF US.
GLOOOOOOOOOW

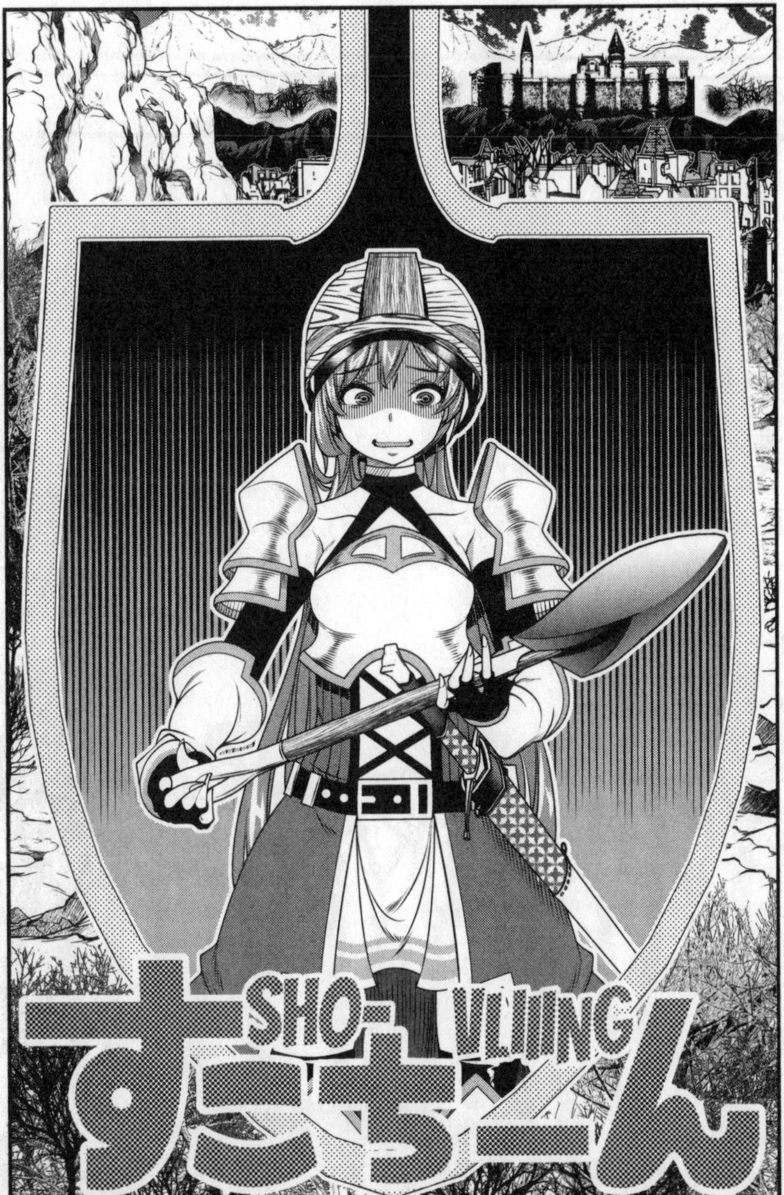
SHO-VLIING

CONTENTS

DESIGN: YUUKO MUCADEYA + HIDEYUKI UEKUSA (MUSICAGO GRAPHICS)

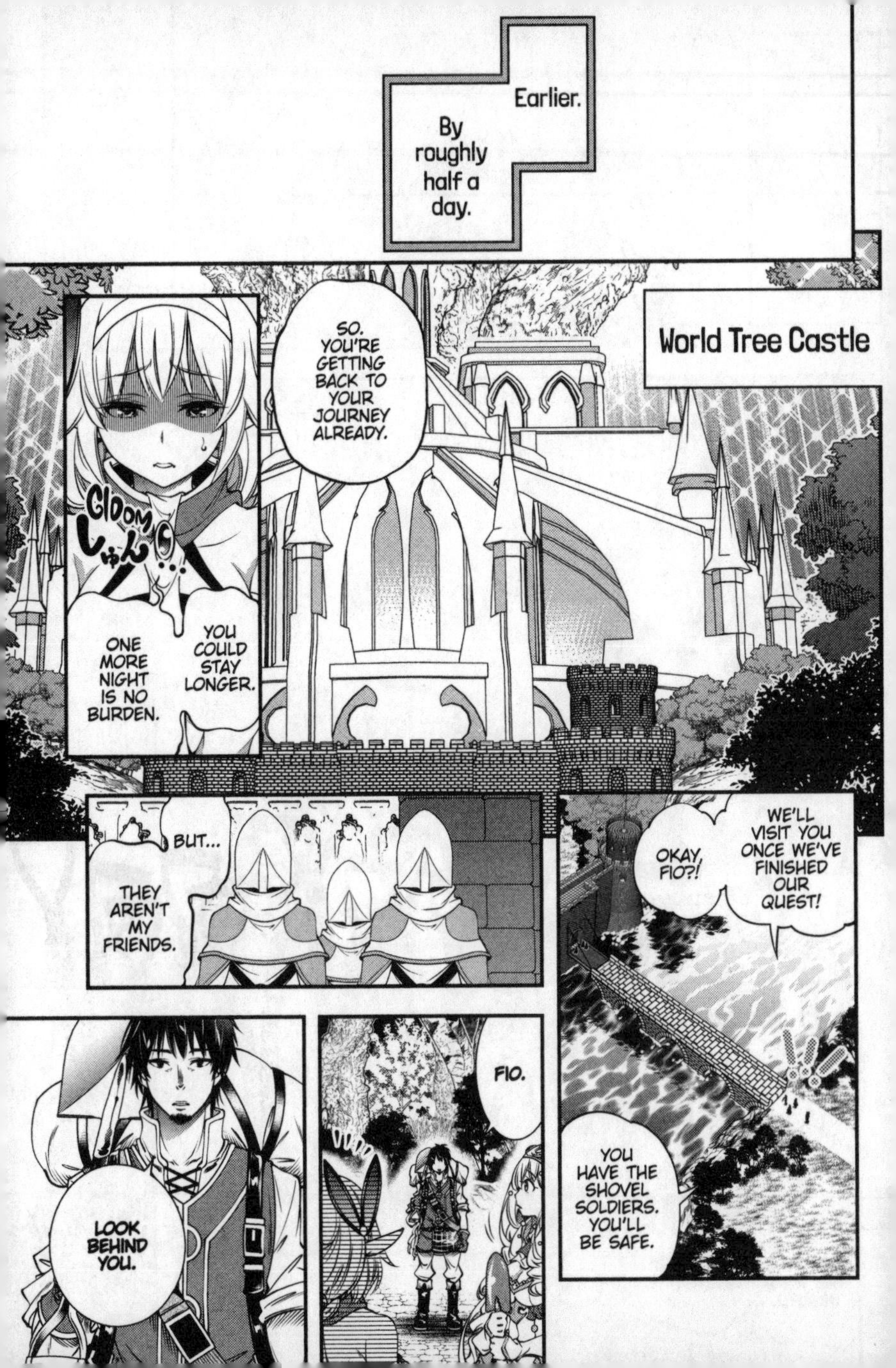
Earlier.
By roughly half a day.
World Tree Castle
SO. YOU'RE GETTING BACK TO YOUR JOURNEY ALREADY.
GLOOM
しゅん...
YOU COULD STAY LONGER.
ONE MORE NIGHT IS NO BURDEN.
WE'LL VISIT YOU ONCE WE'VE FINISHED OUR QUEST!
OKAY, FIO?!
YOU HAVE THE SHOVEL SOLDIERS. YOU'LL BE SAFE.
BUT...
THEY AREN'T MY FRIENDS.
FIO.
LOOK BEHIND YOU.

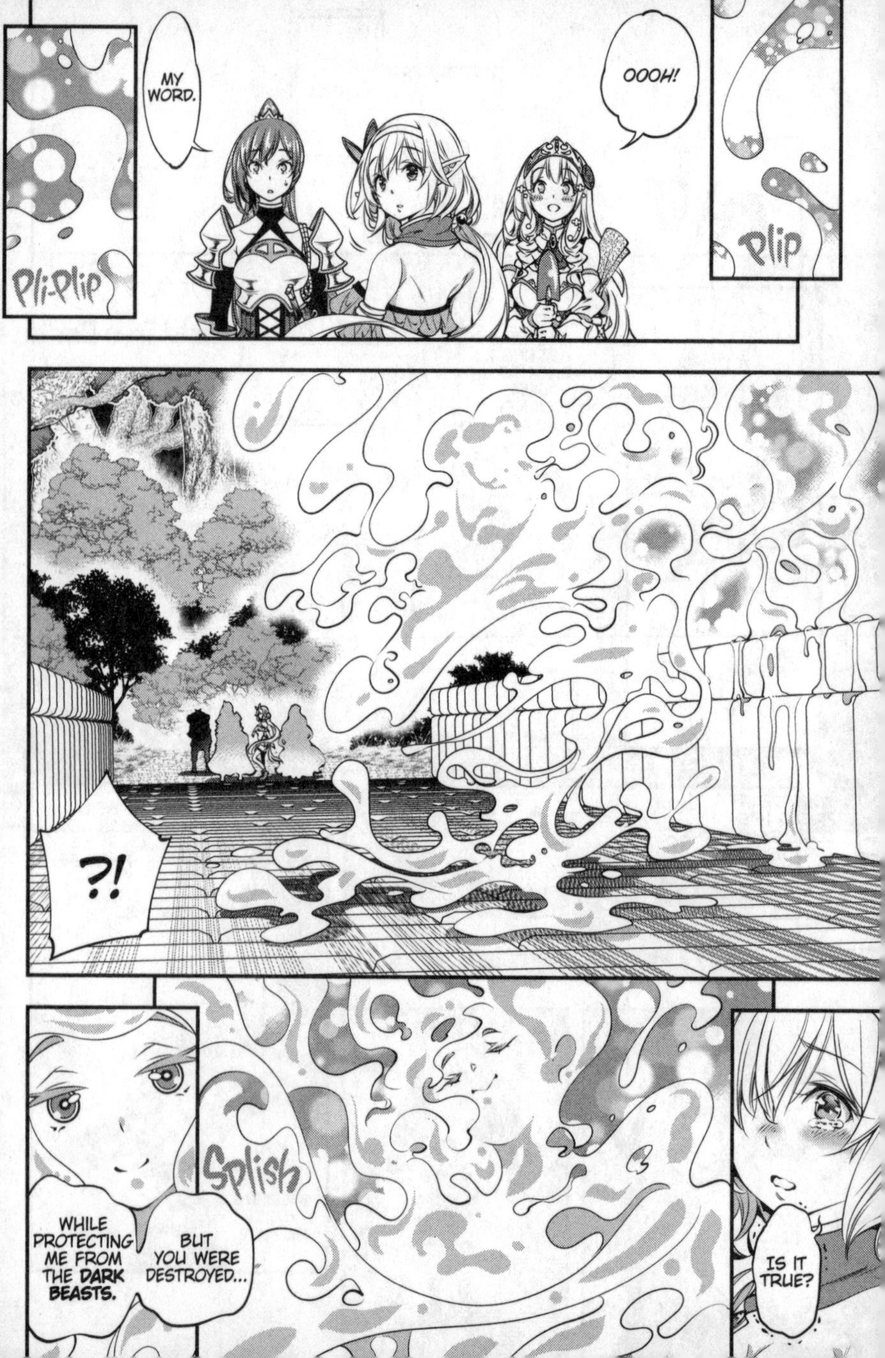
Plip
OOOH!
MY WORD.
Pli-Plip
?!
IS IT TRUE?
Splish
BUT YOU WERE DESTROYED...
WHILE PROTECTING ME FROM THE DARK BEASTS.

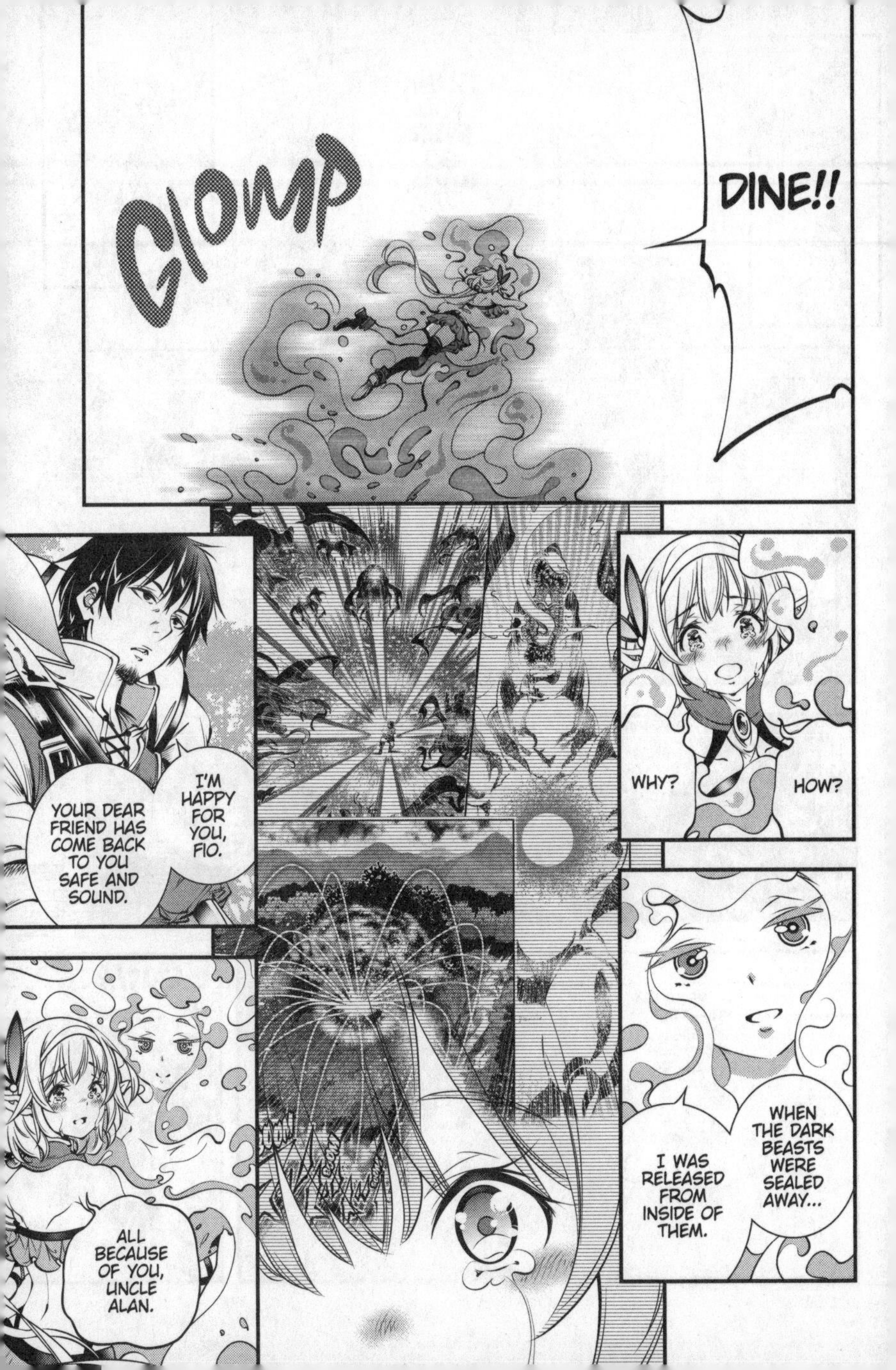
DINE!!
GLOMP
HOW?
WHY?
WHEN THE DARK BEASTS WERE SEALED AWAY...
I WAS RELEASED FROM INSIDE OF THEM.
I'M HAPPY FOR YOU, FIO.
YOUR DEAR FRIEND HAS COME BACK TO YOU SAFE AND SOUND.
ALL BECAUSE OF YOU, UNCLE ALAN.

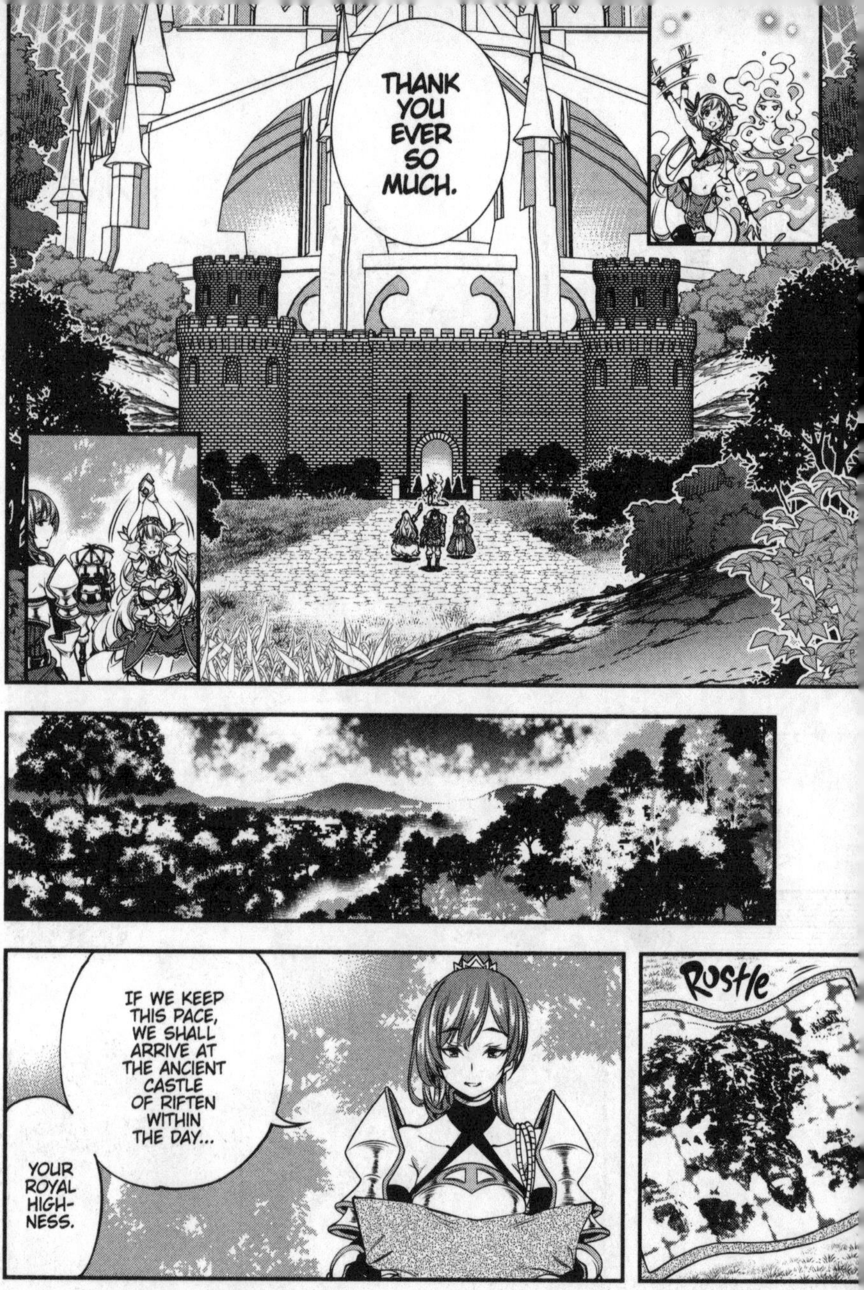
THANK YOU EVER SO MUCH.
Rustle
IF WE KEEP THIS PACE, WE SHALL ARRIVE AT THE ANCIENT CASTLE OF RIFTEN WITHIN THE DAY...
YOUR ROYAL HIGH-NESS.

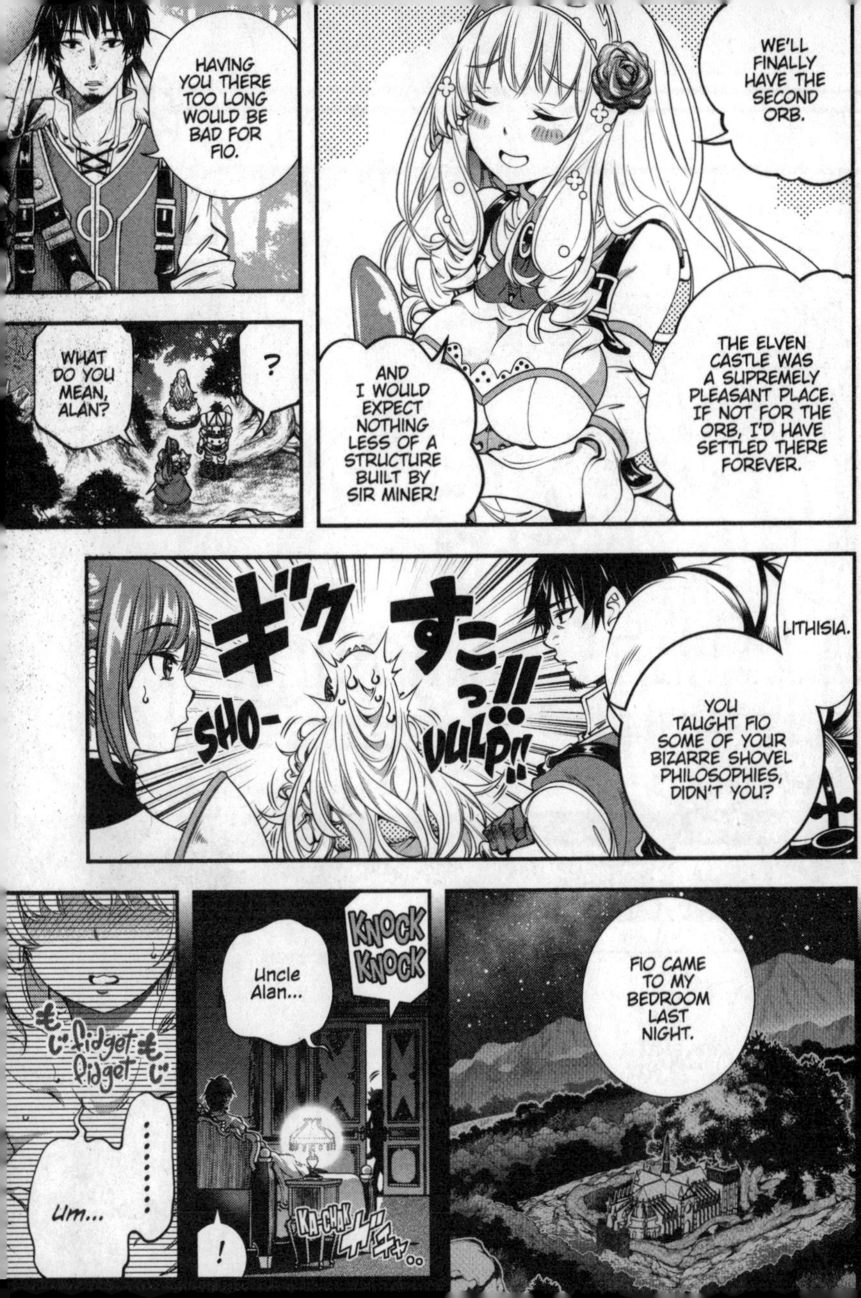
WE'LL FINALLY HAVE THE SECOND ORB.
THE ELVEN CASTLE WAS A SUPREMELY PLEASANT PLACE. IF NOT FOR THE ORB, I'D HAVE SETTLED THERE FOREVER.
AND I WOULD EXPECT NOTHING LESS OF A STRUCTURE BUILT BY SIR MINER!
HAVING YOU THERE TOO LONG WOULD BE BAD FOR FIO.
?
WHAT DO YOU MEAN, ALAN?
LITHISIA.
YOU TAUGHT FIO SOME OF YOUR BIZARRE SHOVEL PHILOSOPHIES, DIDN'T YOU?
すこっ!!
VULP!!
ギク
SHO-
FIO CAME TO MY BEDROOM LAST NIGHT.
KNOCK KNOCK
Uncle Alan...
!
KA-CHAK
ガチャ..
もじ fidget もじ
fidget
....
Um...

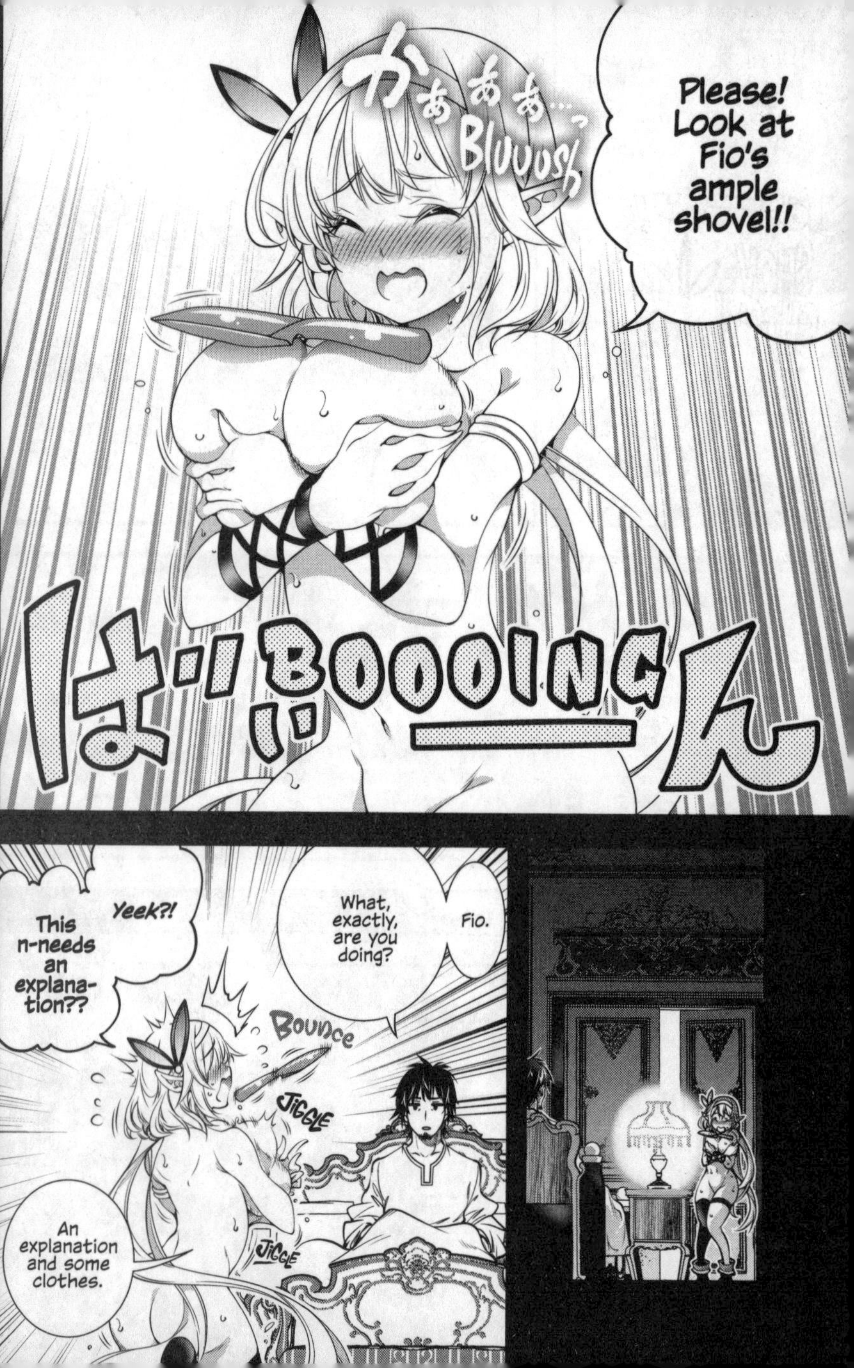
Please! Look at Fio's ample shovel!!
かあああ…っ
Bluuush
はっ
BOOOING
ん
Fio.
What, exactly, are you doing?
Yeek?!
This n-needs an explanation??
Bounce
Jiggle
An explanation and some clothes.
Jiggle

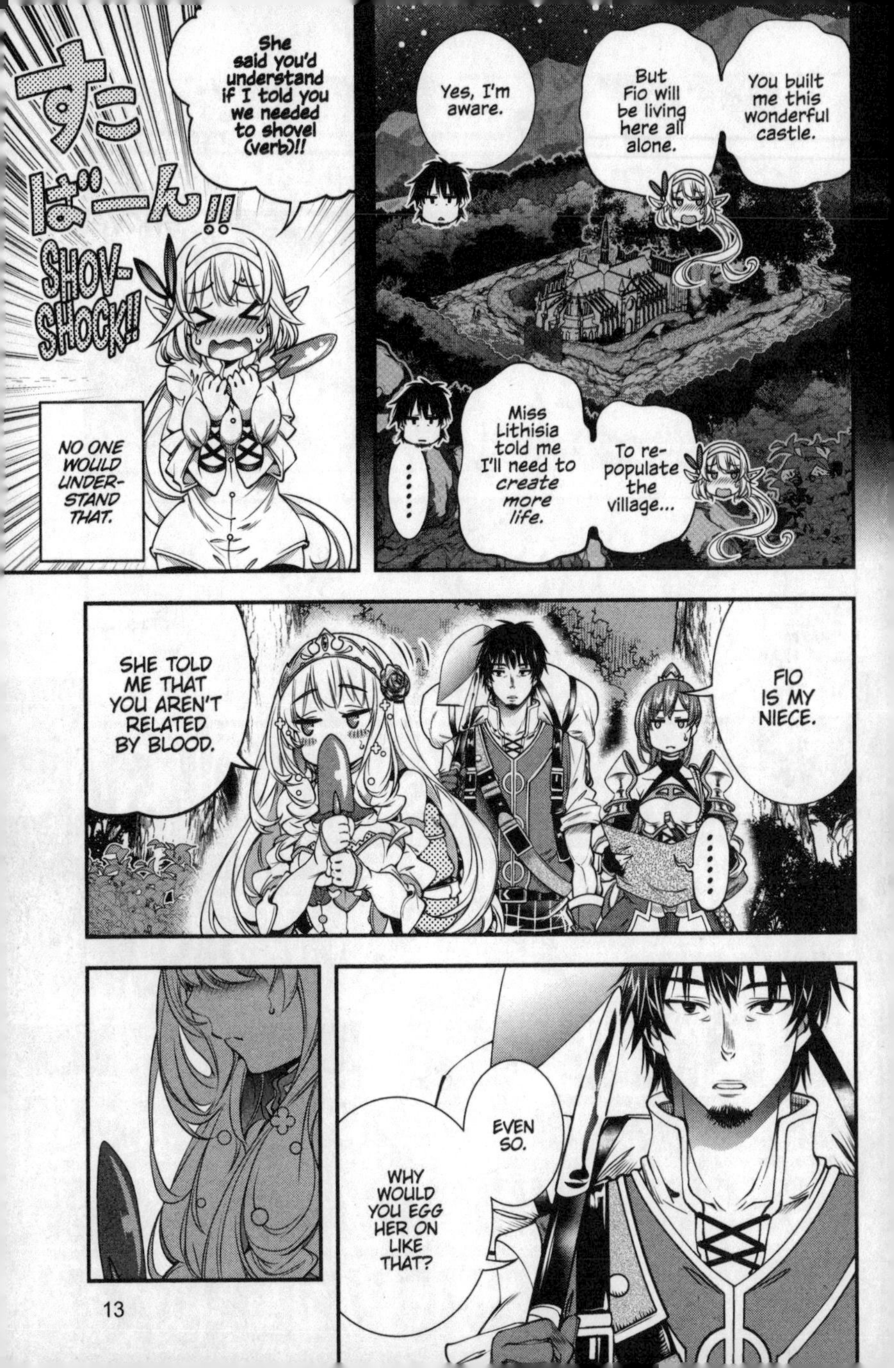
You built me this wonderful castle.
But Fio will be living here all alone.
Yes, I'm aware.
To re-populate the village...
Miss Lithisia told me I'll need to *create more life.*
......
She said you'd understand if I told you we needed to shovel (verb)!!
すこばーん!!
SHOV-SHOCK!!
NO ONE WOULD UNDERSTAND THAT.
FIO IS MY NIECE.
......
SHE TOLD ME THAT YOU AREN'T RELATED BY BLOOD.
EVEN SO.
WHY WOULD YOU EGG HER ON LIKE THAT?

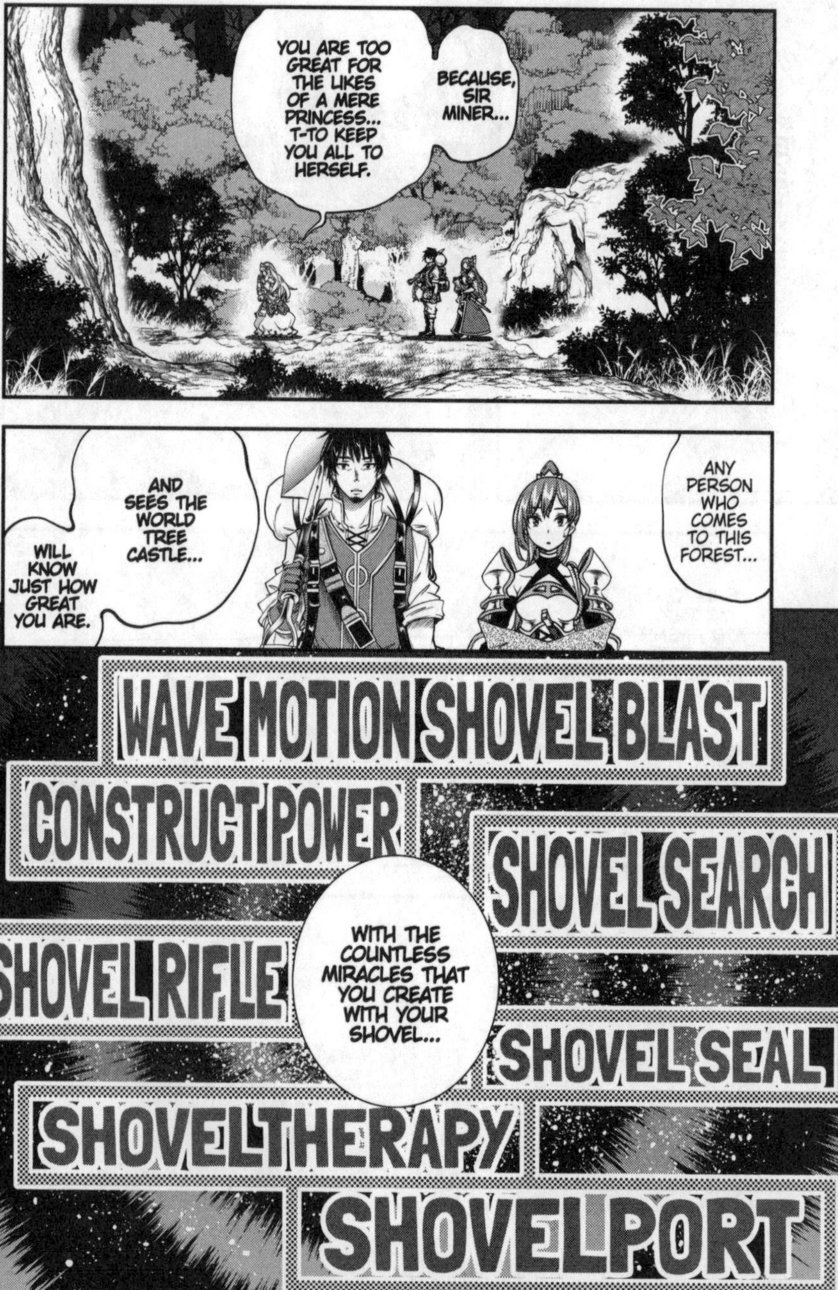
BECAUSE, SIR MINER...
YOU ARE TOO GREAT FOR THE LIKES OF A MERE PRINCESS... T-TO KEEP YOU ALL TO HERSELF.
ANY PERSON WHO COMES TO THIS FOREST...
AND SEES THE WORLD TREE CASTLE...
WILL KNOW JUST HOW GREAT YOU ARE.
WAVE MOTION SHOVEL BLAST
CONSTRUCT POWER
SHOVEL SEARCH
WITH THE COUNTLESS MIRACLES THAT YOU CREATE WITH YOUR SHOVEL...
SHOVEL RIFLE
SHOVEL SEAL
SHOVELTHERAPY
SHOVELPORT

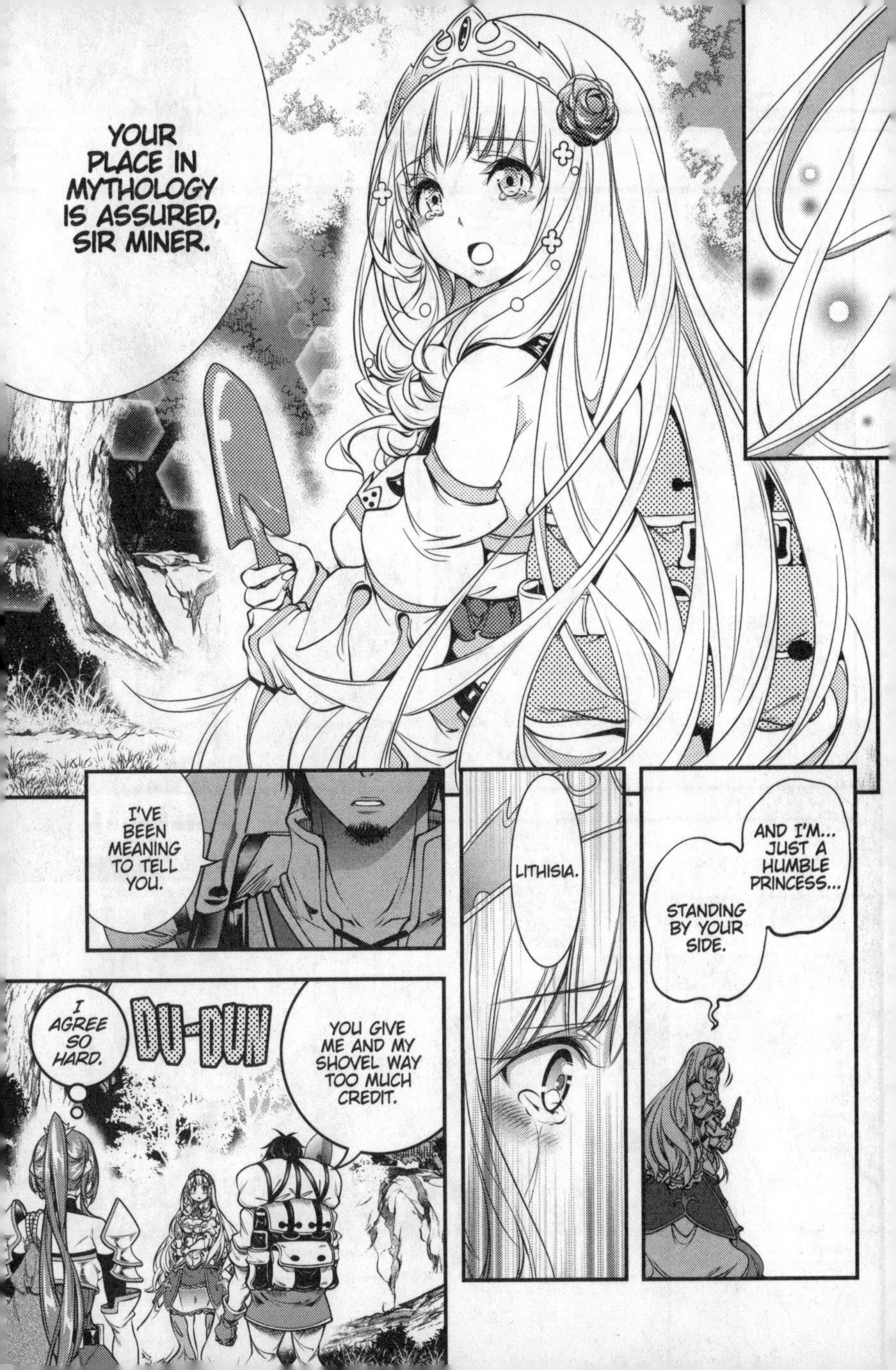
YOUR PLACE IN MYTHOLOGY IS ASSURED, SIR MINER.
AND I'M... JUST A HUMBLE PRINCESS...
STANDING BY YOUR SIDE.
LITHISIA.
I'VE BEEN MEANING TO TELL YOU.
YOU GIVE ME AND MY SHOVEL WAY TOO MUCH CREDIT.
DU-DUN
I AGREE SO HARD.

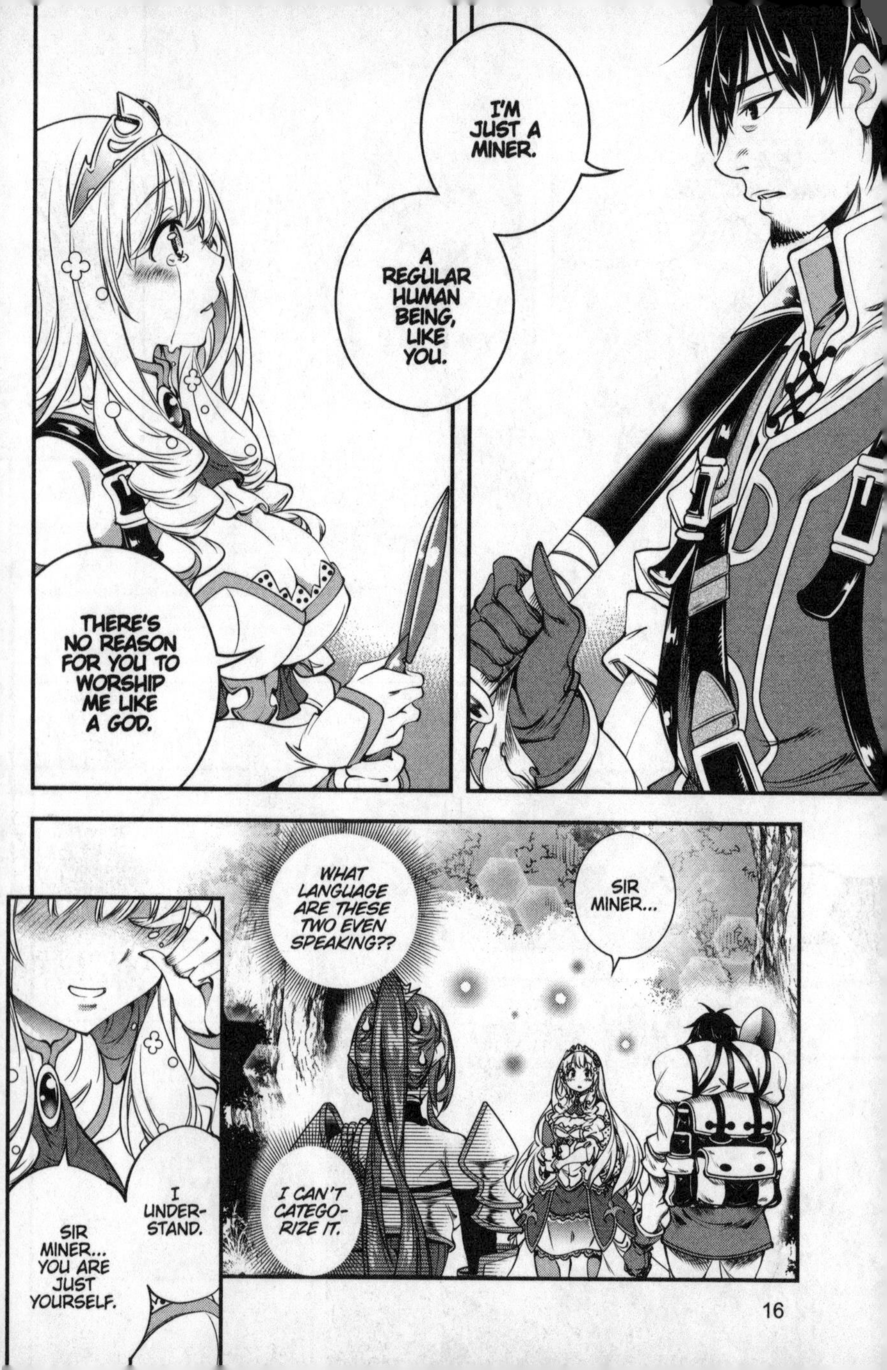
I'M JUST A MINER.
A REGULAR HUMAN BEING, LIKE YOU.
THERE'S NO REASON FOR YOU TO WORSHIP ME LIKE A GOD.
SIR MINER...
WHAT LANGUAGE ARE THESE TWO EVEN SPEAKING??
I CAN'T CATEGO-RIZE IT.
I UNDER-STAND.
SIR MINER... YOU ARE JUST YOURSELF.

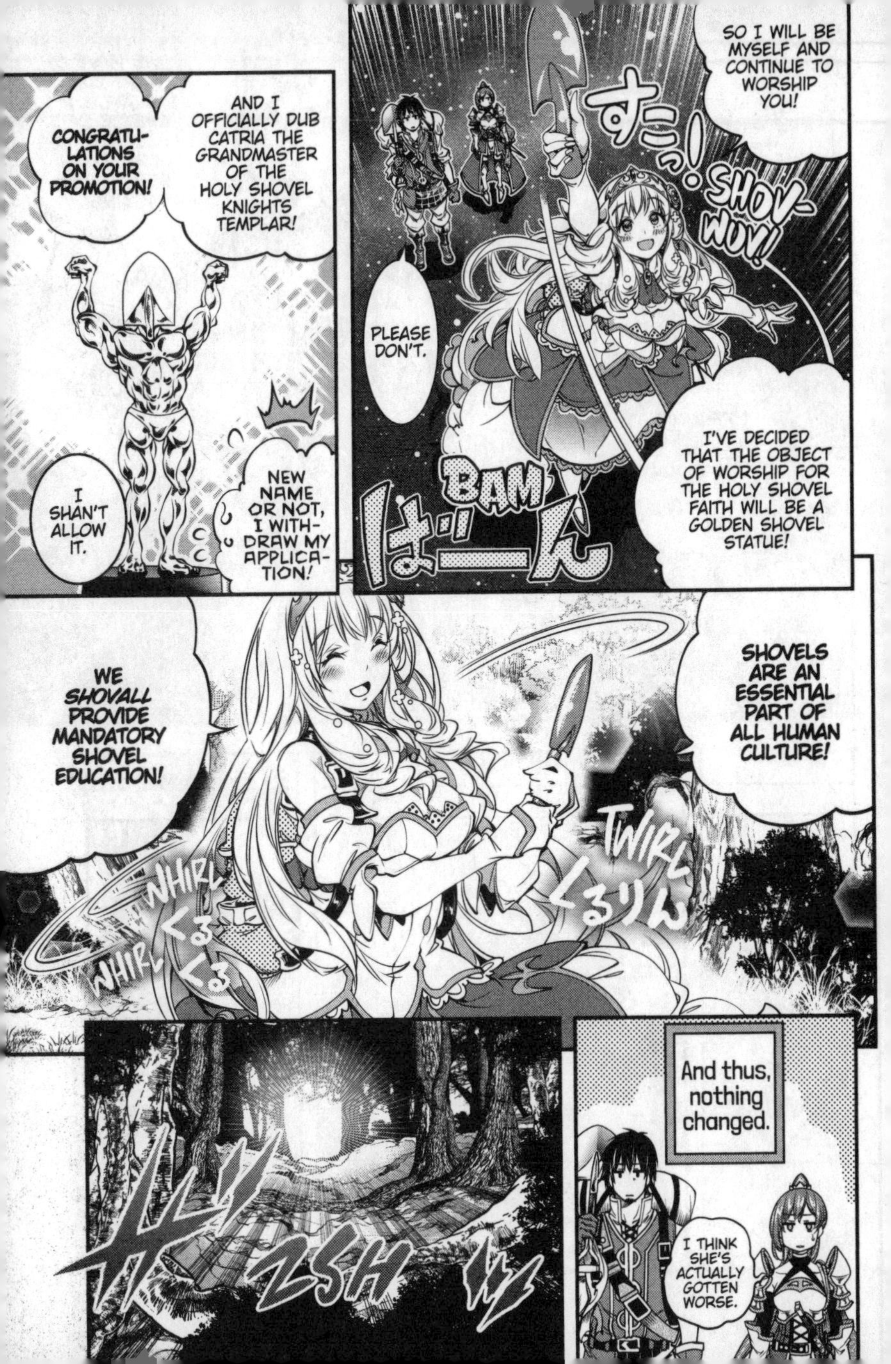
SO I WILL BE MYSELF AND CONTINUE TO WORSHIP YOU!
すこっ! SHOV-WUV!
PLEASE DON'T.
I'VE DECIDED THAT THE OBJECT OF WORSHIP FOR THE HOLY SHOVEL FAITH WILL BE A GOLDEN SHOVEL STATUE!
BAM ばーん
AND I OFFICIALLY DUB CATRIA THE GRANDMASTER OF THE HOLY SHOVEL KNIGHTS TEMPLAR!
CONGRATULATIONS ON YOUR PROMOTION!
NEW NAME OR NOT, I WITHDRAW MY APPLICATION!
I SHAN'T ALLOW IT.
SHOVELS ARE AN ESSENTIAL PART OF ALL HUMAN CULTURE!
WE SHOVALL PROVIDE MANDATORY SHOVEL EDUCATION!
TWIRL くるりん
WHIRL くる WHIRL くる
And thus, nothing changed.
I THINK SHE'S ACTUALLY GOTTEN WORSE.
ZSH

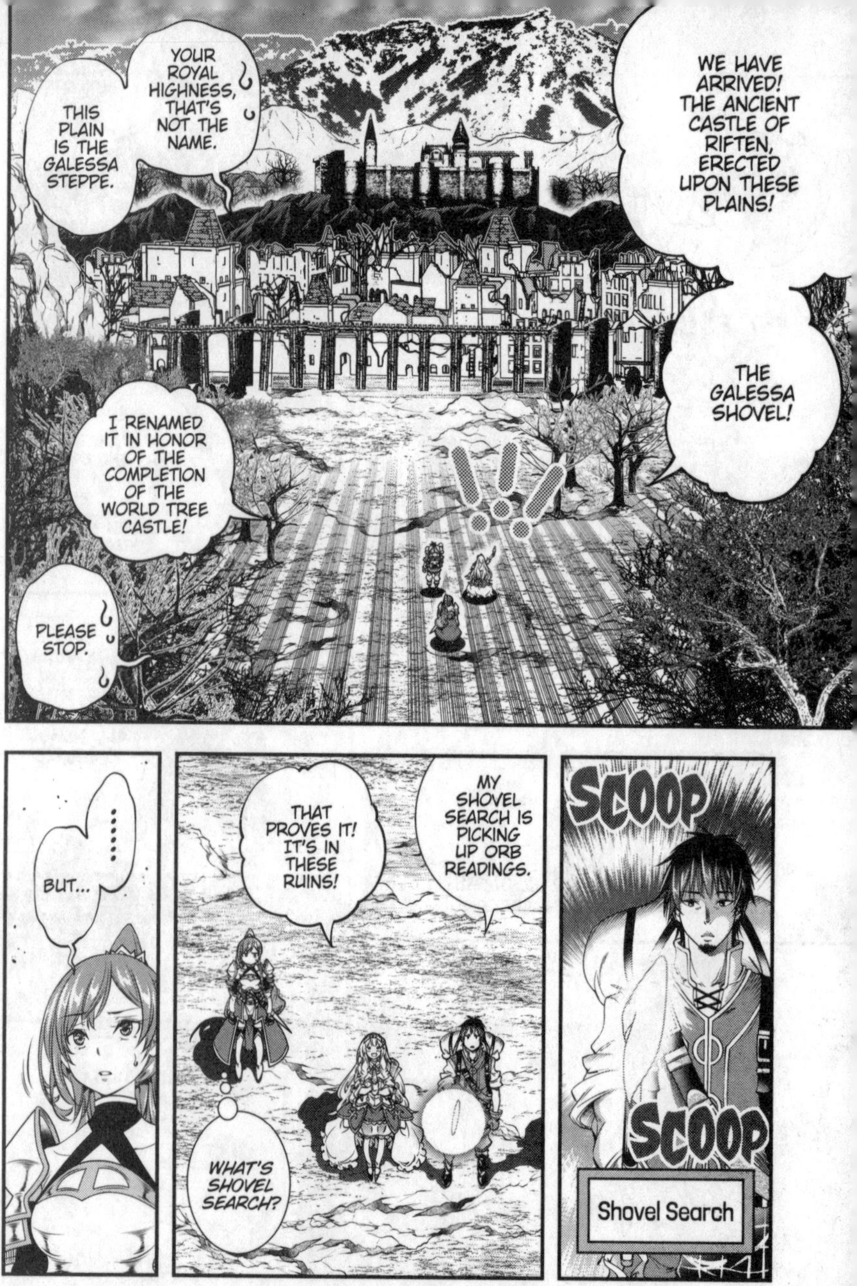
WE HAVE ARRIVED! THE ANCIENT CASTLE OF RIFTEN, ERECTED UPON THESE PLAINS!
THE GALESSA SHOVEL!
YOUR ROYAL HIGHNESS, THAT'S NOT THE NAME.
THIS PLAIN IS THE GALESSA STEPPE.
!!
I RENAMED IT IN HONOR OF THE COMPLETION OF THE WORLD TREE CASTLE!
PLEASE STOP.
SCOOP
SCOOP
Shovel Search
MY SHOVEL SEARCH IS PICKING UP ORB READINGS.
THAT PROVES IT! IT'S IN THESE RUINS!
WHAT'S SHOVEL SEARCH?
......
BUT...

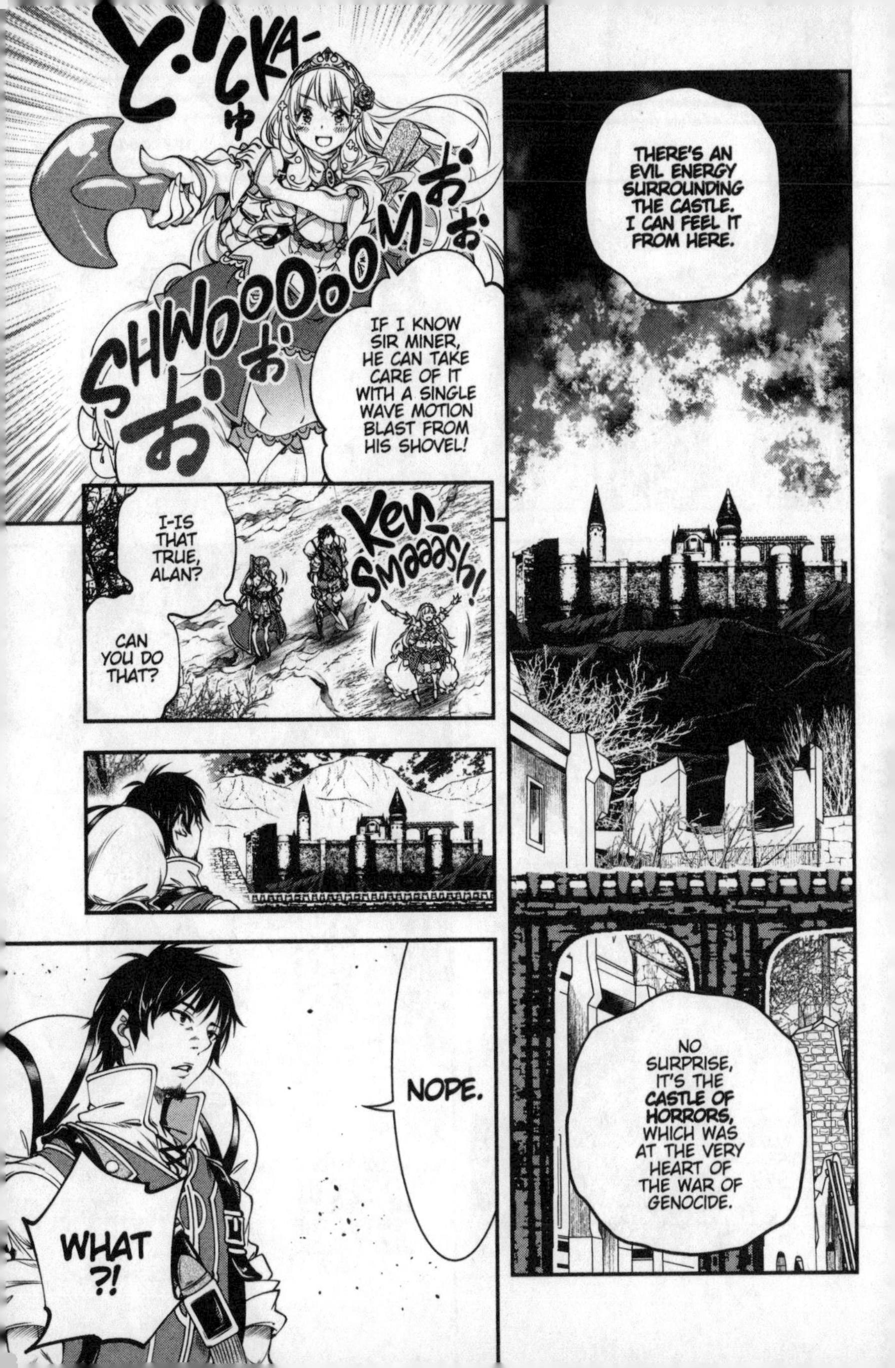
THERE'S AN EVIL ENERGY SURROUNDING THE CASTLE. I CAN FEEL IT FROM HERE.
NO SURPRISE, IT'S THE CASTLE OF HORRORS, WHICH WAS AT THE VERY HEART OF THE WAR OF GENOCIDE.
KA-
SHWOOOOOOM
IF I KNOW SIR MINER, HE CAN TAKE CARE OF IT WITH A SINGLE WAVE MOTION BLAST FROM HIS SHOVEL!
Ken-Smaaash!
I-IS THAT TRUE, ALAN?
CAN YOU DO THAT?
NOPE.
WHAT ?!

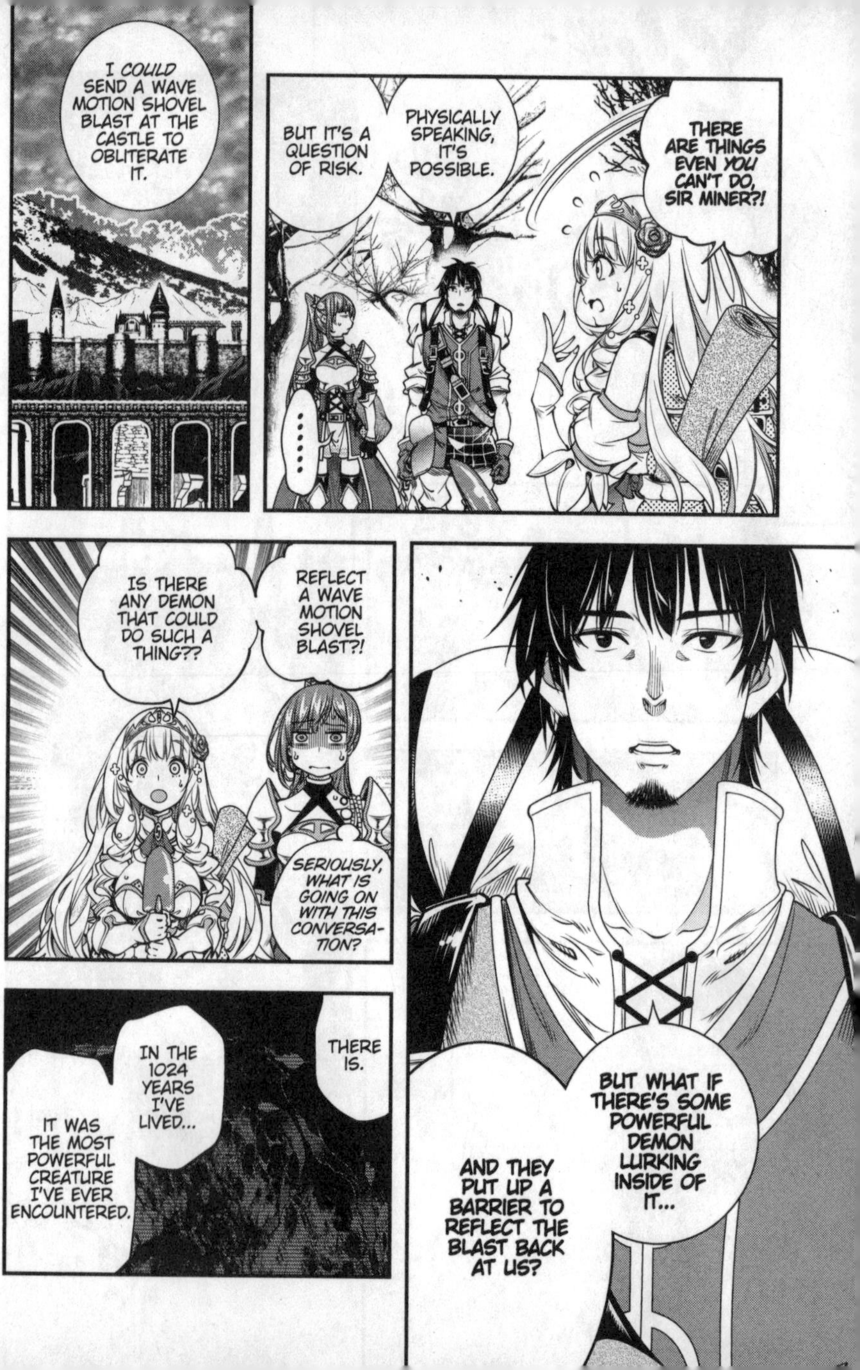
THERE ARE THINGS EVEN YOU CAN'T DO, SIR MINER?!
PHYSICALLY SPEAKING, IT'S POSSIBLE.
BUT IT'S A QUESTION OF RISK.
......
I COULD SEND A WAVE MOTION SHOVEL BLAST AT THE CASTLE TO OBLITERATE IT.
BUT WHAT IF THERE'S SOME POWERFUL DEMON LURKING INSIDE OF IT...
AND THEY PUT UP A BARRIER TO REFLECT THE BLAST BACK AT US?
REFLECT A WAVE MOTION SHOVEL BLAST?!
IS THERE ANY DEMON THAT COULD DO SUCH A THING??
SERIOUSLY, WHAT IS GOING ON WITH THIS CONVERSATION?
THERE IS.
IN THE 1024 YEARS I'VE LIVED...
IT WAS THE MOST POWERFUL CREATURE I'VE EVER ENCOUNTERED.

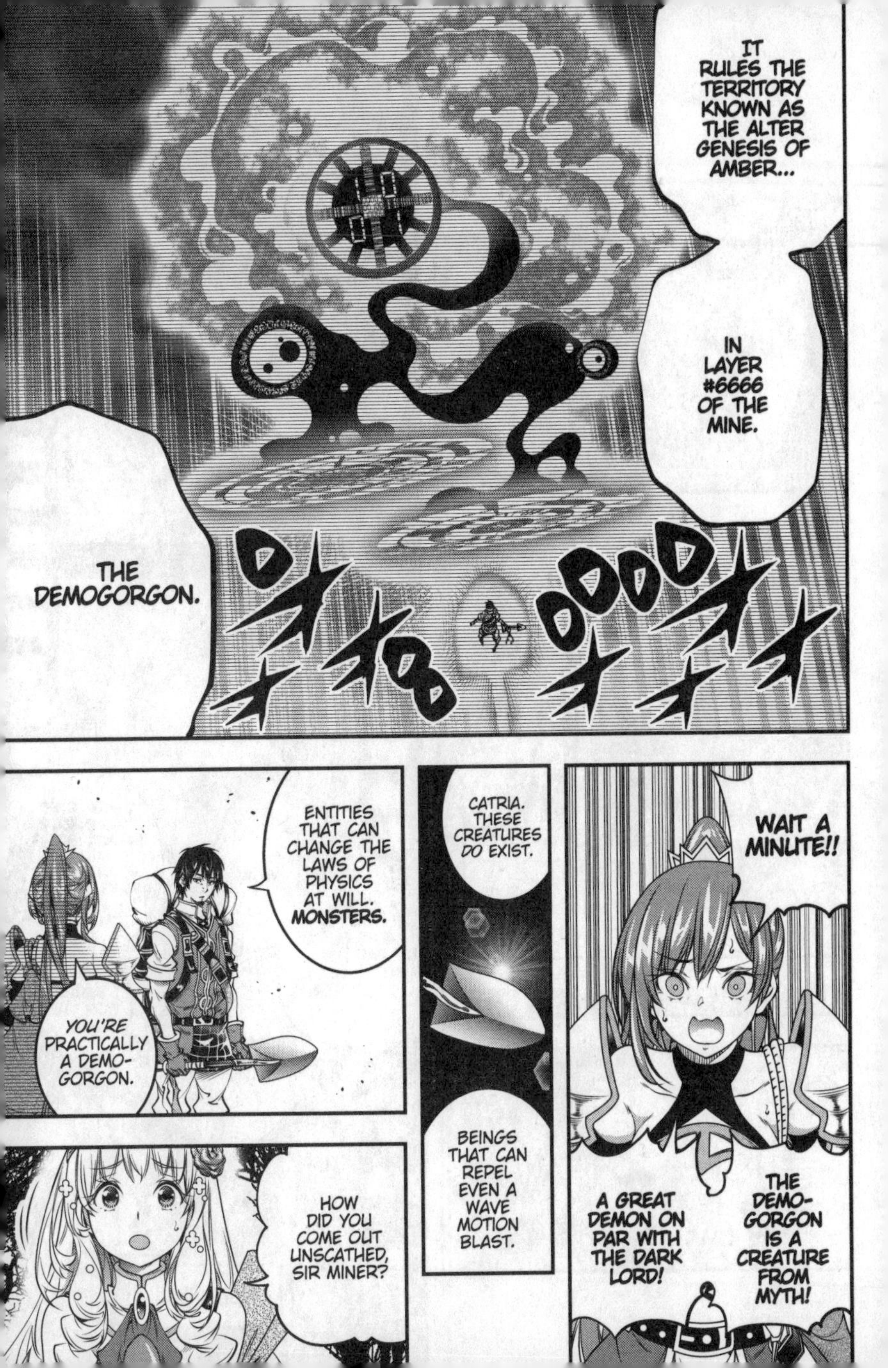
IT RULES THE TERRITORY KNOWN AS THE ALTER GENESIS OF AMBER...
IN LAYER #6666 OF THE MINE.
THE DEMOGORGON.
WAIT A MINUTE!!
THE DEMO-GORGON IS A CREATURE FROM MYTH!
A GREAT DEMON ON PAR WITH THE DARK LORD!
CATRIA. THESE CREATURES *DO* EXIST.
BEINGS THAT CAN REPEL EVEN A WAVE MOTION BLAST.
ENTITIES THAT CAN CHANGE THE LAWS OF PHYSICS AT WILL. **MONSTERS.**
YOU'RE PRACTICALLY A DEMO-GORGON.
HOW DID YOU COME OUT UNSCATHED, SIR MINER?

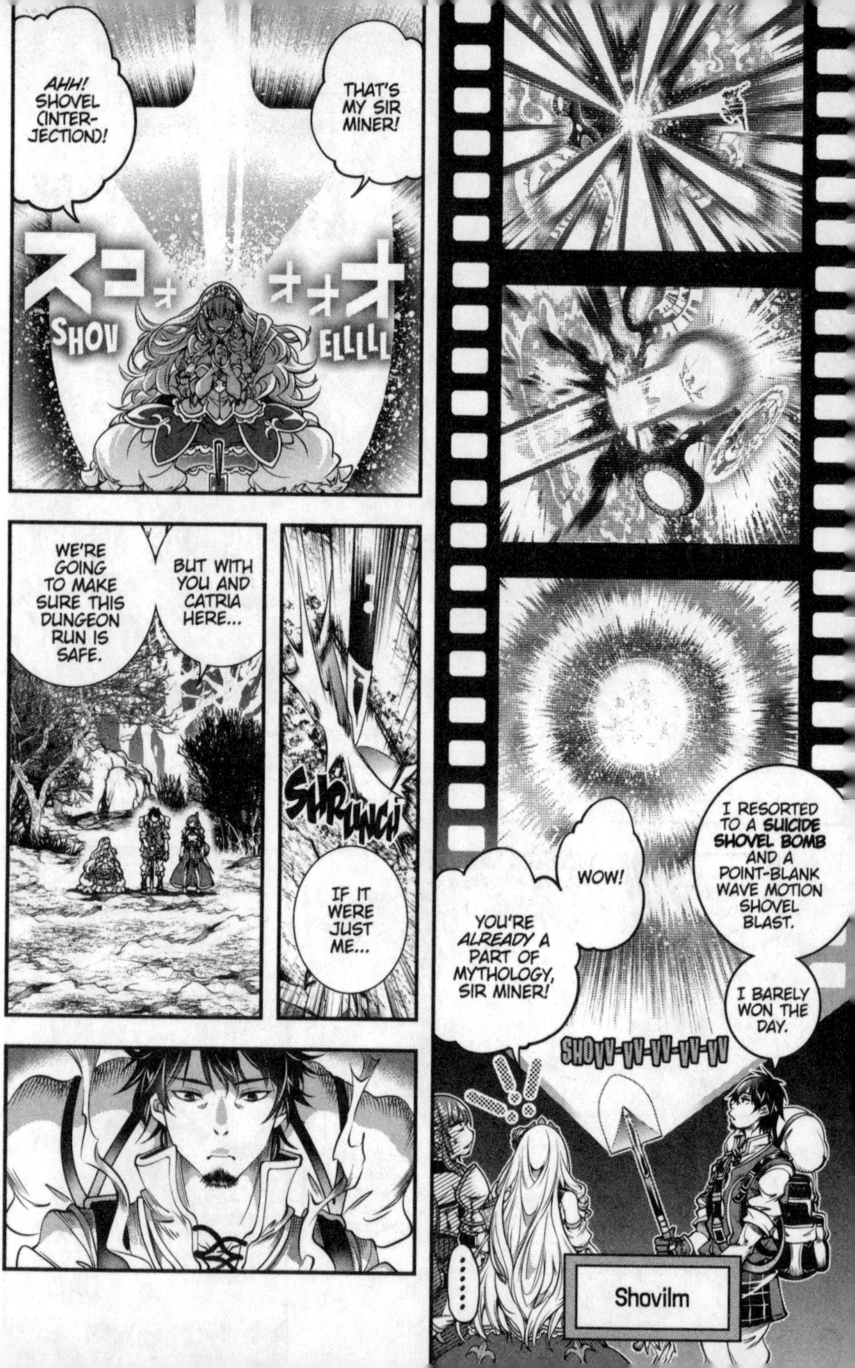

THAT'S MY SIR MINER!
AHH! SHOVEL (INTER-JECTION)!
スコォ
SHOV
ォォオ
ELLLLL
SHRUNCH
IF IT WERE JUST ME...
BUT WITH YOU AND CATRIA HERE...
WE'RE GOING TO MAKE SURE THIS DUNGEON RUN IS SAFE.
I RESORTED TO A **SUICIDE SHOVEL BOMB** AND A POINT-BLANK WAVE MOTION SHOVEL BLAST.
WOW!
I BARELY WON THE DAY.
YOU'RE *ALREADY* A PART OF MYTHOLOGY, SIR MINER!
SHOVV-VV-VV-VV-VV
!!
......
Shovilm

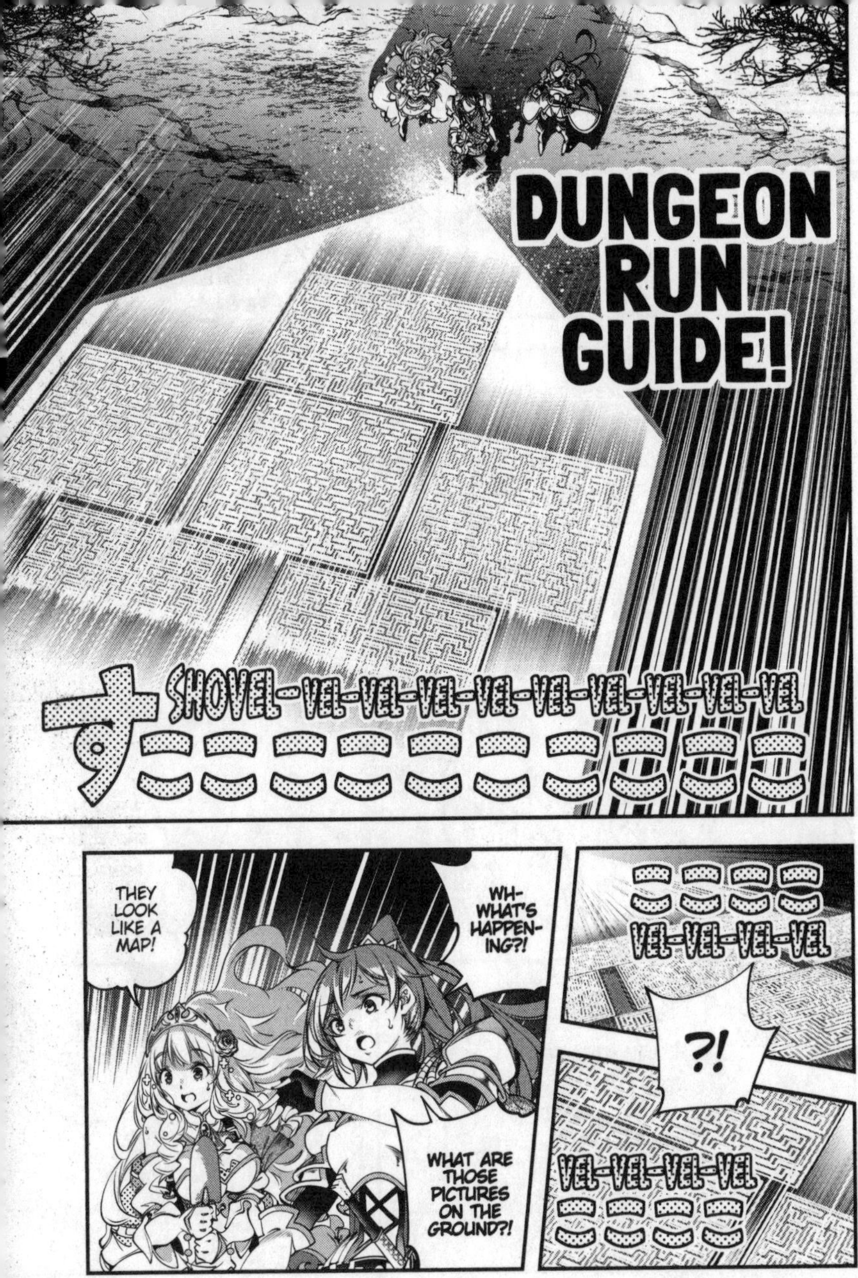

DUNGEON RUN GUIDE!
SHOVEL-VEL-VEL-VEL-VEL-VEL-VEL-VEL-VEL-VEL
す
VEL-VEL-VEL-VEL
?!
VEL-VEL-VEL-VEL
WH- WHAT'S HAPPENING?!
THEY LOOK LIKE A MAP!
WHAT ARE THOSE PICTURES ON THE GROUND?!

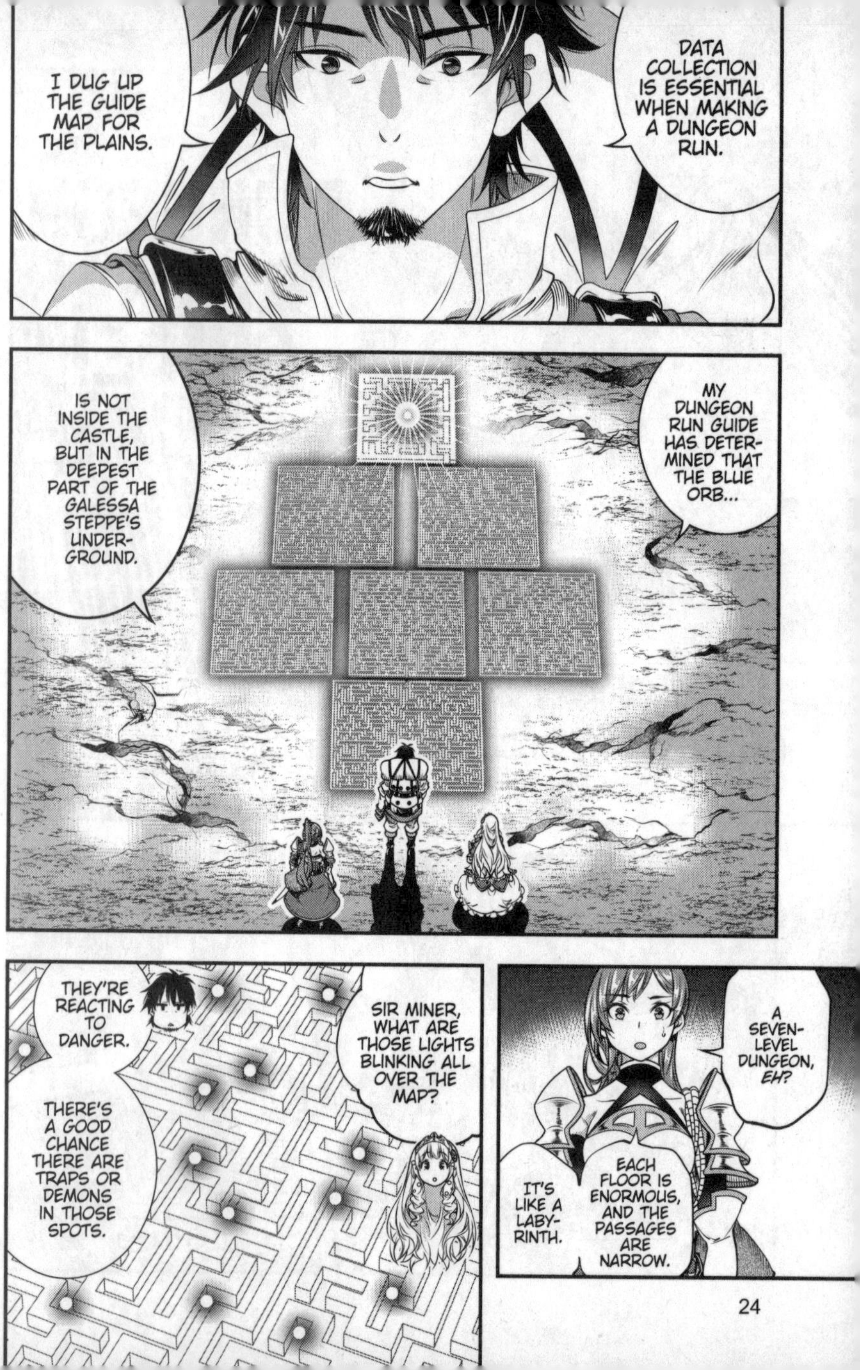
DATA COLLECTION IS ESSENTIAL WHEN MAKING A DUNGEON RUN.
I DUG UP THE GUIDE MAP FOR THE PLAINS.
MY DUNGEON RUN GUIDE HAS DETERMINED THAT THE BLUE ORB...
IS NOT INSIDE THE CASTLE, BUT IN THE DEEPEST PART OF THE GALESSA STEPPE'S UNDERGROUND.
A SEVEN-LEVEL DUNGEON, *EH*?
EACH FLOOR IS ENORMOUS, AND THE PASSAGES ARE NARROW.
IT'S LIKE A LABYRINTH.
SIR MINER, WHAT ARE THOSE LIGHTS BLINKING ALL OVER THE MAP?
THEY'RE REACTING TO DANGER.
THERE'S A GOOD CHANCE THERE ARE TRAPS OR DEMONS IN THOSE SPOTS.

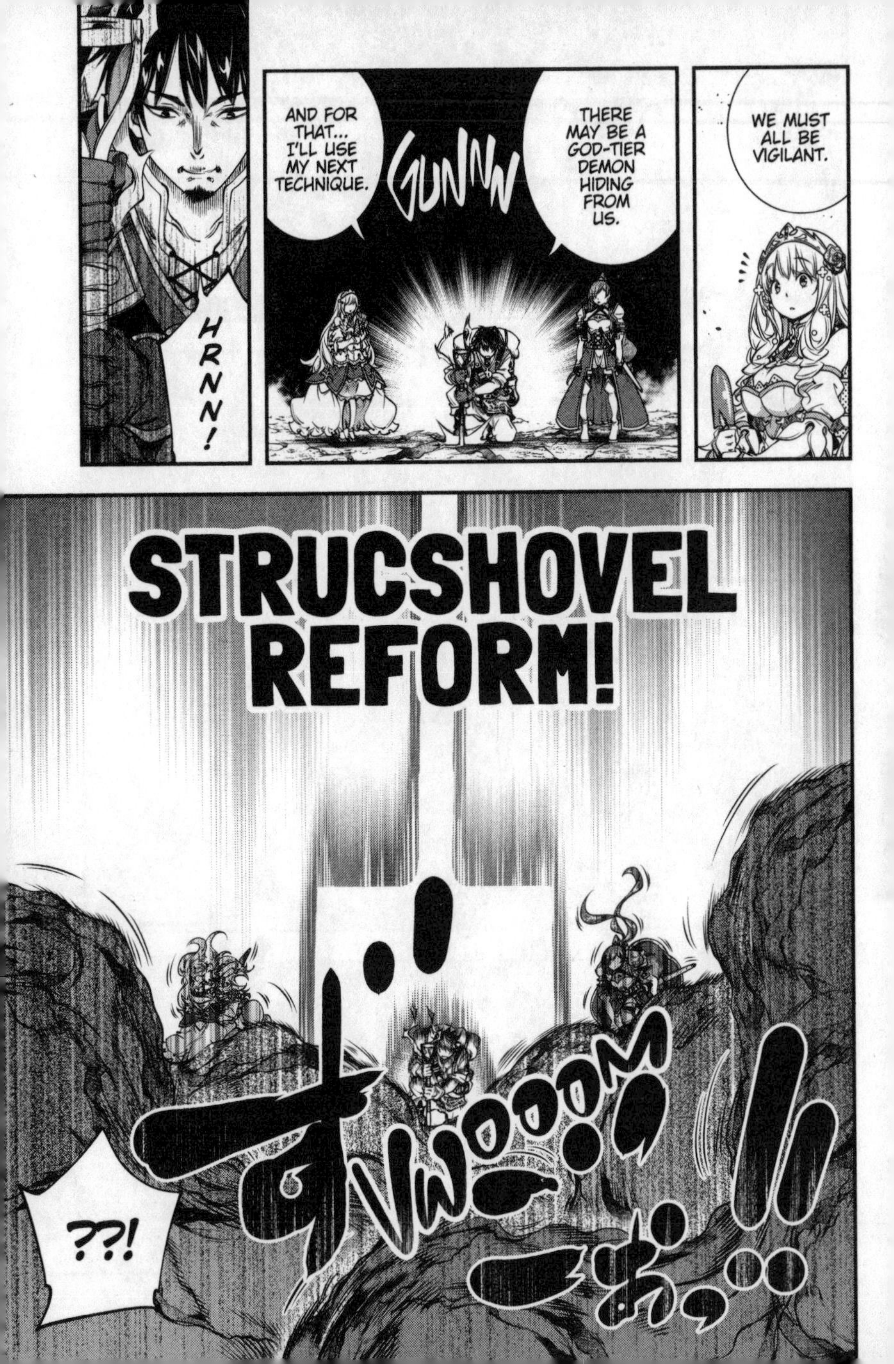
WE MUST ALL BE VIGILANT.
THERE MAY BE A GOD-TIER DEMON HIDING FROM US.
GUNNN
AND FOR THAT... I'LL USE MY NEXT TECHNIQUE.
HRNNN!
STRUCSHOVEL REFORM!
VWOOOOM!!
??!

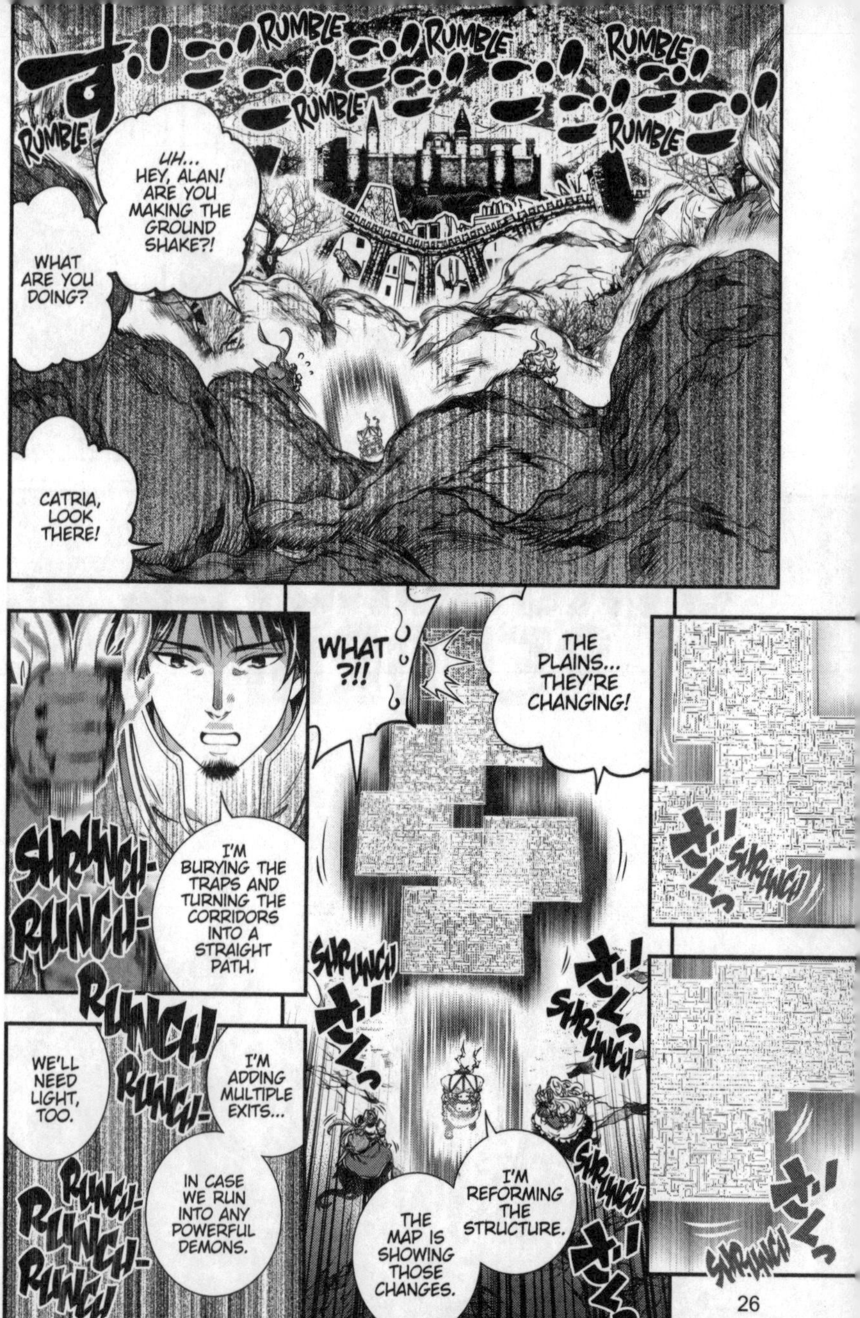
RUMBLE RUMBLE RUMBLE RUMBLE RUMBLE RUMBLE
UH... HEY, ALAN! ARE YOU MAKING THE GROUND SHAKE?!
WHAT ARE YOU DOING?
CATRIA, LOOK THERE!
SHRUNCH
SHRUNCH
THE PLAINS... THEY'RE CHANGING!
WHAT?!!
SHRUNCH
SHRUNCH
SHRUNCH
I'M REFORMING THE STRUCTURE.
THE MAP IS SHOWING THOSE CHANGES.
SHRUNCH
I'M BURYING THE TRAPS AND TURNING THE CORRIDORS INTO A STRAIGHT PATH.
SHRUNCH-RUNCH-
RUNCH RUNCH-
I'M ADDING MULTIPLE EXITS...
WE'LL NEED LIGHT, TOO.
IN CASE WE RUN INTO ANY POWERFUL DEMONS.
RUNCH-RUNCH-RUNCH

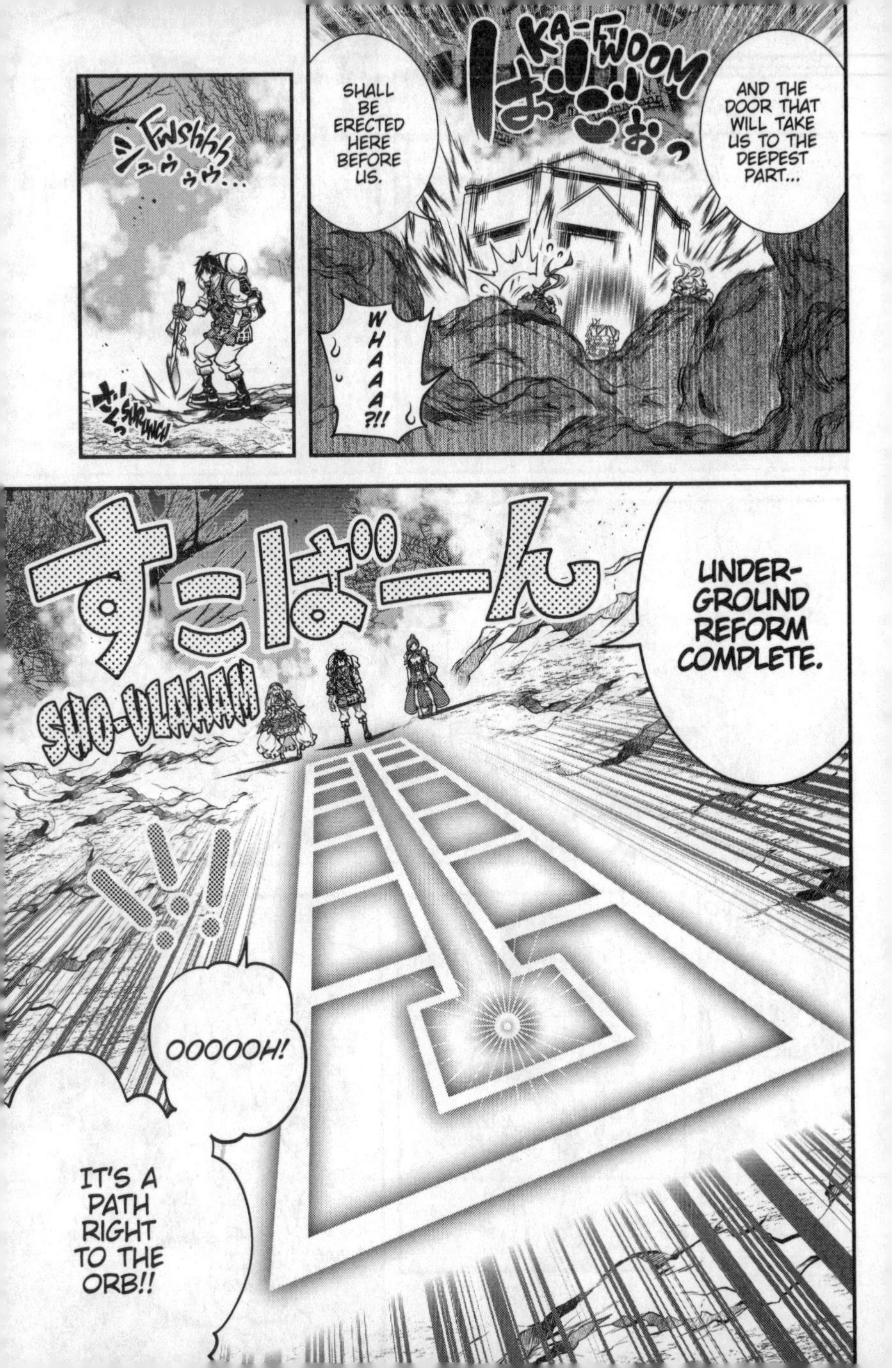
AND THE DOOR THAT WILL TAKE US TO THE DEEPEST PART...
KA-FWOOM
SHALL BE ERECTED HERE BEFORE US.
WHAAAA?!!
FWSHHH
シュウゥゥウ...
SHRUNCH
UNDER-GROUND REFORM COMPLETE.
すこばーん
SHO-DLAAAM
!!
OOOOOH!
IT'S A PATH RIGHT TO THE ORB!!

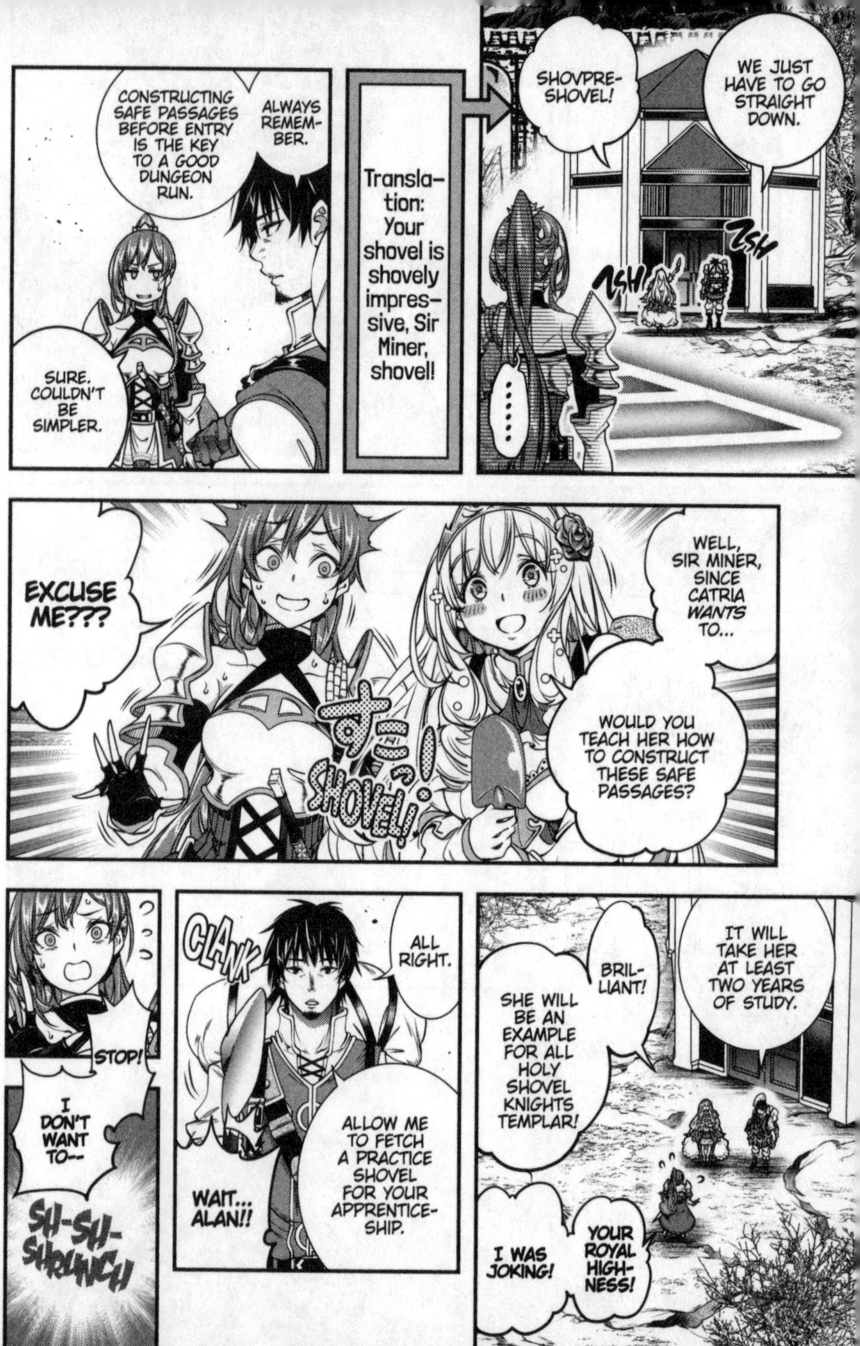
WE JUST HAVE TO GO STRAIGHT DOWN.
SHOVPRE-SHOVEL!
ZSH
ZSH
......
Translation: Your shovel is shovely impressive, Sir Miner, shovel!
ALWAYS REMEMBER.
CONSTRUCTING SAFE PASSAGES BEFORE ENTRY IS THE KEY TO A GOOD DUNGEON RUN.
SURE. COULDN'T BE SIMPLER.
WELL, SIR MINER, SINCE CATRIA *WANTS* TO...
WOULD YOU TEACH HER HOW TO CONSTRUCT THESE SAFE PASSAGES?
SHOVEL!
EXCUSE ME???
IT WILL TAKE HER AT LEAST TWO YEARS OF STUDY.
BRILLIANT!
SHE WILL BE AN EXAMPLE FOR ALL HOLY SHOVEL KNIGHTS TEMPLAR!
YOUR ROYAL HIGHNESS!
I WAS JOKING!
ALL RIGHT.
CLANK
ALLOW ME TO FETCH A PRACTICE SHOVEL FOR YOUR APPRENTICESHIP.
WAIT... ALAN!!
STOP!
I DON'T WANT TO--
SH-SH-SHRUNCH

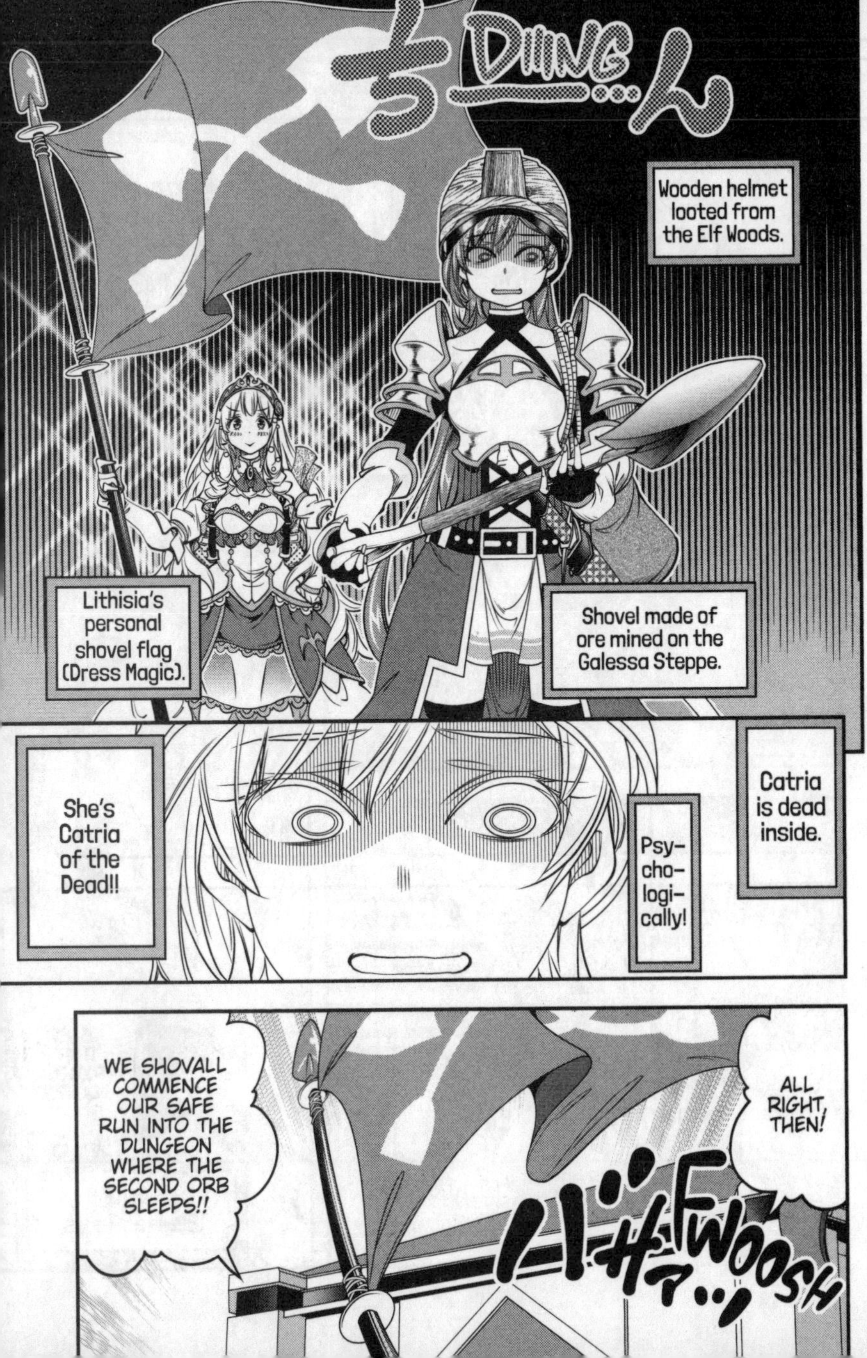
DIING
Wooden helmet looted from the Elf Woods.
Shovel made of ore mined on the Galessa Steppe.
Lithisia's personal shovel flag (Dress Magic).
Catria is dead inside.
Psychologically!
She's Catria of the Dead!!
ALL RIGHT, THEN!
WE SHOVALL COMMENCE OUR SAFE RUN INTO THE DUNGEON WHERE THE SECOND ORB SLEEPS!!
FWOOSH

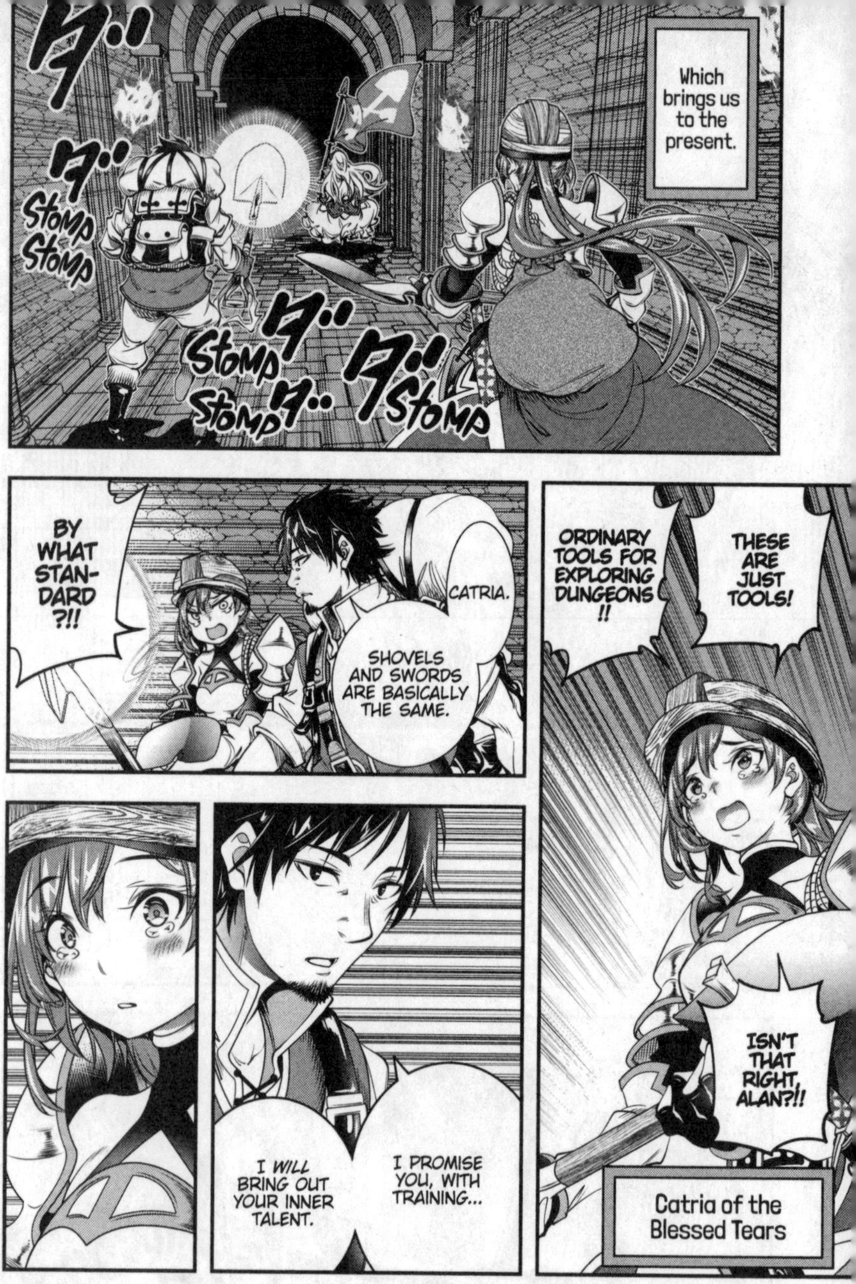

Which brings us to the present.
Stomp Stomp
Stomp Stomp
Stomp
THESE ARE JUST TOOLS!
ORDINARY TOOLS FOR EXPLORING DUNGEONS!!
ISN'T THAT RIGHT, ALAN?!!
Catria of the Blessed Tears
CATRIA.
SHOVELS AND SWORDS ARE BASICALLY THE SAME.
BY WHAT STAN-DARD?!!
I PROMISE YOU, WITH TRAINING...
I *WILL* BRING OUT YOUR INNER TALENT.

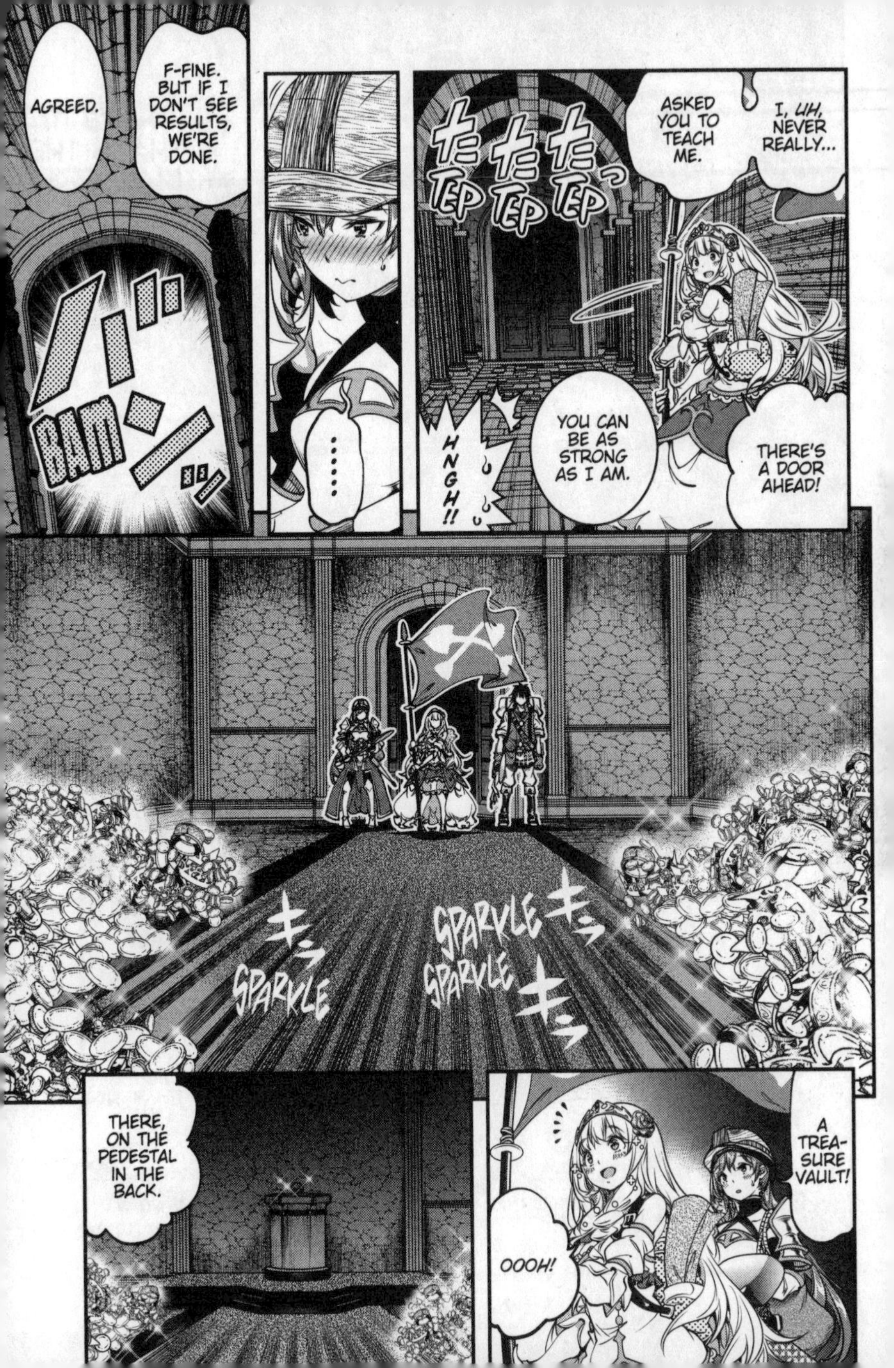
I, UH, NEVER REALLY...
ASKED YOU TO TEACH ME.
TEP TEP TEP
YOU CAN BE AS STRONG AS I AM.
HNGH!!
THERE'S A DOOR AHEAD!
......
F-FINE. BUT IF I DON'T SEE RESULTS, WE'RE DONE.
AGREED.
BAM
SPARKLE
SPARKLE
SPARKLE
A TREASURE VAULT!
OOOH!
THERE, ON THE PEDESTAL IN THE BACK.

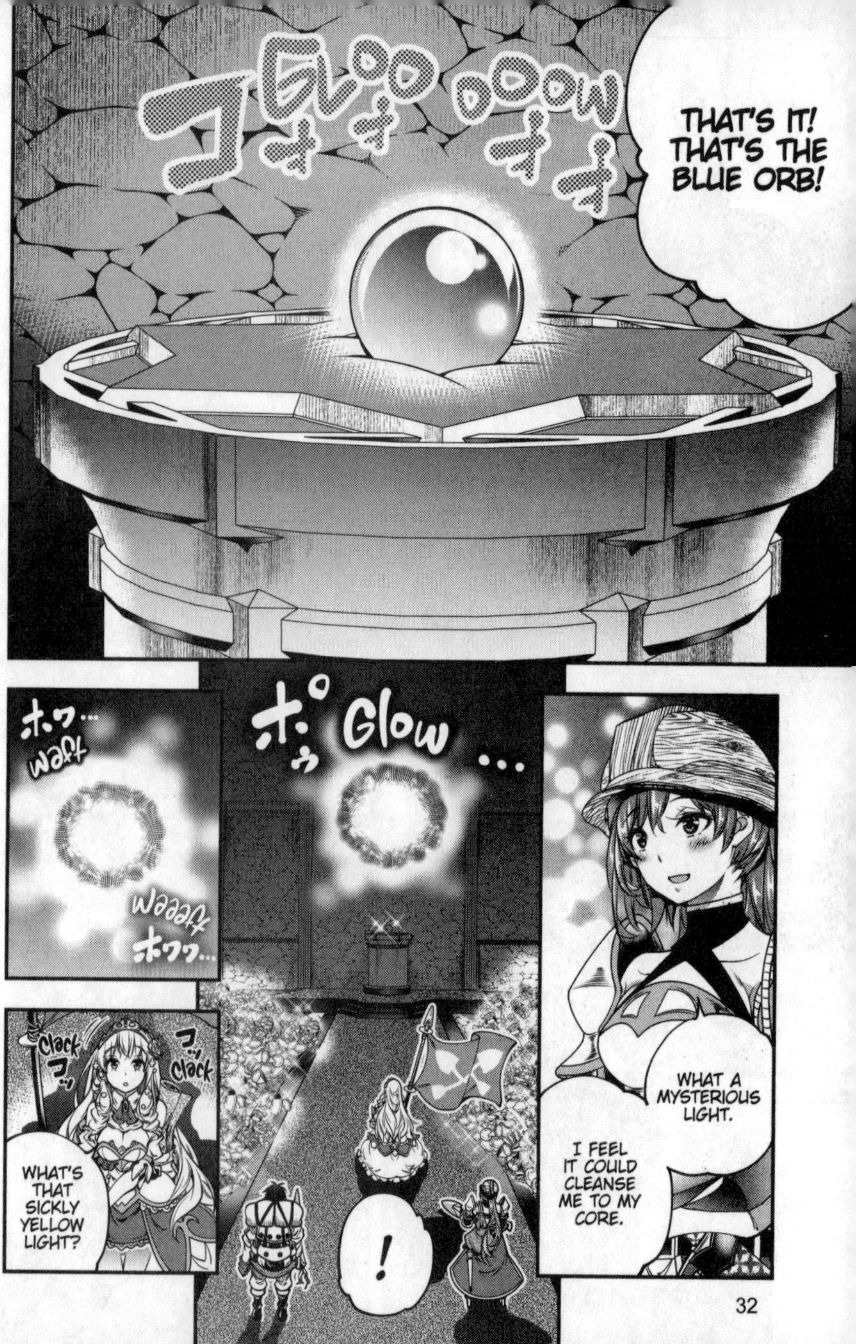
DOOOW
THAT'S IT! THAT'S THE BLUE ORB!
WHAT A MYSTERIOUS LIGHT.
I FEEL IT COULD CLEANSE ME TO MY CORE.
ポゥ Glow ...
!
ホワ… waft
waaaft ホワワ…
Clack Clack
WHAT'S THAT SICKLY YELLOW LIGHT?

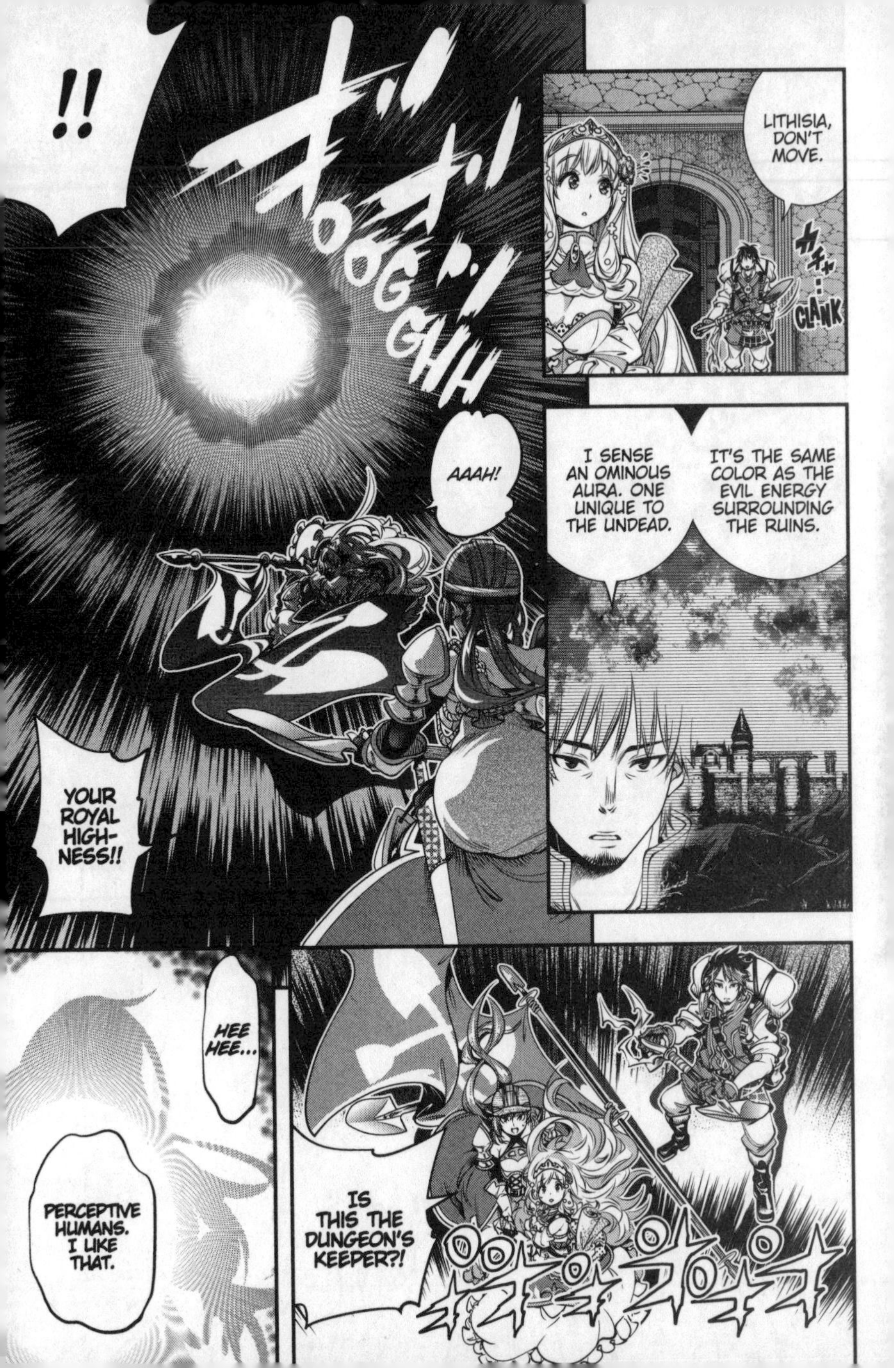
LITHISIA, DON'T MOVE.
CLANK
I SENSE AN OMINOUS AURA. ONE UNIQUE TO THE UNDEAD.
IT'S THE SAME COLOR AS THE EVIL ENERGY SURROUNDING THE RUINS.
!!
OOGGHH
AAAH!
YOUR ROYAL HIGHNESS!!
IS THIS THE DUNGEON'S KEEPER?!
HEE HEE...
PERCEPTIVE HUMANS. I LIKE THAT.

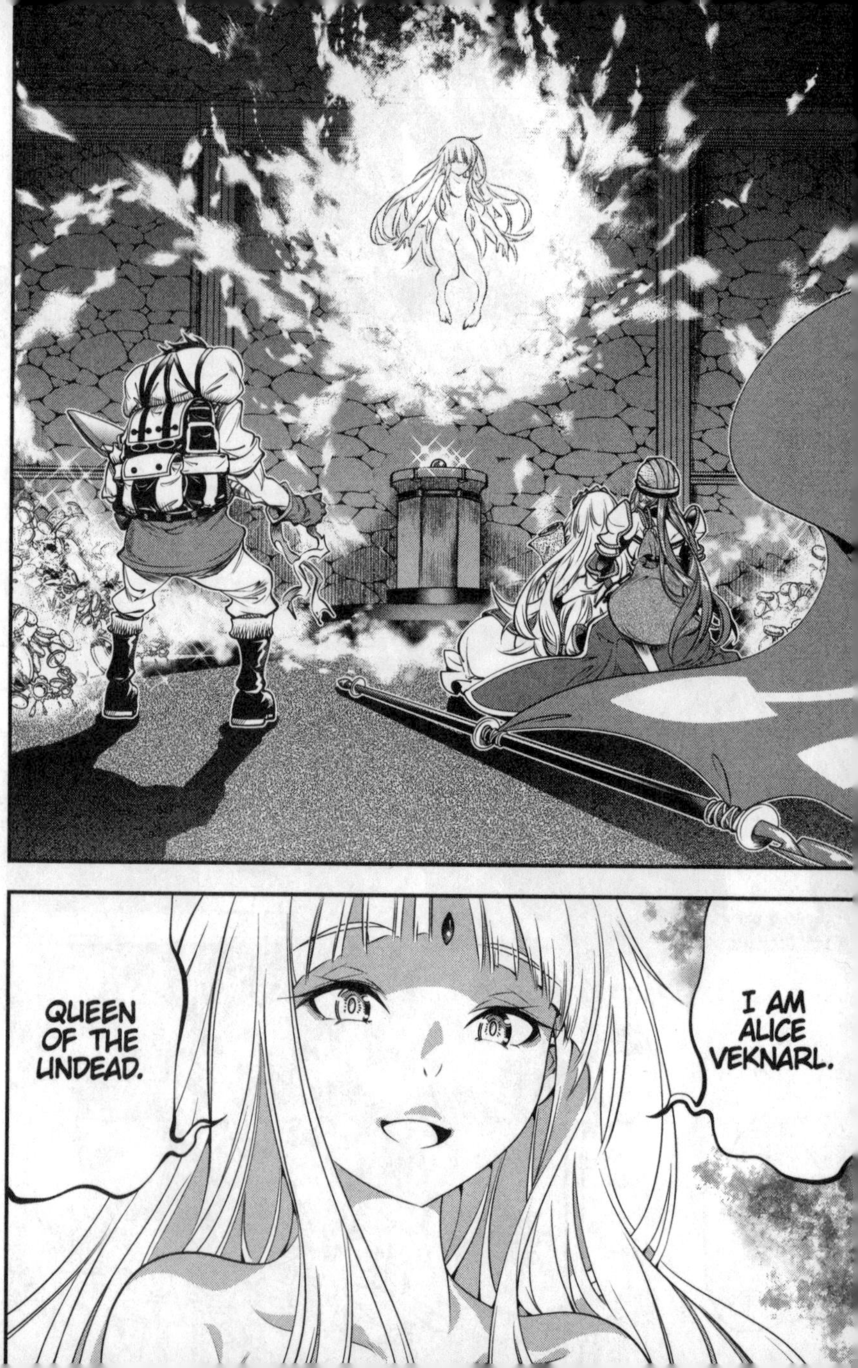
I AM ALICE VEKNARL.
QUEEN OF THE UNDEAD.

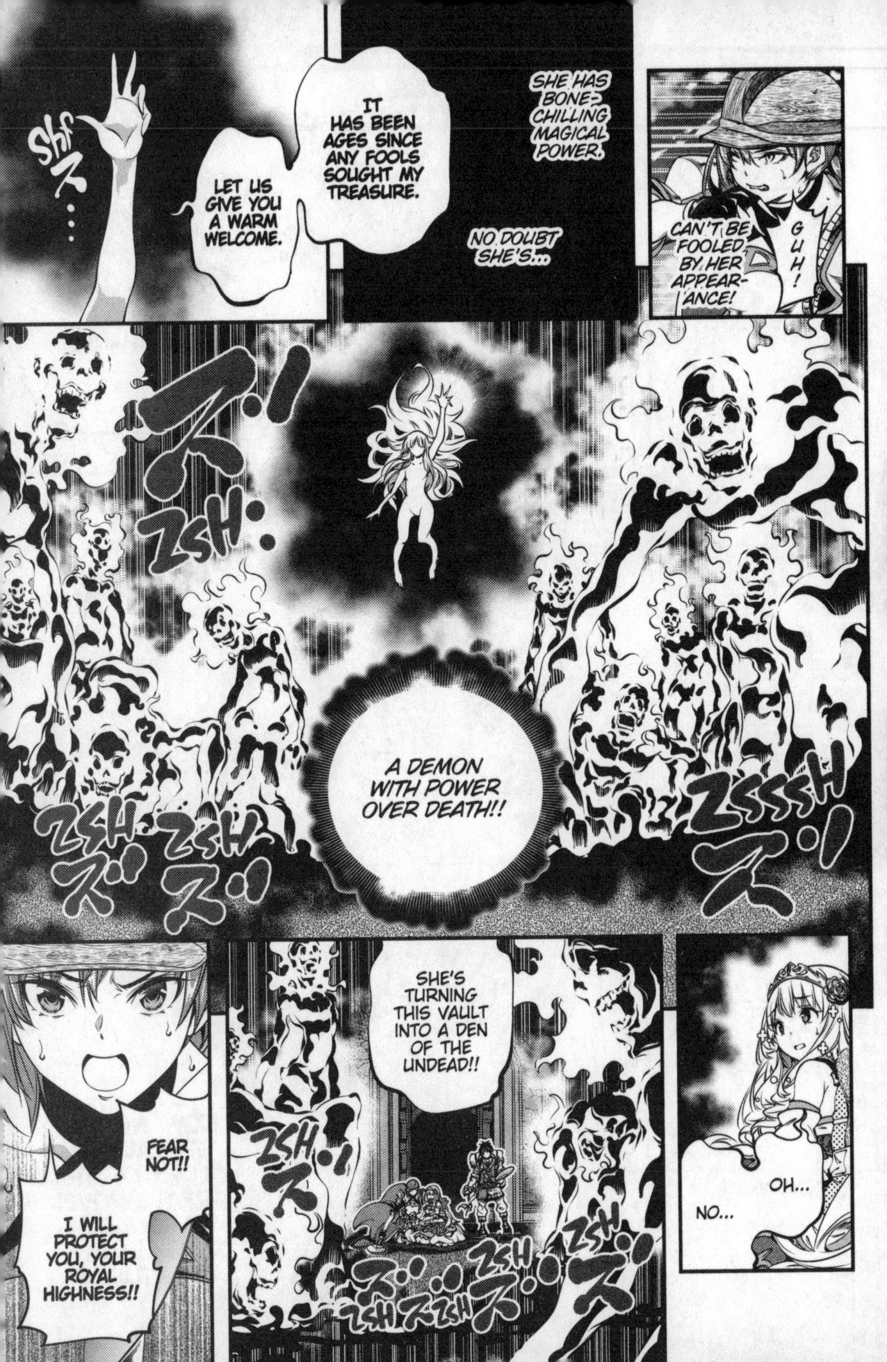
GUH!
CAN'T BE FOOLED BY HER APPEARANCE!
SHE HAS BONE-CHILLING MAGICAL POWER.
NO DOUBT SHE'S...
IT HAS BEEN AGES SINCE ANY FOOLS SOUGHT MY TREASURE.
LET US GIVE YOU A WARM WELCOME.
Shf...
ZSH
ZSSSSH
A DEMON WITH POWER OVER DEATH!!
ZSH
ZSH
OH...
NO...
SHE'S TURNING THIS VAULT INTO A DEN OF THE UNDEAD!!
ZSH
ZSH
ZSH
ZSH
ZSH
FEAR NOT!!
I WILL PROTECT YOU, YOUR ROYAL HIGHNESS!!

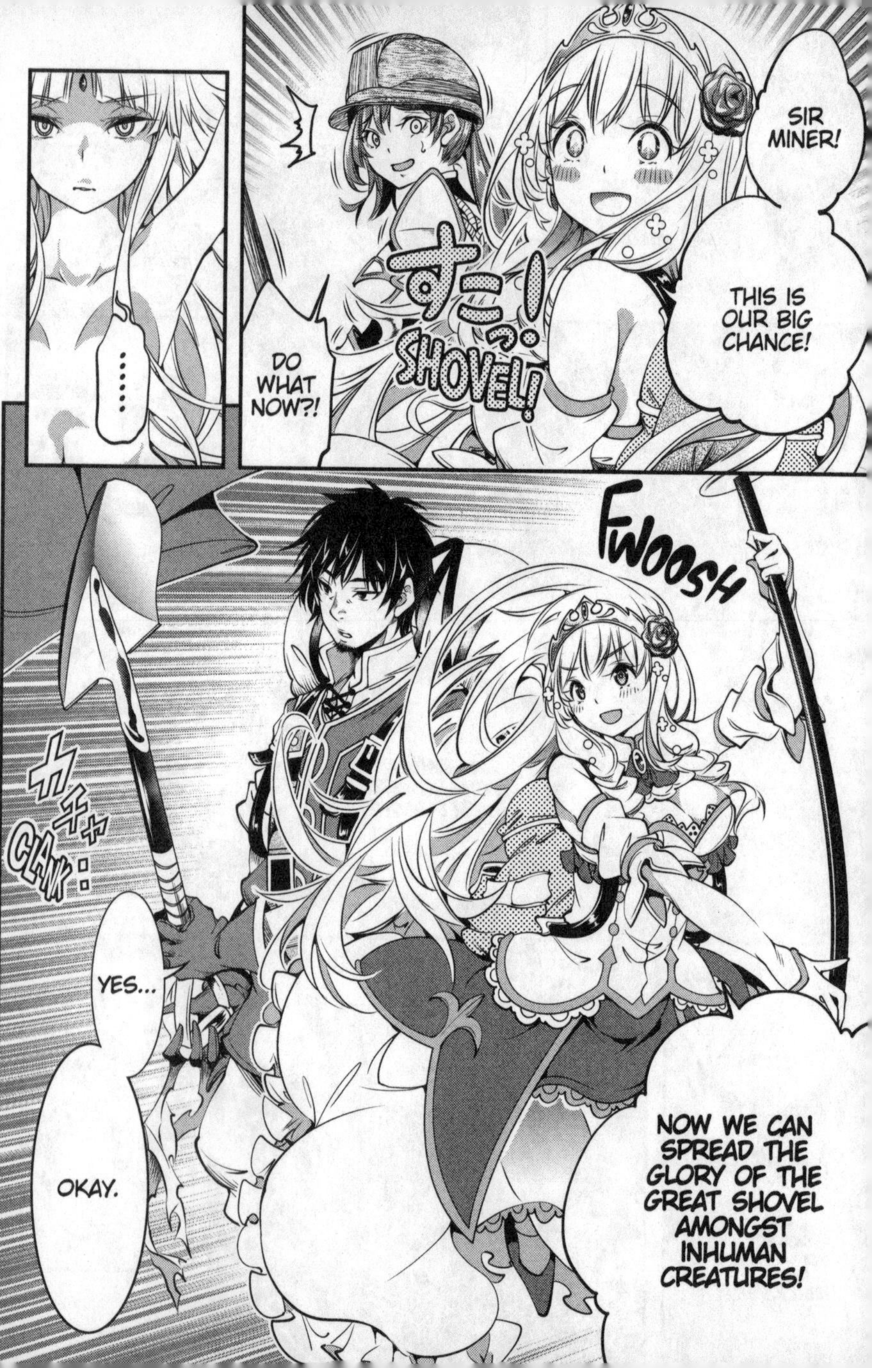
SIR MINER!
THIS IS OUR BIG CHANCE!
すこっ! SHOVEL!
DO WHAT NOW?!
……
FWOOSH
NOW WE CAN SPREAD THE GLORY OF THE GREAT SHOVEL AMONGST INHUMAN CREATURES!
カチャ… CLANK
YES...
OKAY.

THE INVINCIBLE SHOVEL

SHOVEL

"WAVE MOTION SHOVEL BLAST!"
(˙･ω･˙)σ≡≡≡★('д ：;;:).:．KA-CHOOOM

THE INVINCIBLE SHOVEL

"WAVE MOTION SHOVEL BLAST!"

(｀・ω・´)♂=====★(ﾟДﾟ ;;;).:∴ KA-CHOOOM

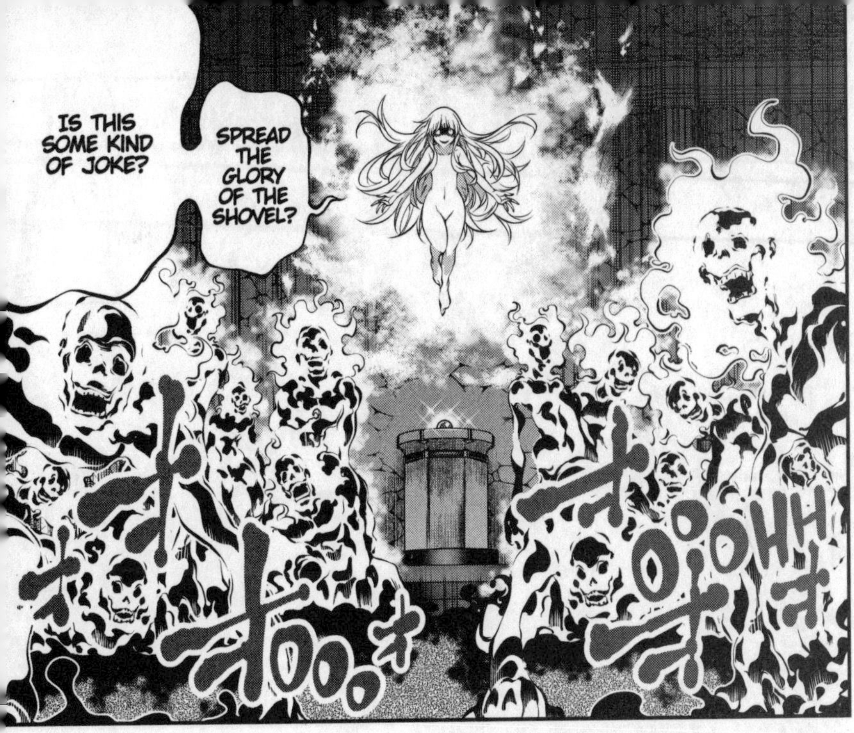
SPREAD THE GLORY OF THE SHOVEL?
IS THIS SOME KIND OF JOKE?
OOOHH

Chapter 7: The Immortal Girl Alice

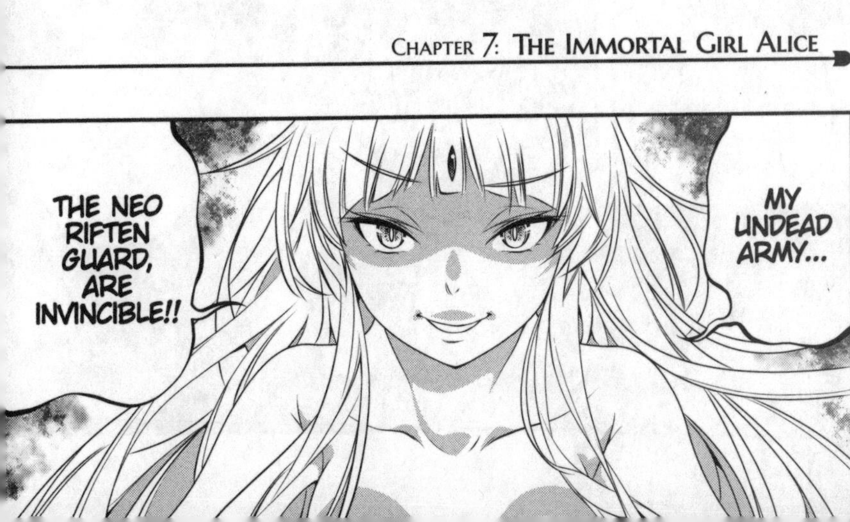
MY UNDEAD ARMY...
THE NEO RIFTEN GUARD, ARE INVINCIBLE!!

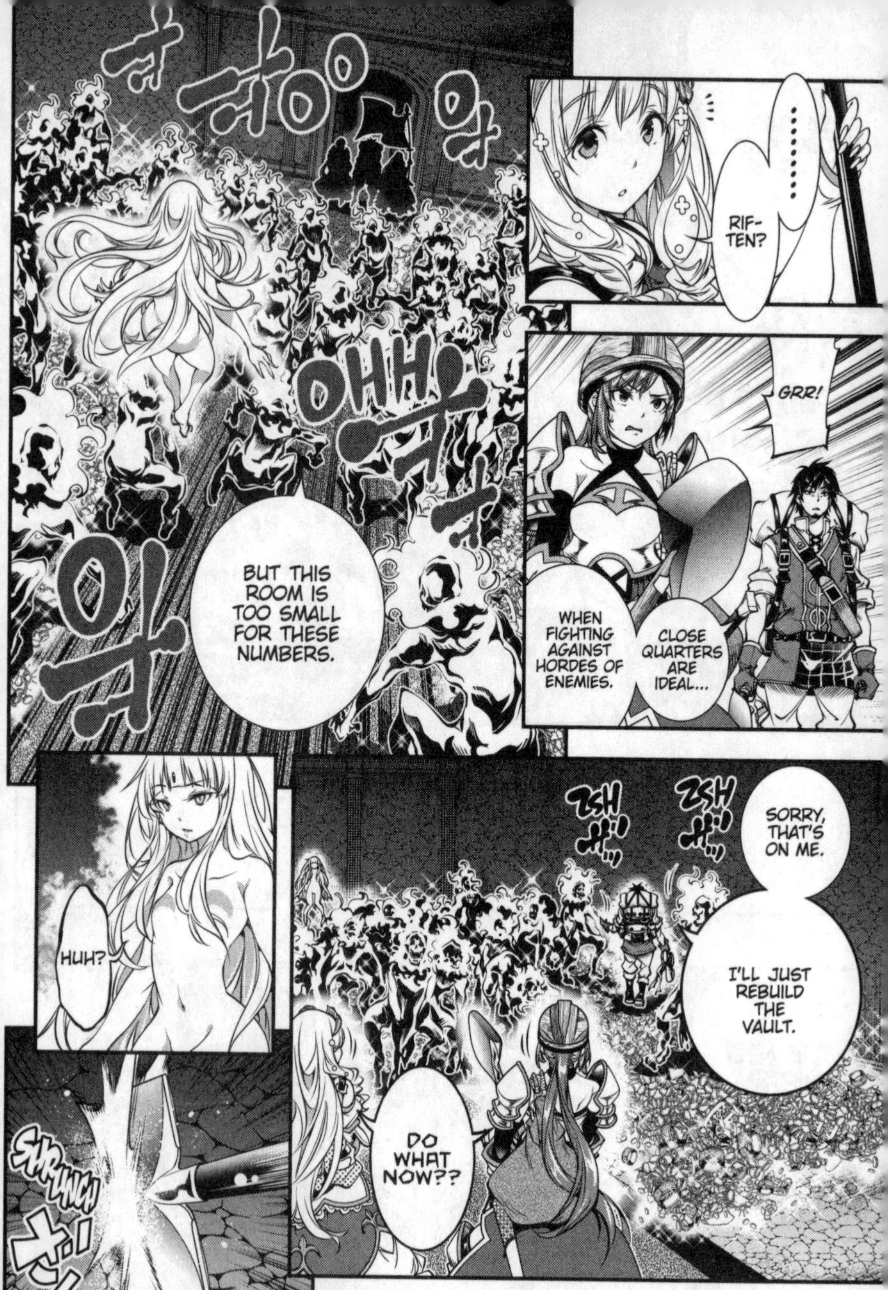

...
......
RIF-TEN?
GRR!
CLOSE QUARTERS ARE IDEAL...
WHEN FIGHTING AGAINST HORDES OF ENEMIES.
OHH
BUT THIS ROOM IS TOO SMALL FOR THESE NUMBERS.
ZSH
ZSH
SORRY, THAT'S ON ME.
I'LL JUST REBUILD THE VAULT.
DO WHAT NOW??
HUH?
SHRUNCH

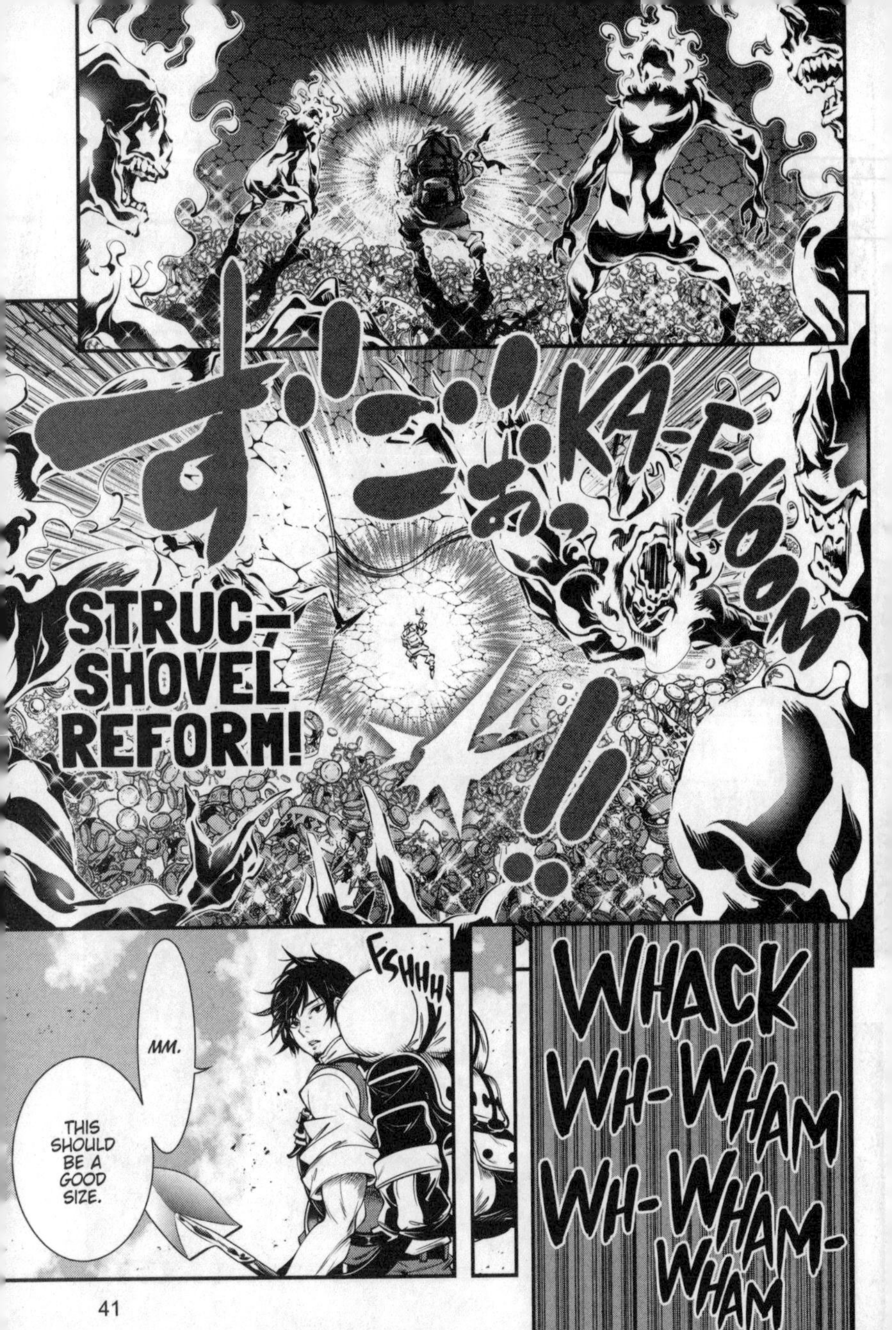
KA-FWOOM!!
STRUC-SHOVEL REFORM!
WHACK WH-WHAM WH-WHAM-WHAM
FSHHH
MM.
THIS SHOULD BE A GOOD SIZE.

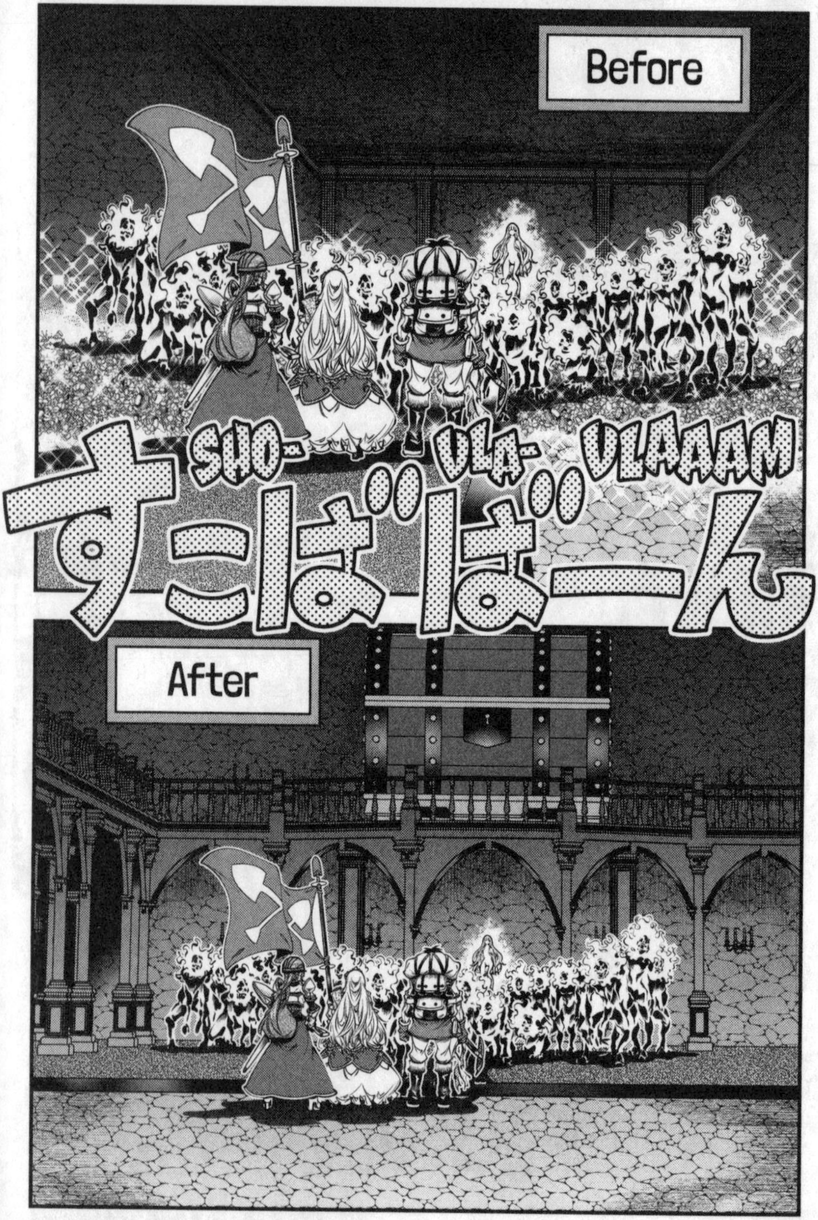
Before
SHO-
VLA-
VLAAAM
すこばばーん
After

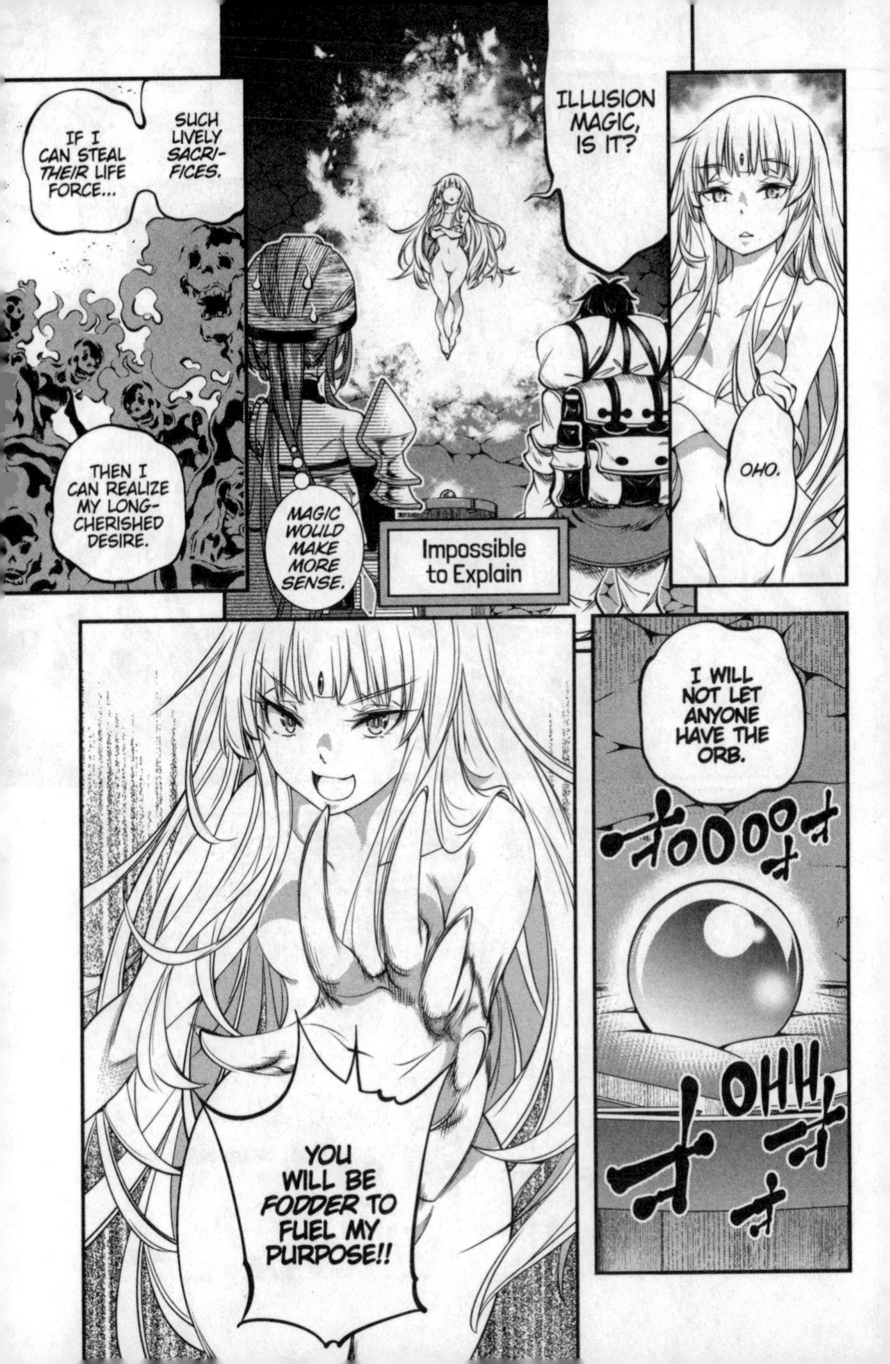

OHO.
ILLUSION MAGIC, IS IT?
MAGIC WOULD MAKE MORE SENSE.
Impossible to Explain
SUCH LIVELY SACRIFICES.
IF I CAN STEAL THEIR LIFE FORCE...
THEN I CAN REALIZE MY LONG-CHERISHED DESIRE.
I WILL NOT LET ANYONE HAVE THE ORB.
OHH
YOU WILL BE FODDER TO FUEL MY PURPOSE!!

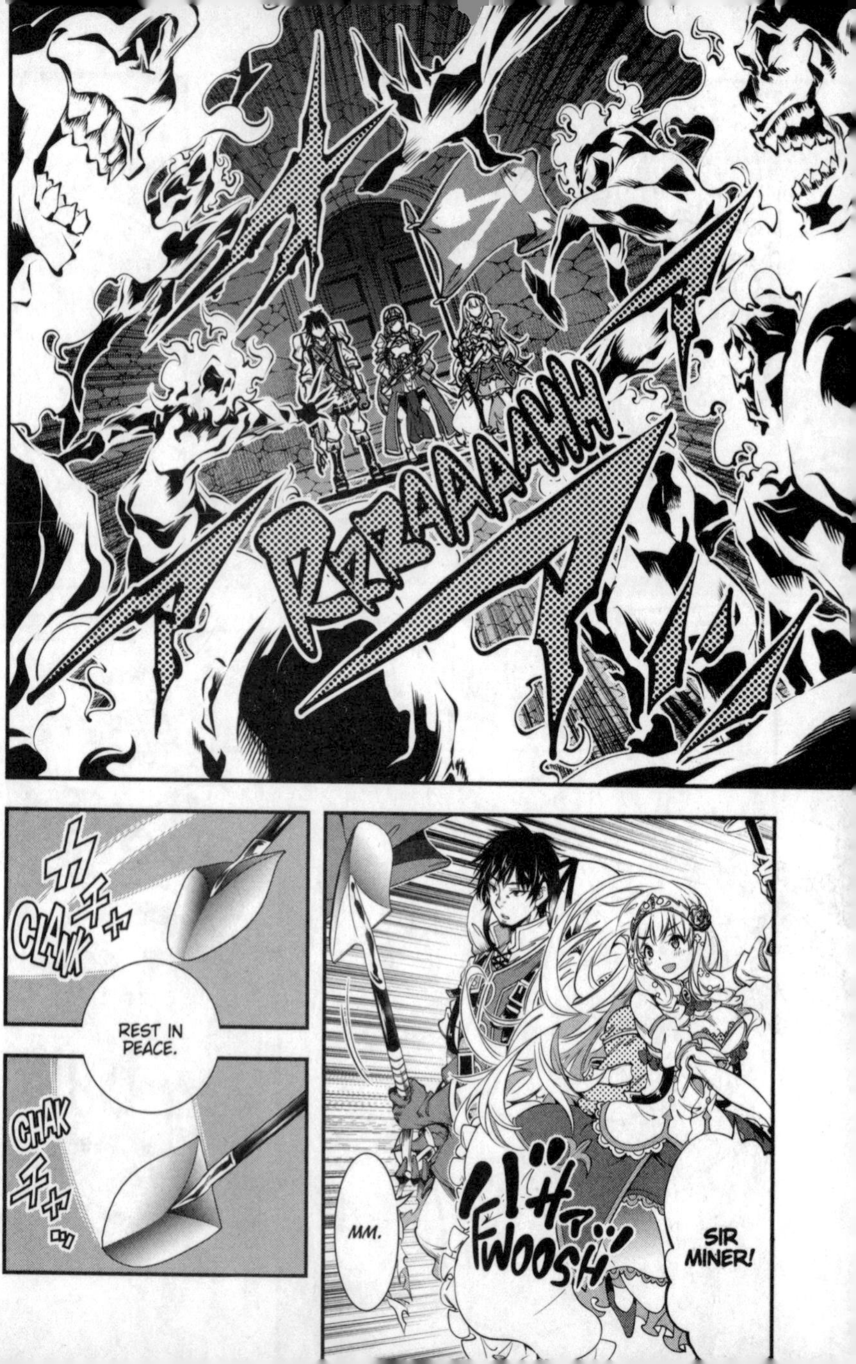
RZZAAAAAHH
SIR MINER!
FWOOSH
MM.
CLANK
REST IN PEACE.
CHAK

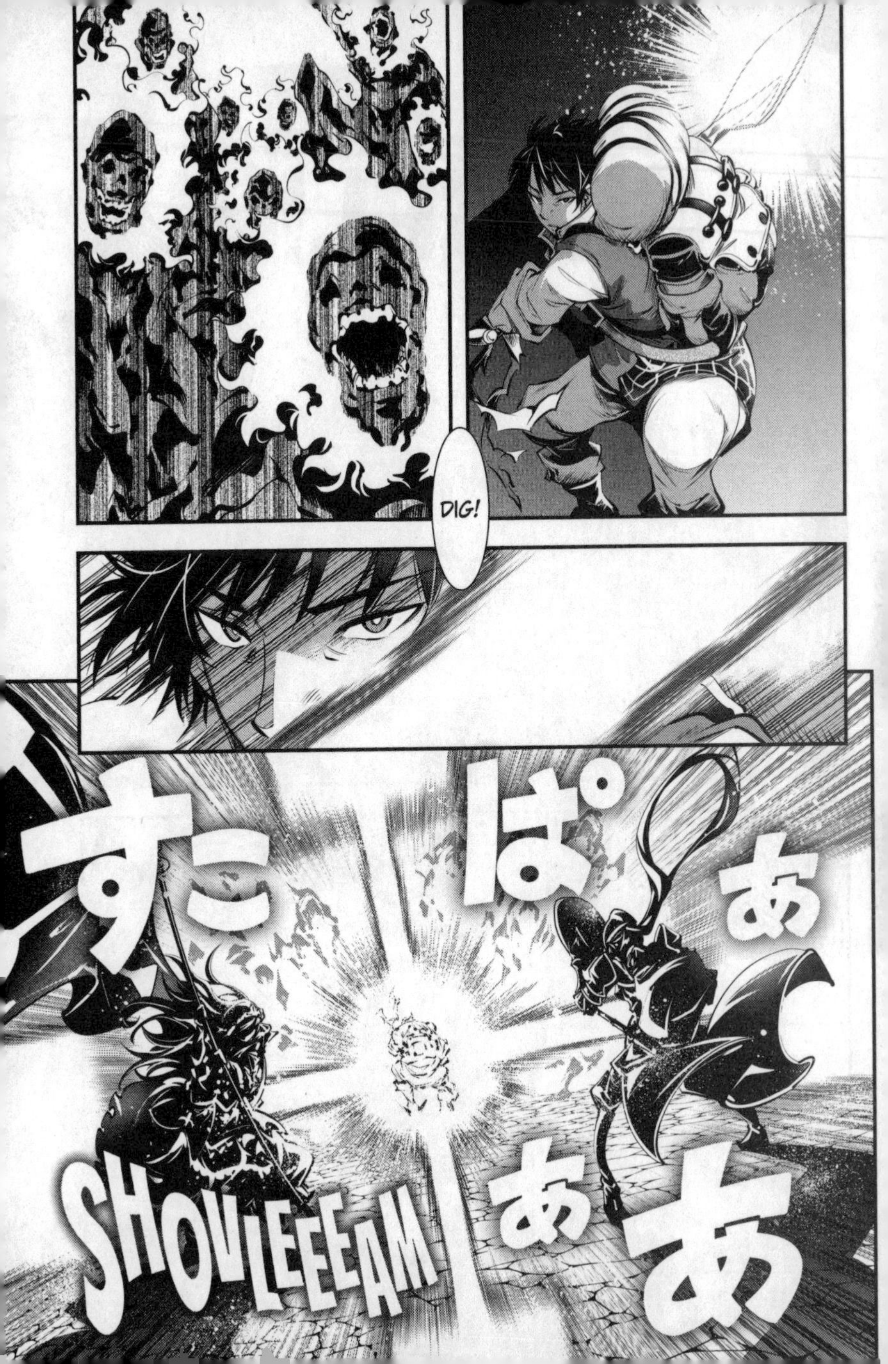
DIG!
すこぱぁぁあ
SHOVLEEEAM

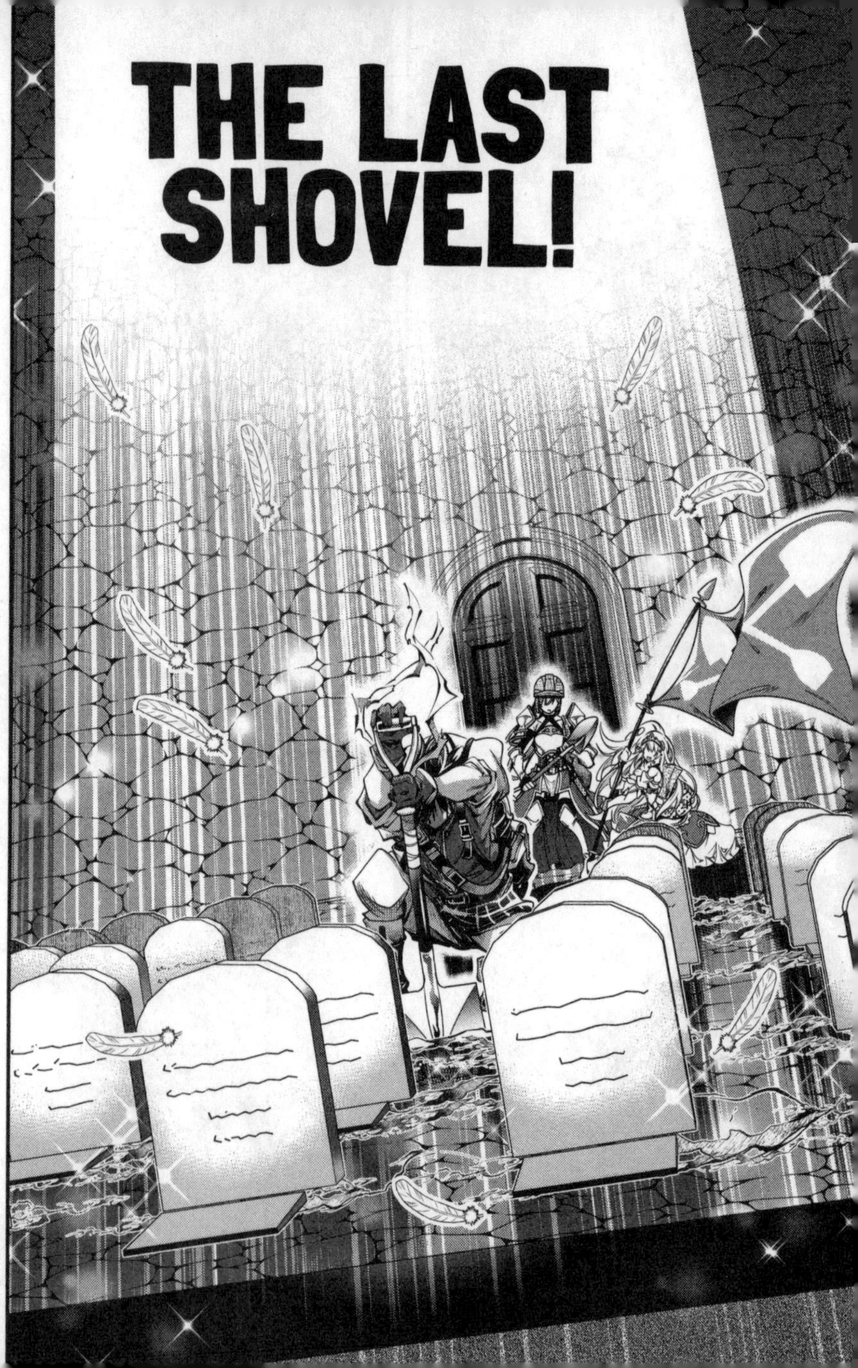
THE LAST SHOVEL!

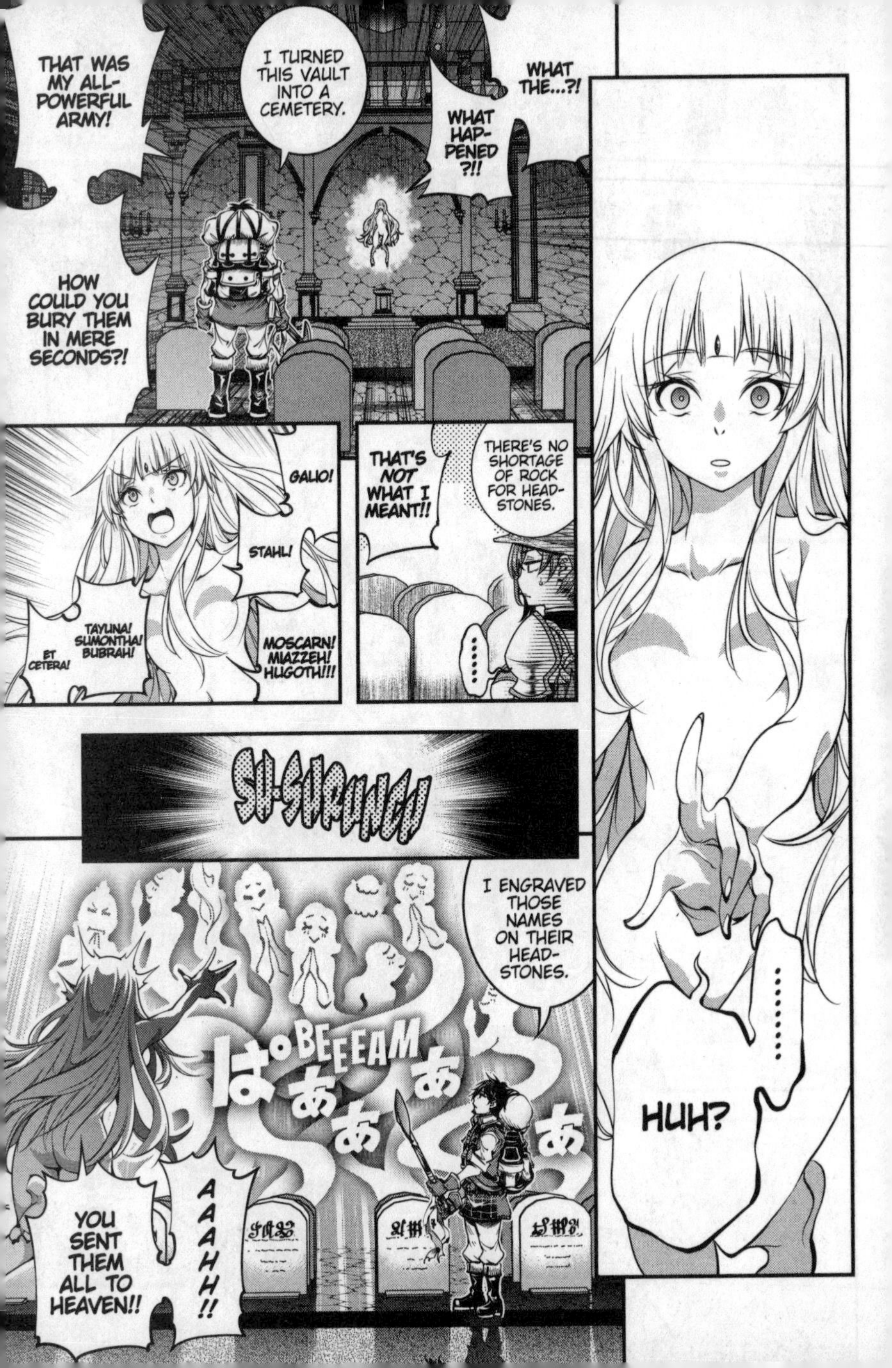

WHAT THE...?!
WHAT HAPPENED?!!
I TURNED THIS VAULT INTO A CEMETERY.
THAT WAS MY ALL-POWERFUL ARMY!
HOW COULD YOU BURY THEM IN MERE SECONDS?!
THERE'S NO SHORTAGE OF ROCK FOR HEADSTONES.
THAT'S *NOT* WHAT I MEANT!!
......
GALIO!
STAHL!
MOSCARN! MIAZZEH! HUGOTH!!!
TAYUNA! SUMONTHA! BUBRAH!
ET CETERA!
SU-SHRUNCH
I ENGRAVED THOSE NAMES ON THEIR HEADSTONES.
BEEEAM
はあああああ
AAAAHH!!
YOU SENT THEM ALL TO HEAVEN!!
......
HUH?

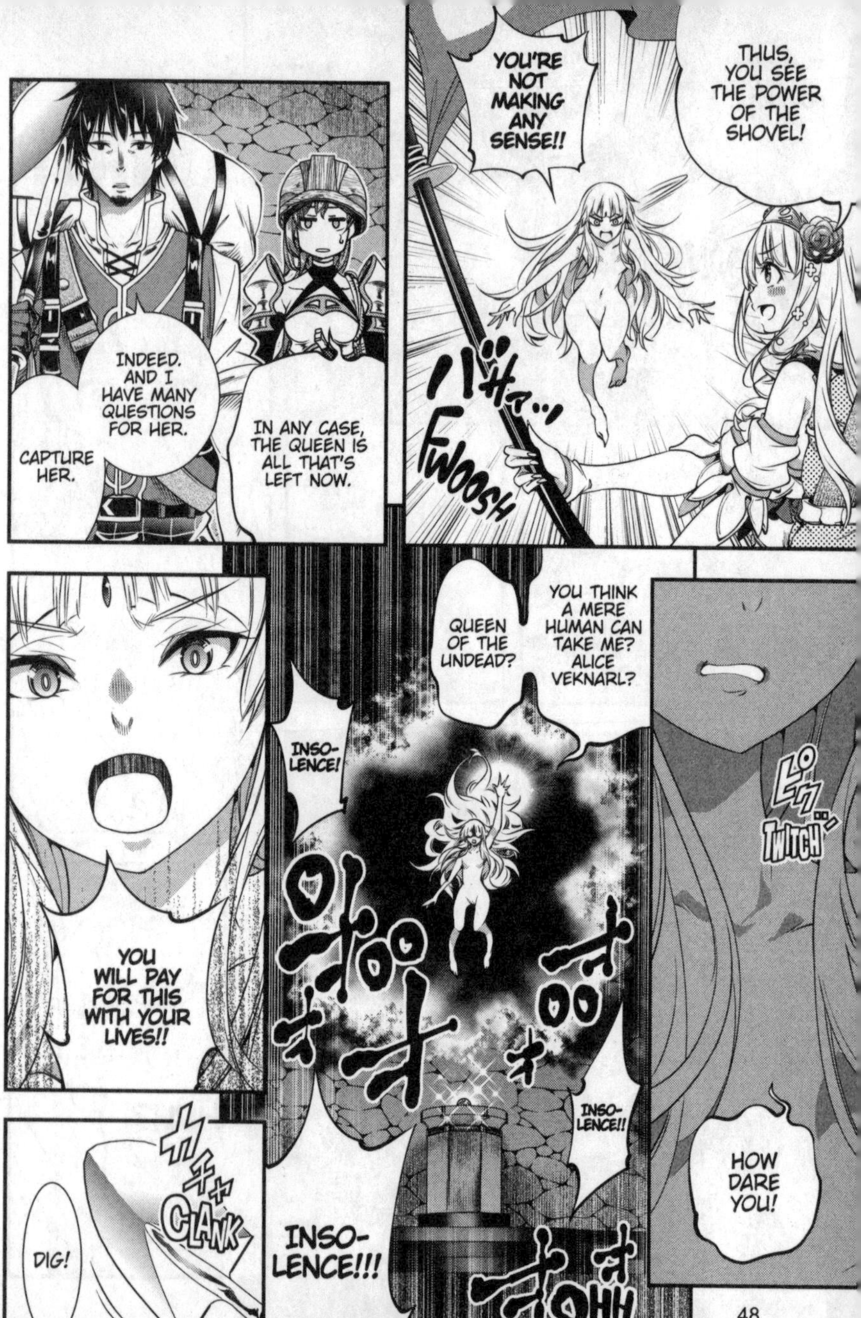
THUS, YOU SEE THE POWER OF THE SHOVEL!
YOU'RE NOT MAKING ANY SENSE!!
FWOOSH
IN ANY CASE, THE QUEEN IS ALL THAT'S LEFT NOW.
INDEED. AND I HAVE MANY QUESTIONS FOR HER.
CAPTURE HER.
TWITCH
HOW DARE YOU!
YOU THINK A MERE HUMAN CAN TAKE ME? ALICE VEKNARL?
QUEEN OF THE UNDEAD?
INSO-LENCE!
INSO-LENCE!!
INSO-LENCE!!!
OHH
YOU WILL PAY FOR THIS WITH YOUR LIVES!!
CLANK
DIG!

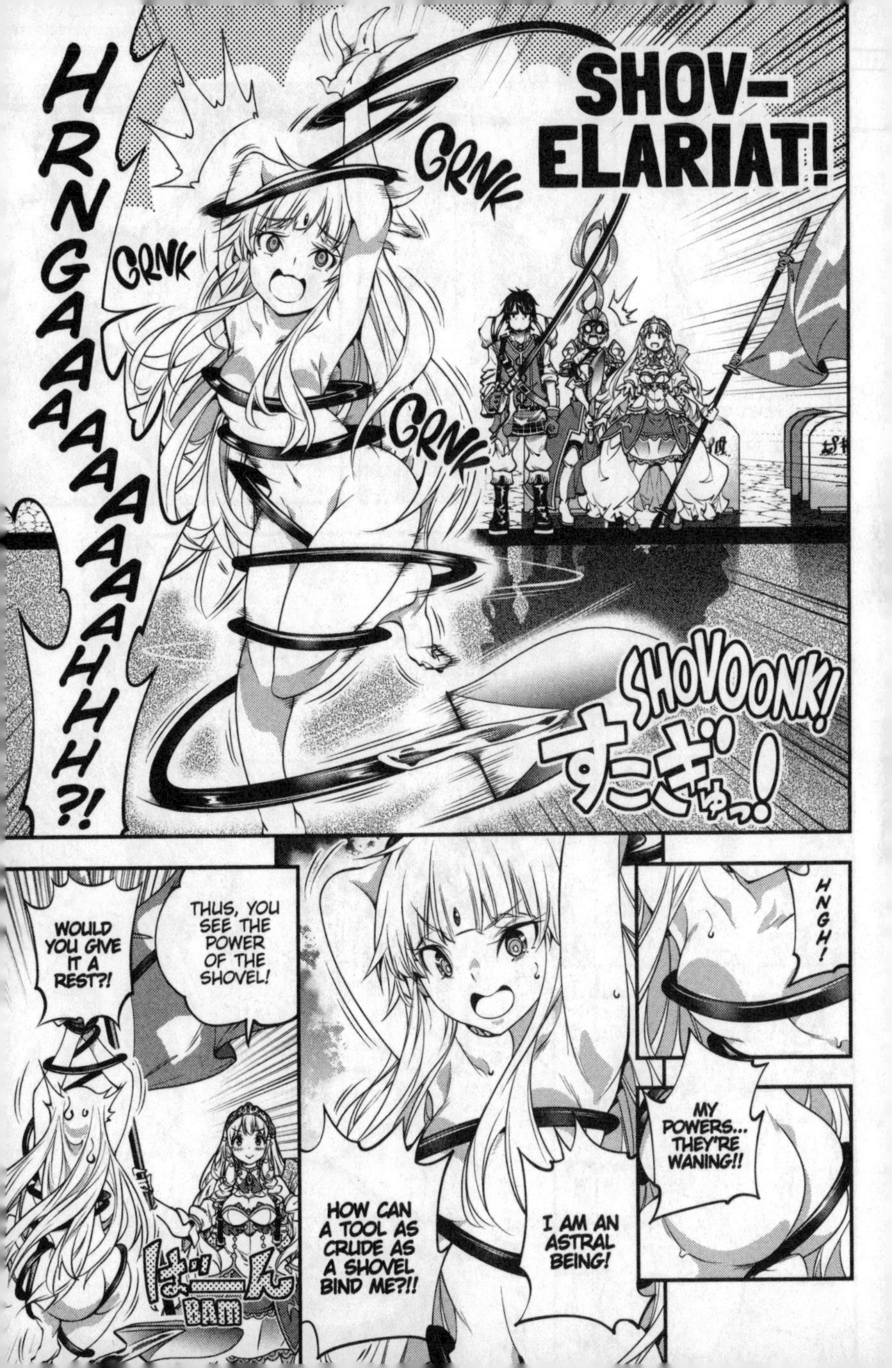
SHOV-
ELARIAT!
GRNK
GRNK
GRNK
SHOVOONK!
すこぎゅっ!
HRNGAAAAAAAAAHHH?!
HNGH!
MY POWERS... THEY'RE WANING!!
I AM AN ASTRAL BEING!
HOW CAN A TOOL AS CRUDE AS A SHOVEL BIND ME?!!
THUS, YOU SEE THE POWER OF THE SHOVEL!
WOULD YOU GIVE IT A REST?!
ばーん
BAM

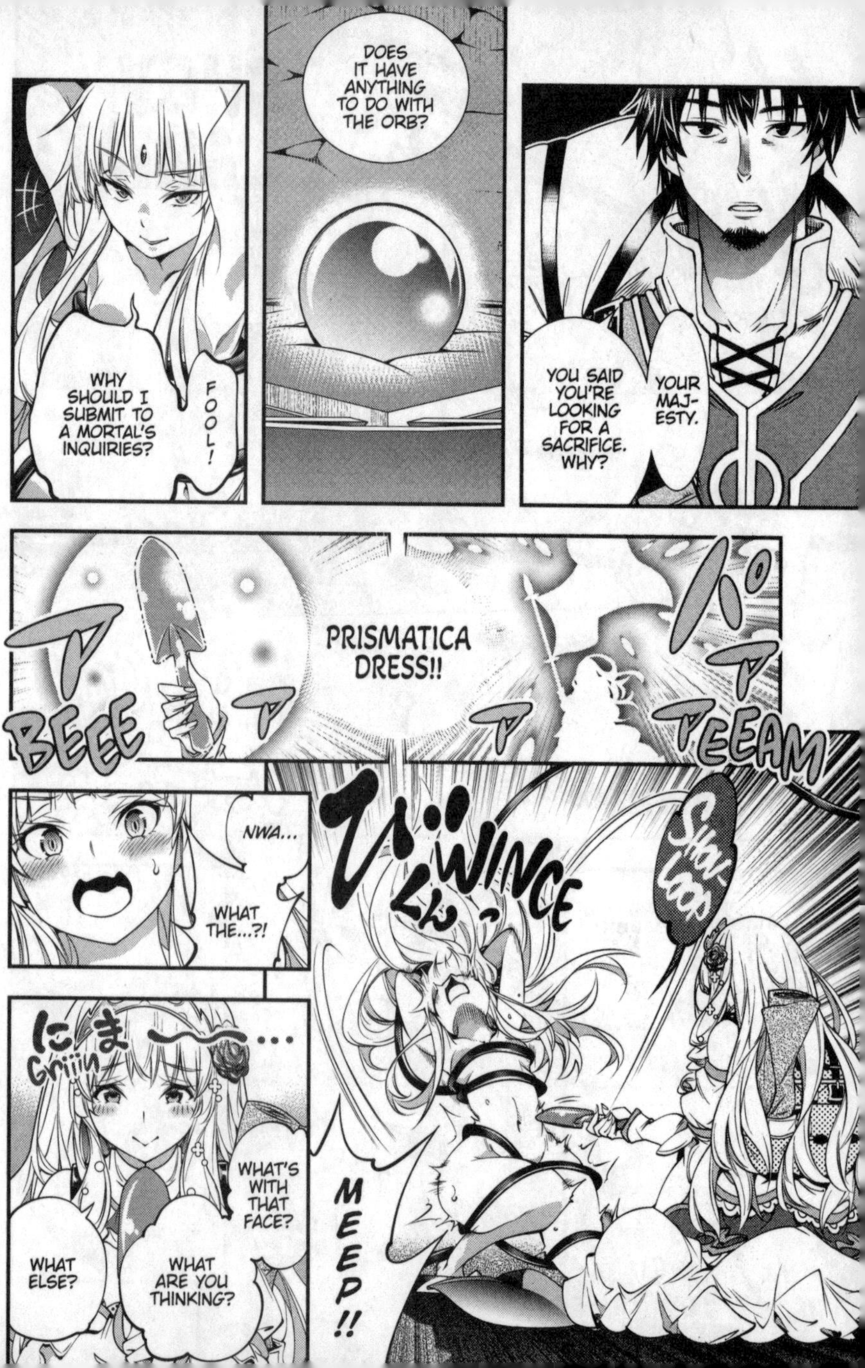

YOUR MAJESTY.
YOU SAID YOU'RE LOOKING FOR A SACRIFICE. WHY?
DOES IT HAVE ANYTHING TO DO WITH THE ORB?
FOOL!
WHY SHOULD I SUBMIT TO A MORTAL'S INQUIRIES?
パァ
TEEAM
ア
PRISMATICA DRESS!!
ア
ア
BEEE
ぴ
WINCE
くんっ
MEEP!!
NWA...
WHAT THE...?!
にま〜〜…
Griiin
WHAT'S WITH THAT FACE?
WHAT ARE YOU THINKING?
WHAT ELSE?

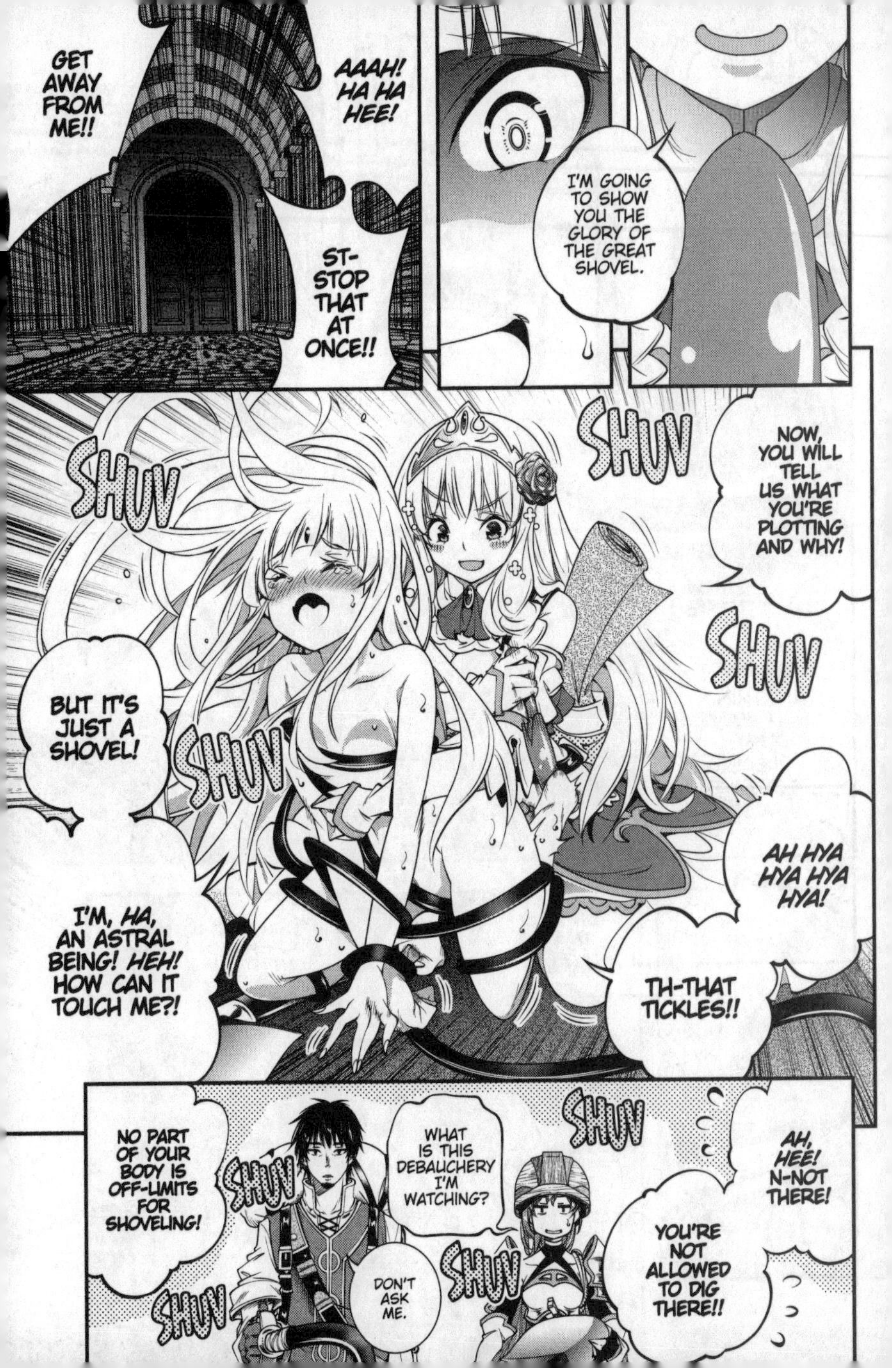
I'M GOING TO SHOW YOU THE GLORY OF THE GREAT SHOVEL.
AAAH! HA HA HEE!
GET AWAY FROM ME!!
ST-STOP THAT AT ONCE!!
NOW, YOU WILL TELL US WHAT YOU'RE PLOTTING AND WHY!
SHUV
SHUV
SHUV
BUT IT'S JUST A SHOVEL!
SHUV
AH HYA HYA HYA HYA!
TH-THAT TICKLES!!
I'M, HA, AN ASTRAL BEING! HEH! HOW CAN IT TOUCH ME?!
SHUV
AH, HEE! N-NOT THERE!
WHAT IS THIS DEBAUCHERY I'M WATCHING?
NO PART OF YOUR BODY IS OFF-LIMITS FOR SHOVELING!
SHUV
YOU'RE NOT ALLOWED TO DIG THERE!!
SHUV
DON'T ASK ME.
SHUV

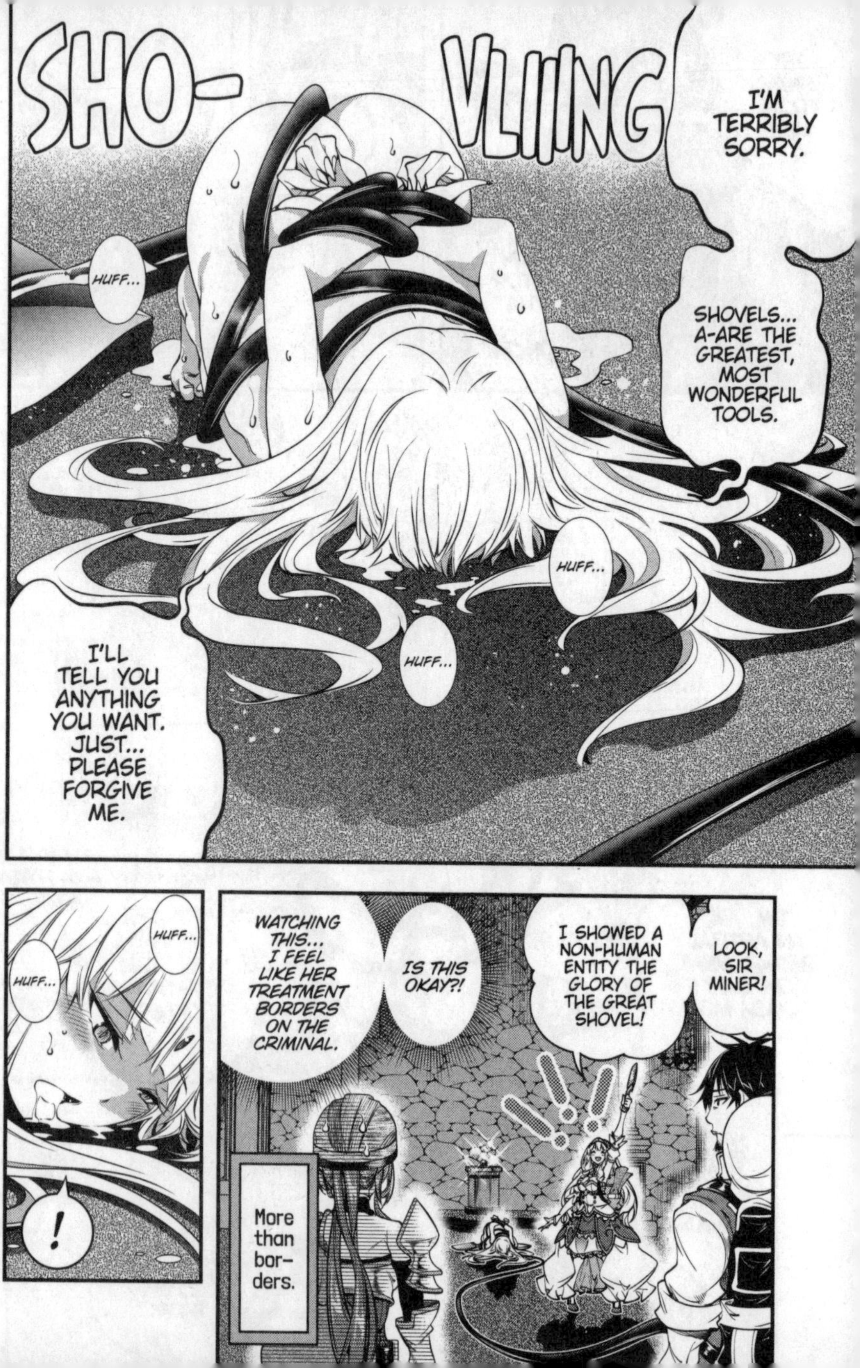
SHO-
VLIIING
I'M TERRIBLY SORRY.
SHOVELS... A-ARE THE GREATEST, MOST WONDERFUL TOOLS.
HUFF...
HUFF...
HUFF...
I'LL TELL YOU ANYTHING YOU WANT. JUST... PLEASE FORGIVE ME.
LOOK, SIR MINER!
I SHOWED A NON-HUMAN ENTITY THE GLORY OF THE GREAT SHOVEL!
IS THIS OKAY?!
WATCHING THIS... I FEEL LIKE HER TREATMENT BORDERS ON THE CRIMINAL.
More than bor-ders.
HUFF...
HUFF...
!

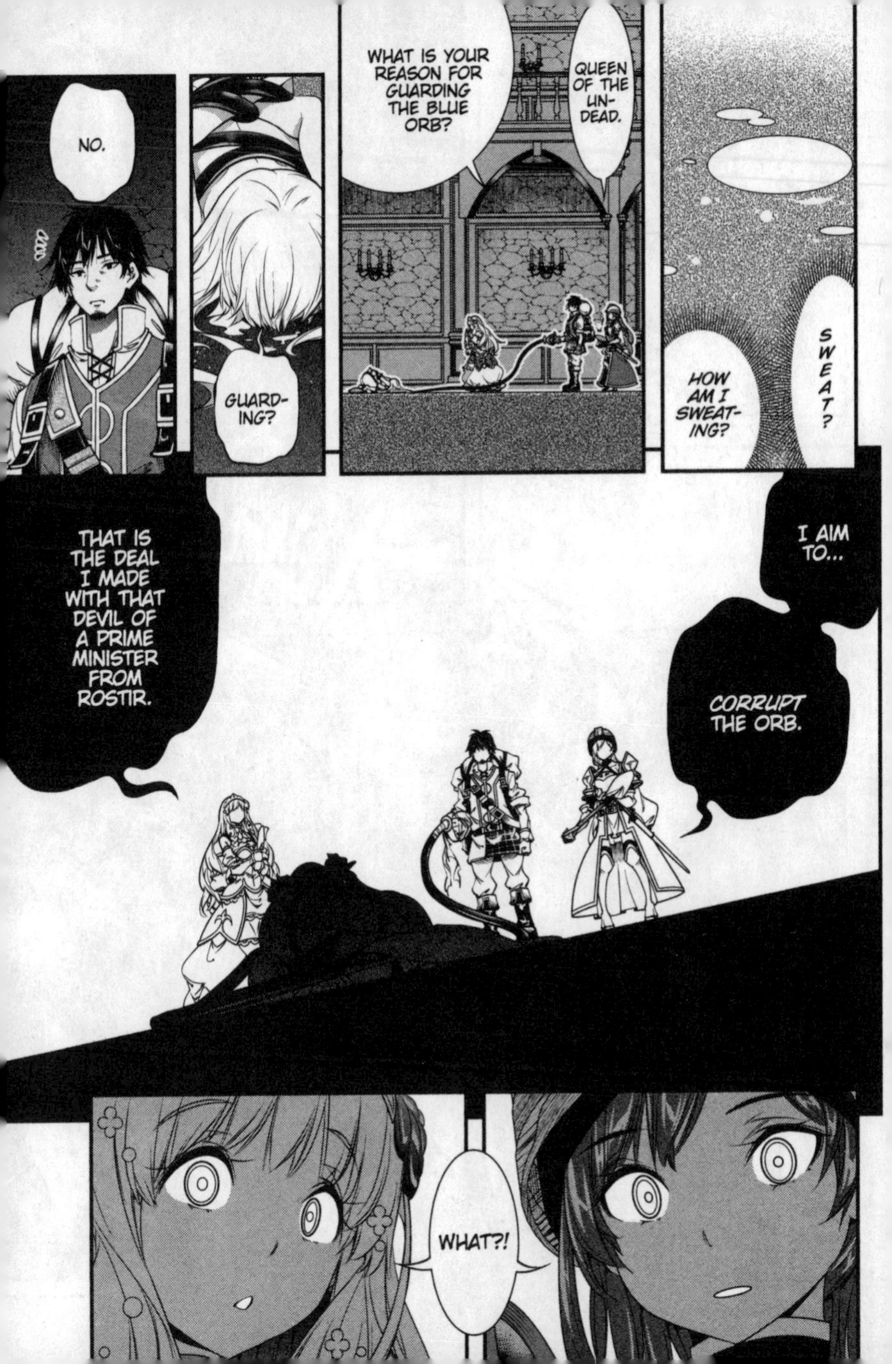
SWEAT?
HOW AM I SWEATING?
QUEEN OF THE UNDEAD.
WHAT IS YOUR REASON FOR GUARDING THE BLUE ORB?
GUARDING?
NO.
I AIM TO...
CORRUPT THE ORB.
THAT IS THE DEAL I MADE WITH THAT DEVIL OF A PRIME MINISTER FROM ROSTIR.
WHAT?!

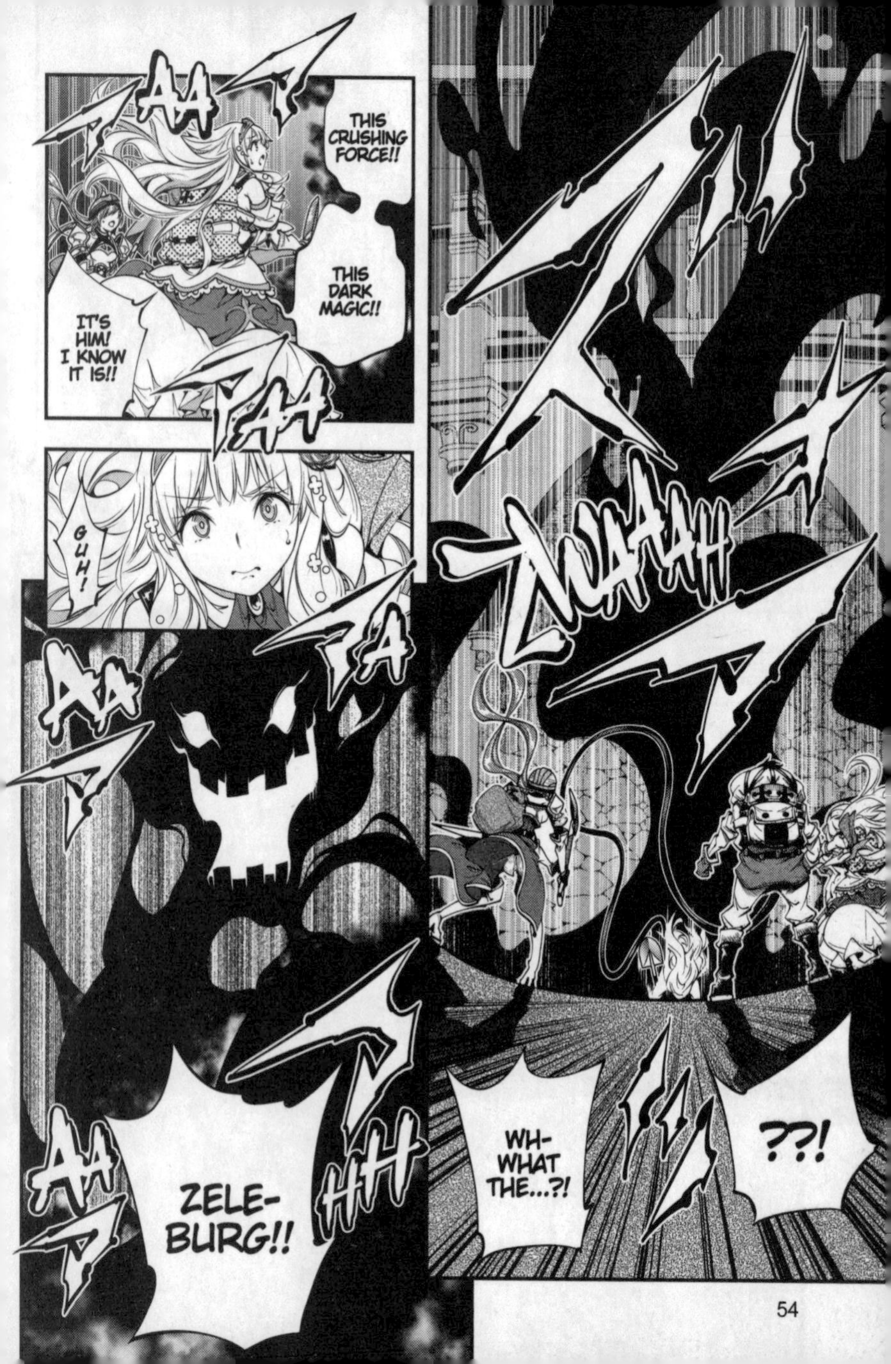

ZWAAAH
??!
WH-
WHAT
THE...?!
THIS
CRUSHING
FORCE!!
THIS
DARK
MAGIC!!
IT'S
HIM!
I KNOW
IT IS!!
GUH!
ZELE-
BURG!!

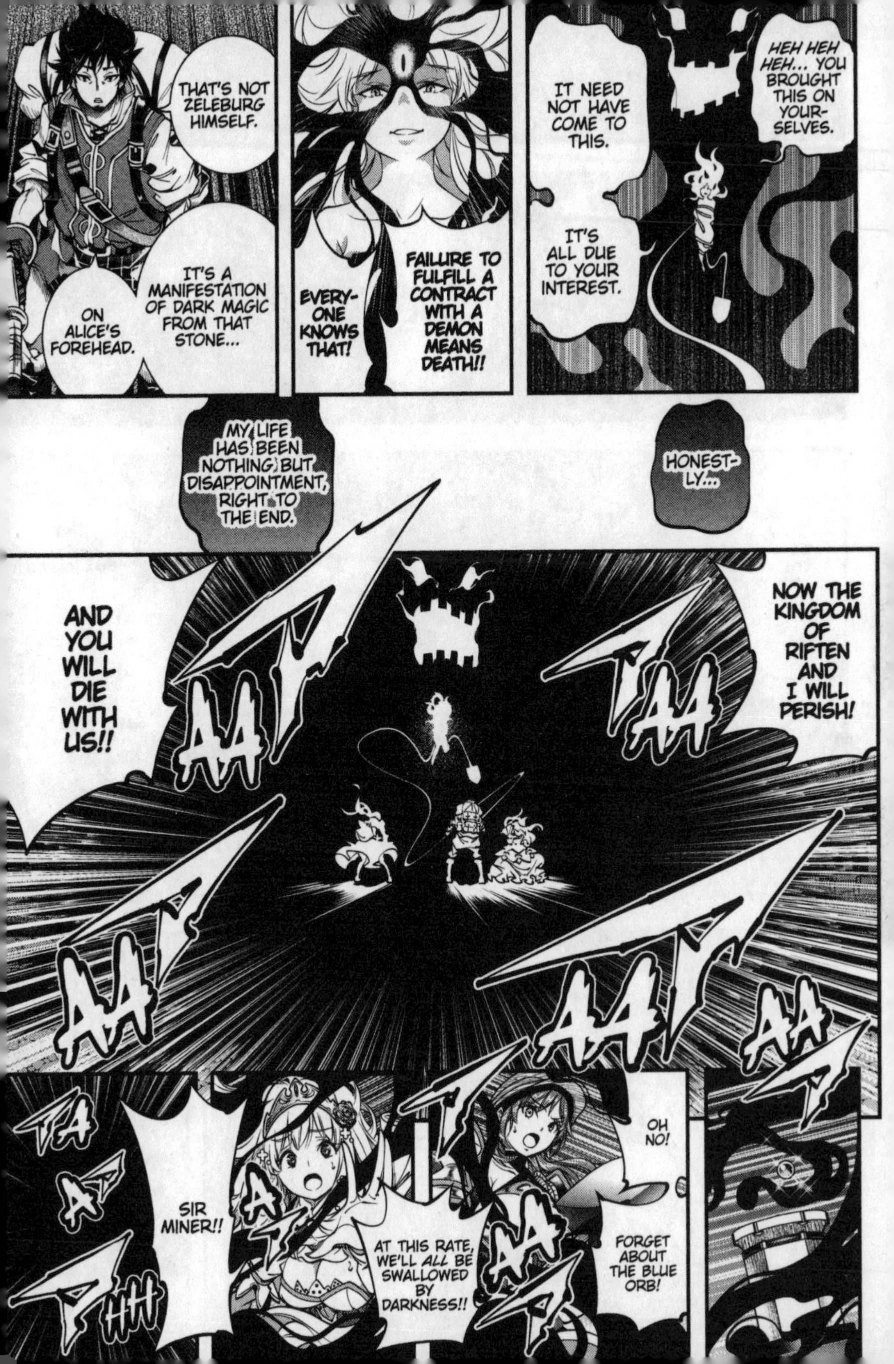

HEH HEH HEH... YOU BROUGHT THIS ON YOURSELVES.
IT NEED NOT HAVE COME TO THIS.
IT'S ALL DUE TO YOUR INTEREST.
FAILURE TO FULFILL A CONTRACT WITH A DEMON MEANS DEATH!!
EVERYONE KNOWS THAT!
THAT'S NOT ZELEBURG HIMSELF.
IT'S A MANIFESTATION OF DARK MAGIC FROM THAT STONE...
ON ALICE'S FOREHEAD.
HONESTLY...
MY LIFE HAS BEEN NOTHING BUT DISAPPOINTMENT, RIGHT TO THE END.
NOW THE KINGDOM OF RIFTEN AND I WILL PERISH!
AA
AA
AND YOU WILL DIE WITH US!!
AA
AA
AA
OH NO!
FORGET ABOUT THE BLUE ORB!
AA
AT THIS RATE, WE'LL *ALL* BE SWALLOWED BY DARKNESS!!
SIR MINER!!

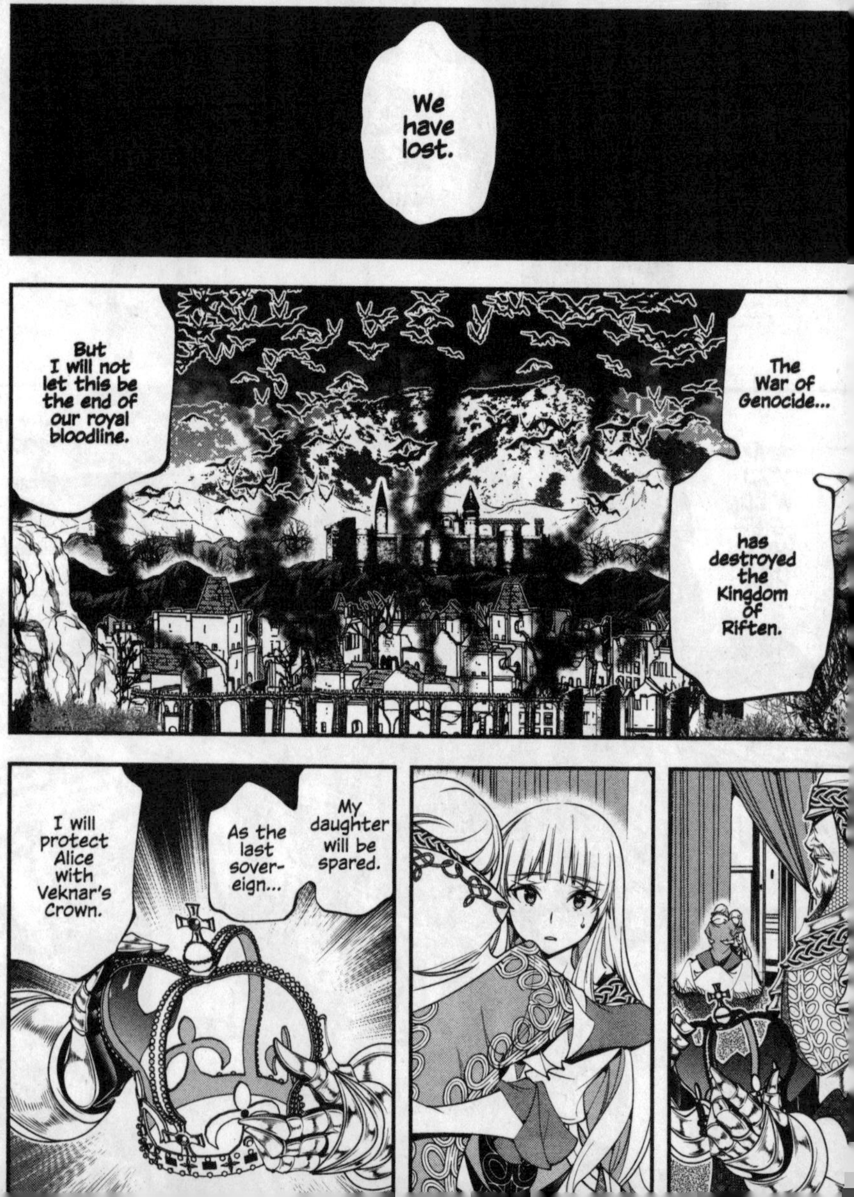
We have lost.
The War of Genocide...
has destroyed the Kingdom of Riften.
But I will not let this be the end of our royal bloodline.
My daughter will be spared.
As the last sover-eign...
I will protect Alice with Veknar's Crown.

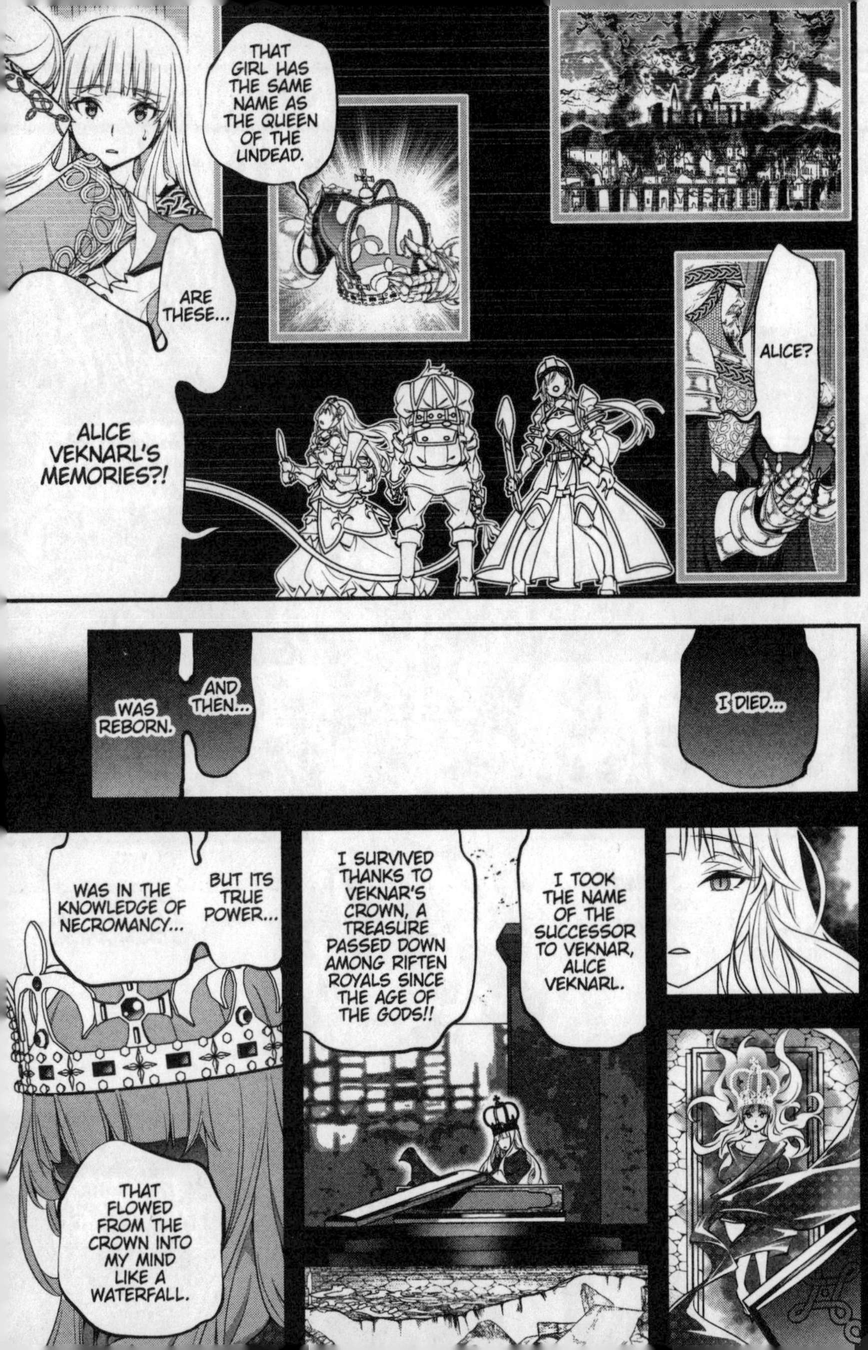
ALICE?
THAT GIRL HAS THE SAME NAME AS THE QUEEN OF THE UNDEAD.
ARE THESE...
ALICE VEKNARL'S MEMORIES?!
I DIED...
AND THEN...
WAS REBORN.
I TOOK THE NAME OF THE SUCCESSOR TO VEKNAR, ALICE VEKNARL.
I SURVIVED THANKS TO VEKNAR'S CROWN, A TREASURE PASSED DOWN AMONG RIFTEN ROYALS SINCE THE AGE OF THE GODS!!
BUT ITS TRUE POWER...
WAS IN THE KNOWLEDGE OF NECROMANCY...
THAT FLOWED FROM THE CROWN INTO MY MIND LIKE A WATERFALL.

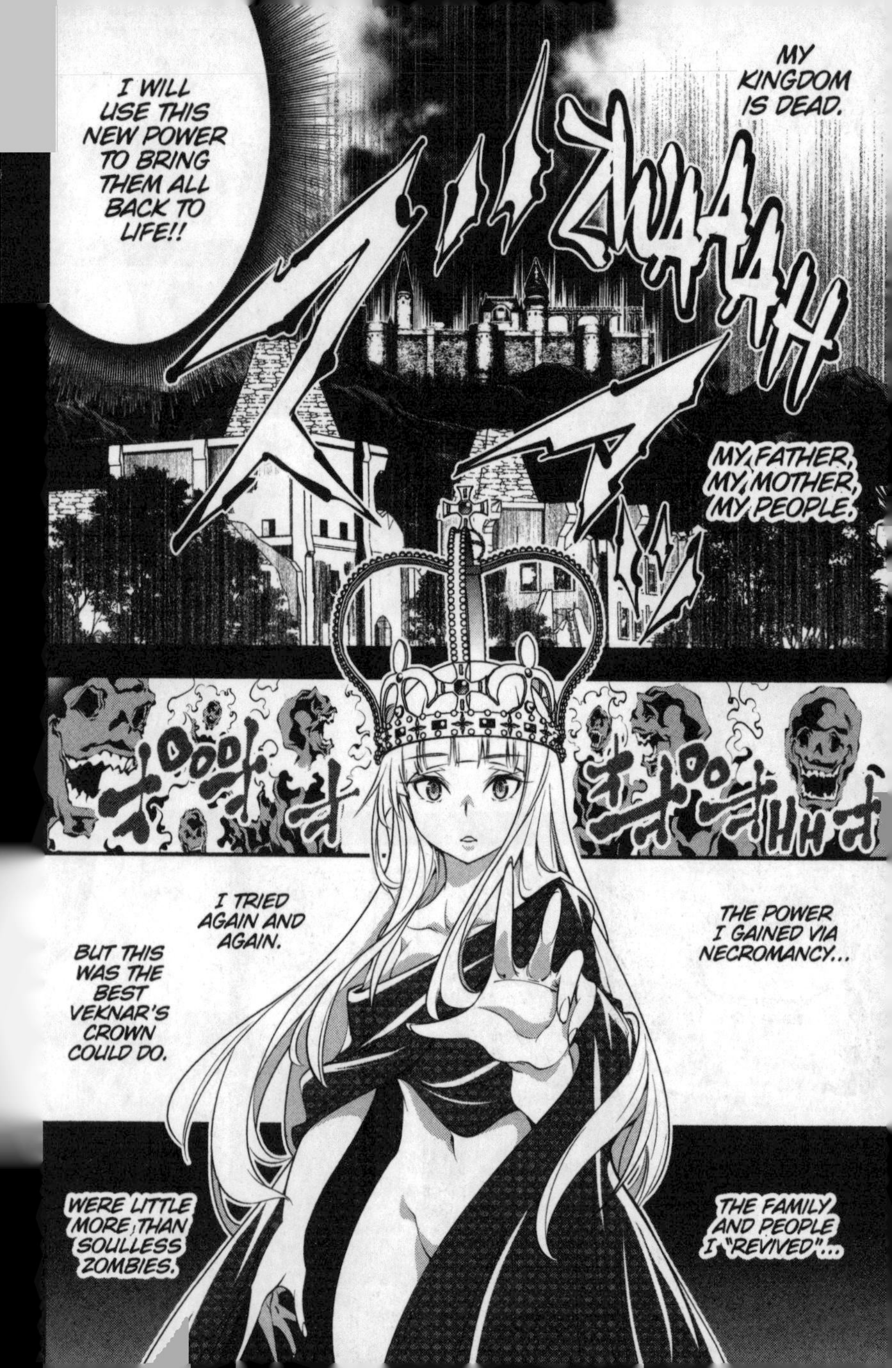
MY KINGDOM IS DEAD.
I WILL USE THIS NEW POWER TO BRING THEM ALL BACK TO LIFE!!
MY FATHER, MY MOTHER, MY PEOPLE.
THE POWER I GAINED VIA NECROMANCY...
I TRIED AGAIN AND AGAIN.
BUT THIS WAS THE BEST VEKNAR'S CROWN COULD DO.
THE FAMILY AND PEOPLE I "REVIVED"...
WERE LITTLE MORE THAN SOULLESS ZOMBIES.

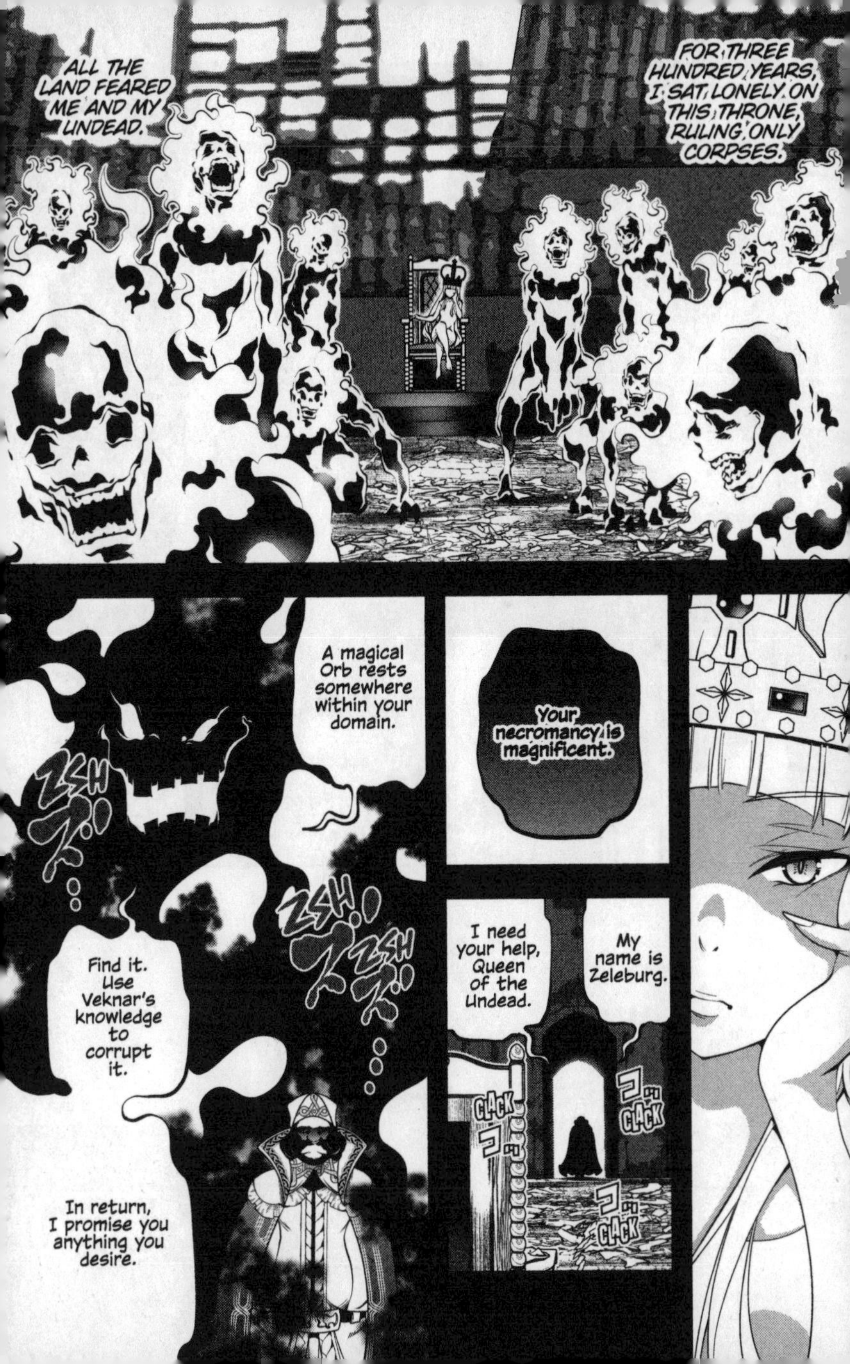
FOR THREE HUNDRED YEARS, I SAT LONELY ON THIS THRONE, RULING ONLY CORPSES.
ALL THE LAND FEARED ME AND MY UNDEAD.
Your necromancy is magnificent.
My name is Zeleburg.
I need your help, Queen of the Undead.
CLACK
CLACK
CLACK
A magical Orb rests somewhere within your domain.
ZSH
ZSH!
ZSH
Find it. Use Veknar's knowledge to corrupt it.
In return, I promise you anything you desire.

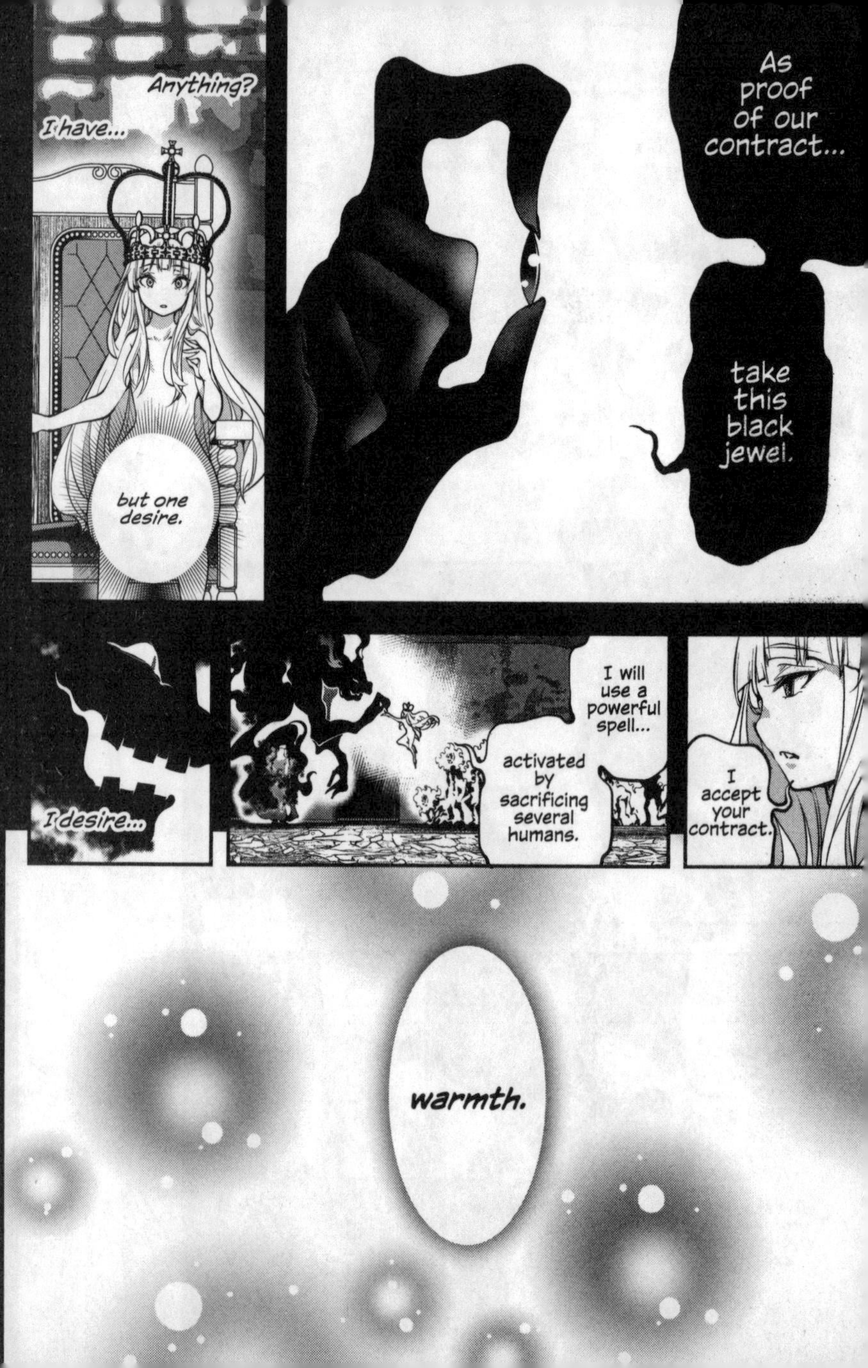
As proof of our contract...
take this black jewel.
Anything?
I have...
but one desire.
I accept your contract.
I will use a powerful spell...
activated by sacrificing several humans.
I desire...
warmth.

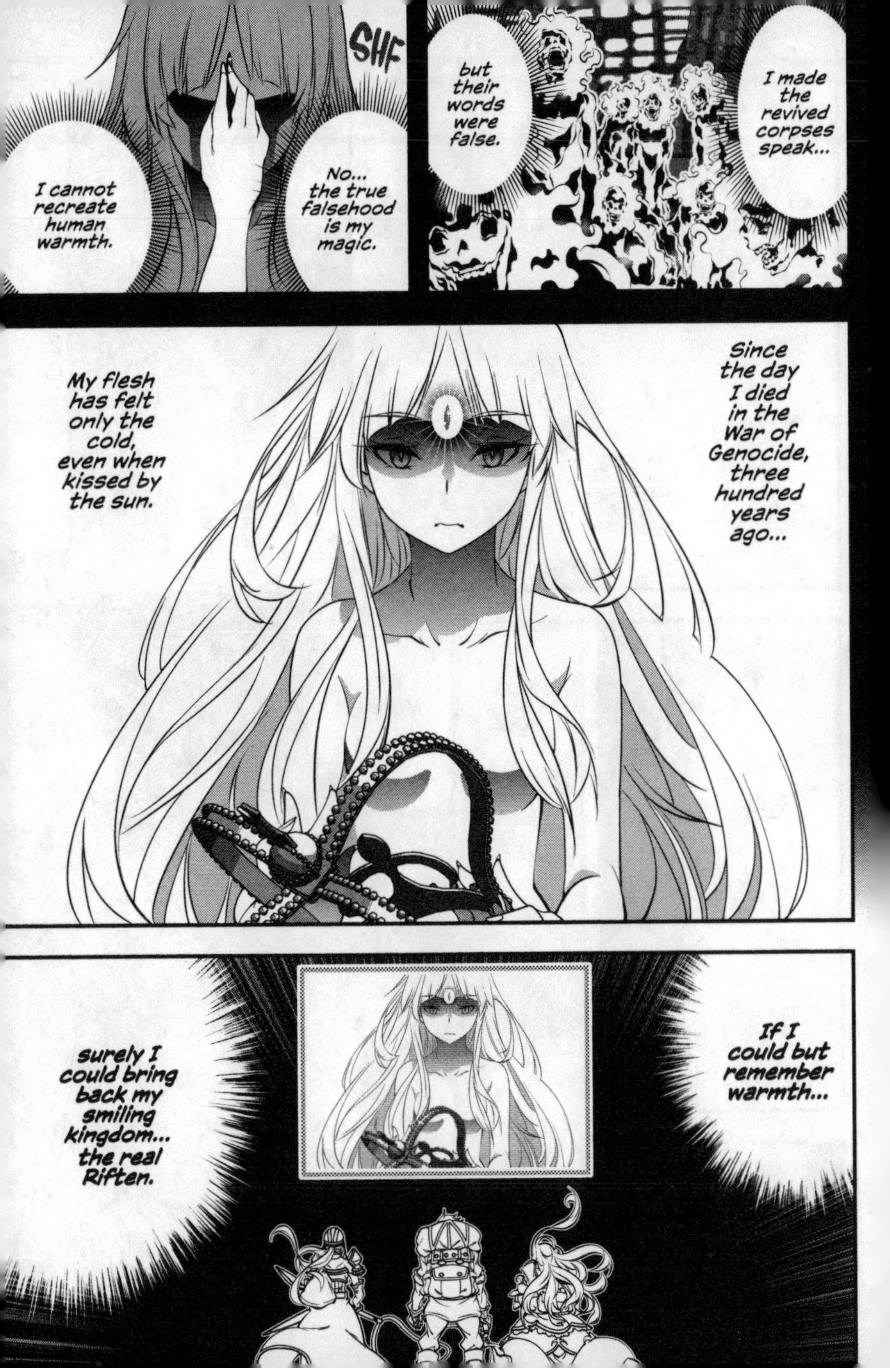
I made the revived corpses speak...
but their words were false.
SHF
No... the true falsehood is my magic.
I cannot recreate human warmth.
Since the day I died in the War of Genocide, three hundred years ago...
My flesh has felt only the cold, even when kissed by the sun.
If I could but remember warmth...
surely I could bring back my smiling kingdom... the real Riften.

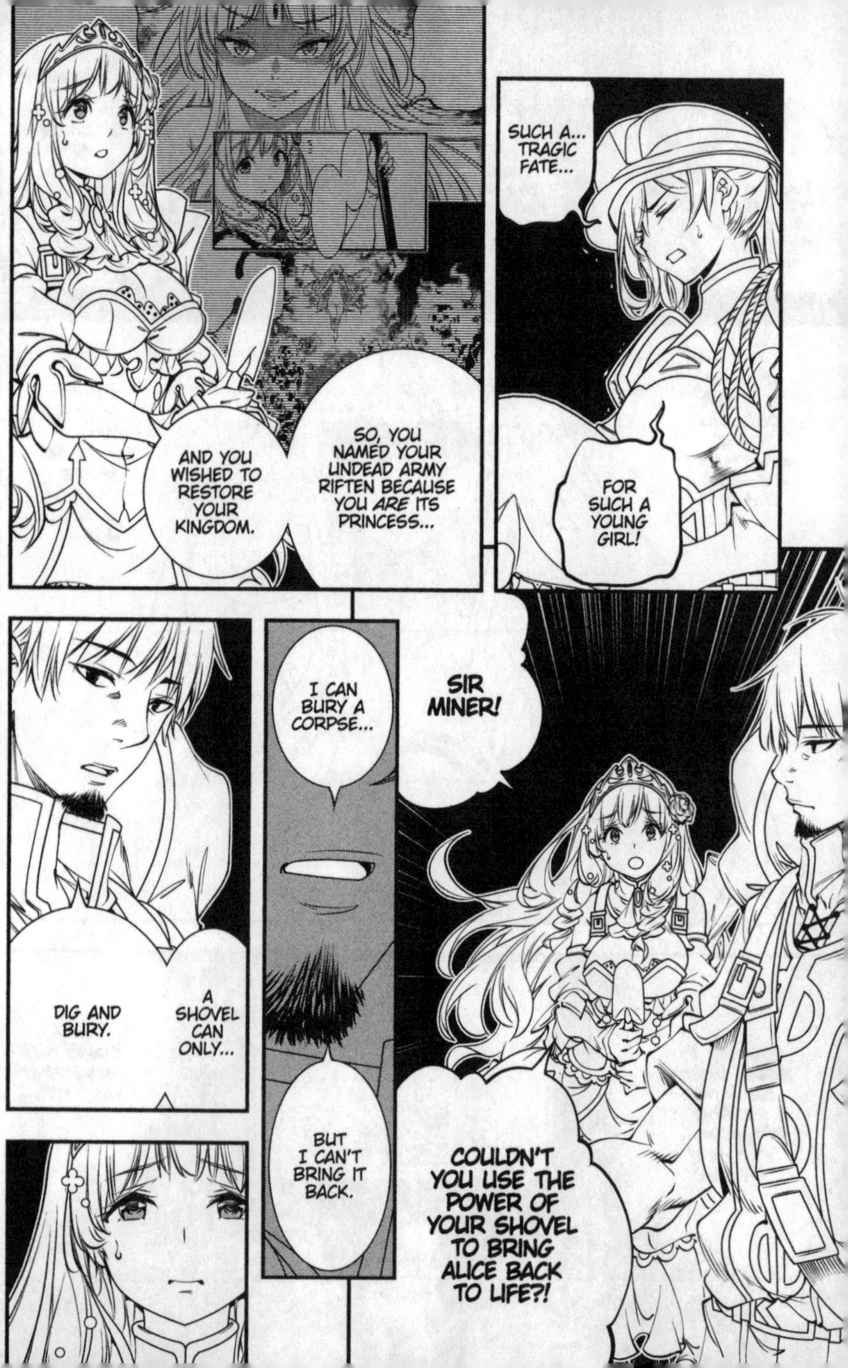

SUCH A... TRAGIC FATE...
FOR SUCH A YOUNG GIRL!
SO, YOU NAMED YOUR UNDEAD ARMY RIFTEN BECAUSE YOU *ARE* ITS PRINCESS...
AND YOU WISHED TO RESTORE YOUR KINGDOM.
SIR MINER!
COULDN'T YOU USE THE POWER OF YOUR SHOVEL TO BRING ALICE BACK TO LIFE?!
I CAN BURY A CORPSE...
BUT I CAN'T BRING IT BACK.
A SHOVEL CAN ONLY...
DIG AND BURY.

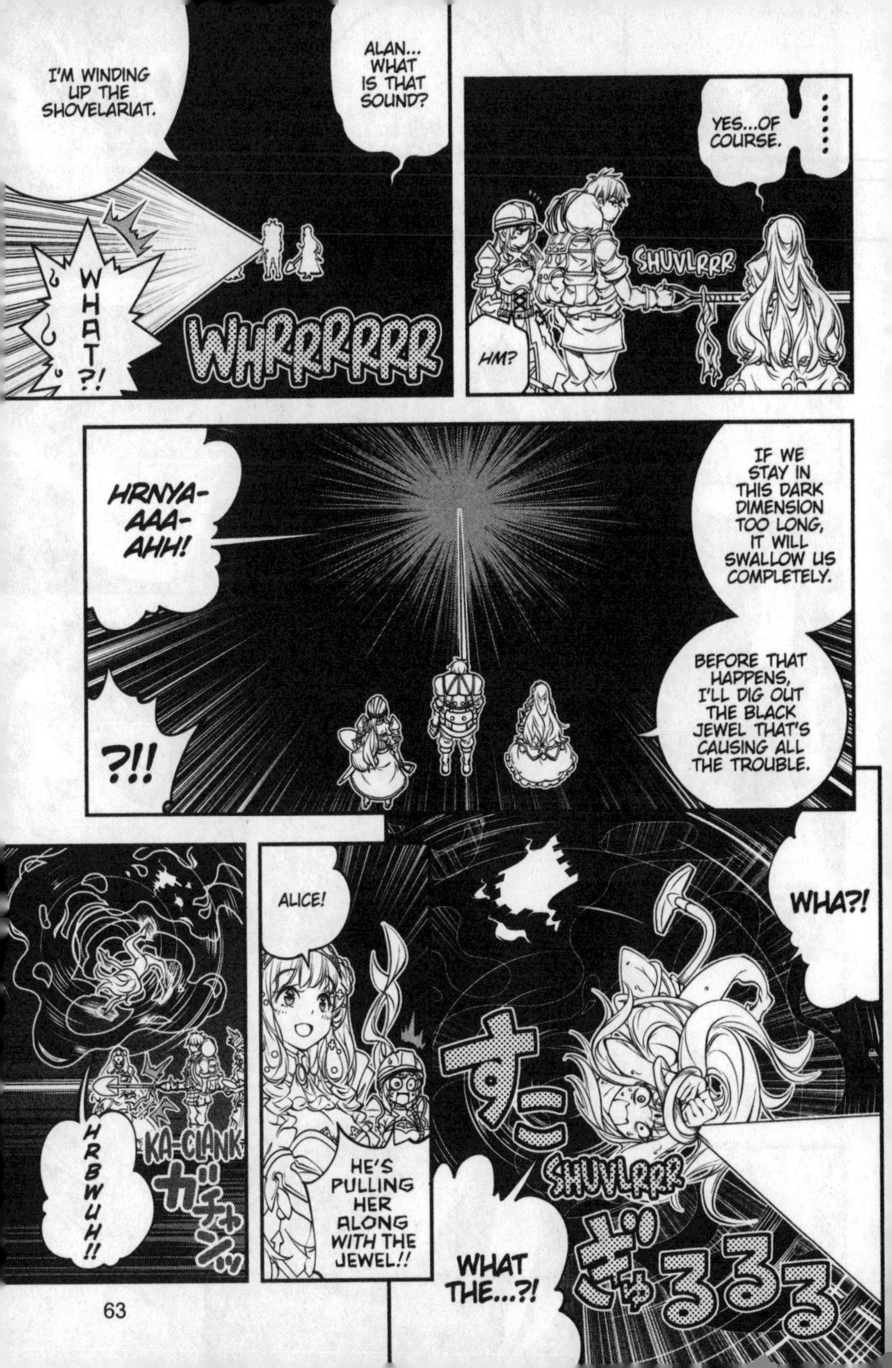
YES...OF COURSE.
......
SHUVLRRR
HM?
ALAN... WHAT IS THAT SOUND?
I'M WINDING UP THE SHOVELARIAT.
WHAT?!
WHRRRRRR
IF WE STAY IN THIS DARK DIMENSION TOO LONG, IT WILL SWALLOW US COMPLETELY.
BEFORE THAT HAPPENS, I'LL DIG OUT THE BLACK JEWEL THAT'S CAUSING ALL THE TROUBLE.
HRNYA-AAA-AHH!
?!!
WHA?!
すこ
SHUVLRRR
ぎゅるるる
WHAT THE...?!
ALICE!
HE'S PULLING HER ALONG WITH THE JEWEL!!
KA-CLANK
ガチャッ
HRBWUH!!

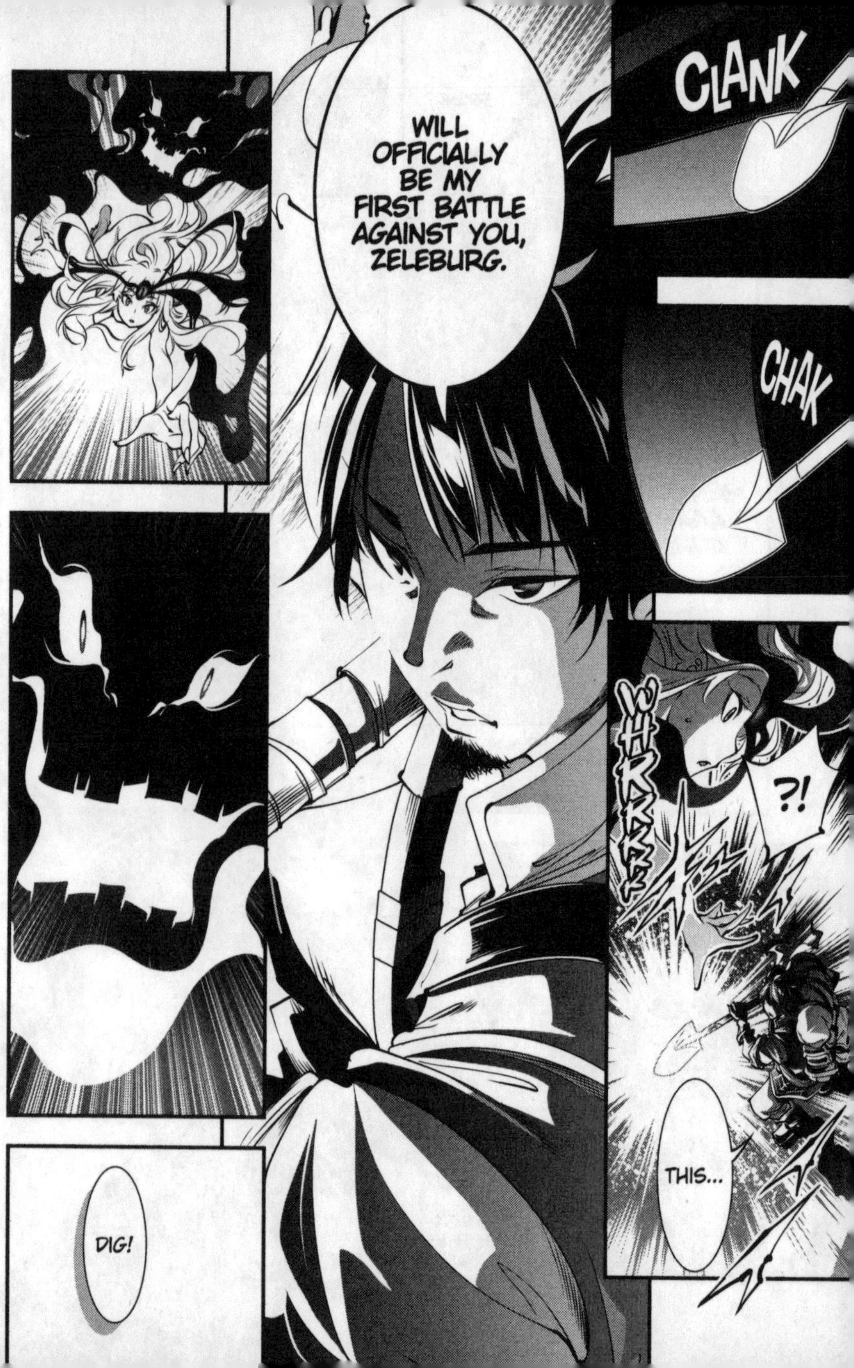
CLANK
CHAK
WILL OFFICIALLY BE MY FIRST BATTLE AGAINST YOU, ZELEBURG.
WHRRRR
?!
THIS...
DIG!

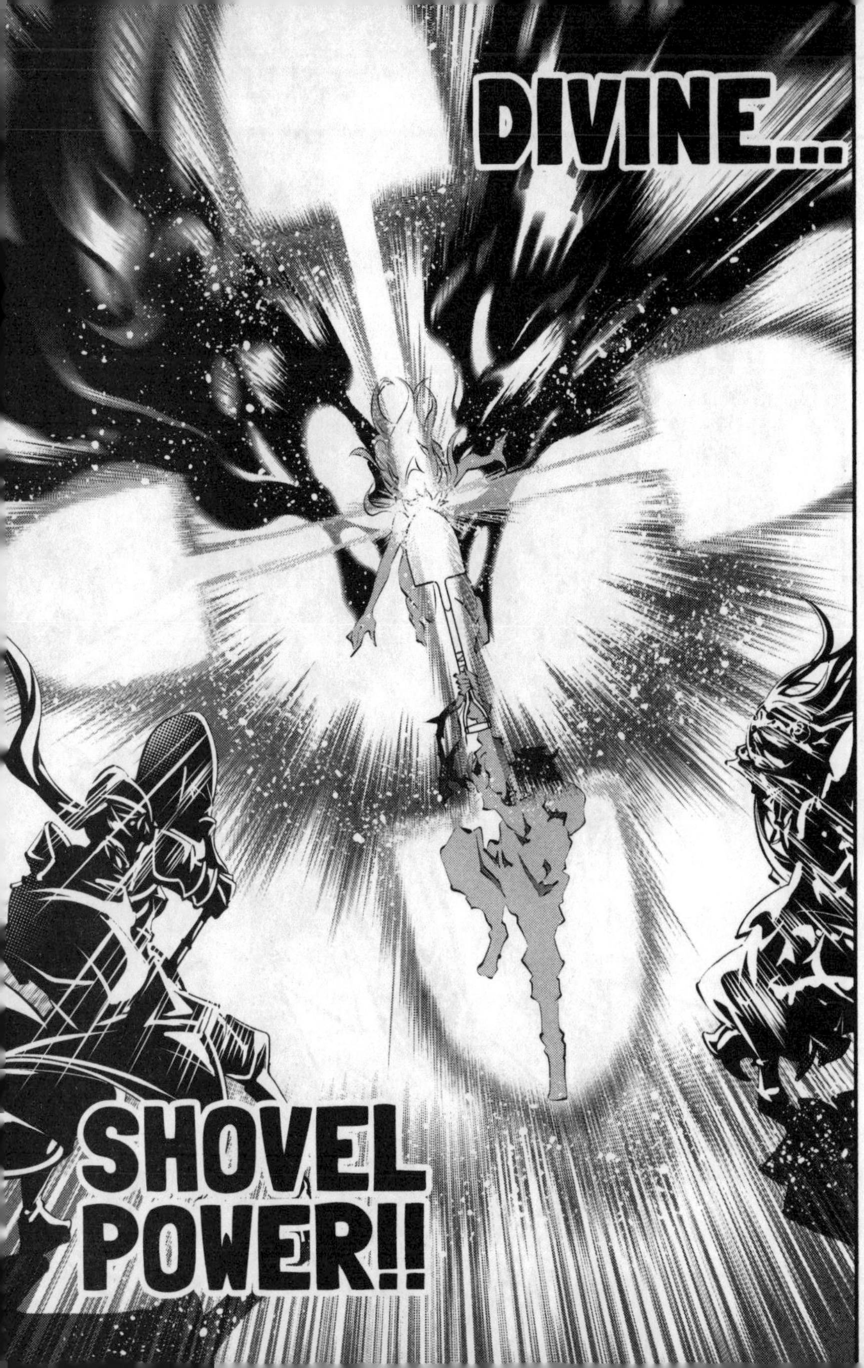
DIVINE...
SHOVEL POWER!!

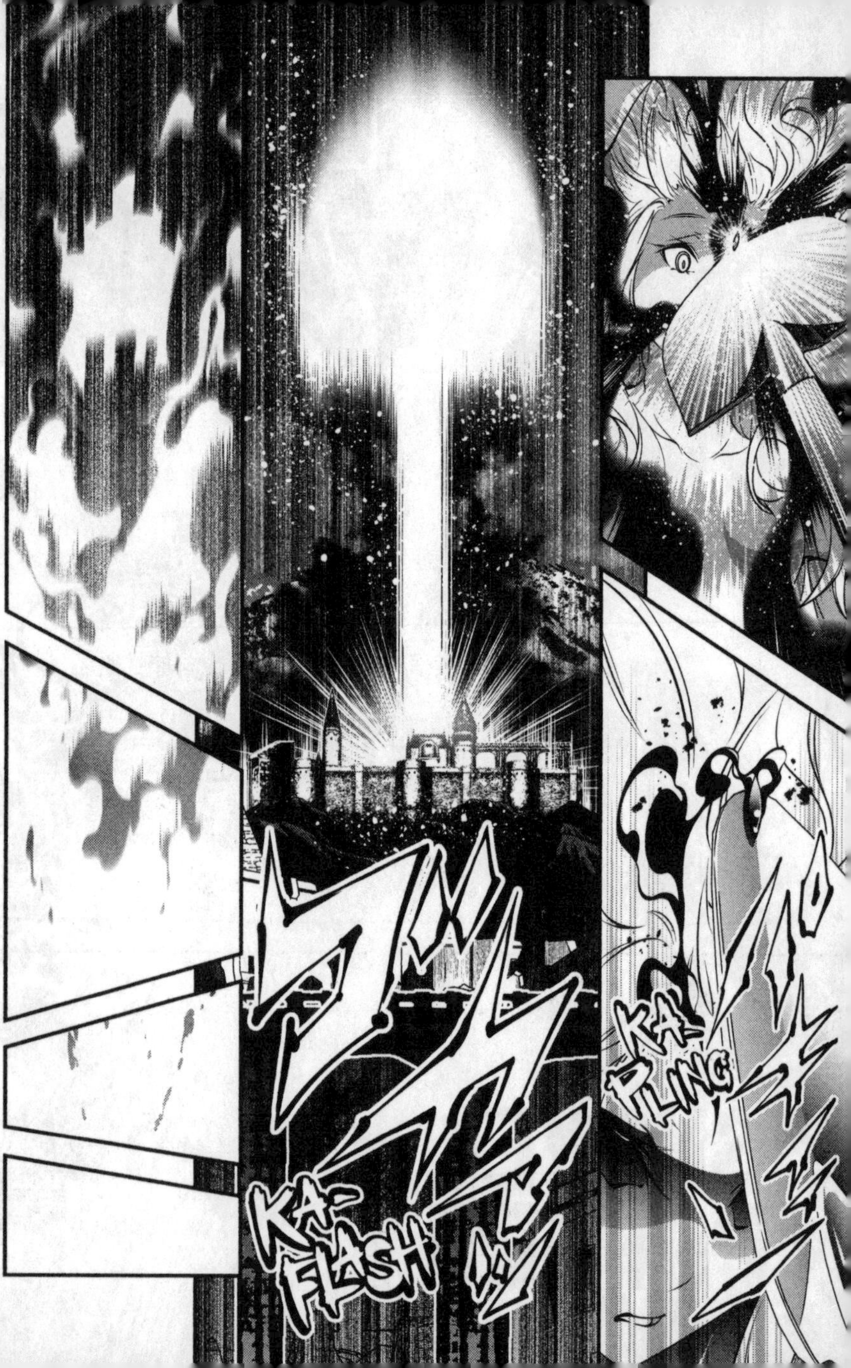
KA-
PLING
KA-
FLASH

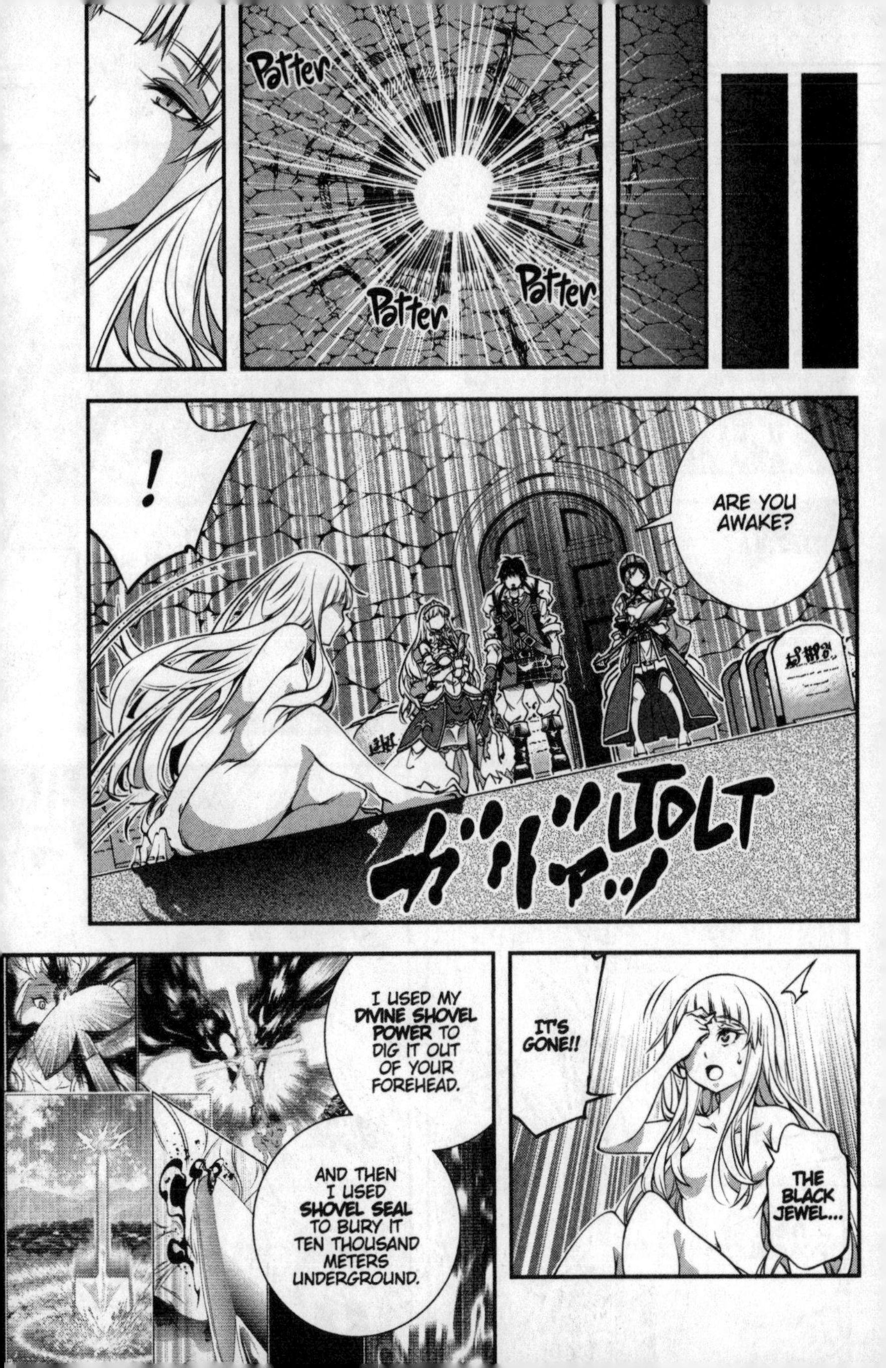
Patter
Patter
Patter
ARE YOU AWAKE?
!
JOLT
IT'S GONE!!
THE BLACK JEWEL...
I USED MY DIVINE SHOVEL POWER TO DIG IT OUT OF YOUR FOREHEAD.
AND THEN I USED SHOVEL SEAL TO BURY IT TEN THOUSAND METERS UNDERGROUND.

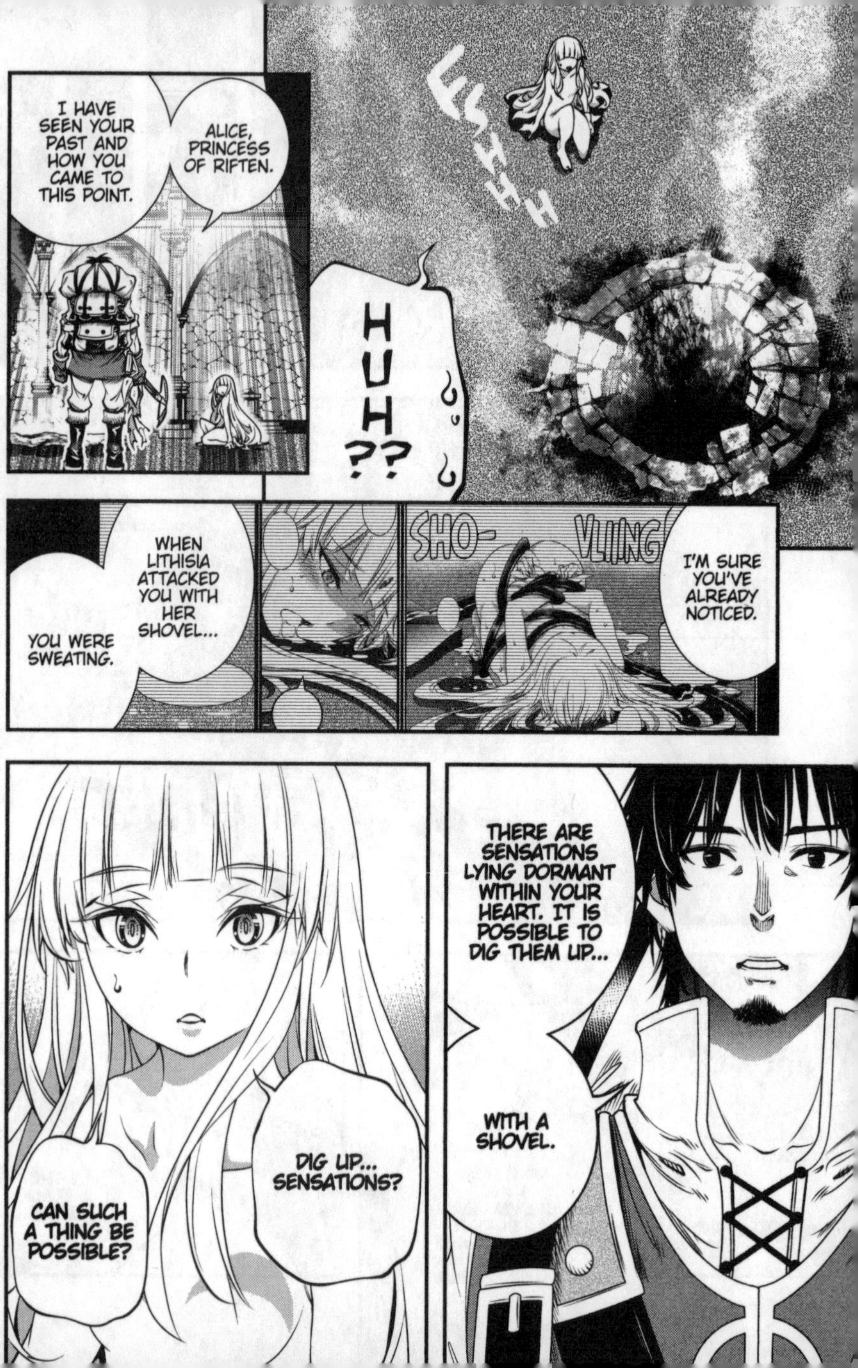
HUH??
ALICE, PRINCESS OF RIFTEN.
I HAVE SEEN YOUR PAST AND HOW YOU CAME TO THIS POINT.
SHO-VLING
I'M SURE YOU'VE ALREADY NOTICED.
WHEN LITHISIA ATTACKED YOU WITH HER SHOVEL...
YOU WERE SWEATING.
THERE ARE SENSATIONS LYING DORMANT WITHIN YOUR HEART. IT IS POSSIBLE TO DIG THEM UP...
WITH A SHOVEL.
DIG UP... SENSATIONS?
CAN SUCH A THING BE POSSIBLE?

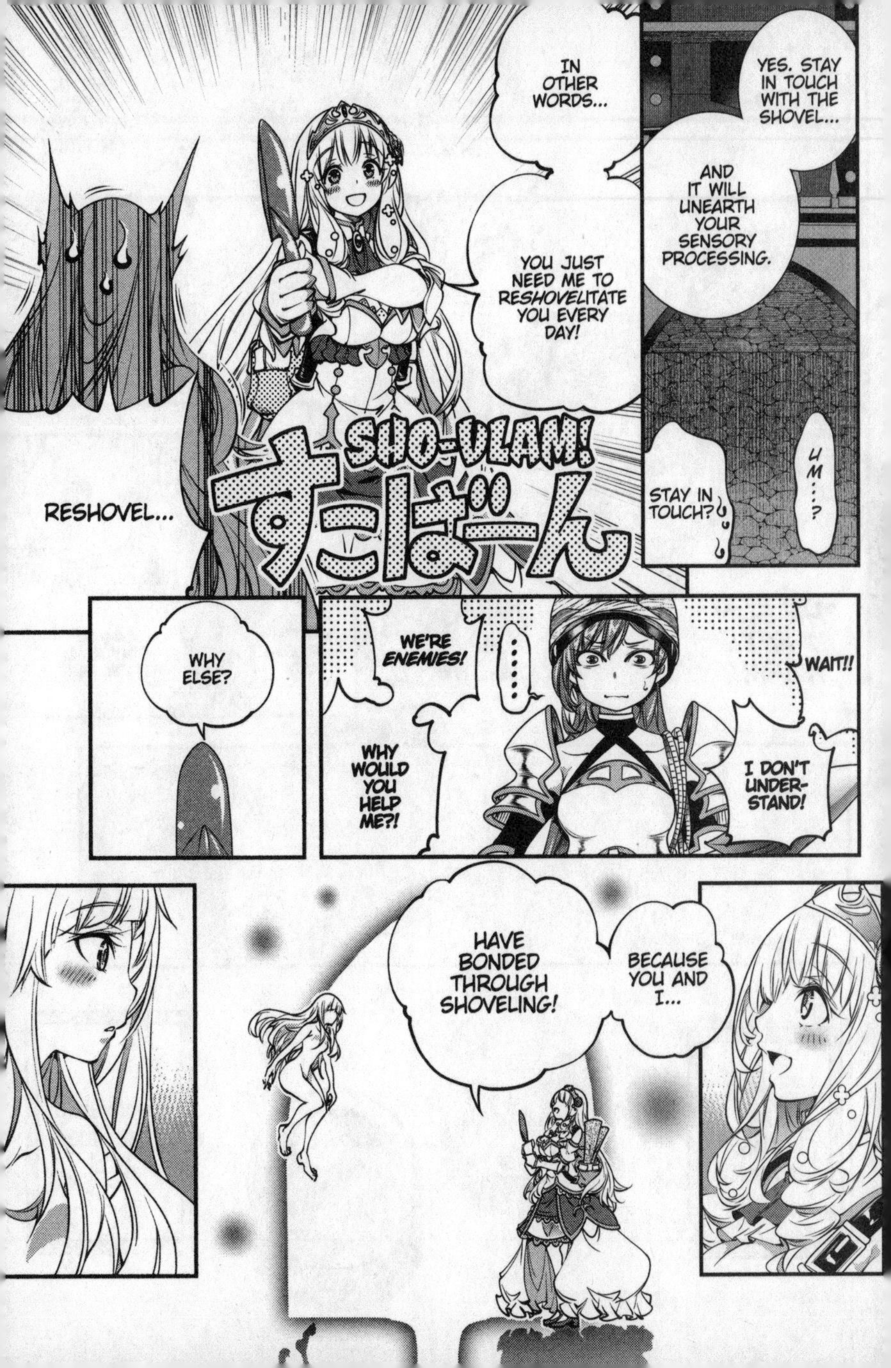
YES. STAY IN TOUCH WITH THE SHOVEL...
AND IT WILL UNEARTH YOUR SENSORY PROCESSING.
UM...?
STAY IN TOUCH?
IN OTHER WORDS...
YOU JUST NEED ME TO RESHOVELITATE YOU EVERY DAY!
SHO-VLAM!
すこばーん
RESHOVEL...
WAIT!!
I DON'T UNDERSTAND!
......
WE'RE ENEMIES!
WHY WOULD YOU HELP ME?!
WHY ELSE?
BECAUSE YOU AND I...
HAVE BONDED THROUGH SHOVELING!

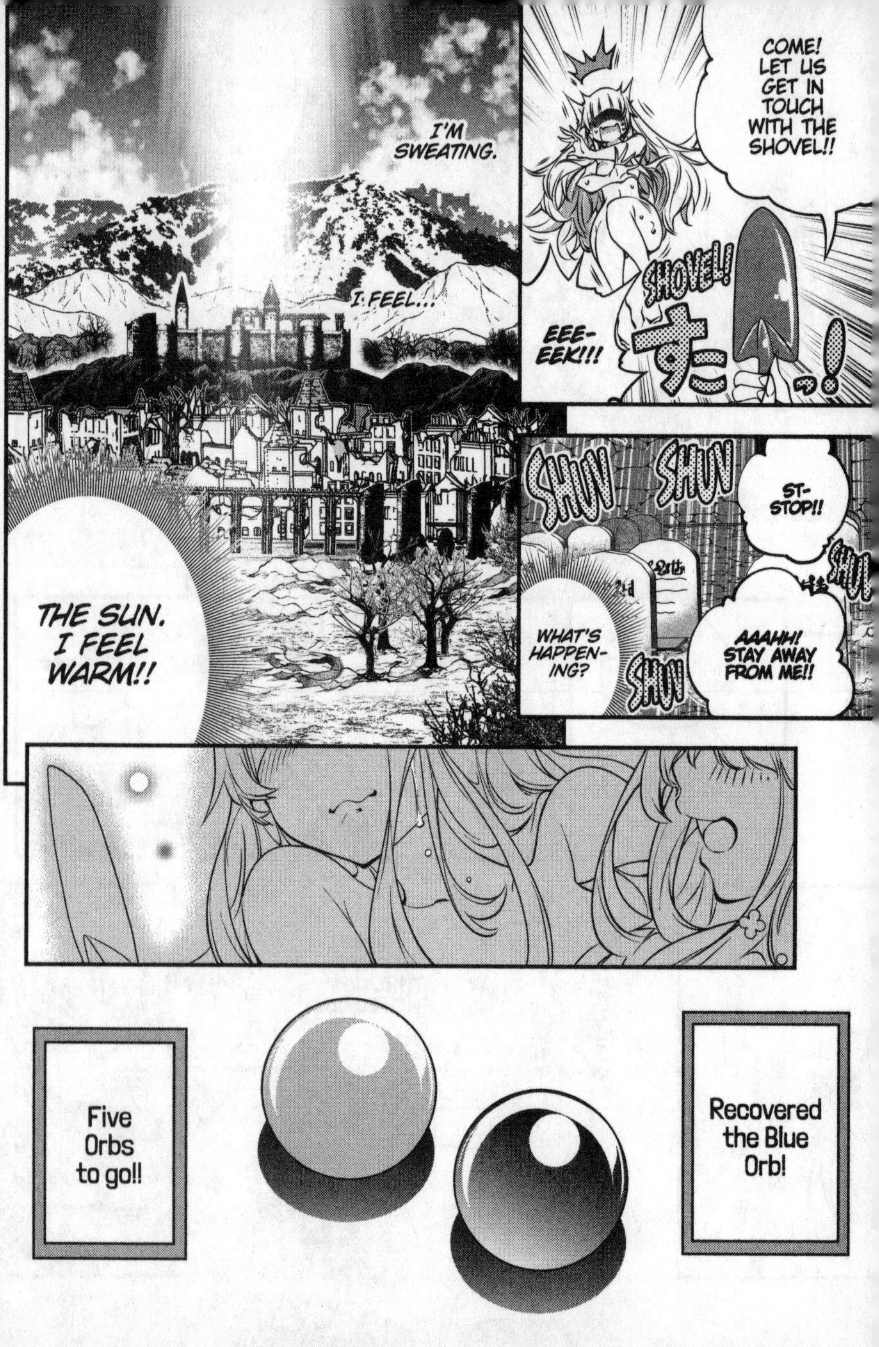
COME! LET US GET IN TOUCH WITH THE SHOVEL!!
SHOVEL!
EEE-EEK!!!
すたっ!
SHUV
SHUV
ST- STOP!!
SHUV
AAAHH! STAY AWAY FROM ME!!
WHAT'S HAPPEN- ING?
SHUV
I'M SWEATING.
I FEEL...
THE SUN. I FEEL WARM!!
Recovered the Blue Orb!
Five Orbs to go!!

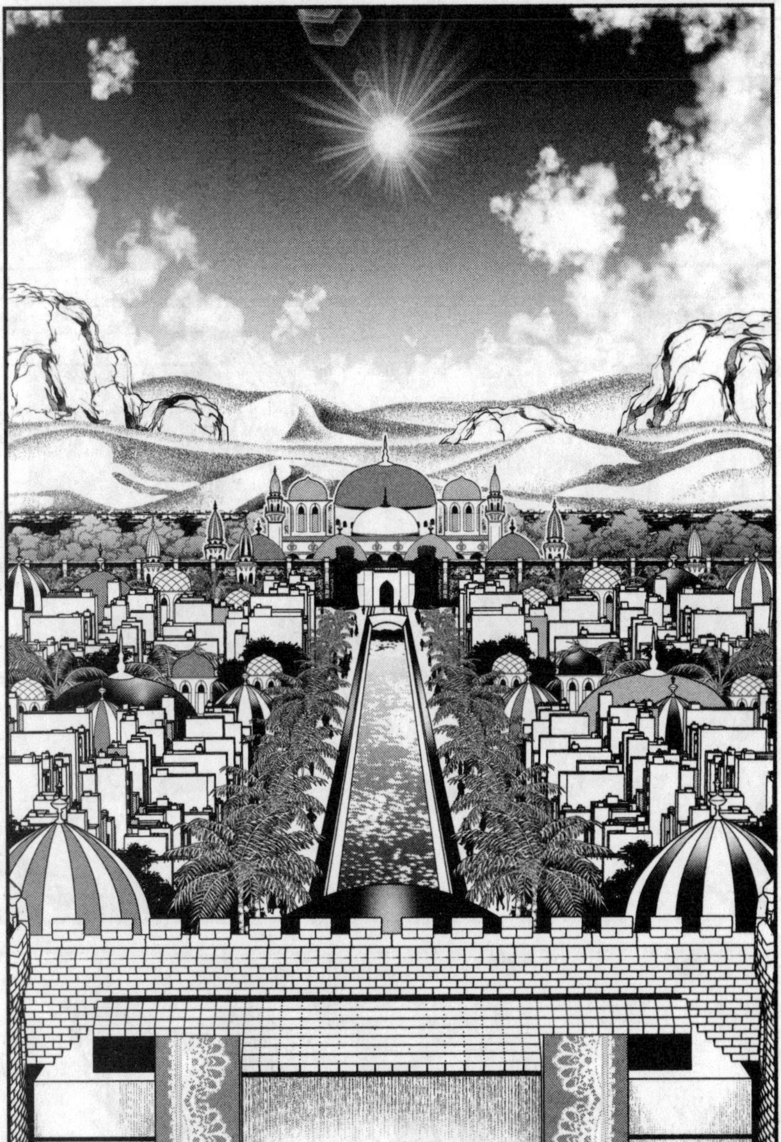
Chapter 8: The Shovel in Desertopia

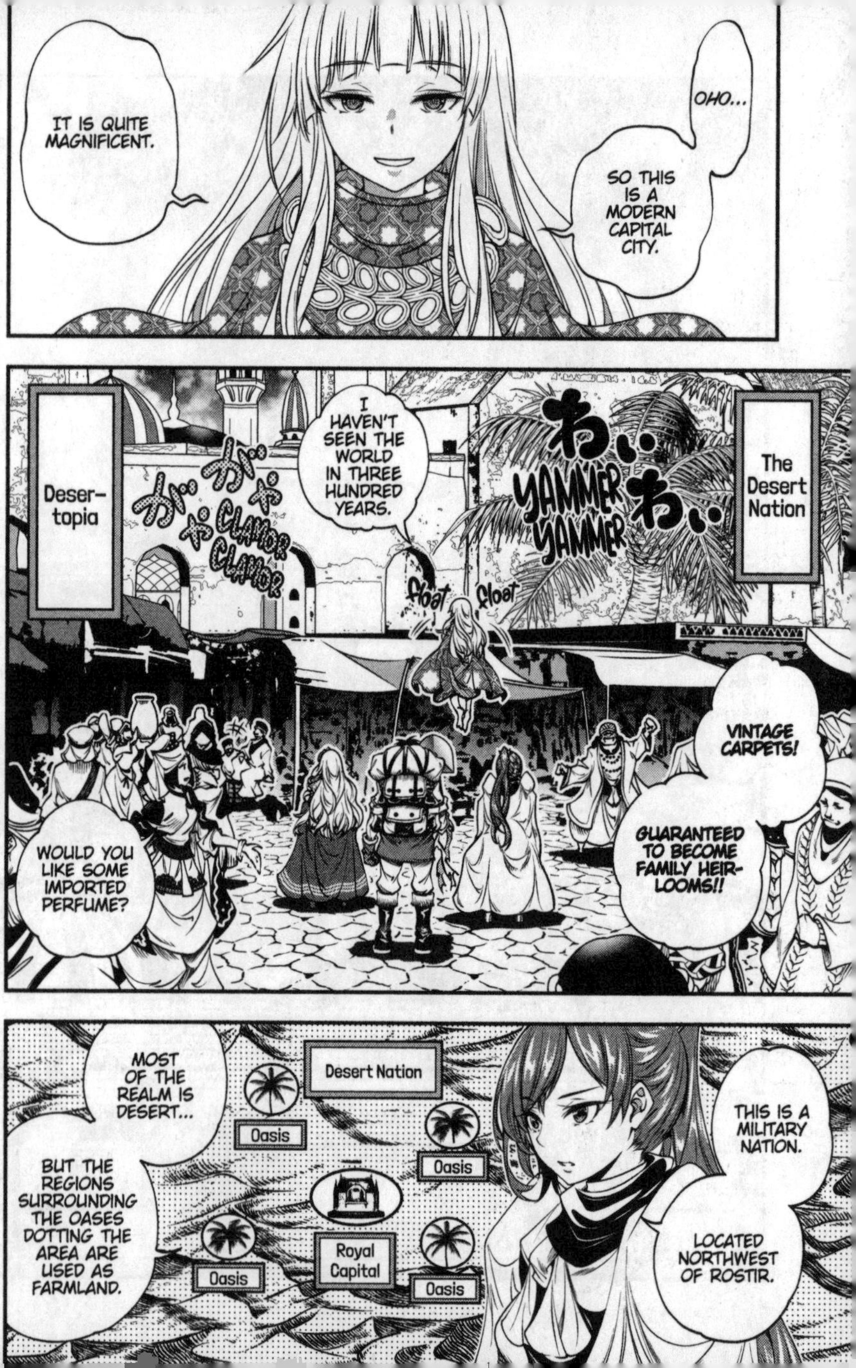

OHO... SO THIS IS A MODERN CAPITAL CITY.
IT IS QUITE MAGNIFICENT.
The Desert Nation
わいわい YAMMER YAMMER
I HAVEN'T SEEN THE WORLD IN THREE HUNDRED YEARS.
float float
Deser-topia
がやがや CLAMOR CLAMOR
VINTAGE CARPETS!
GUARANTEED TO BECOME FAMILY HEIR-LOOMS!!
WOULD YOU LIKE SOME IMPORTED PERFUME?
THIS IS A MILITARY NATION.
LOCATED NORTHWEST OF ROSTIR.
Desert Nation
Oasis
Oasis
Royal Capital
Oasis
Oasis
MOST OF THE REALM IS DESERT...
BUT THE REGIONS SURROUNDING THE OASES DOTTING THE AREA ARE USED AS FARMLAND.

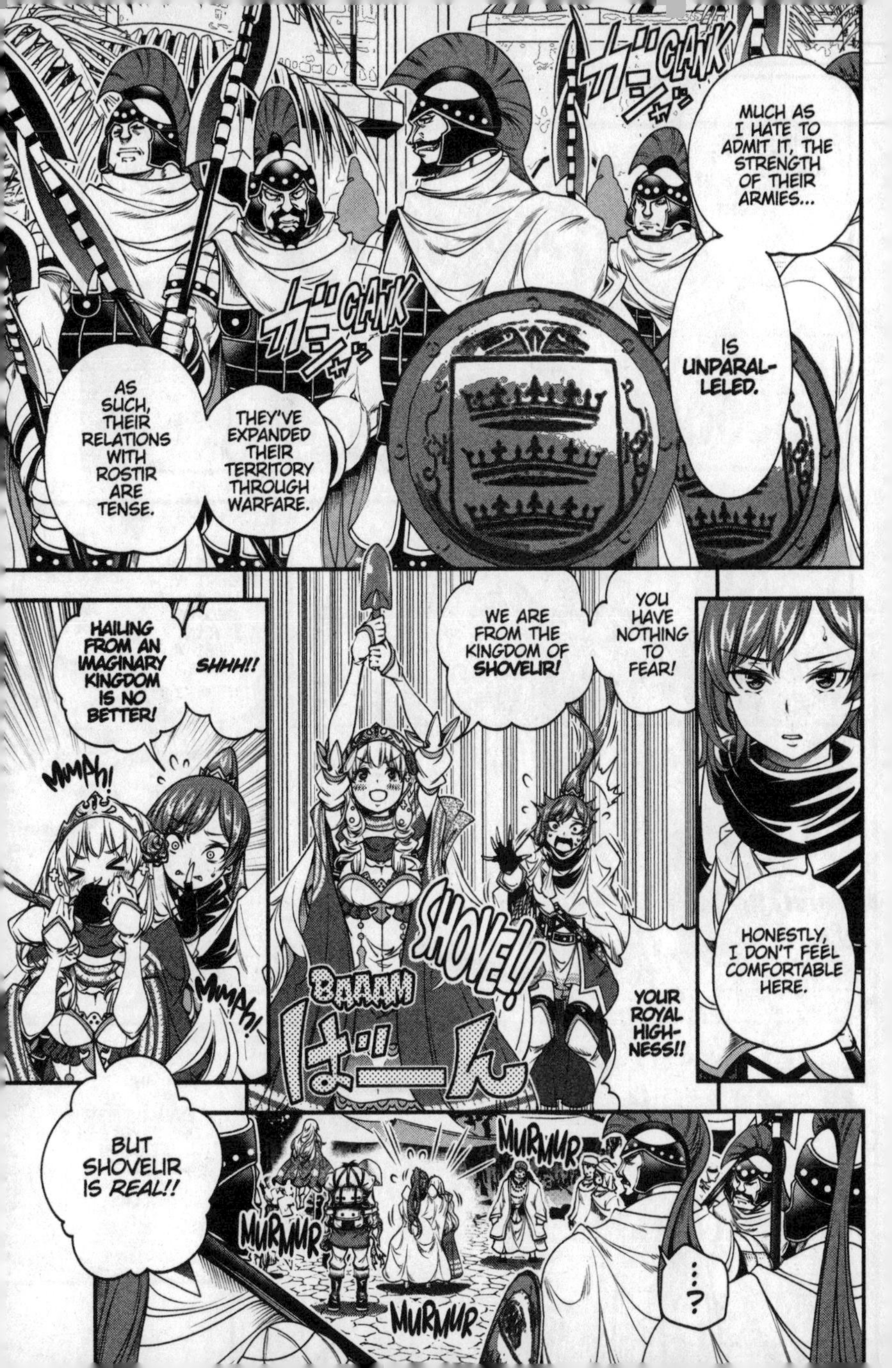

CLANK
MUCH AS I HATE TO ADMIT IT, THE STRENGTH OF THEIR ARMIES...
IS UNPARAL-LELED.
CLANK
THEY'VE EXPANDED THEIR TERRITORY THROUGH WARFARE.
AS SUCH, THEIR RELATIONS WITH ROSTIR ARE TENSE.
HONESTLY, I DON'T FEEL COMFORTABLE HERE.
YOU HAVE NOTHING TO FEAR!
WE ARE FROM THE KINGDOM OF SHOVELIR!
SHOVEL!!
YOUR ROYAL HIGH-NESS!!
BAAAM
HAILING FROM AN IMAGINARY KINGDOM IS NO BETTER!
SHHH!!
MMPH!
MMPH!
...?
MURMUR
MURMUR
MURMUR
BUT SHOVELIR IS REAL!!

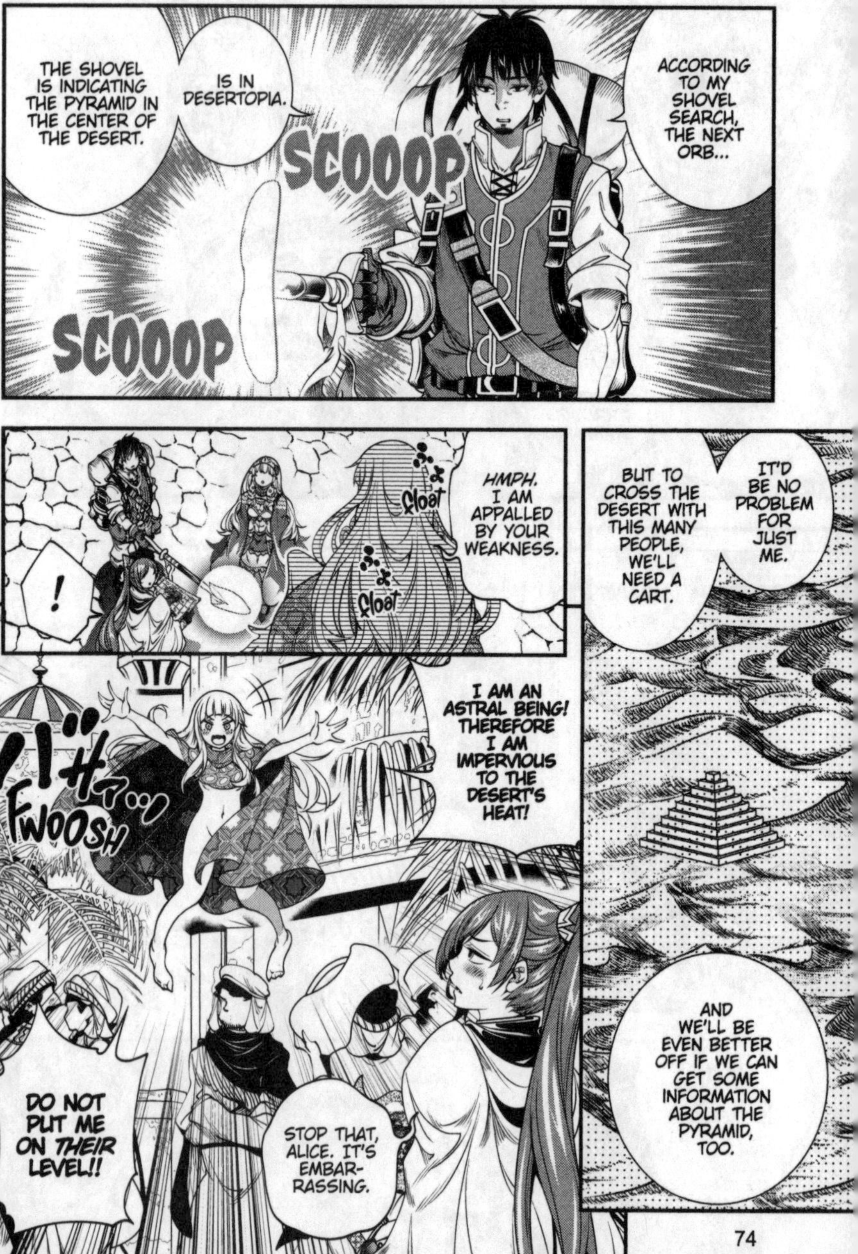
ACCORDING TO MY SHOVEL SEARCH, THE NEXT ORB...
IS IN DESERTOPIA.
THE SHOVEL IS INDICATING THE PYRAMID IN THE CENTER OF THE DESERT.
SCOOOP
SCOOOP
IT'D BE NO PROBLEM FOR JUST ME.
BUT TO CROSS THE DESERT WITH THIS MANY PEOPLE, WE'LL NEED A CART.
AND WE'LL BE EVEN BETTER OFF IF WE CAN GET SOME INFORMATION ABOUT THE PYRAMID, TOO.
HMPH. I AM APPALLED BY YOUR WEAKNESS.
float
float
!
I AM AN ASTRAL BEING! THEREFORE I AM IMPERVIOUS TO THE DESERT'S HEAT!
FWOOSH
STOP THAT, ALICE. IT'S EMBARRASSING.
DO NOT PUT ME ON *THEIR* LEVEL!!

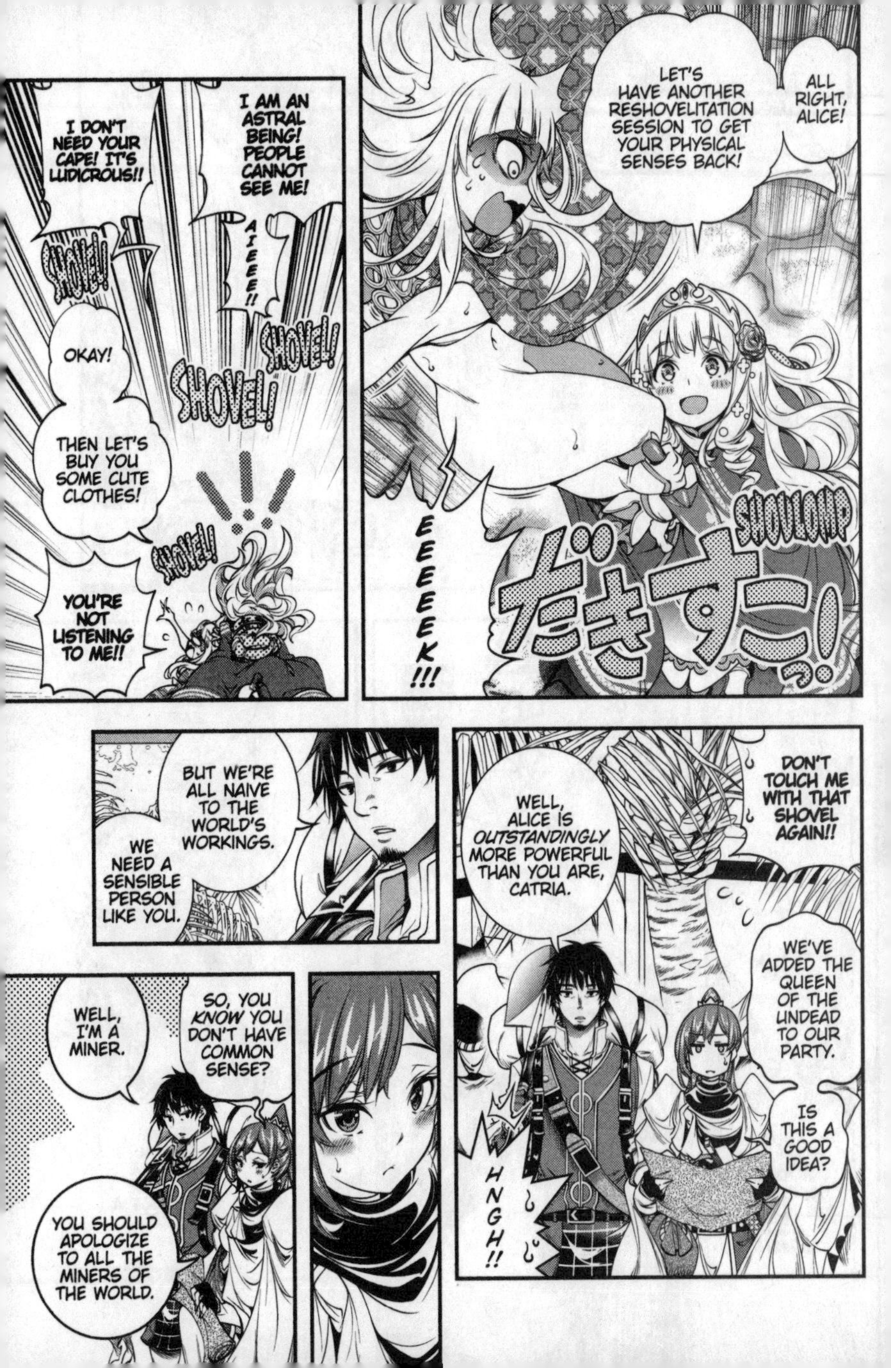
ALL RIGHT, ALICE!
LET'S HAVE ANOTHER RESHOVELITATION SESSION TO GET YOUR PHYSICAL SENSES BACK!
EEEEEEK!!!
SHOVLOMP
だきすこっ!
I AM AN ASTRAL BEING! PEOPLE CANNOT SEE ME!
I DON'T NEED YOUR CAPE! IT'S LUDICROUS!!
AIEEEE!!
SHOVEL!
SHOVEL!
SHOVEL!
OKAY!
THEN LET'S BUY YOU SOME CUTE CLOTHES!
SHOVEL!
YOU'RE NOT LISTENING TO ME!!
DON'T TOUCH ME WITH THAT SHOVEL AGAIN!!
WELL, ALICE IS *OUTSTANDINGLY* MORE POWERFUL THAN YOU ARE, CATRIA.
WE'VE ADDED THE QUEEN OF THE UNDEAD TO OUR PARTY.
IS THIS A GOOD IDEA?
HNGH!!
BUT WE'RE ALL NAIVE TO THE WORLD'S WORKINGS.
WE NEED A SENSIBLE PERSON LIKE YOU.
SO, YOU *KNOW* YOU DON'T HAVE COMMON SENSE?
WELL, I'M A MINER.
YOU SHOULD APOLOGIZE TO ALL THE MINERS OF THE WORLD.

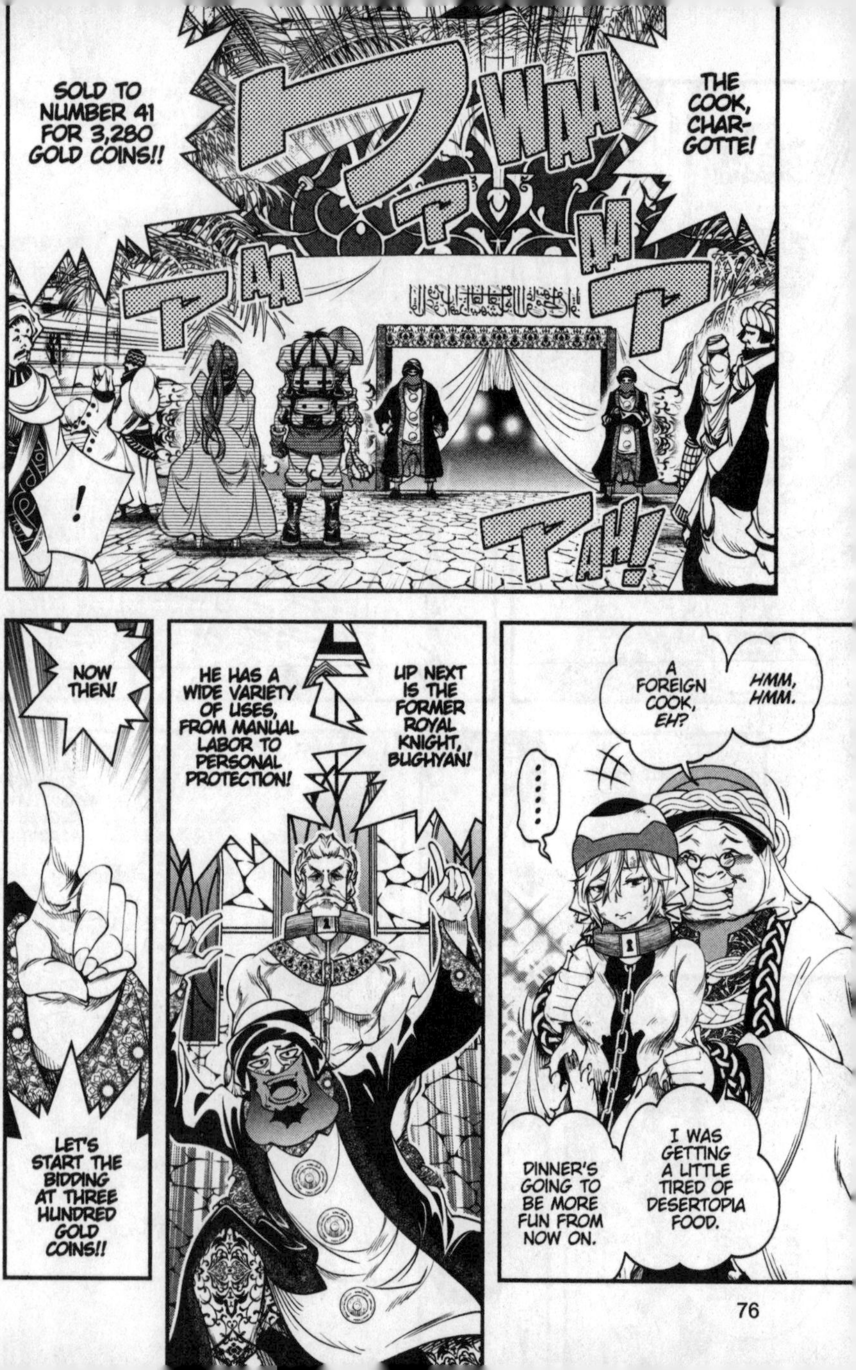
THE COOK, CHARGOTTE!
WAA
AA
AA
AH!!
SOLD TO NUMBER 41 FOR 3,280 GOLD COINS!!
!
HMM, HMM.
A FOREIGN COOK, EH?
......
I WAS GETTING A LITTLE TIRED OF DESERTOPIA FOOD.
DINNER'S GOING TO BE MORE FUN FROM NOW ON.
UP NEXT IS THE FORMER ROYAL KNIGHT, BUGHYAN!
HE HAS A WIDE VARIETY OF USES, FROM MANUAL LABOR TO PERSONAL PROTECTION!
NOW THEN!
LET'S START THE BIDDING AT THREE HUNDRED GOLD COINS!!

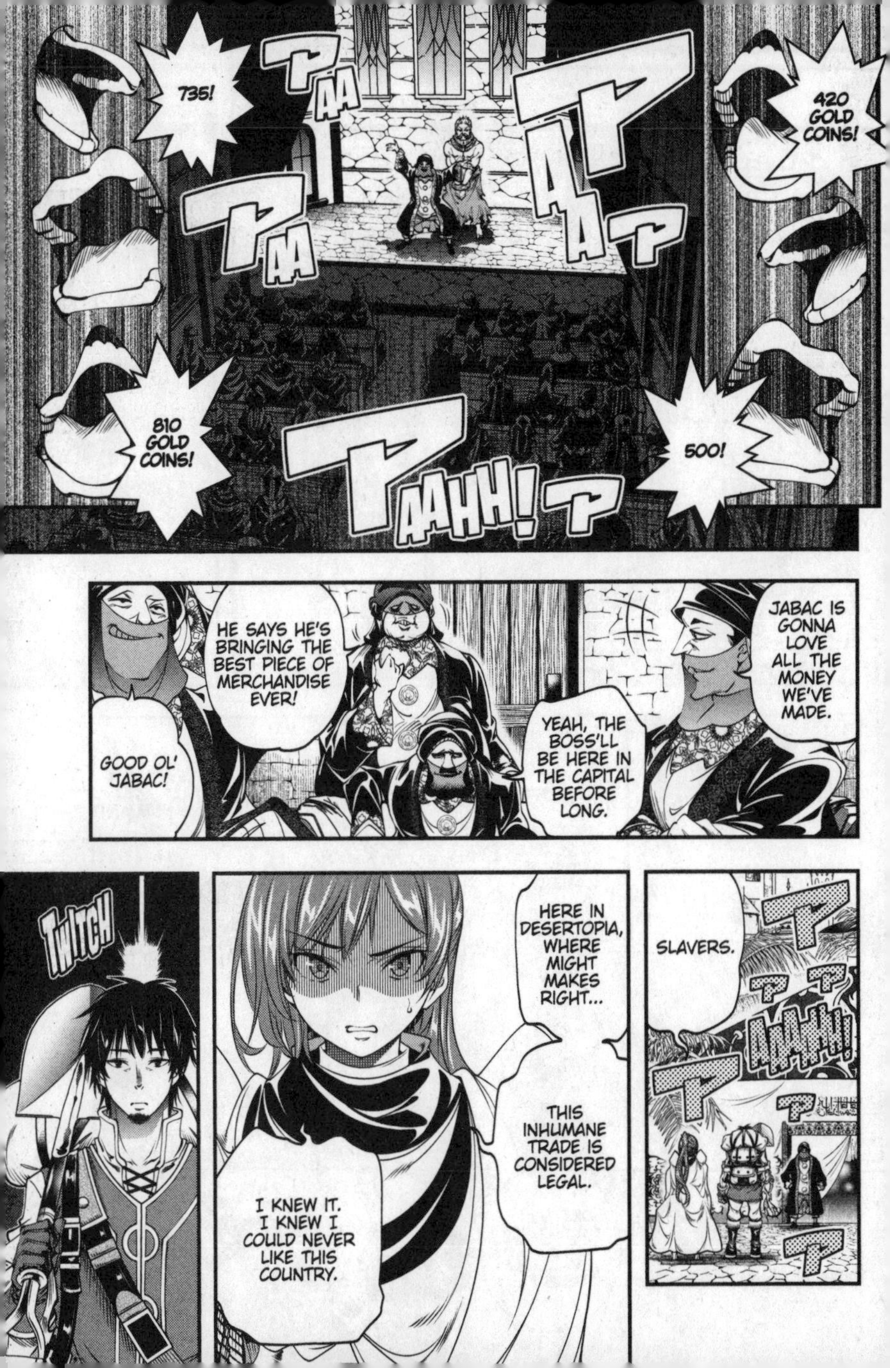
420 GOLD COINS!
AA
735!
AA
AA
500!
AAHH!
810 GOLD COINS!
JABAC IS GONNA LOVE ALL THE MONEY WE'VE MADE.
YEAH, THE BOSS'LL BE HERE IN THE CAPITAL BEFORE LONG.
HE SAYS HE'S BRINGING THE BEST PIECE OF MERCHANDISE EVER!
GOOD OL' JABAC!
SLAVERS.
AAHH!
HERE IN DESERTOPIA, WHERE MIGHT MAKES RIGHT...
THIS INHUMANE TRADE IS CONSIDERED LEGAL.
I KNEW IT. I KNEW I COULD NEVER LIKE THIS COUNTRY.
TWITCH

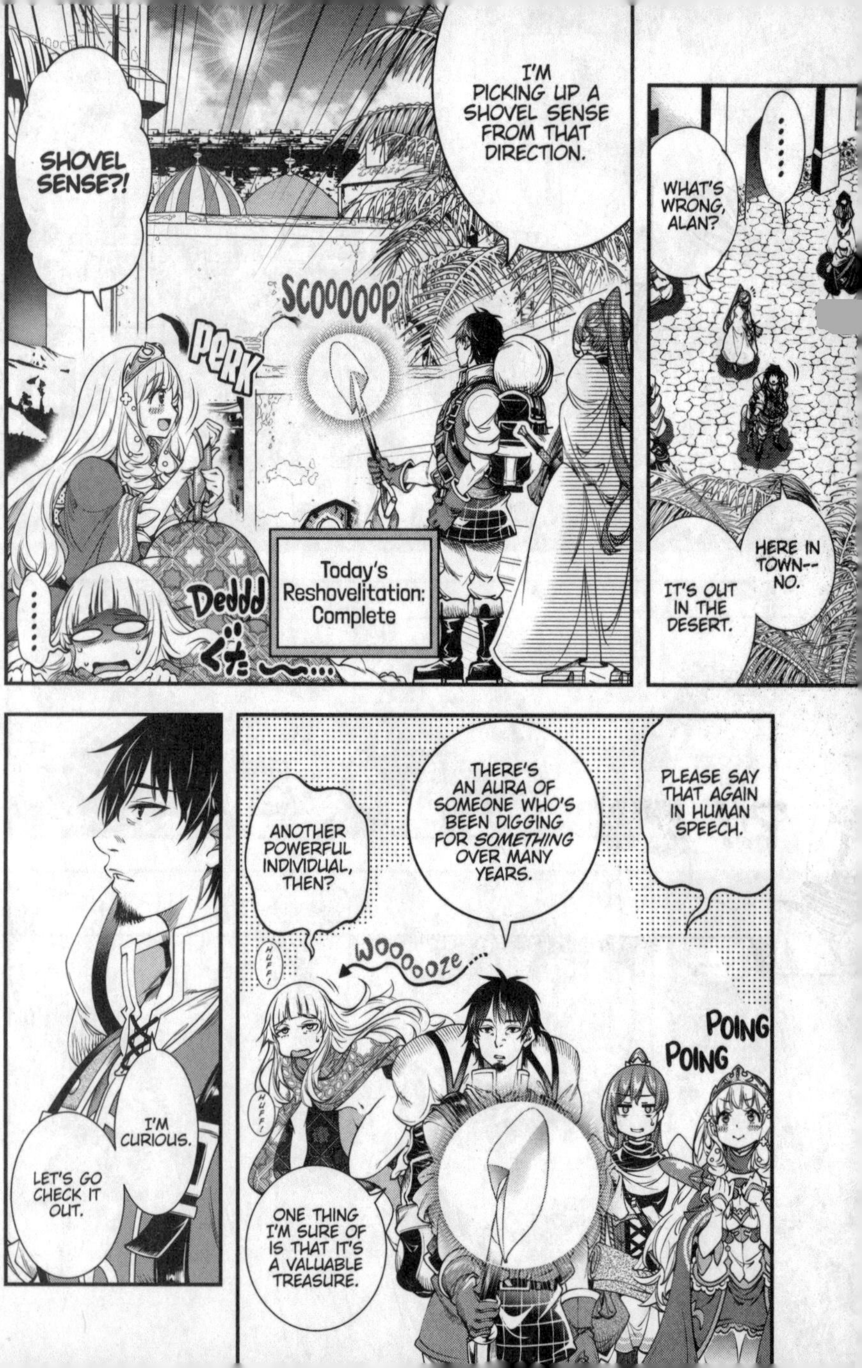
......
WHAT'S WRONG, ALAN?
HERE IN TOWN-- NO.
IT'S OUT IN THE DESERT.
I'M PICKING UP A SHOVEL SENSE FROM THAT DIRECTION.
SHOVEL SENSE?!
SCOOOOOP
PERK
Today's Reshovelitation: Complete
Deddd
......
PLEASE SAY THAT AGAIN IN HUMAN SPEECH.
THERE'S AN AURA OF SOMEONE WHO'S BEEN DIGGING FOR *SOMETHING* OVER MANY YEARS.
ANOTHER POWERFUL INDIVIDUAL, THEN?
WOOOOOZE...
HUFF!
HUFF!
POING
POING
ONE THING I'M SURE OF IS THAT IT'S A VALUABLE TREASURE.
I'M CURIOUS.
LET'S GO CHECK IT OUT.

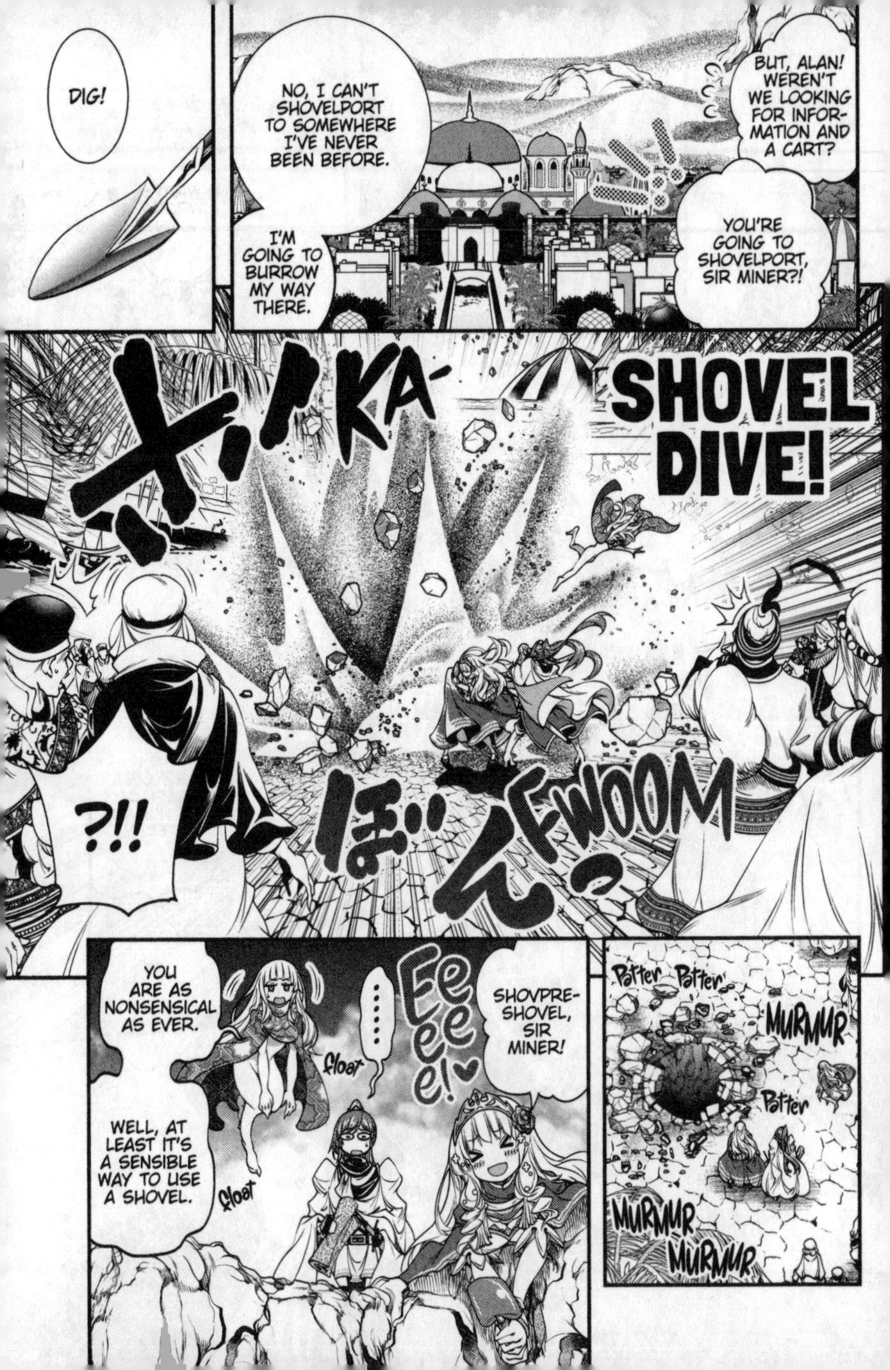
BUT, ALAN! WEREN'T WE LOOKING FOR INFORMATION AND A CART?
YOU'RE GOING TO SHOVELPORT, SIR MINER?!
NO, I CAN'T SHOVELPORT TO SOMEWHERE I'VE NEVER BEEN BEFORE.
I'M GOING TO BURROW MY WAY THERE.
DIG!
SHOVEL DIVE!
KA-
?!!
FWOOM
Patter Patter
MURMUR
Patter
MURMUR MURMUR
SHOVPRE-SHOVEL, SIR MINER!
Feeeee!♥
......
YOU ARE AS NONSENSICAL AS EVER.
float
WELL, AT LEAST IT'S A SENSIBLE WAY TO USE A SHOVEL.
float

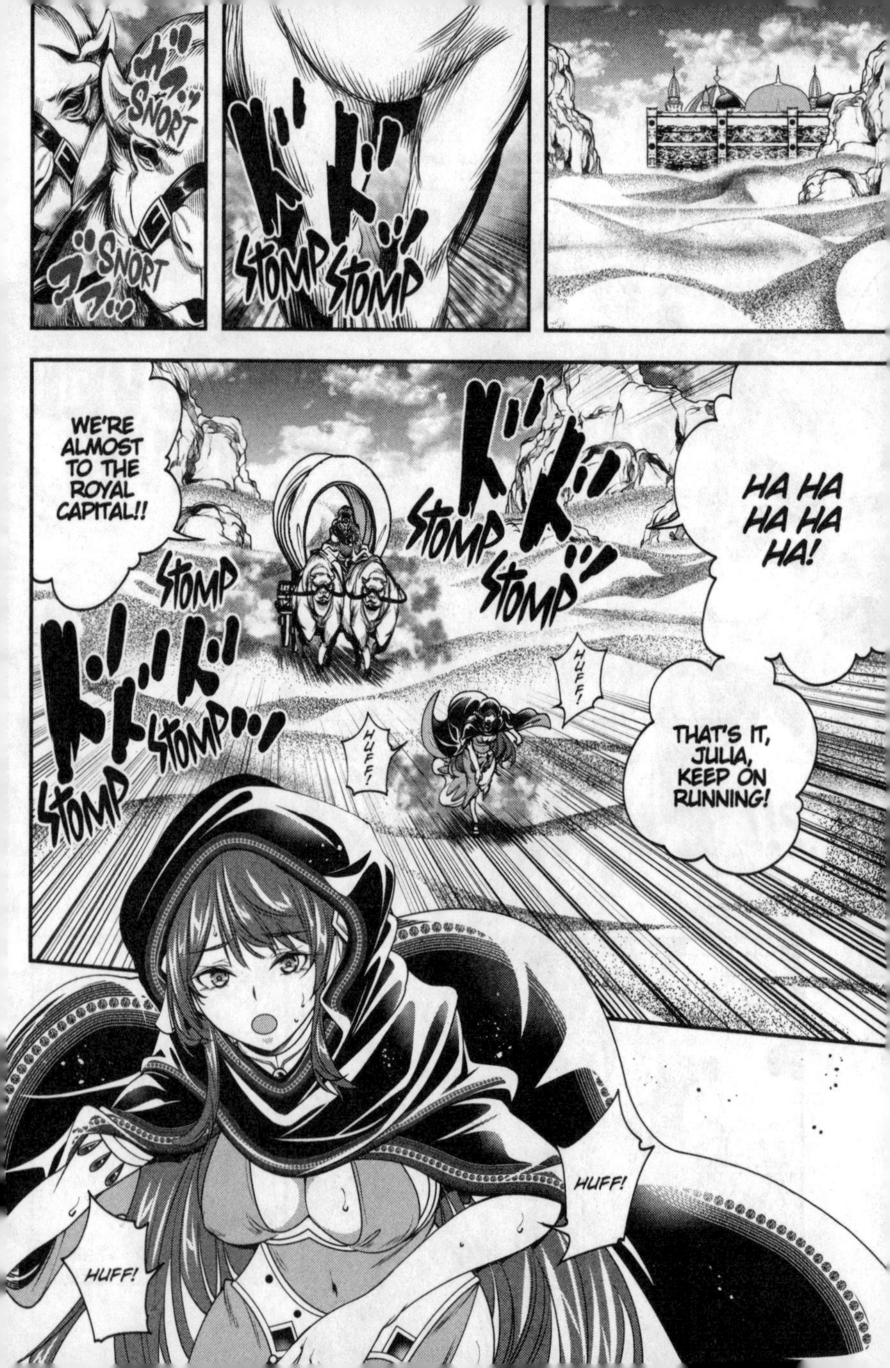
STOMP STOMP
SNORT
SNORT
HA HA HA HA HA!
WE'RE ALMOST TO THE ROYAL CAPITAL!!
STOMP STOMP
STOMP
HUFF!
THAT'S IT, JULIA, KEEP ON RUNNING!
HUFF!
STOMP STOMP
HUFF!
HUFF!

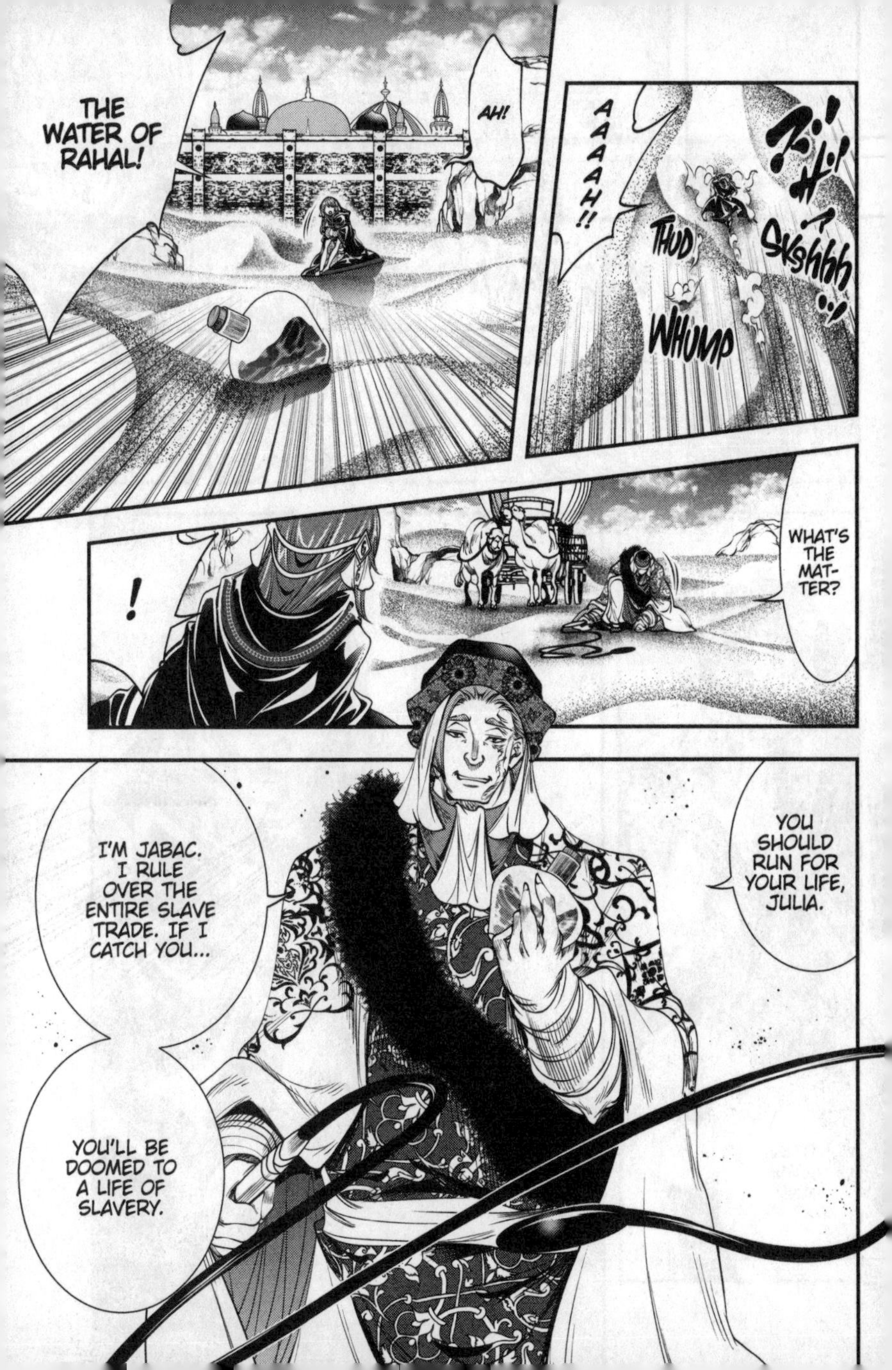
AAAAAH!!
Skshhh..!
THUD
WHUMP
AH!
THE WATER OF RAHAL!
WHAT'S THE MAT-TER?
!
YOU SHOULD RUN FOR YOUR LIFE, JULIA.
I'M JABAC. I RULE OVER THE ENTIRE SLAVE TRADE. IF I CATCH YOU...
YOU'LL BE DOOMED TO A LIFE OF SLAVERY.

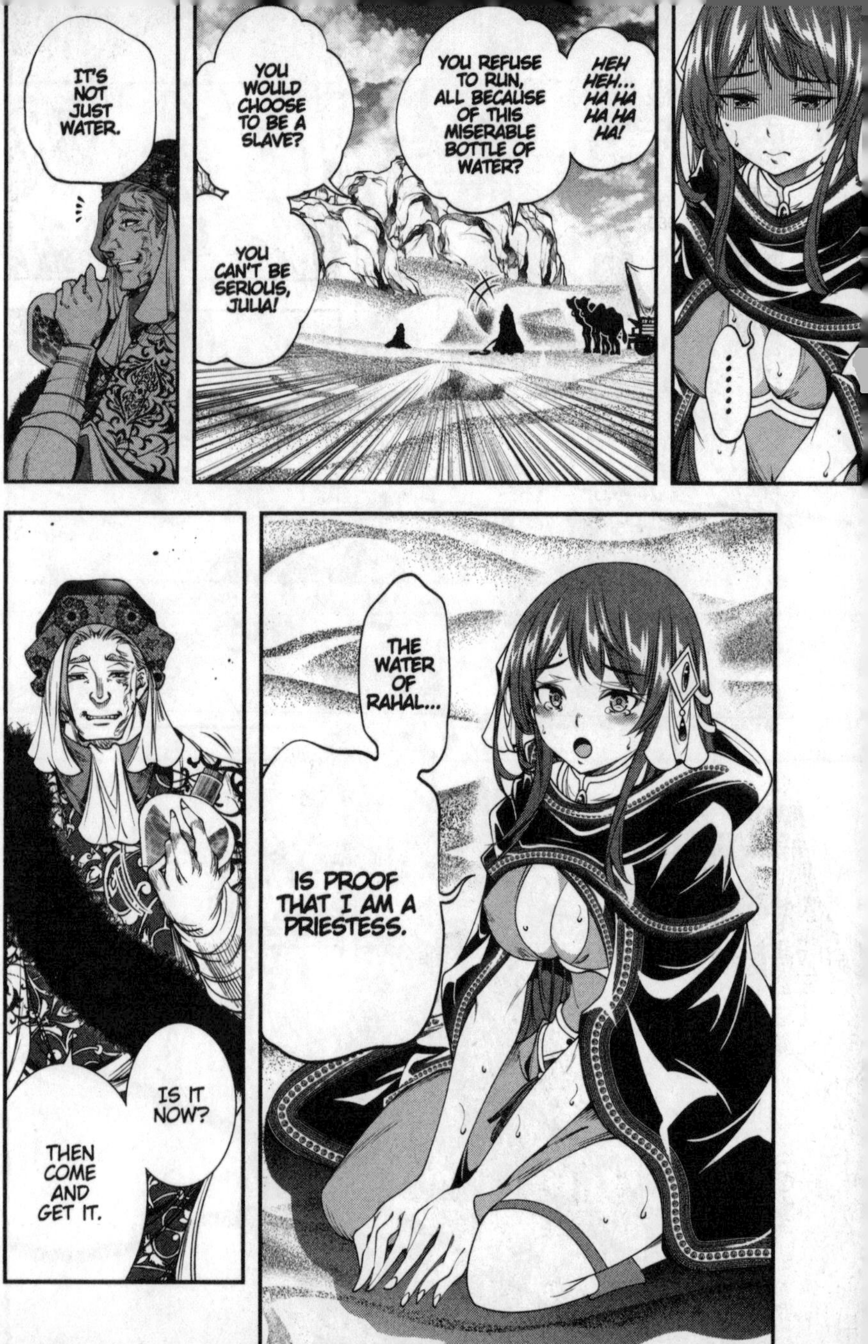
......
HEH HEH... HA HA HA HA HA!
YOU REFUSE TO RUN, ALL BECAUSE OF THIS MISERABLE BOTTLE OF WATER?
YOU WOULD CHOOSE TO BE A SLAVE?
YOU CAN'T BE SERIOUS, JULIA!
IT'S NOT JUST WATER.
THE WATER OF RAHAL...
IS PROOF THAT I AM A PRIESTESS.
IS IT NOW?
THEN COME AND GET IT.

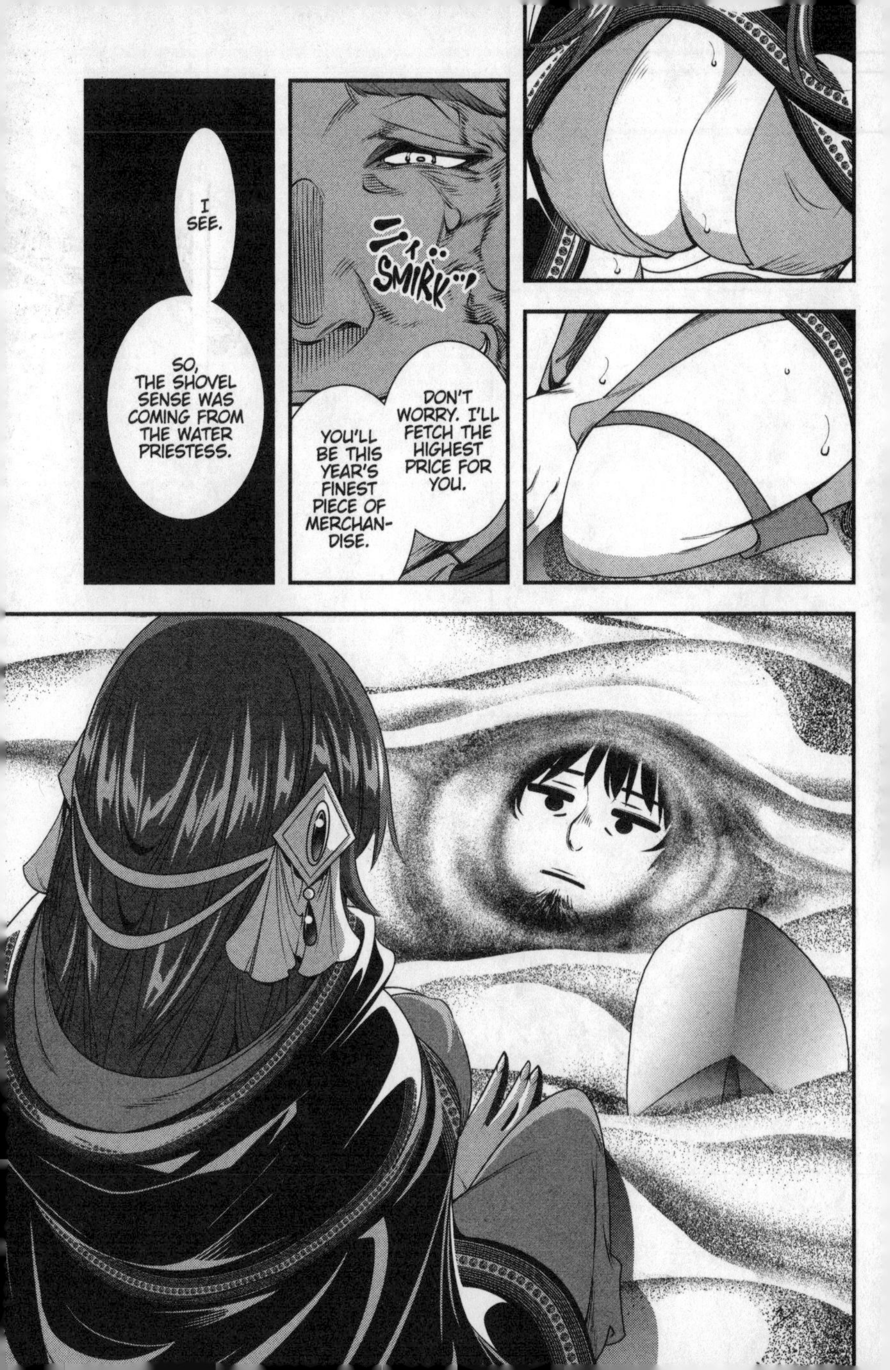
SMIRK
DON'T WORRY. I'LL FETCH THE HIGHEST PRICE FOR YOU.
YOU'LL BE THIS YEAR'S FINEST PIECE OF MERCHAN-DISE.
I SEE.
SO, THE SHOVEL SENSE WAS COMING FROM THE WATER PRIESTESS.

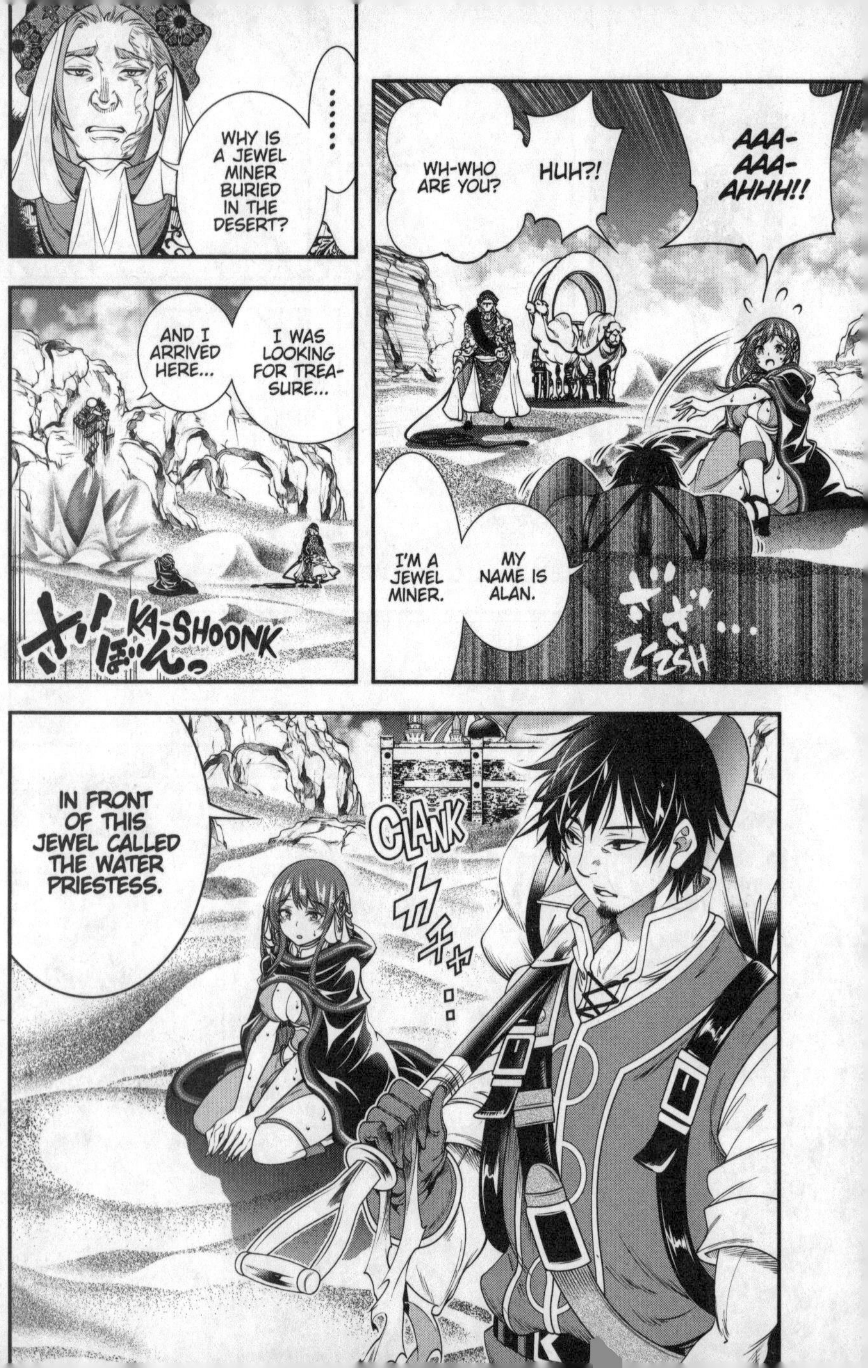

AAA-AAA-AHHH!!
HUH?!
WH-WHO ARE YOU?
MY NAME IS ALAN.
I'M A JEWEL MINER.
ZZSH
......
WHY IS A JEWEL MINER BURIED IN THE DESERT?
I WAS LOOKING FOR TREASURE...
AND I ARRIVED HERE...
KA-SHOONK
IN FRONT OF THIS JEWEL CALLED THE WATER PRIESTESS.
CLANK

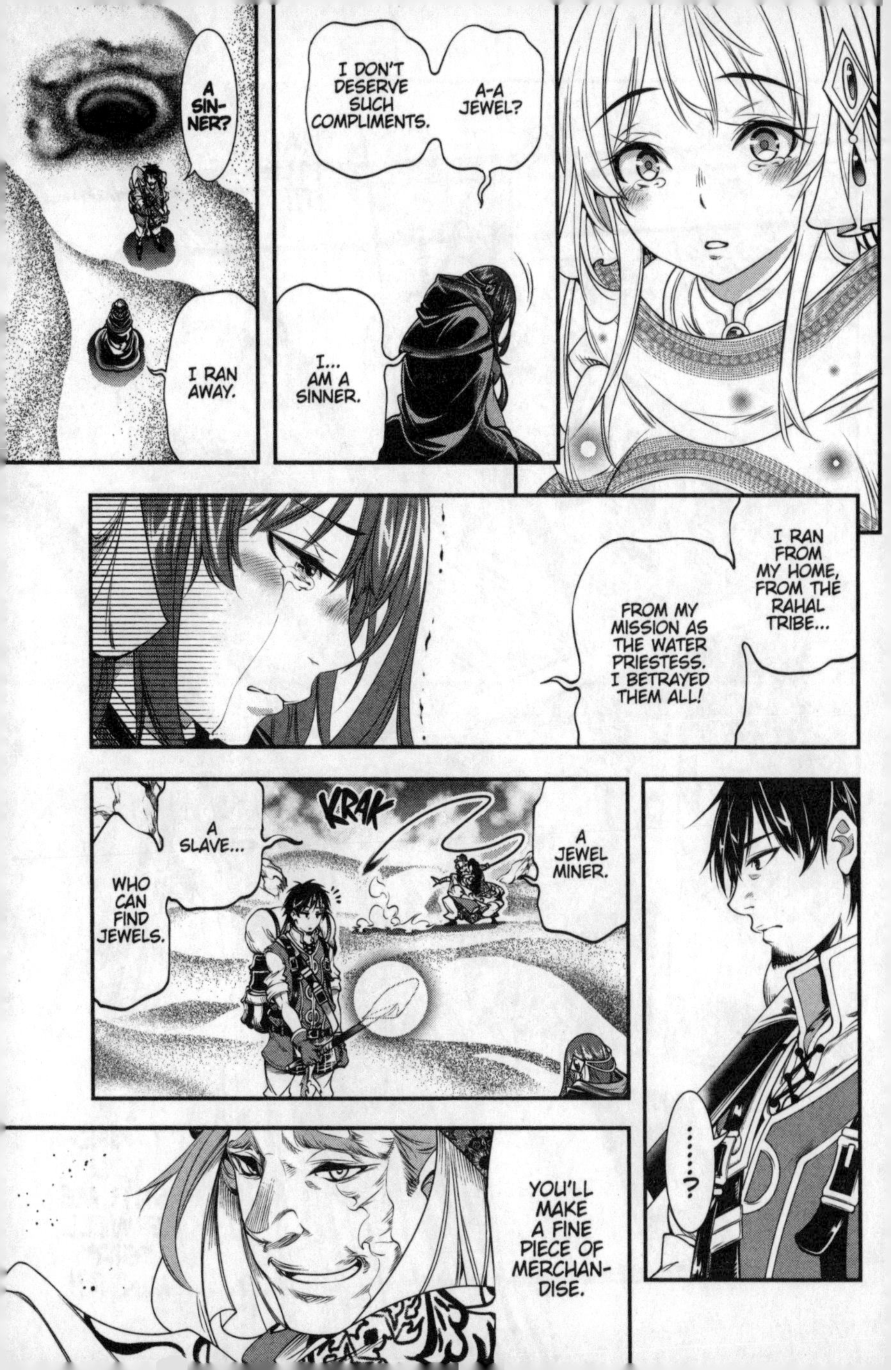
A-A JEWEL?
I DON'T DESERVE SUCH COMPLIMENTS.
I... AM A SINNER.
A SINNER?
I RAN AWAY.
I RAN FROM MY HOME, FROM THE RAHAL TRIBE...
FROM MY MISSION AS THE WATER PRIESTESS. I BETRAYED THEM ALL!
......?
A JEWEL MINER.
KRAK
A SLAVE...
WHO CAN FIND JEWELS.
YOU'LL MAKE A FINE PIECE OF MERCHANDISE.

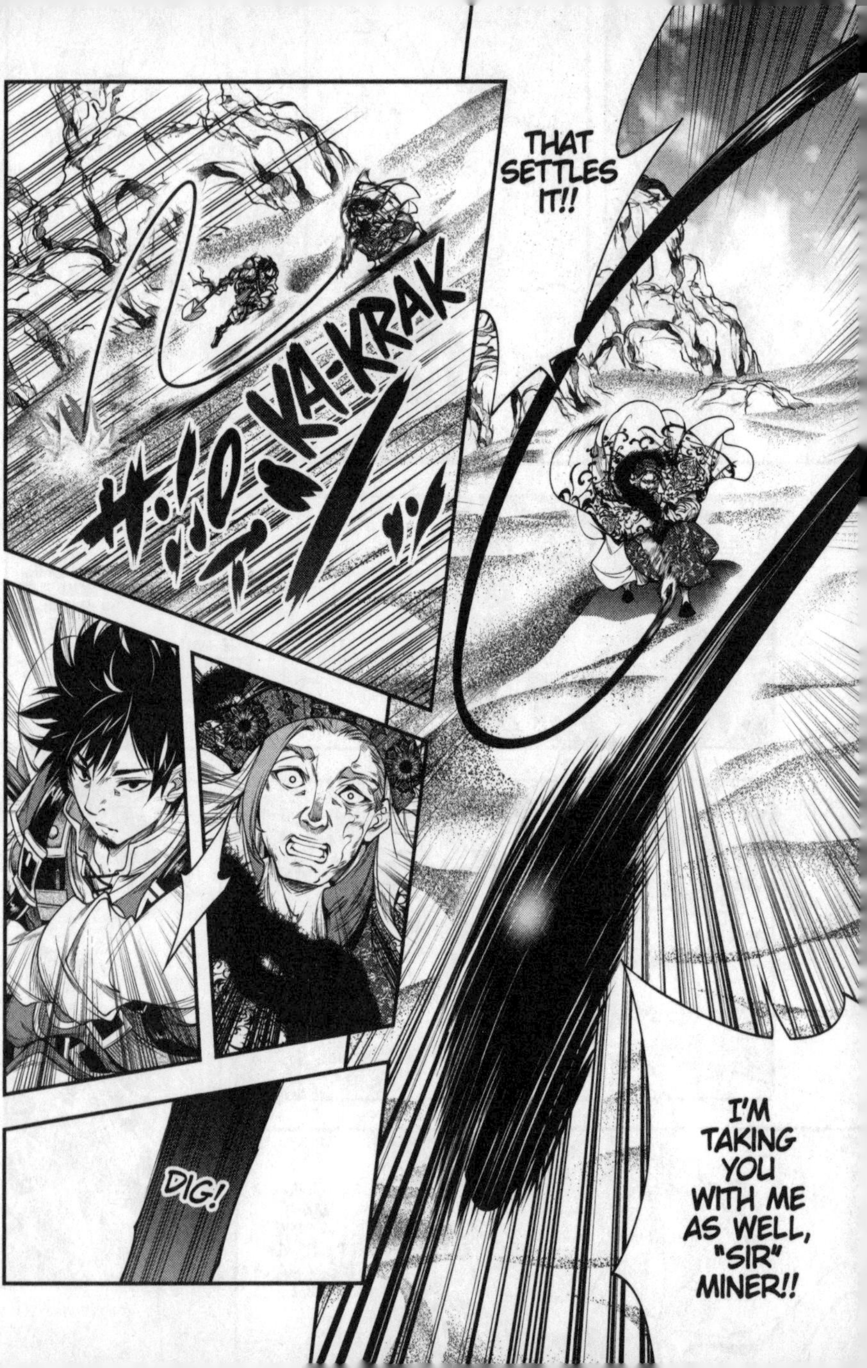
THAT SETTLES IT!!
I'M TAKING YOU WITH ME AS WELL, "SIR" MINER!!
KA-KRAK
DIG!

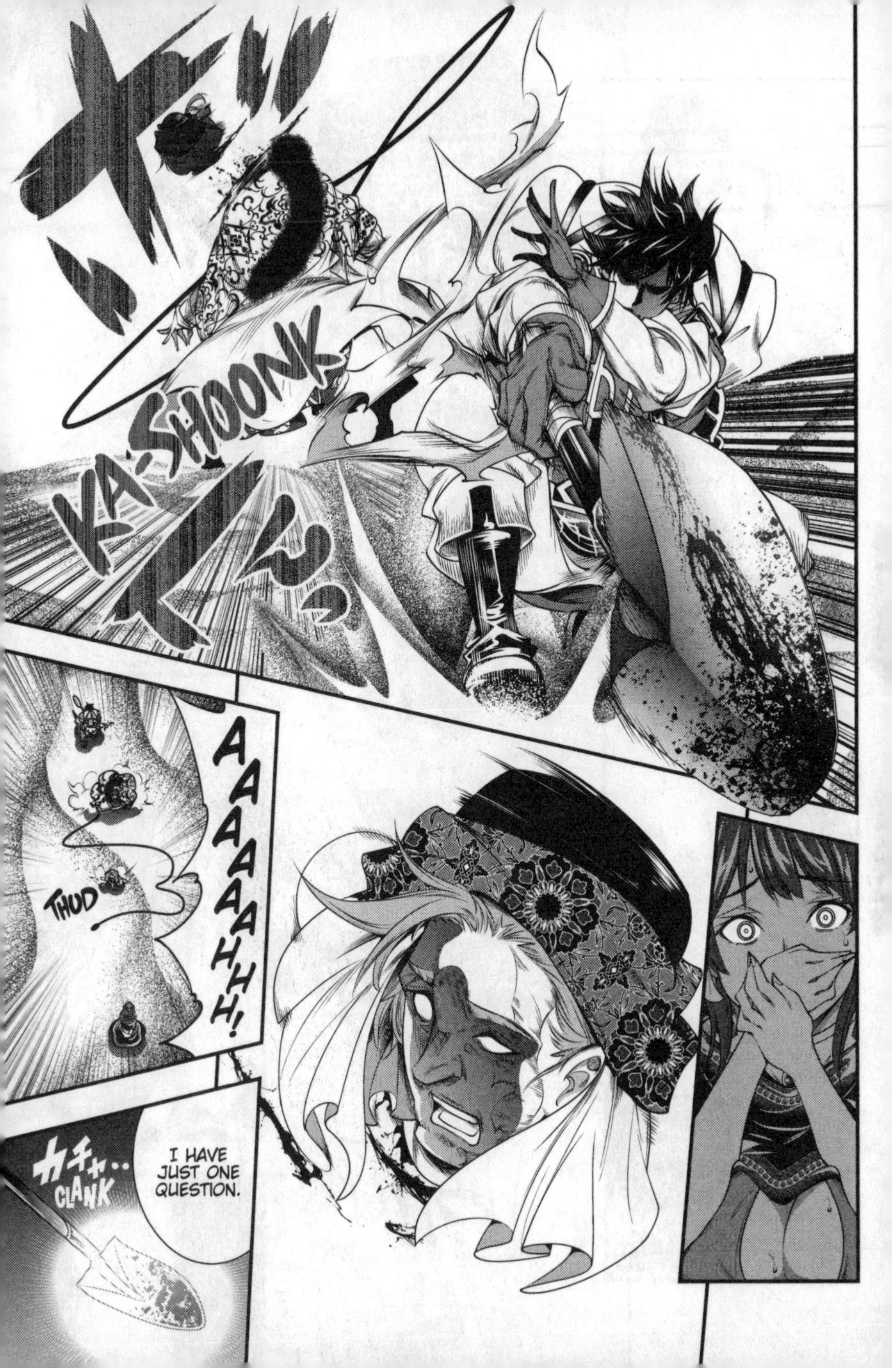
KA-SHOONK
AAAAAAAHHH!
THUD
I HAVE JUST ONE QUESTION.
カチャ..
CLANK

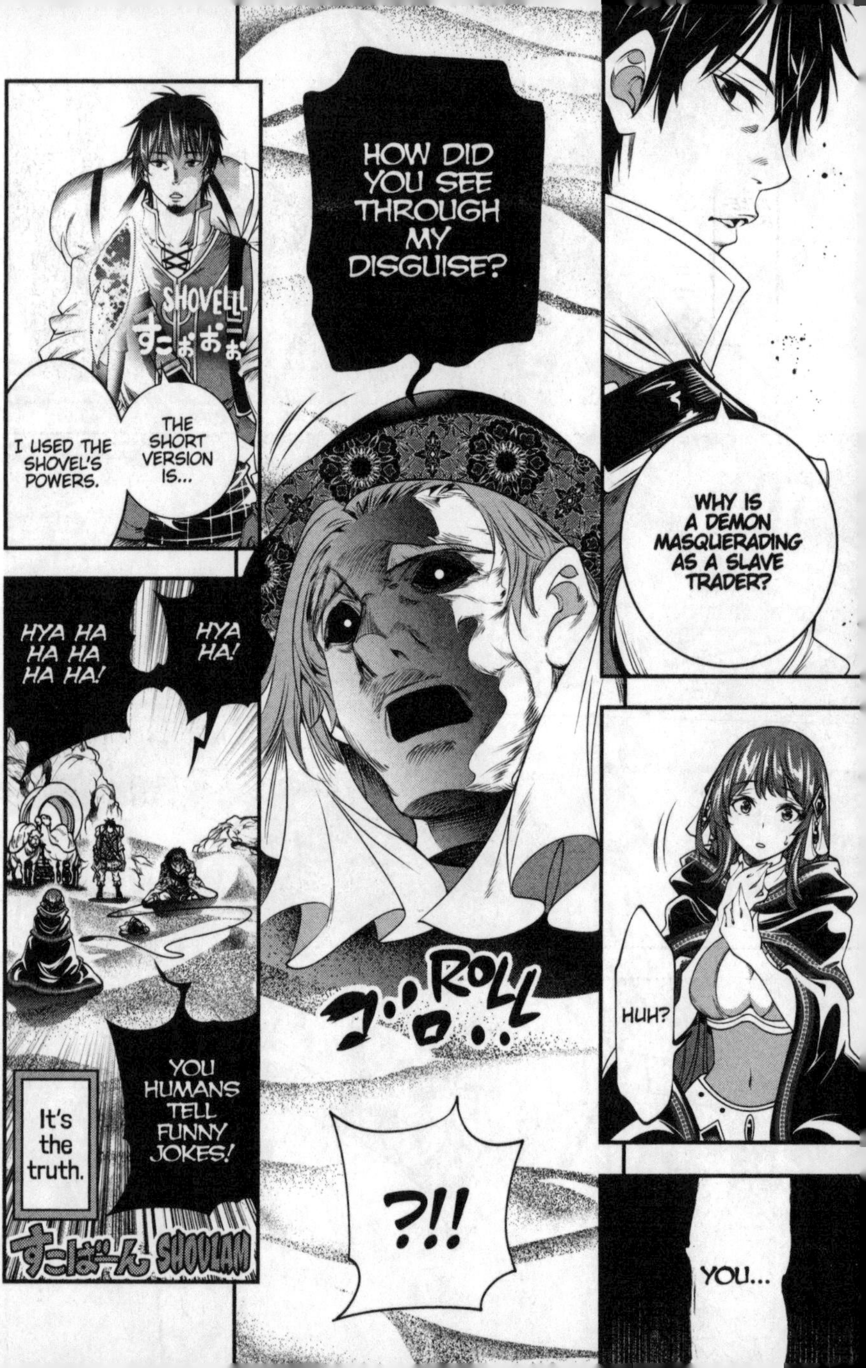
WHY IS A DEMON MASQUERADING AS A SLAVE TRADER?
HUH?
YOU...
HOW DID YOU SEE THROUGH MY DISGUISE?
ROLL
?!!
SHOVELLL
THE SHORT VERSION IS...
I USED THE SHOVEL'S POWERS.
HYA HA HA HA HA HA!
HYA HA!
YOU HUMANS TELL FUNNY JOKES!
It's the truth.
SHOVLAM

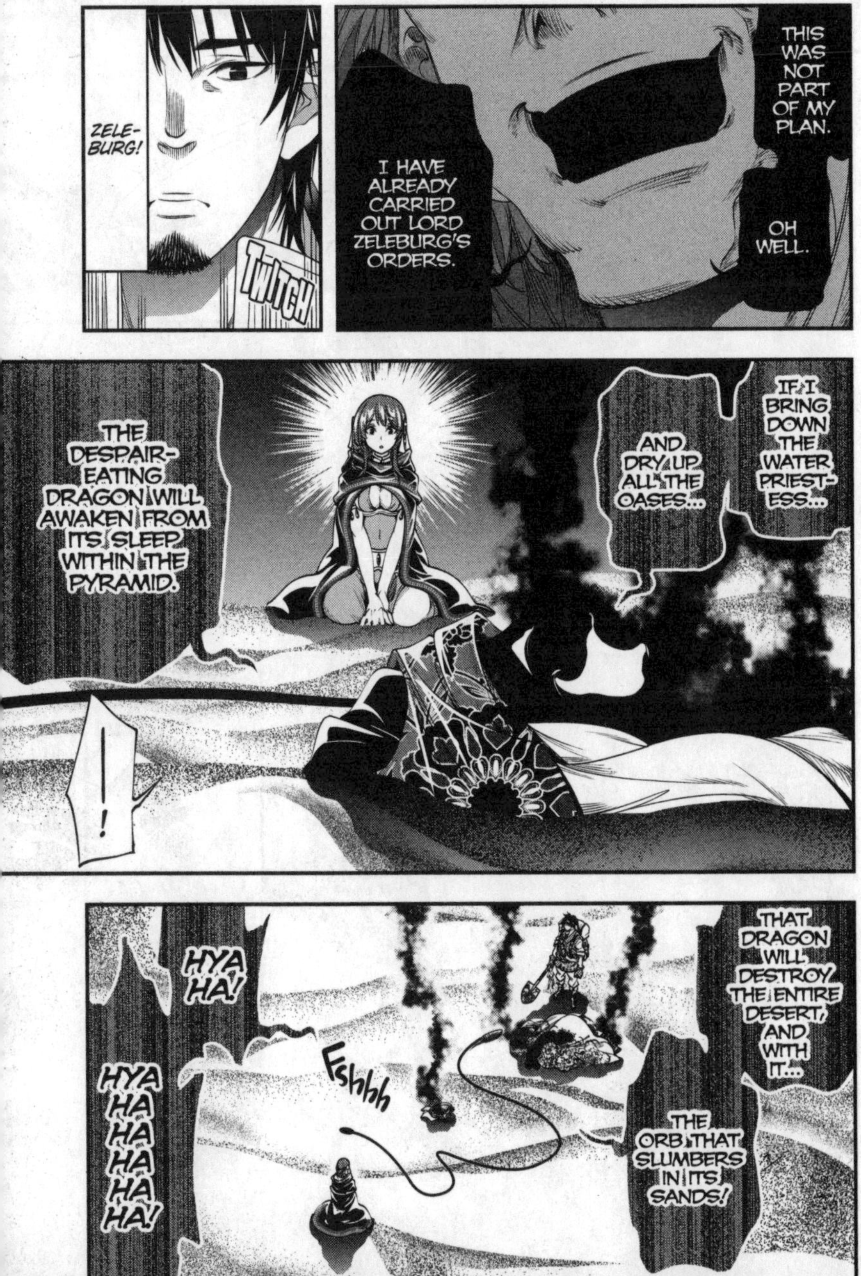
THIS WAS NOT PART OF MY PLAN.
I HAVE ALREADY CARRIED OUT LORD ZELEBURG'S ORDERS.
OH WELL.
ZELE-BURG!
TWITCH
IF I BRING DOWN THE WATER PRIEST-ESS...
AND DRY UP ALL THE OASES...
THE DESPAIR-EATING DRAGON WILL AWAKEN FROM ITS SLEEP WITHIN THE PYRAMID.
!
THAT DRAGON WILL DESTROY THE ENTIRE DESERT, AND WITH IT...
THE ORB THAT SLUMBERS IN ITS SANDS!
Fshhh
HYA HA!
HYA HA HA HA HA HA!

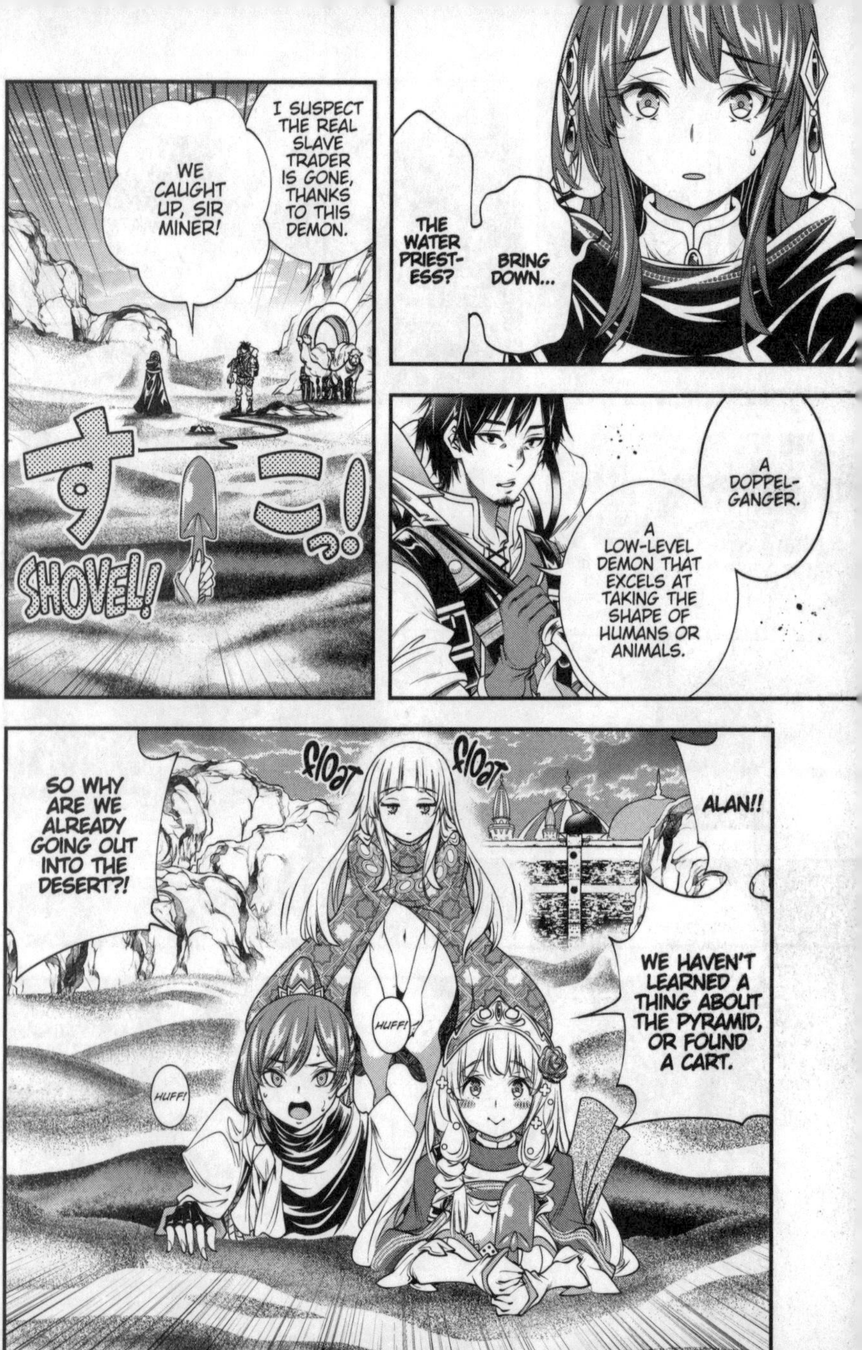
BRING DOWN...
THE WATER PRIESTESS?
A DOPPELGANGER.
A LOW-LEVEL DEMON THAT EXCELS AT TAKING THE SHAPE OF HUMANS OR ANIMALS.
I SUSPECT THE REAL SLAVE TRADER IS GONE, THANKS TO THIS DEMON.
WE CAUGHT UP, SIR MINER!
すこっ!
SHOVEL!
ALAN!!
float
float
SO WHY ARE WE ALREADY GOING OUT INTO THE DESERT?!
WE HAVEN'T LEARNED A THING ABOUT THE PYRAMID, OR FOUND A CART.
HUFF!
HUFF!

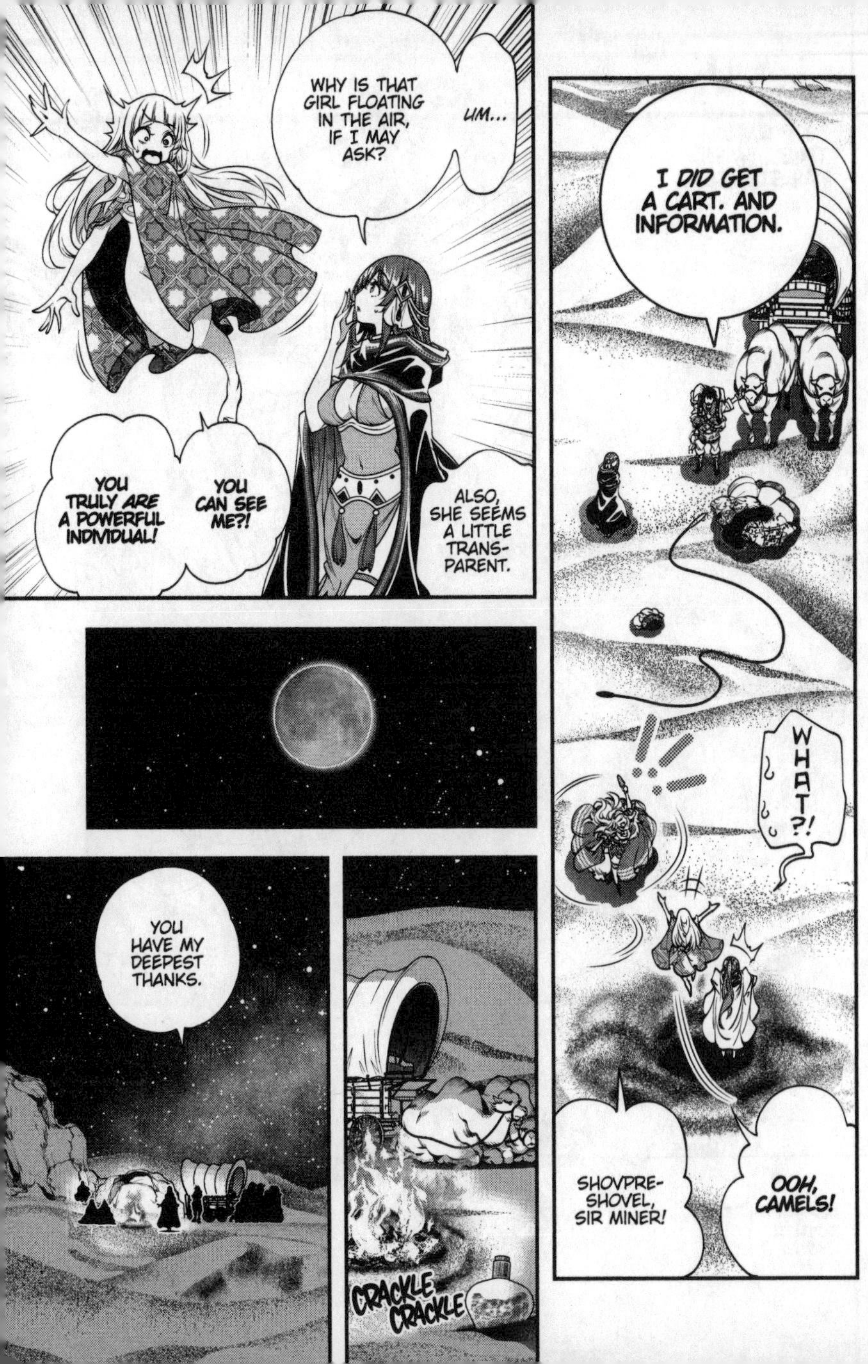
I DID GET A CART. AND INFORMATION.
WHAT?!
OOH, CAMELS!
SHOVPRE-SHOVEL, SIR MINER!
UM...
WHY IS THAT GIRL FLOATING IN THE AIR, IF I MAY ASK?
ALSO, SHE SEEMS A LITTLE TRANS-PARENT.
YOU CAN SEE ME?!
YOU TRULY ARE A POWERFUL INDIVIDUAL!
CRACKLE CRACKLE
YOU HAVE MY DEEPEST THANKS.

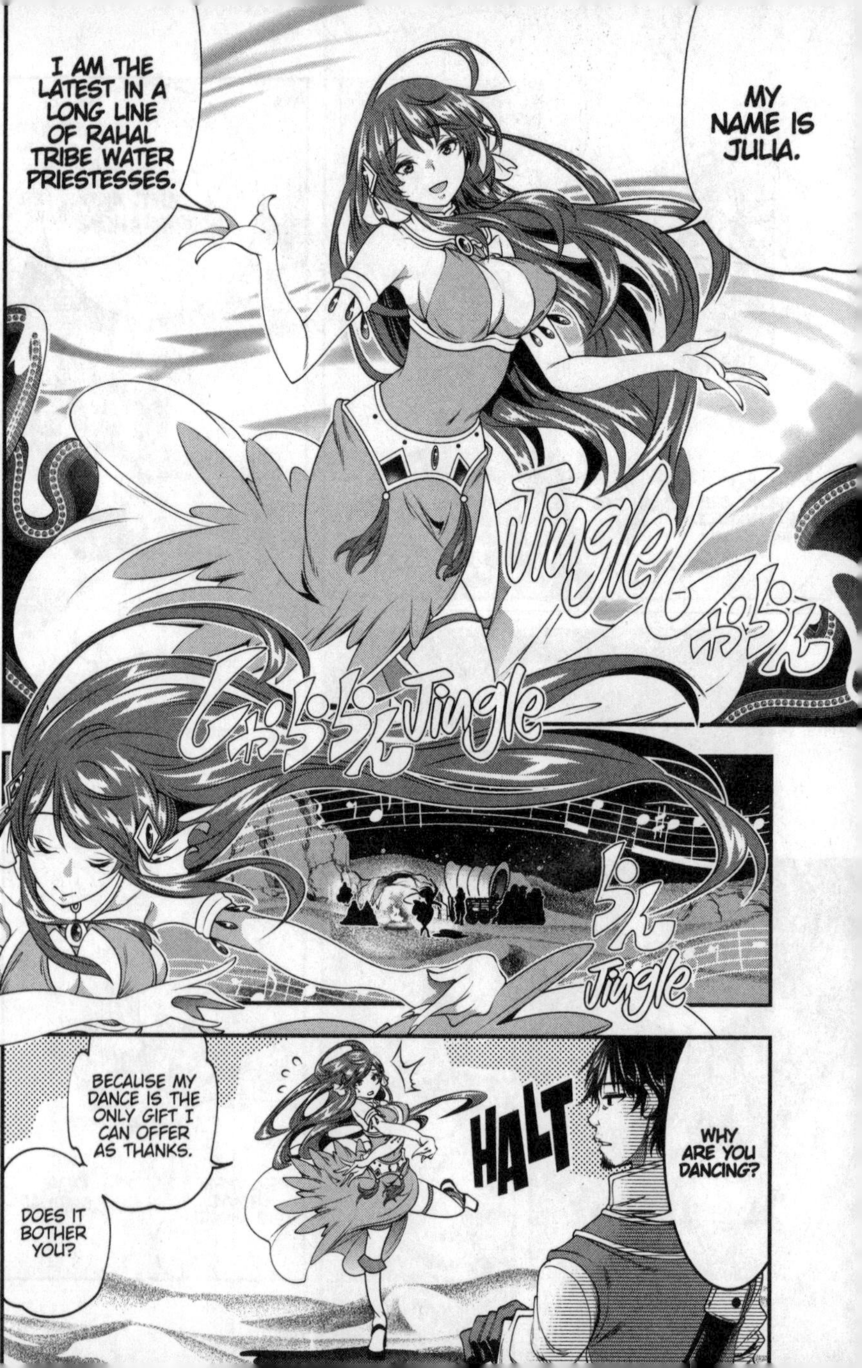

MY NAME IS JULIA.
I AM THE LATEST IN A LONG LINE OF RAHAL TRIBE WATER PRIESTESSES.
Jingle
しゃらん
しゃららん
Jingle
らん
Jingle
WHY ARE YOU DANCING?
HALT
BECAUSE MY DANCE IS THE ONLY GIFT I CAN OFFER AS THANKS.
DOES IT BOTHER YOU?

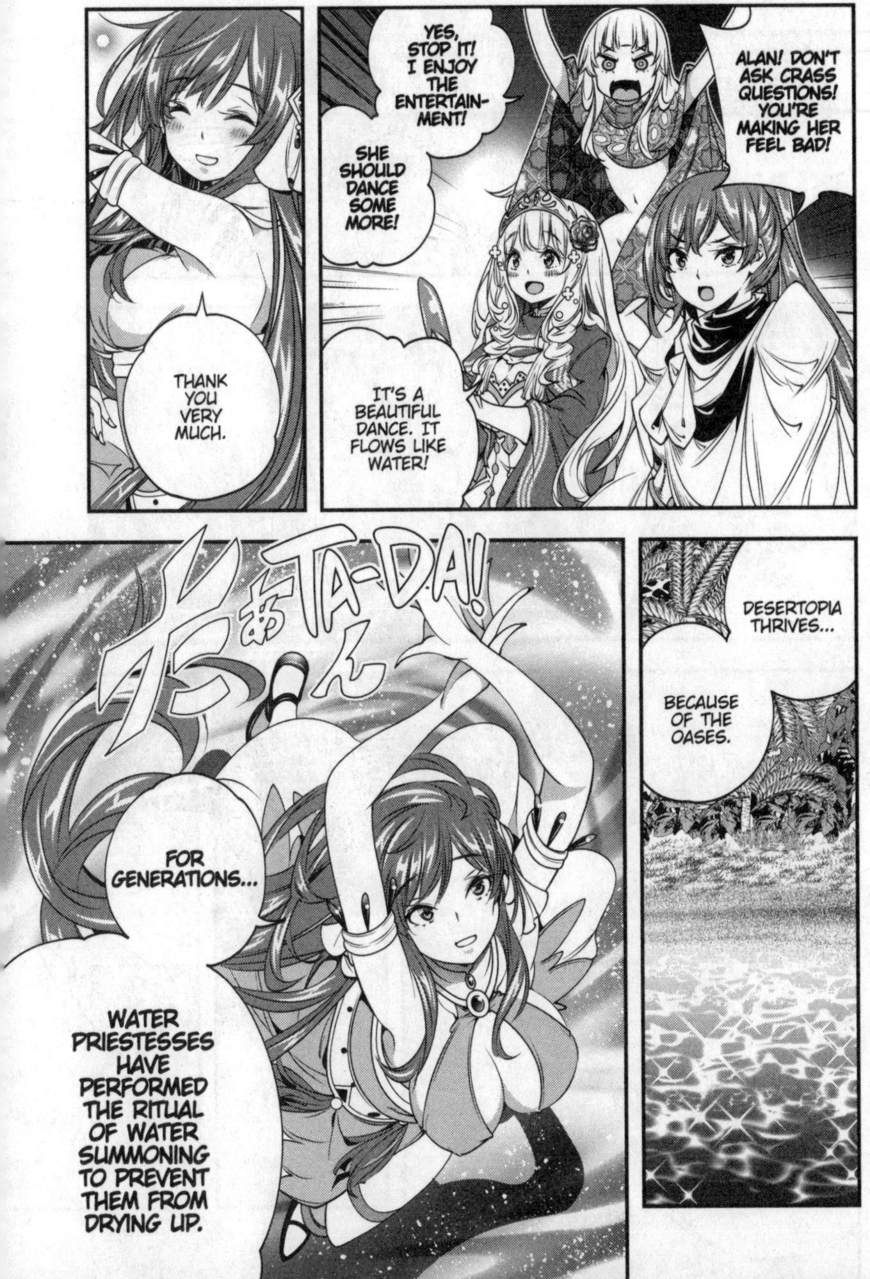
ALAN! DON'T ASK CRASS QUESTIONS! YOU'RE MAKING HER FEEL BAD!
YES, STOP IT! I ENJOY THE ENTERTAINMENT!
SHE SHOULD DANCE SOME MORE!
IT'S A BEAUTIFUL DANCE. IT FLOWS LIKE WATER!
THANK YOU VERY MUCH.
DESERTOPIA THRIVES...
BECAUSE OF THE OASES.
TA-DA!
FOR GENERATIONS...
WATER PRIESTESSES HAVE PERFORMED THE RITUAL OF WATER SUMMONING TO PREVENT THEM FROM DRYING UP.

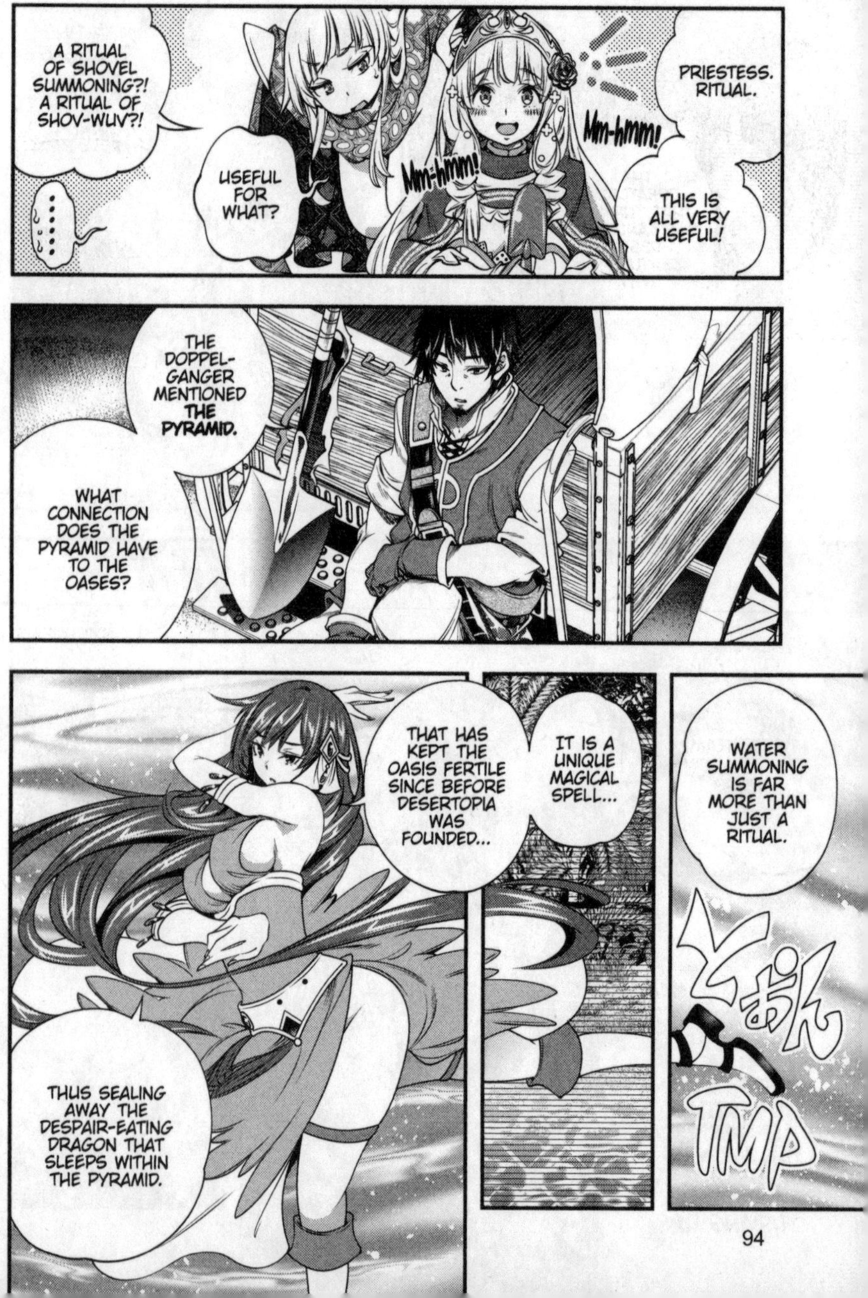
PRIESTESS. RITUAL.
Mm-hmm!
Mm-hmm!
THIS IS ALL VERY USEFUL!
USEFUL FOR WHAT?
A RITUAL OF SHOVEL SUMMONING?! A RITUAL OF SHOV-WUV?!
......
THE DOPPEL-GANGER MENTIONED THE PYRAMID.
WHAT CONNECTION DOES THE PYRAMID HAVE TO THE OASES?
WATER SUMMONING IS FAR MORE THAN JUST A RITUAL.
とぉん
TMP
IT IS A UNIQUE MAGICAL SPELL...
THAT HAS KEPT THE OASIS FERTILE SINCE BEFORE DESERTOPIA WAS FOUNDED...
THUS SEALING AWAY THE DESPAIR-EATING DRAGON THAT SLEEPS WITHIN THE PYRAMID.

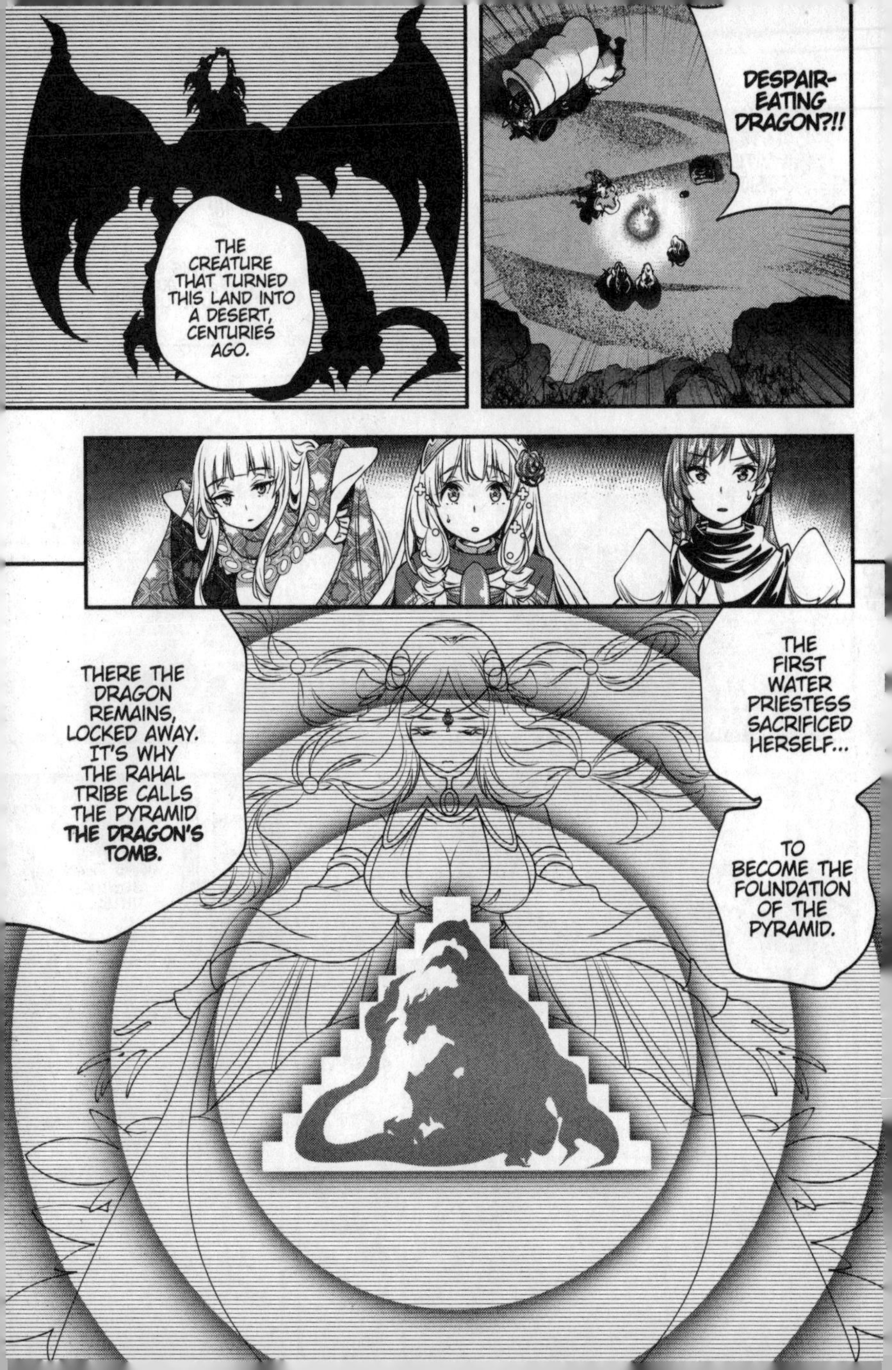

DESPAIR-EATING DRAGON?!!
THE CREATURE THAT TURNED THIS LAND INTO A DESERT, CENTURIES AGO.
THE FIRST WATER PRIESTESS SACRIFICED HERSELF...
TO BECOME THE FOUNDATION OF THE PYRAMID.
THERE THE DRAGON REMAINS, LOCKED AWAY. IT'S WHY THE RAHAL TRIBE CALLS THE PYRAMID **THE DRAGON'S TOMB.**

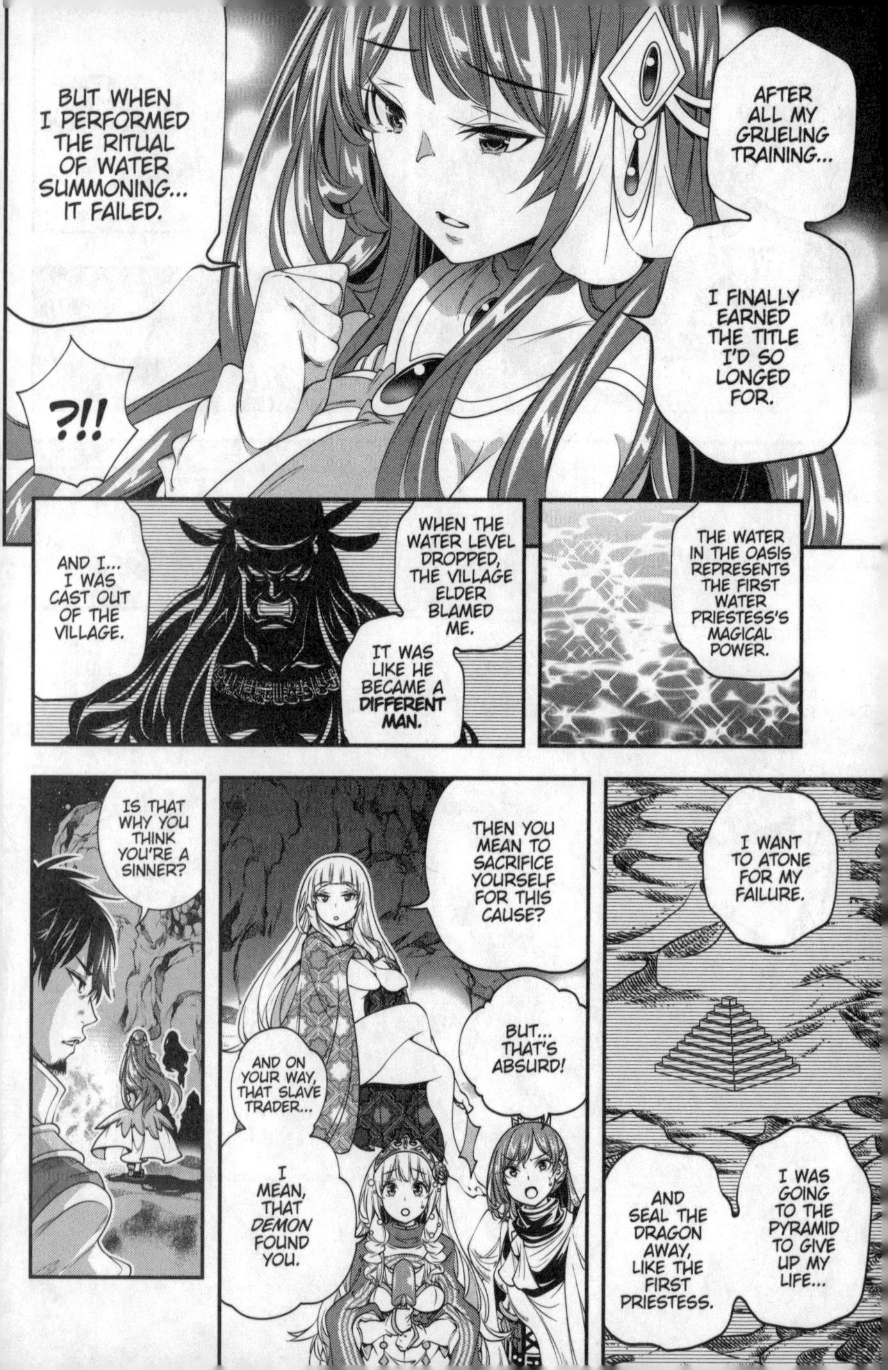
AFTER ALL MY GRUELING TRAINING...
I FINALLY EARNED THE TITLE I'D SO LONGED FOR.
BUT WHEN I PERFORMED THE RITUAL OF WATER SUMMONING... IT FAILED.
?!!
THE WATER IN THE OASIS REPRESENTS THE FIRST WATER PRIESTESS'S MAGICAL POWER.
WHEN THE WATER LEVEL DROPPED, THE VILLAGE ELDER BLAMED ME.
IT WAS LIKE HE BECAME A **DIFFERENT MAN.**
AND I... I WAS CAST OUT OF THE VILLAGE.
I WANT TO ATONE FOR MY FAILURE.
I WAS GOING TO THE PYRAMID TO GIVE UP MY LIFE...
AND SEAL THE DRAGON AWAY, LIKE THE FIRST PRIESTESS.
THEN YOU MEAN TO SACRIFICE YOURSELF FOR THIS CAUSE?
BUT... THAT'S ABSURD!
AND ON YOUR WAY, THAT SLAVE TRADER...
I MEAN, THAT *DEMON* FOUND YOU.
IS THAT WHY YOU THINK YOU'RE A SINNER?

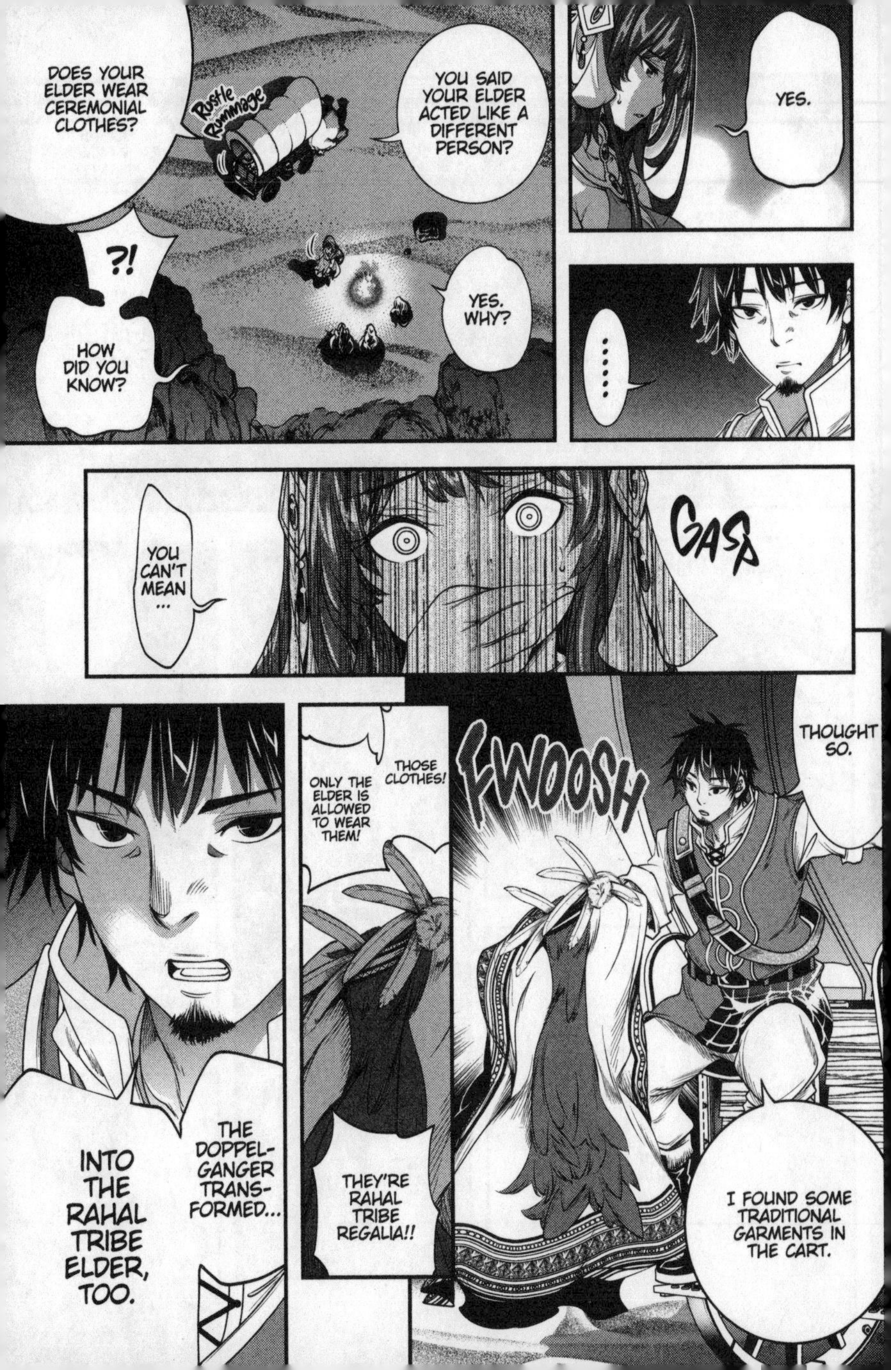
YES.
......
YOU SAID YOUR ELDER ACTED LIKE A DIFFERENT PERSON?
Rustle Rummage
DOES YOUR ELDER WEAR CEREMONIAL CLOTHES?
YES. WHY?
?!
HOW DID YOU KNOW?
GASP
YOU CAN'T MEAN ...
THOUGHT SO.
FWOOSH
I FOUND SOME TRADITIONAL GARMENTS IN THE CART.
THOSE CLOTHES!
ONLY THE ELDER IS ALLOWED TO WEAR THEM!
THEY'RE RAHAL TRIBE REGALIA!!
THE DOPPEL-GANGER TRANS-FORMED...
INTO THE RAHAL TRIBE ELDER, TOO.

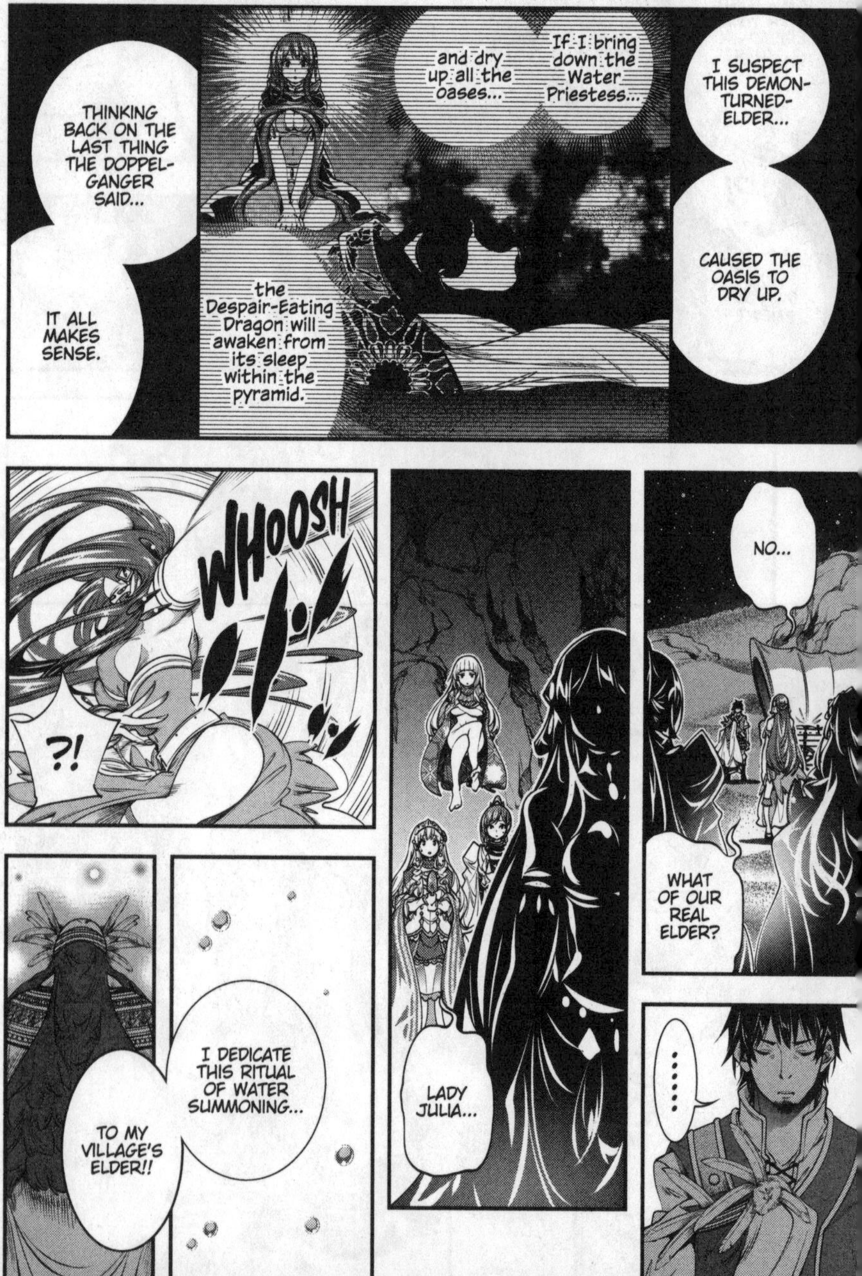

I SUSPECT THIS DEMON-TURNED-ELDER...
CAUSED THE OASIS TO DRY UP.
If I bring down the Water Priestess...
and dry up all the oases...
the Despair-Eating Dragon will awaken from its sleep within the pyramid.
THINKING BACK ON THE LAST THING THE DOPPEL-GANGER SAID...
IT ALL MAKES SENSE.
NO...
WHAT OF OUR REAL ELDER?
......
LADY JULIA...
WHOOSH
?!
I DEDICATE THIS RITUAL OF WATER SUMMONING...
TO MY VILLAGE'S ELDER!!

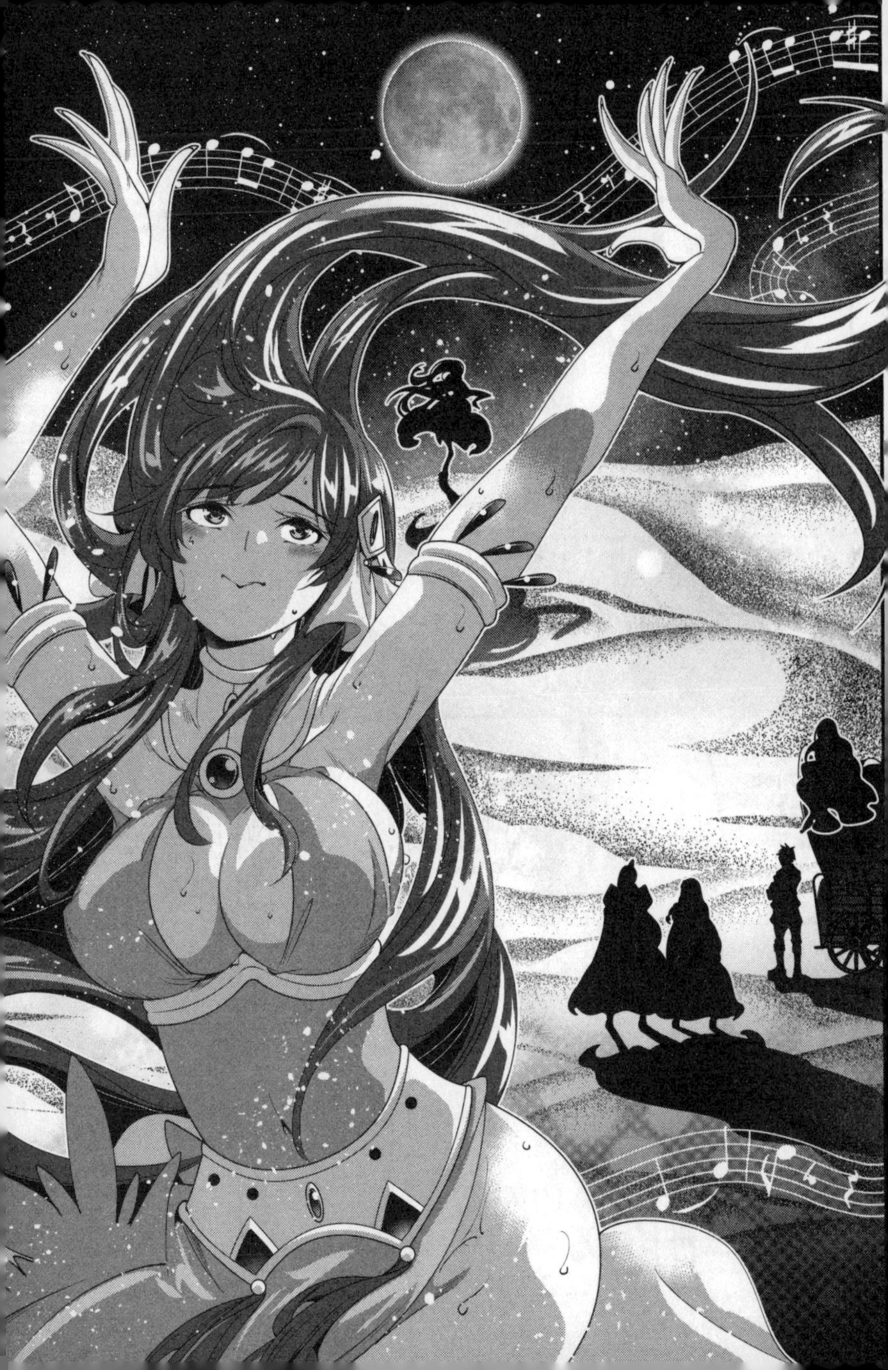

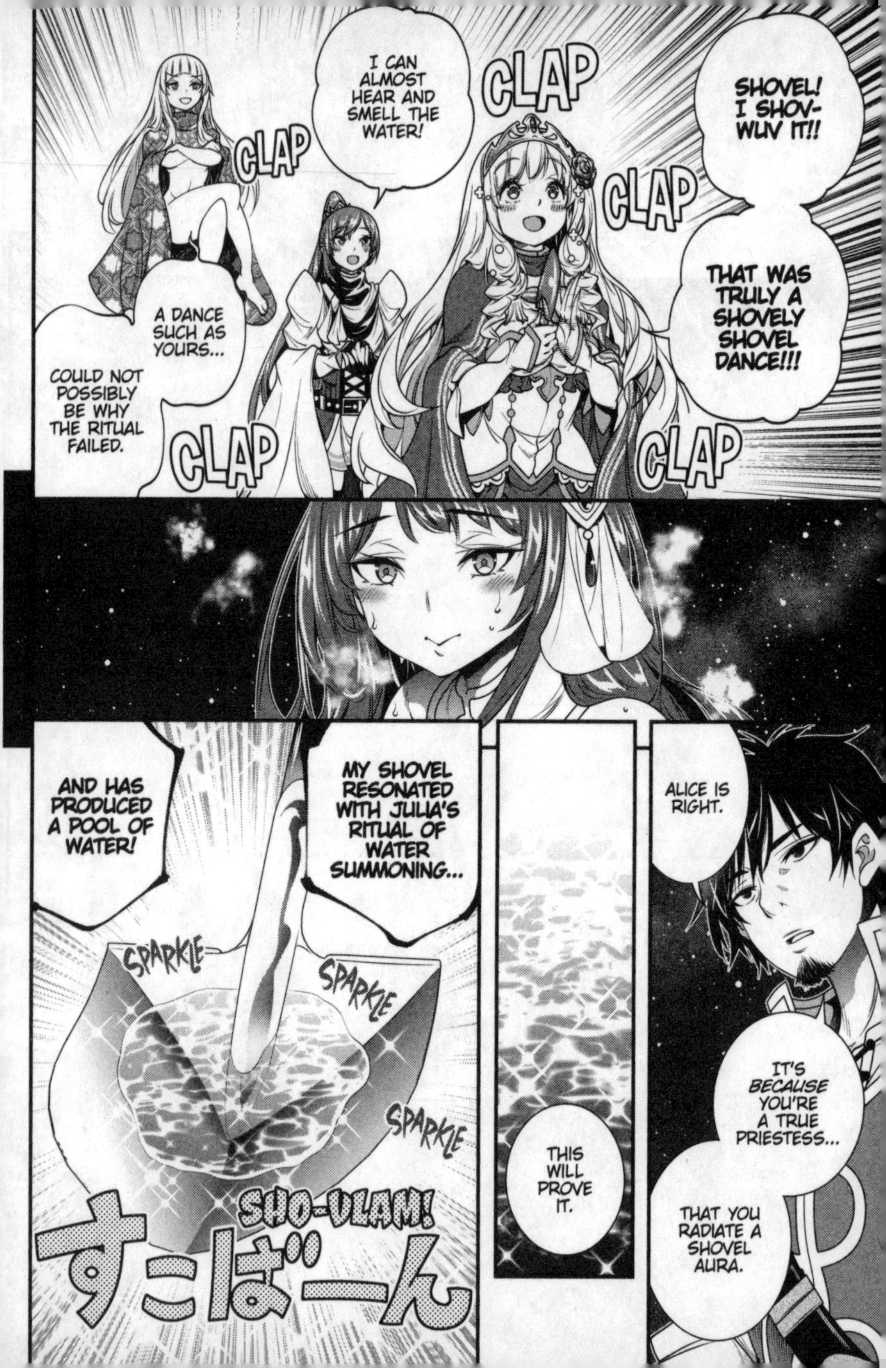
SHOVEL! I SHOV-WUV IT!!
THAT WAS TRULY A SHOVELY SHOVEL DANCE!!!
CLAP
CLAP
CLAP
I CAN ALMOST HEAR AND SMELL THE WATER!
CLAP
A DANCE SUCH AS YOURS...
COULD NOT POSSIBLY BE WHY THE RITUAL FAILED.
CLAP
ALICE IS RIGHT.
IT'S BECAUSE YOU'RE A TRUE PRIESTESS...
THAT YOU RADIATE A SHOVEL AURA.
THIS WILL PROVE IT.
MY SHOVEL RESONATED WITH JULIA'S RITUAL OF WATER SUMMONING...
AND HAS PRODUCED A POOL OF WATER!
SPARKLE
SPARKLE
SPARKLE
SHO-VLAM!
すこばーん

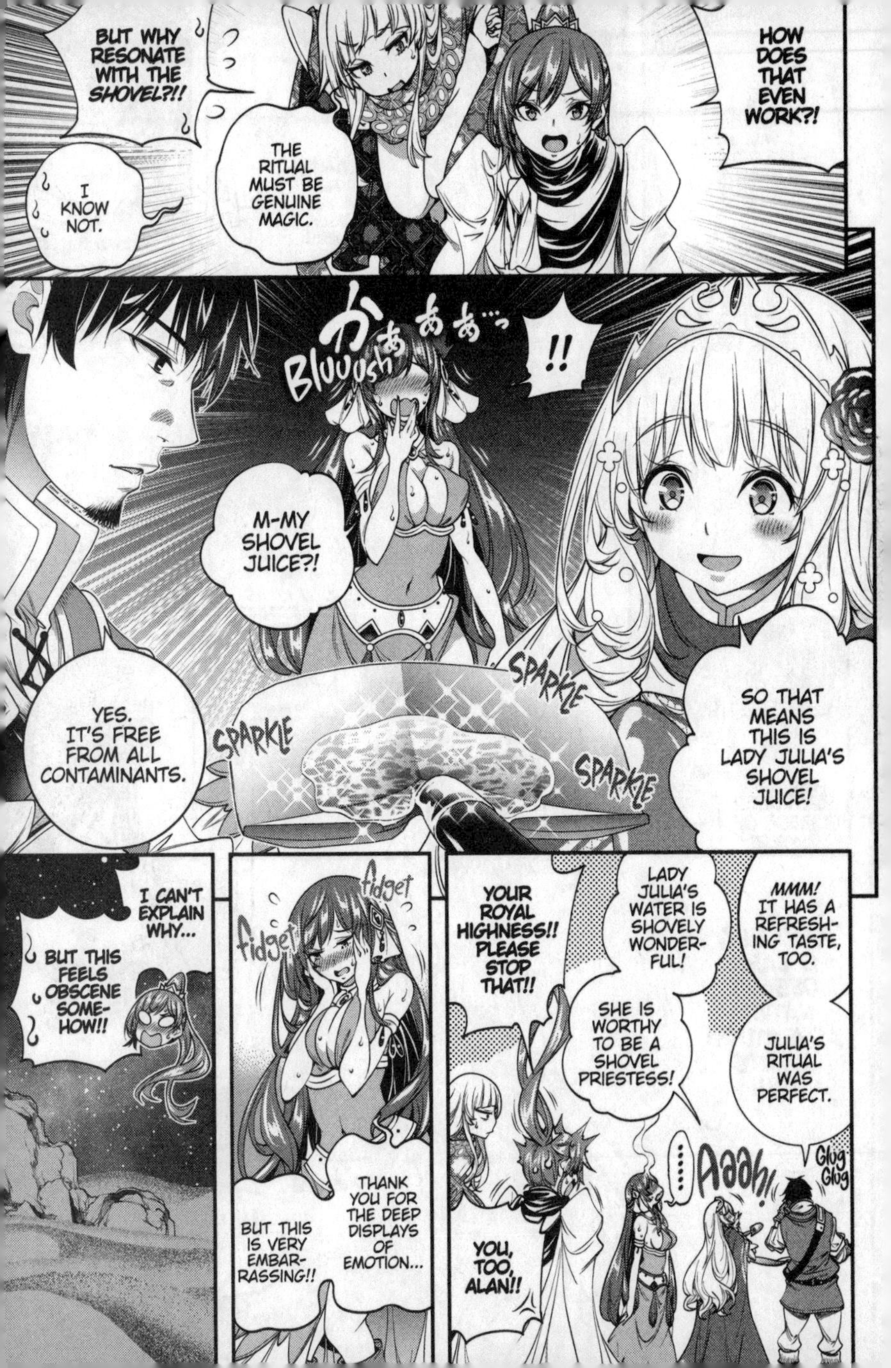
HOW DOES THAT EVEN WORK?!
THE RITUAL MUST BE GENUINE MAGIC.
BUT WHY RESONATE WITH THE *SHOVEL?!!*
I KNOW NOT.
かあぁぁ…っ
Bluuush
!!
M-MY SHOVEL JUICE?!
SO THAT MEANS THIS IS LADY JULIA'S SHOVEL JUICE!
SPARKLE
SPARKLE
SPARKLE
YES. IT'S FREE FROM ALL CONTAMINANTS.
MMM! IT HAS A REFRESHING TASTE, TOO.
LADY JULIA'S WATER IS SHOVELY WONDERFUL!
JULIA'S RITUAL WAS PERFECT.
SHE IS WORTHY TO BE A SHOVEL PRIESTESS!
YOUR ROYAL HIGHNESS!! PLEASE STOP THAT!!
Glug Glug
Aaah!
......
YOU, TOO, ALAN!!
fidget
fidget
THANK YOU FOR THE DEEP DISPLAYS OF EMOTION...
BUT THIS IS VERY EMBARRASSING!!
I CAN'T EXPLAIN WHY...
BUT THIS FEELS OBSCENE SOMEHOW!!

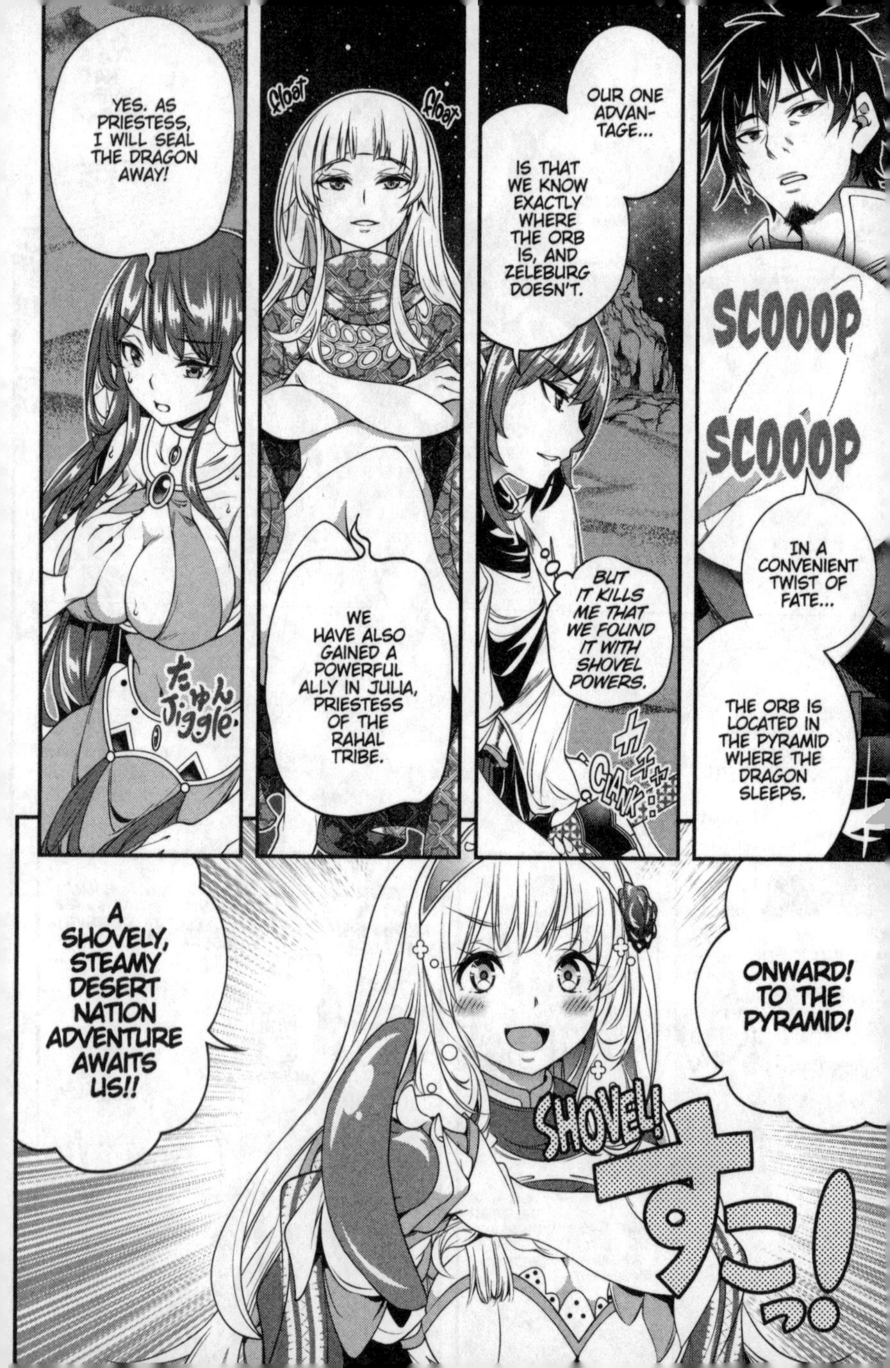
SCOOOP
SCOOOP
IN A CONVENIENT TWIST OF FATE...
THE ORB IS LOCATED IN THE PYRAMID WHERE THE DRAGON SLEEPS.
OUR ONE ADVANTAGE...
IS THAT WE KNOW EXACTLY WHERE THE ORB IS, AND ZELEBURG DOESN'T.
BUT IT KILLS ME THAT WE FOUND IT WITH SHOVEL POWERS.
CLANK
float
float
WE HAVE ALSO GAINED A POWERFUL ALLY IN JULIA, PRIESTESS OF THE RAHAL TRIBE.
YES. AS PRIESTESS, I WILL SEAL THE DRAGON AWAY!
たゆん
Jiggle
ONWARD! TO THE PYRAMID!
A SHOVELY, STEAMY DESERT NATION ADVENTURE AWAITS US!!
SHOVEL!

THE INVINCIBLE

SHOVEL

"WAVE MOTION SHOVEL BLAST!"
(・ω・)σ====★(`д　　 ;;):.: KA-CHOOOM

THE INVINCIBLE
SHOVEL

"WAVE MOTION SHOVEL BLAST!"
(・ω・)σ≡≡≡≡★(д   ::::).:.∴ KA-CHOOOM

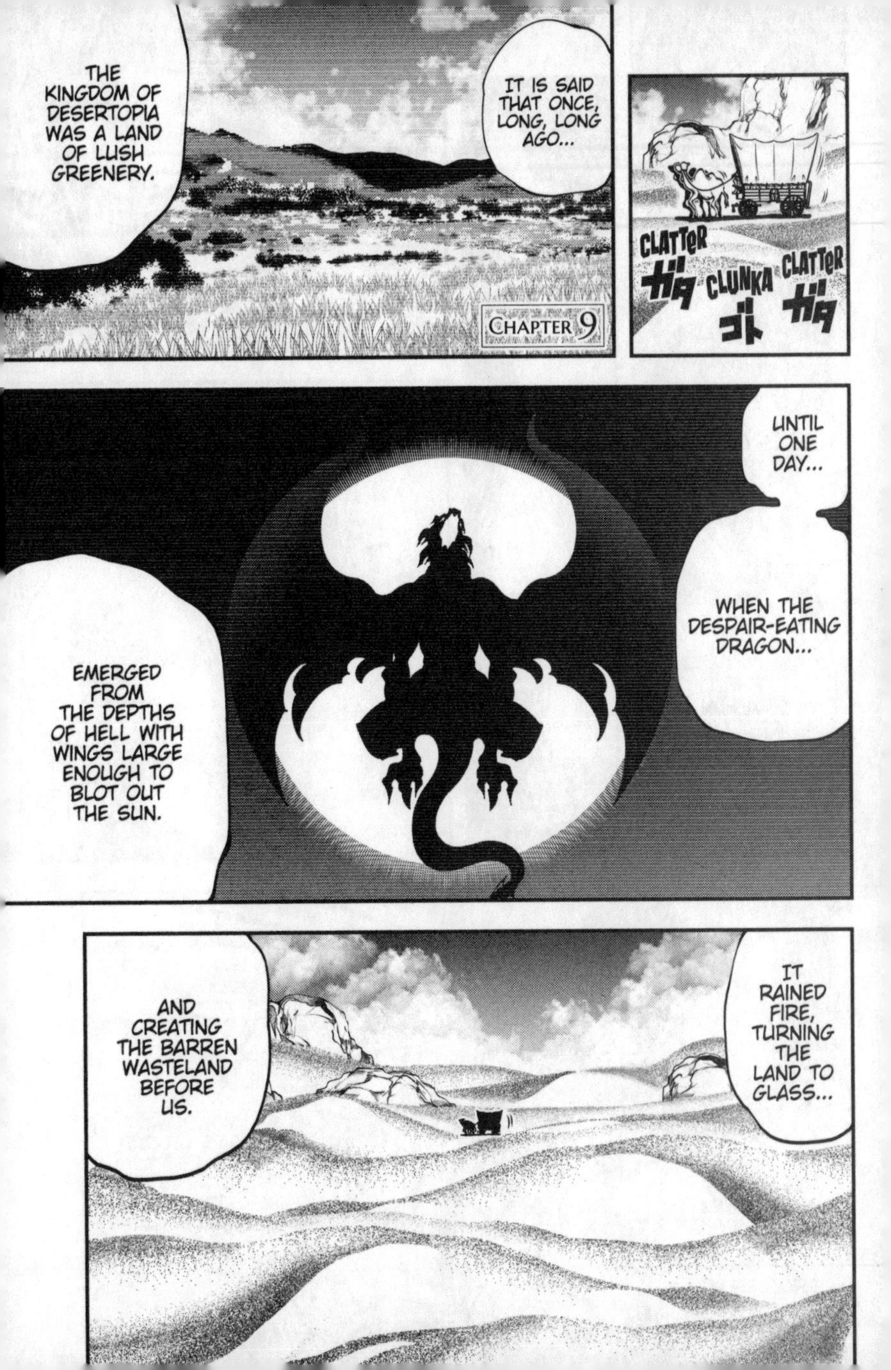
CLATTER ガタ
CLUNKA ゴト
CLATTER ガタ
IT IS SAID THAT ONCE, LONG, LONG AGO...
THE KINGDOM OF DESERTOPIA WAS A LAND OF LUSH GREENERY.
CHAPTER 9
UNTIL ONE DAY...
WHEN THE DESPAIR-EATING DRAGON...
EMERGED FROM THE DEPTHS OF HELL WITH WINGS LARGE ENOUGH TO BLOT OUT THE SUN.
IT RAINED FIRE, TURNING THE LAND TO GLASS...
AND CREATING THE BARREN WASTELAND BEFORE US.

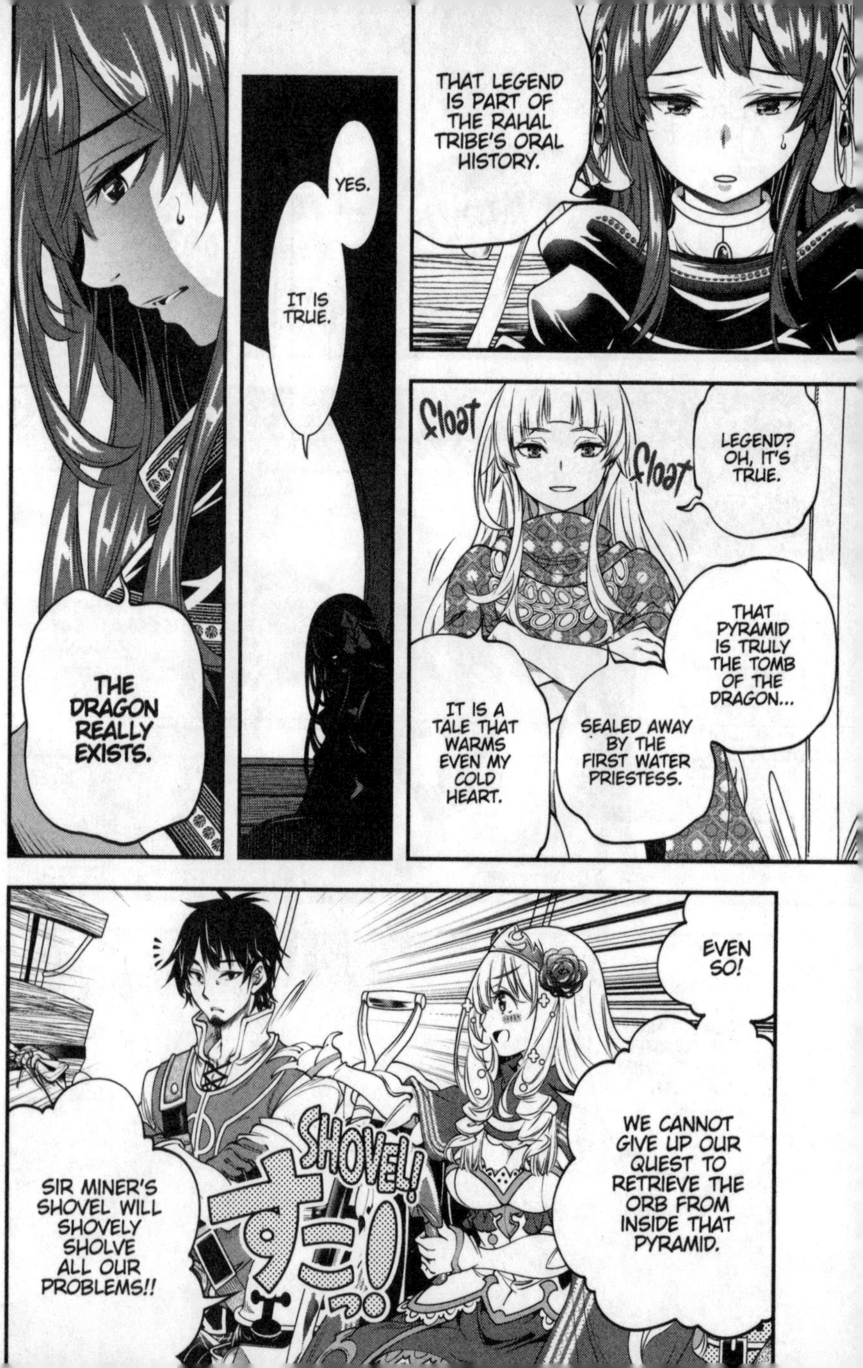
THAT LEGEND IS PART OF THE RAHAL TRIBE'S ORAL HISTORY.
float
float
LEGEND? OH, IT'S TRUE.
THAT PYRAMID IS TRULY THE TOMB OF THE DRAGON...
SEALED AWAY BY THE FIRST WATER PRIESTESS.
IT IS A TALE THAT WARMS EVEN MY COLD HEART.
YES.
IT IS TRUE.
THE DRAGON REALLY EXISTS.
EVEN SO!
WE CANNOT GIVE UP OUR QUEST TO RETRIEVE THE ORB FROM INSIDE THAT PYRAMID.
SHOVEL!
SIR MINER'S SHOVEL WILL SHOVELY SHOLVE ALL OUR PROBLEMS!!

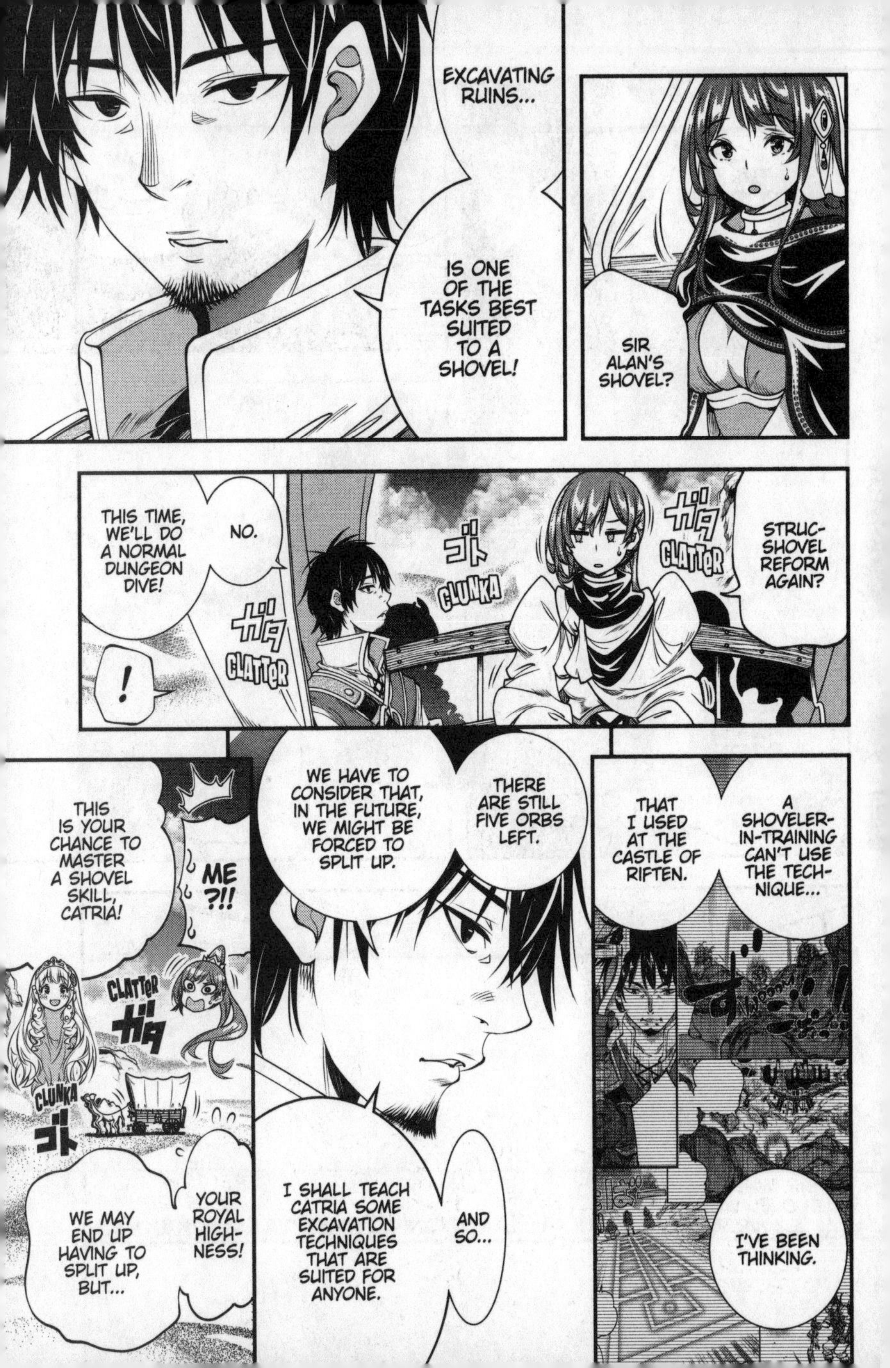
SIR ALAN'S SHOVEL?
EXCAVATING RUINS...
IS ONE OF THE TASKS BEST SUITED TO A SHOVEL!
STRUC-SHOVEL REFORM AGAIN?
ガタ CLATTER
ゴト CLUNKA
NO.
THIS TIME, WE'LL DO A NORMAL DUNGEON DIVE!
ガタ CLATTER
!
A SHOVELER-IN-TRAINING CAN'T USE THE TECHNIQUE...
THAT I USED AT THE CASTLE OF RIFTEN.
I'VE BEEN THINKING.
THERE ARE STILL FIVE ORBS LEFT.
WE HAVE TO CONSIDER THAT, IN THE FUTURE, WE MIGHT BE FORCED TO SPLIT UP.
AND SO...
I SHALL TEACH CATRIA SOME EXCAVATION TECHNIQUES THAT ARE SUITED FOR ANYONE.
THIS IS YOUR CHANCE TO MASTER A SHOVEL SKILL, CATRIA!
ME?!!
CLATTER ガタ
CLUNKA ゴト
YOUR ROYAL HIGHNESS!
WE MAY END UP HAVING TO SPLIT UP, BUT...

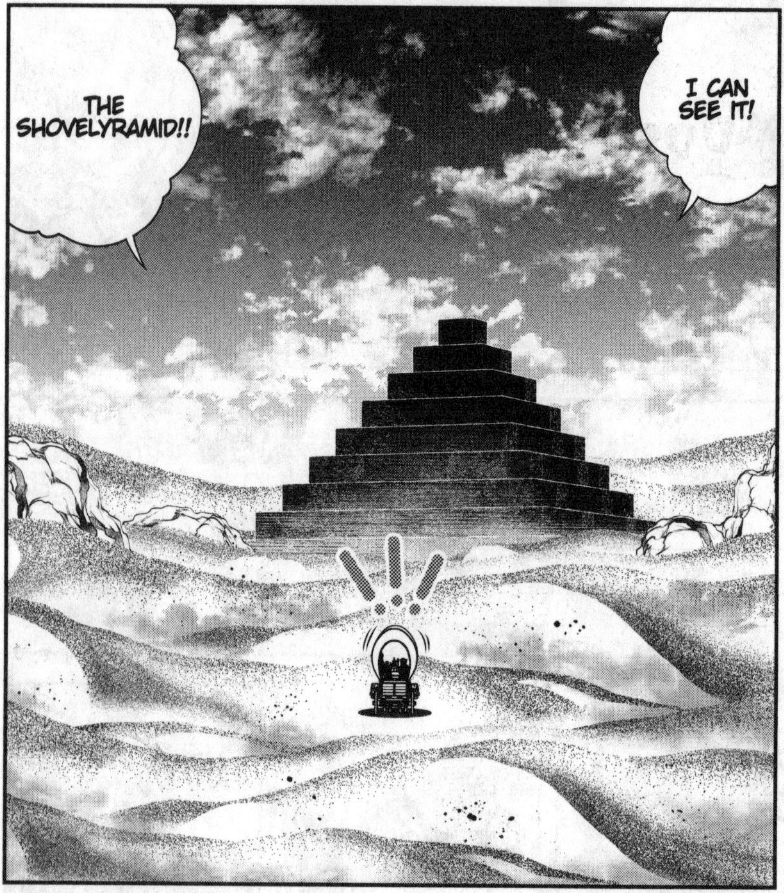
I CAN SEE IT!
THE SHOVELYRAMID!!

Chapter 9: The Shovel Solution to the Pyramid Riddle

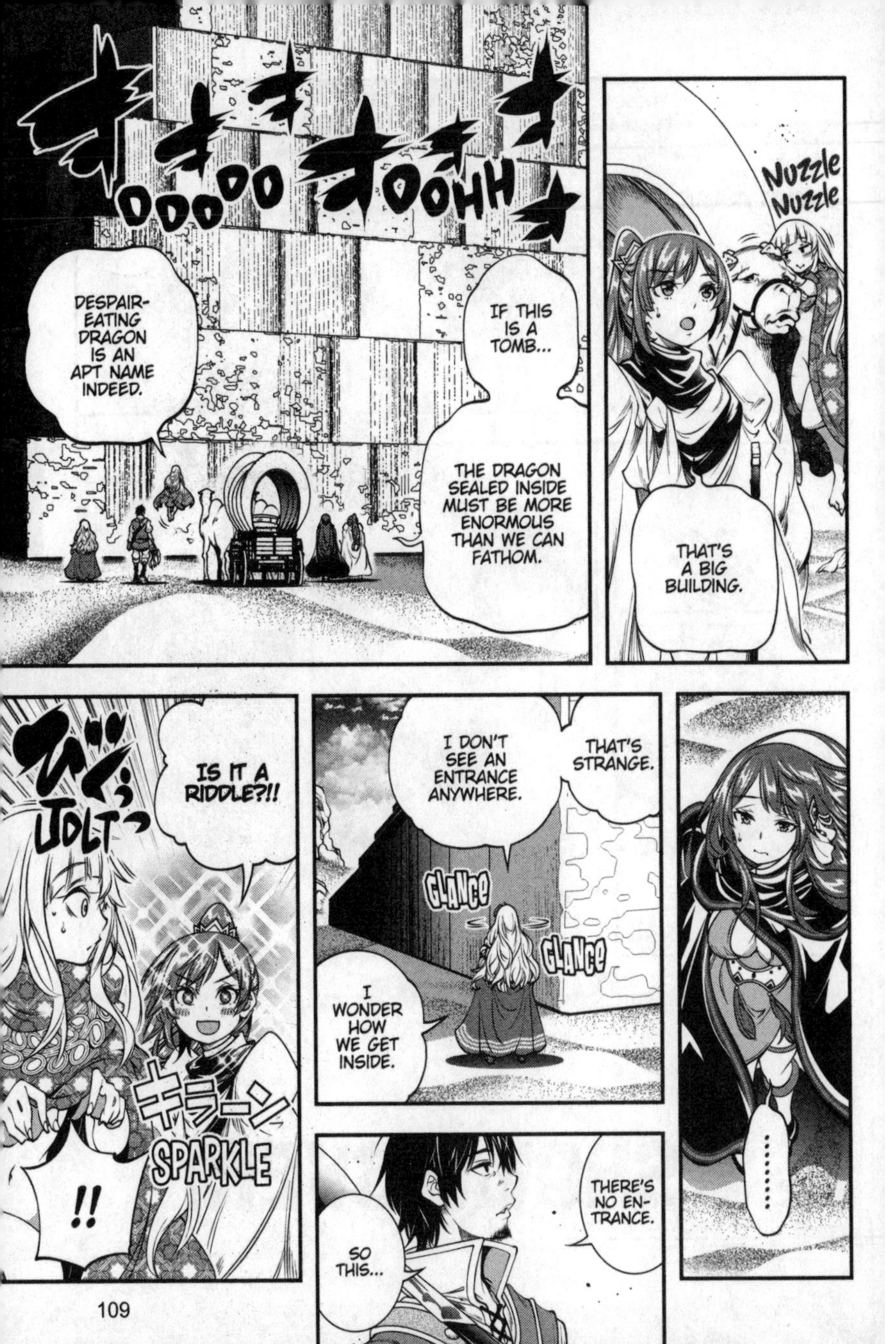
NUZZLE NUZZLE
THAT'S A BIG BUILDING.
OOOOOOOOHH
IF THIS IS A TOMB...
THE DRAGON SEALED INSIDE MUST BE MORE ENORMOUS THAN WE CAN FATHOM.
DESPAIR-EATING DRAGON IS AN APT NAME INDEED.
......
THAT'S STRANGE.
I DON'T SEE AN ENTRANCE ANYWHERE.
GLANCE
GLANCE
I WONDER HOW WE GET INSIDE.
THERE'S NO EN-TRANCE.
SO THIS...
JOLT
IS IT A RIDDLE?!!
キラーン
SPARKLE
!!

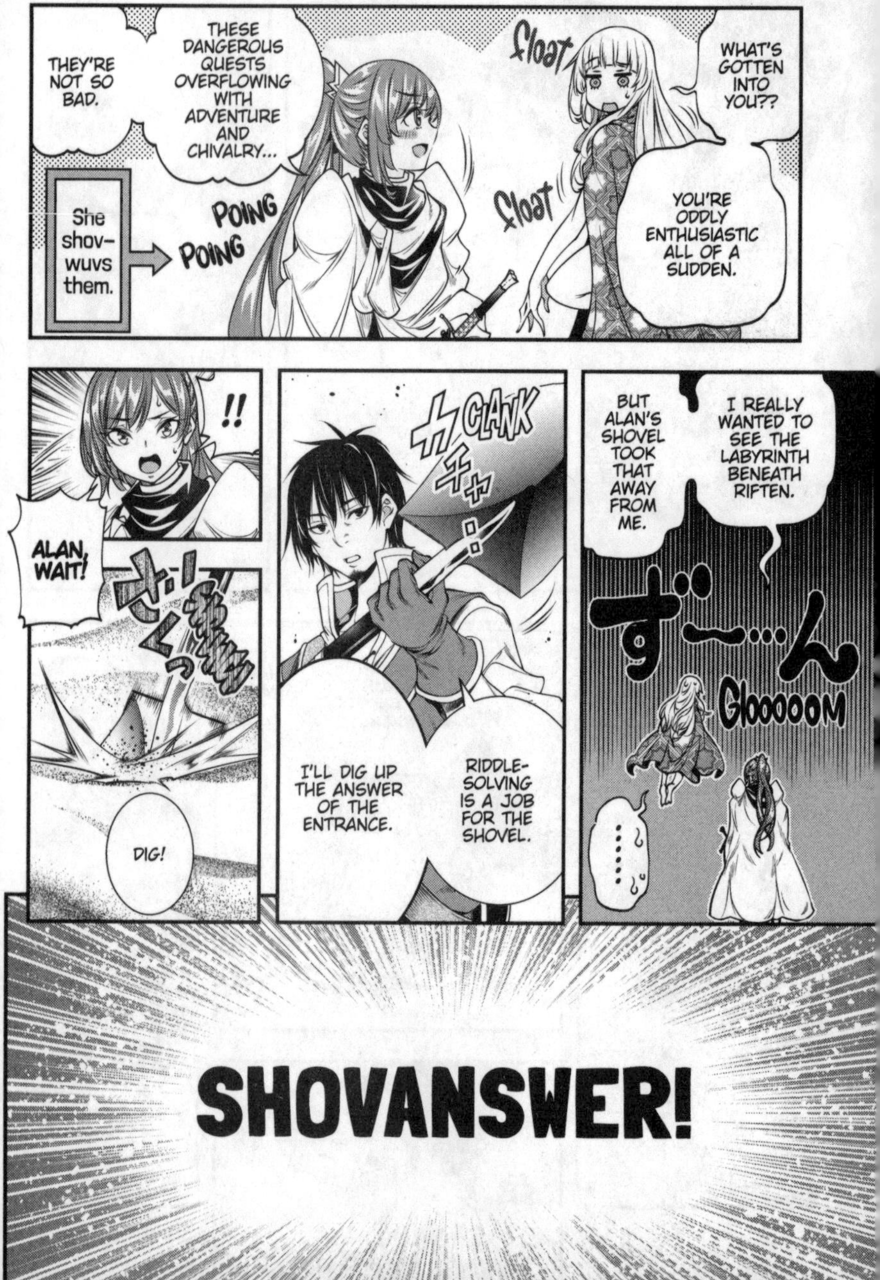
float
WHAT'S GOTTEN INTO YOU??
float
YOU'RE ODDLY ENTHUSIASTIC ALL OF A SUDDEN.
THESE DANGEROUS QUESTS OVERFLOWING WITH ADVENTURE AND CHIVALRY...
THEY'RE NOT SO BAD.
POING
POING
She shov-wuvs them.
I REALLY WANTED TO SEE THE LABYRINTH BENEATH RIFTEN.
BUT ALAN'S SHOVEL TOOK THAT AWAY FROM ME.
ず〜…ん
GLOOOOOM
......
カチャ
CLANK
RIDDLE-SOLVING IS A JOB FOR THE SHOVEL.
I'LL DIG UP THE ANSWER OF THE ENTRANCE.
!!
ALAN, WAIT!
ざくっ
DIG!
SHOVANSWER!

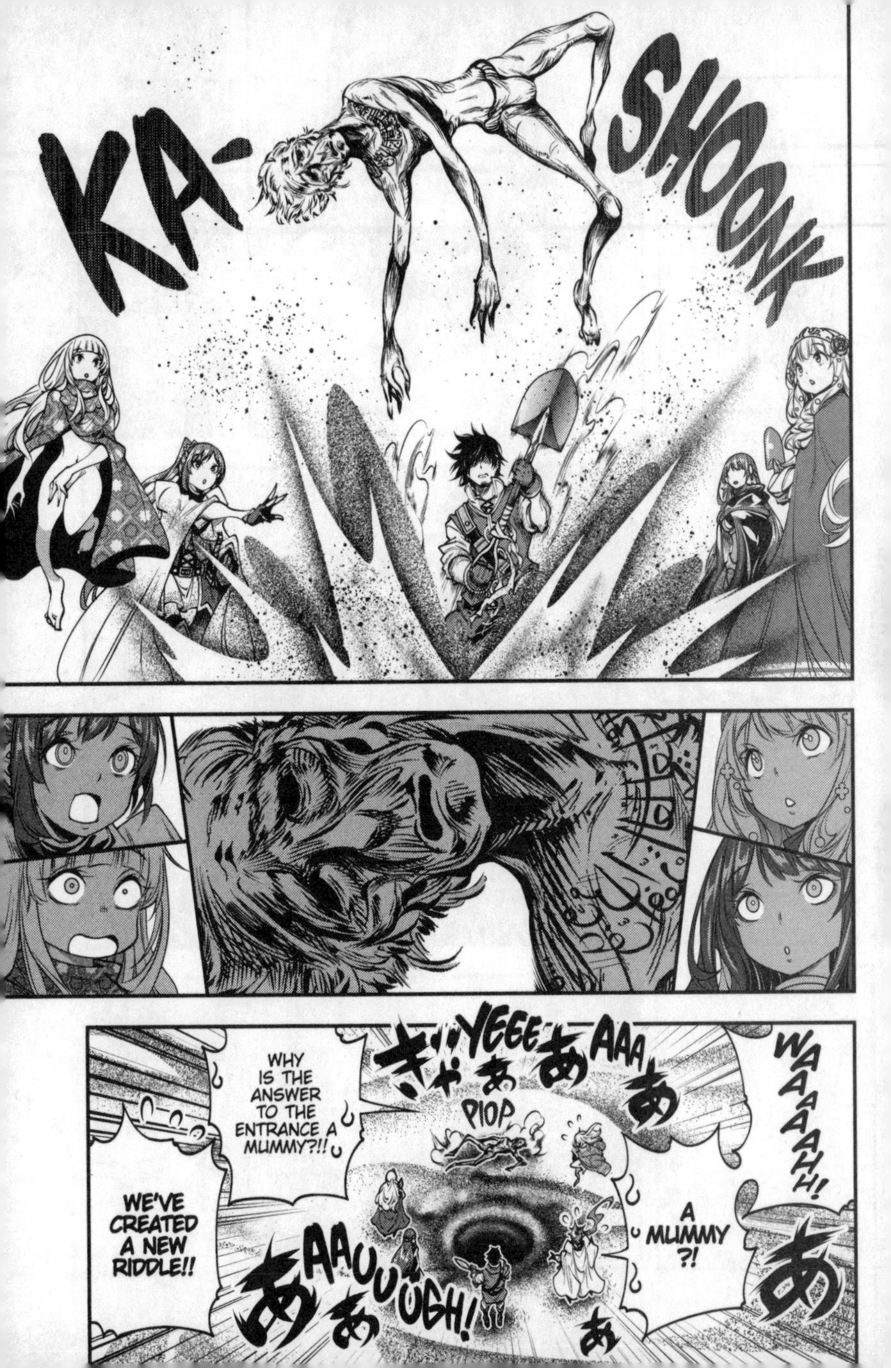
KA-SHOONK
WAAAAAH!
A MUMMY?!
ぎゃあああ YEEEAAA
PLOP
WHY IS THE ANSWER TO THE ENTRANCE A MUMMY?!!
WE'VE CREATED A NEW RIDDLE!!
AAUUUGH!

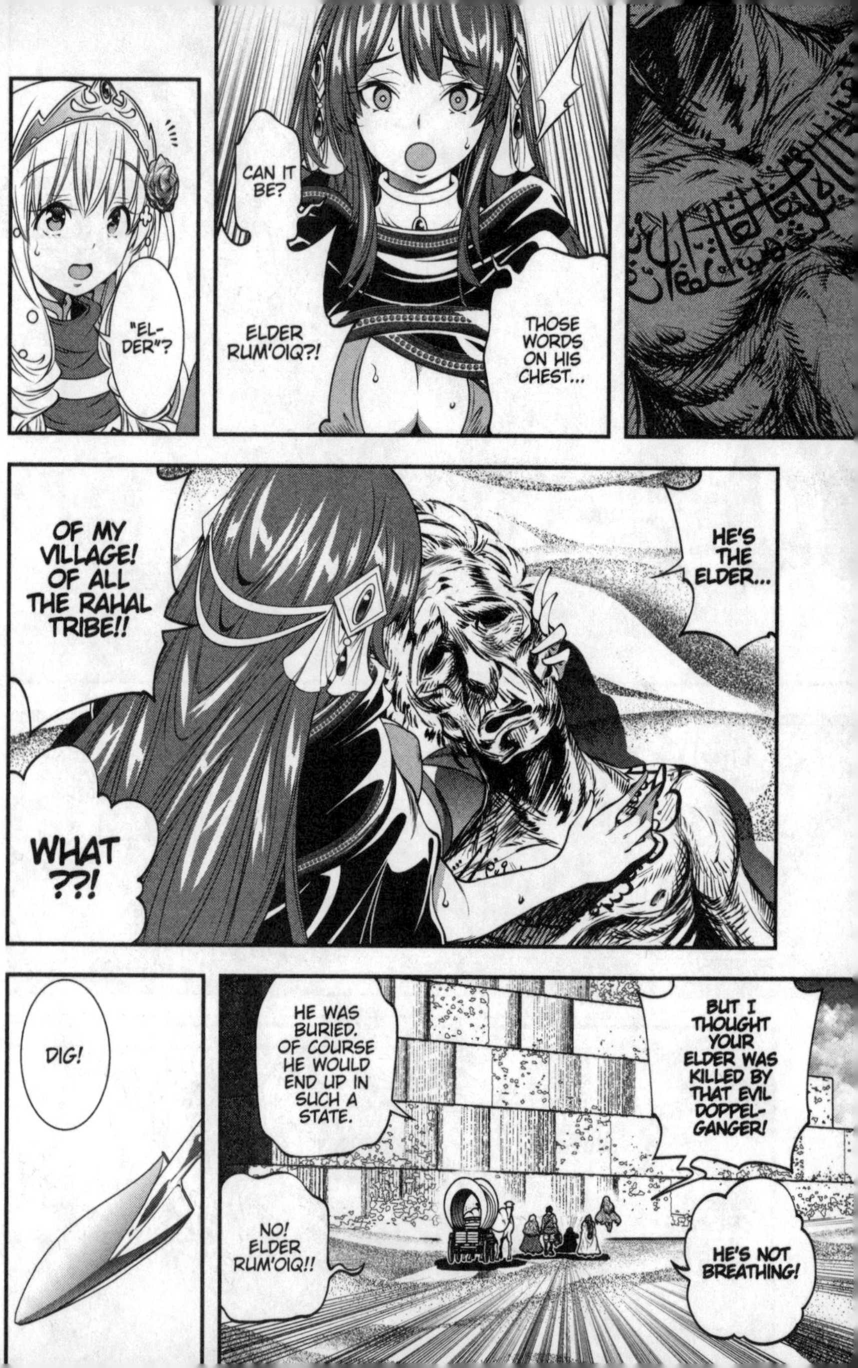
THOSE WORDS ON HIS CHEST...
CAN IT BE?
ELDER RUM'OIQ?!
"EL-DER"?
HE'S THE ELDER...
OF MY VILLAGE! OF ALL THE RAHAL TRIBE!!
WHAT ??!
BUT I THOUGHT YOUR ELDER WAS KILLED BY THAT EVIL DOPPEL-GANGER!
HE WAS BURIED. OF COURSE HE WOULD END UP IN SUCH A STATE.
HE'S NOT BREATHING!
NO! ELDER RUM'OIQ!!
DIG!

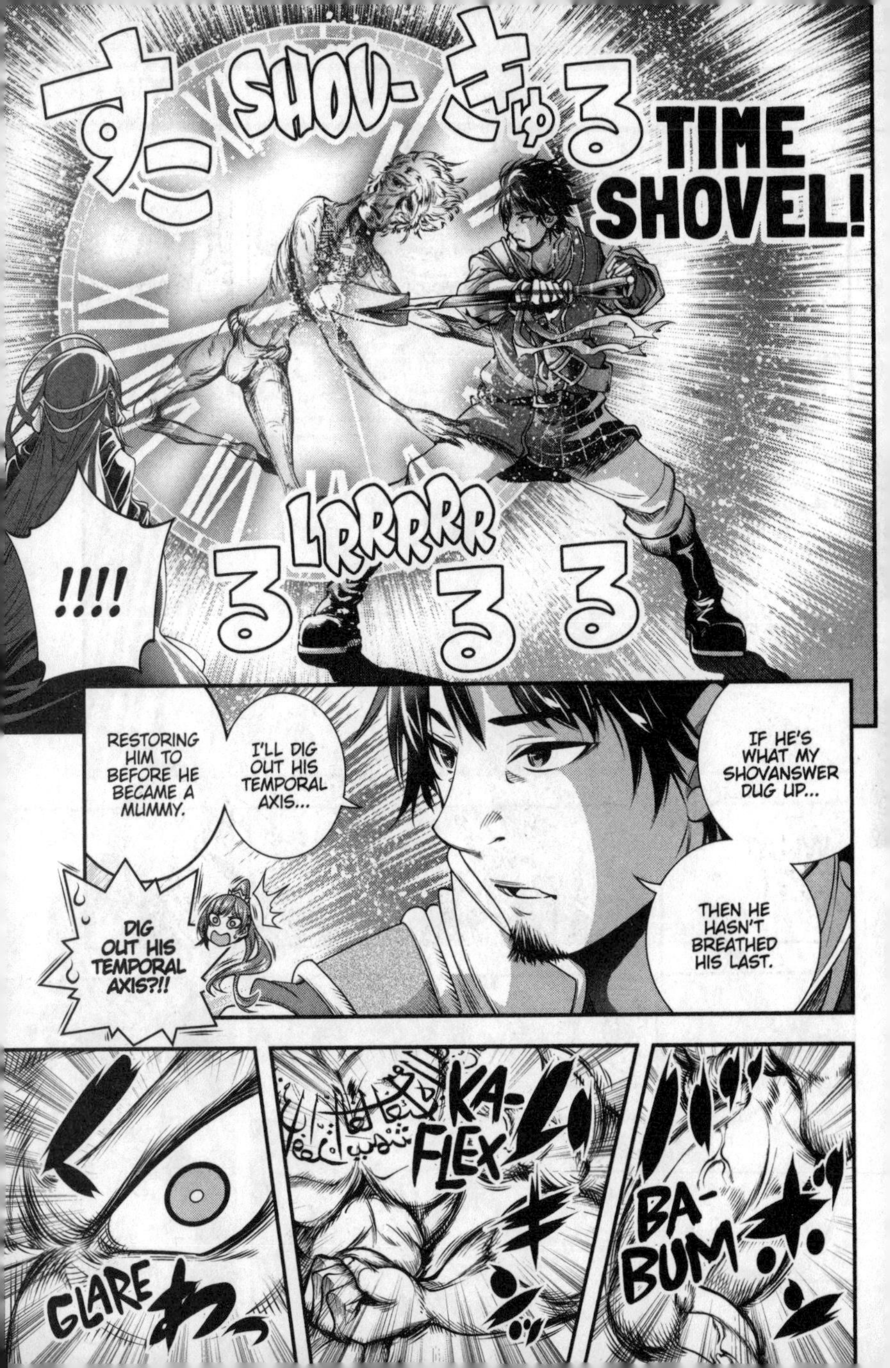
TIME SHOVEL!
きゅる
SHOV-
すー
LRRRRR
るるる
!!!!
IF HE'S WHAT MY SHOVANSWER DUG UP...
THEN HE HASN'T BREATHED HIS LAST.
I'LL DIG OUT HIS TEMPORAL AXIS...
RESTORING HIM TO BEFORE HE BECAME A MUMMY.
DIG OUT HIS TEMPORAL AXIS?!!
BA-BUM
KA-FLEX
GLARE
わっ

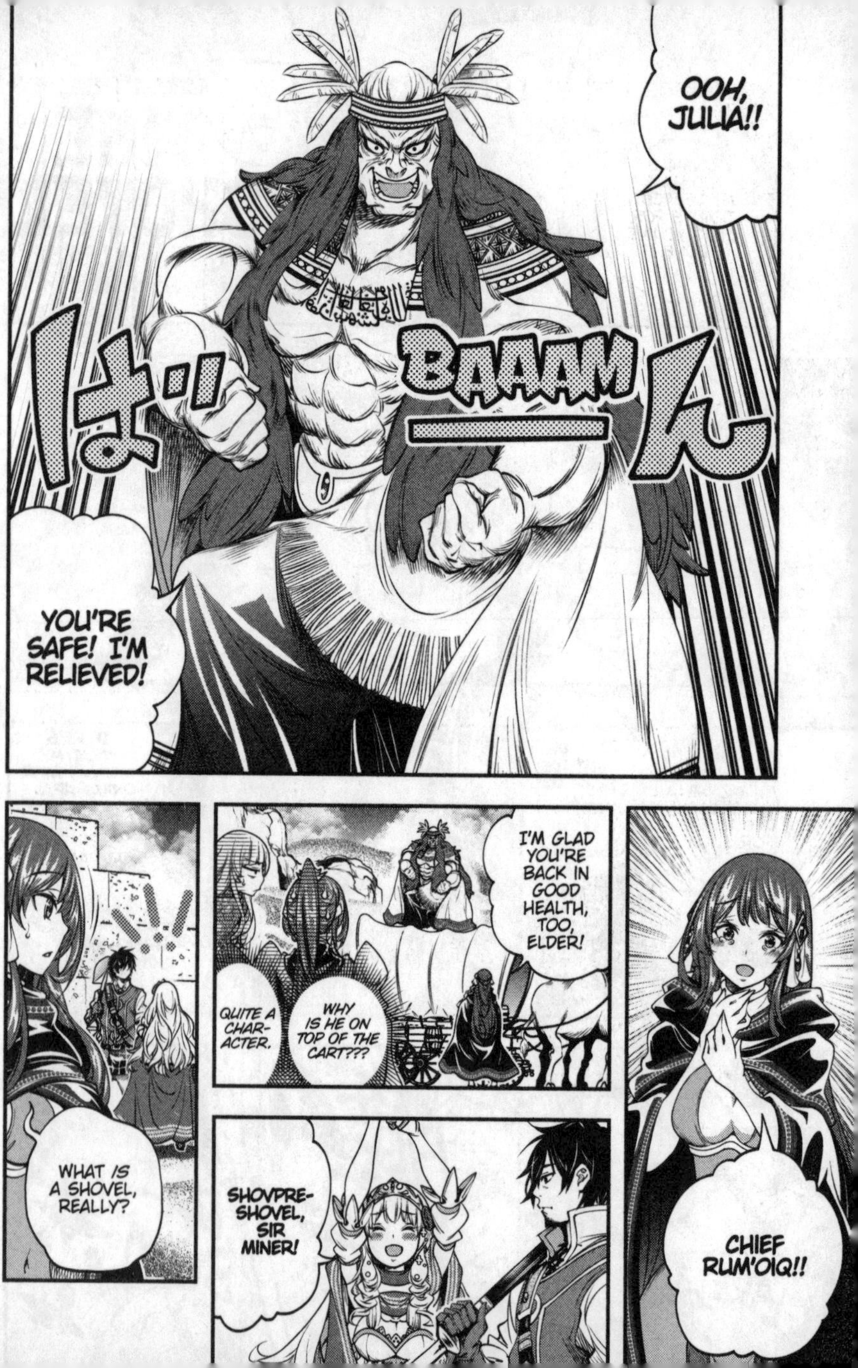
OOH, JULIA!!
BAAAM
YOU'RE SAFE! I'M RELIEVED!
CHIEF RUM'OIQ!!
I'M GLAD YOU'RE BACK IN GOOD HEALTH, TOO, ELDER!
WHY IS HE ON TOP OF THE CART???
QUITE A CHARACTER.
SHOVPRE-SHOVEL, SIR MINER!
WHAT *IS* A SHOVEL, REALLY?

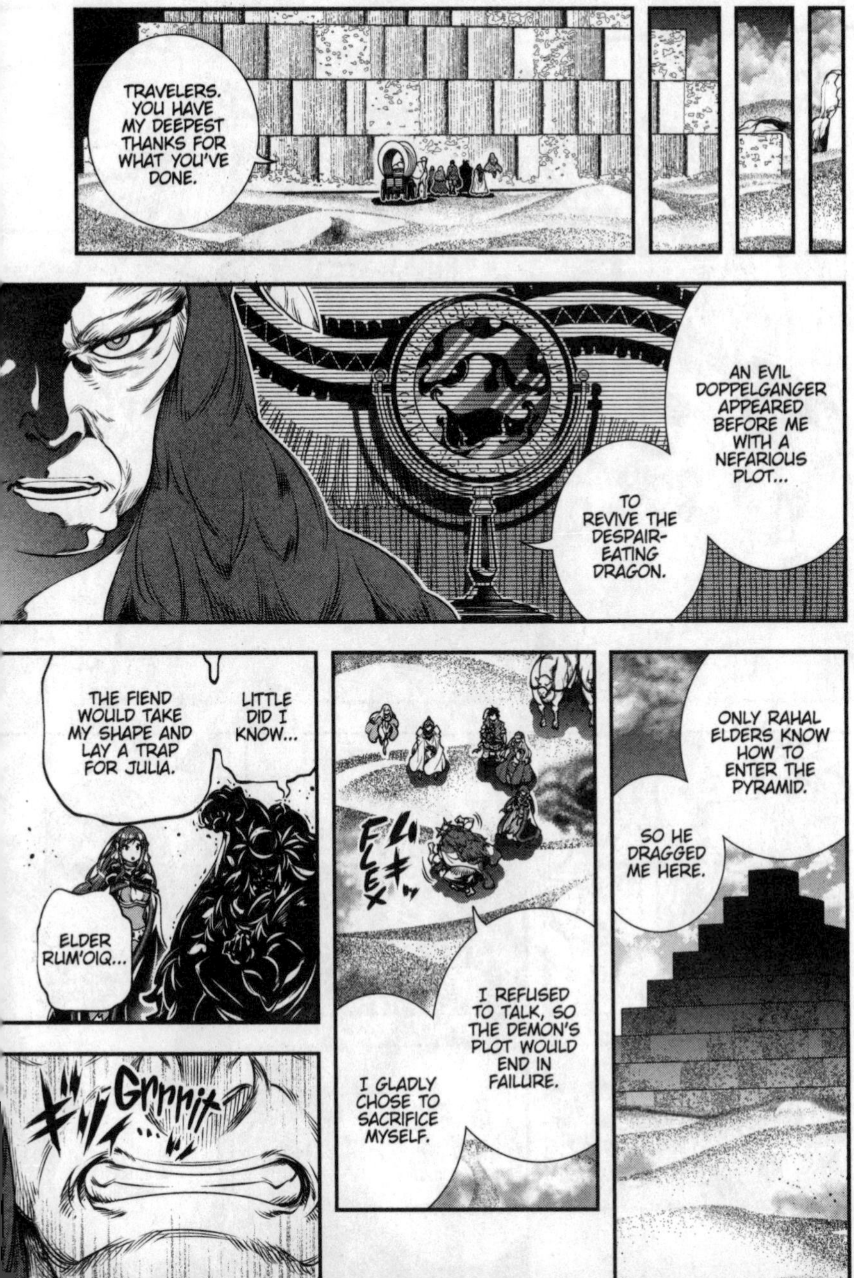

TRAVELERS. YOU HAVE MY DEEPEST THANKS FOR WHAT YOU'VE DONE.
AN EVIL DOPPELGANGER APPEARED BEFORE ME WITH A NEFARIOUS PLOT...
TO REVIVE THE DESPAIR-EATING DRAGON.
ONLY RAHAL ELDERS KNOW HOW TO ENTER THE PYRAMID.
SO HE DRAGGED ME HERE.
FLEX
I REFUSED TO TALK, SO THE DEMON'S PLOT WOULD END IN FAILURE.
I GLADLY CHOSE TO SACRIFICE MYSELF.
LITTLE DID I KNOW...
THE FIEND WOULD TAKE MY SHAPE AND LAY A TRAP FOR JULIA.
ELDER RUM'OIQ...
Grrrit

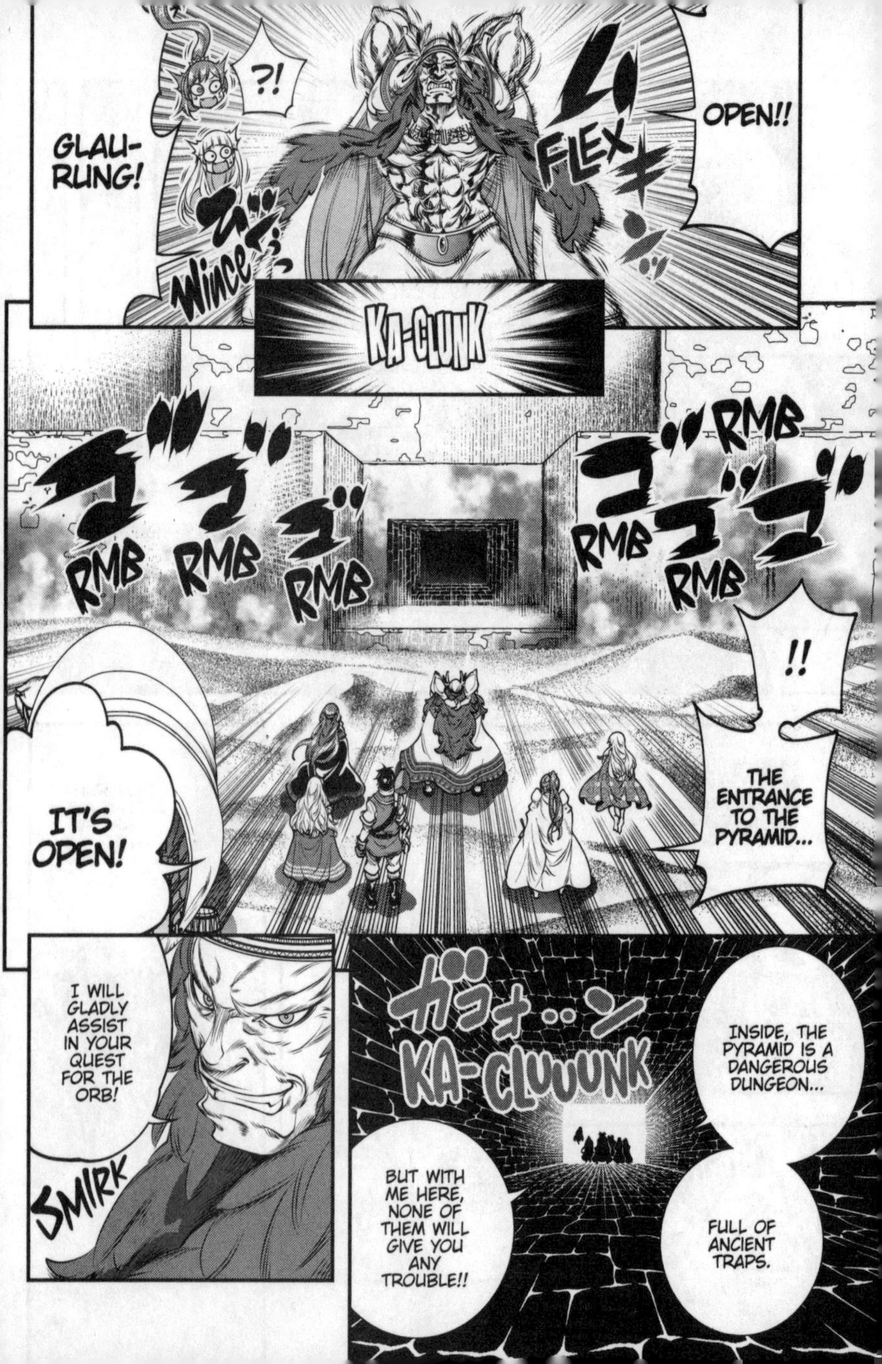
OPEN!!
FLEX
?!
GLAU-RUNG!
Wince
KA-CLUNK
RMB
RMB
RMB
RMB
RMB
RMB
!!
THE ENTRANCE TO THE PYRAMID...
IT'S OPEN!
KA-CLUUUNK
INSIDE, THE PYRAMID IS A DANGEROUS DUNGEON...
FULL OF ANCIENT TRAPS.
BUT WITH ME HERE, NONE OF THEM WILL GIVE YOU ANY TROUBLE!!
I WILL GLADLY ASSIST IN YOUR QUEST FOR THE ORB!
SMIRK

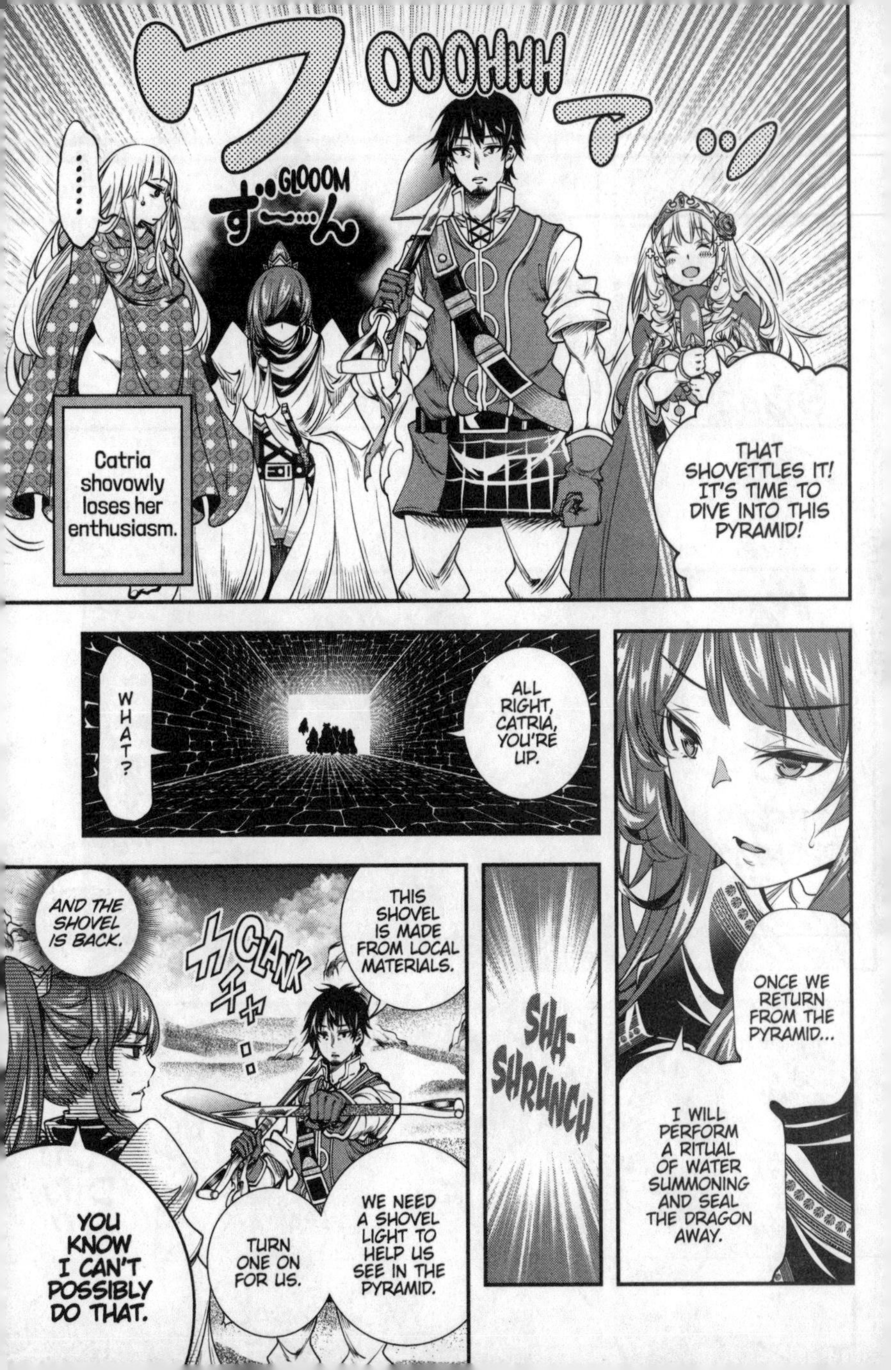
THAT SHOVETTLES IT! IT'S TIME TO DIVE INTO THIS PYRAMID!
OOOHHH
GLOOOM
......
Catria shovowly loses her enthusiasm.
ONCE WE RETURN FROM THE PYRAMID...
I WILL PERFORM A RITUAL OF WATER SUMMONING AND SEAL THE DRAGON AWAY.
ALL RIGHT, CATRIA, YOU'RE UP.
WHAT?
SHA-SHRUNCH
THIS SHOVEL IS MADE FROM LOCAL MATERIALS.
CLANK
AND THE SHOVEL IS BACK.
WE NEED A SHOVEL LIGHT TO HELP US SEE IN THE PYRAMID.
TURN ONE ON FOR US.
YOU KNOW I CAN'T POSSIBLY DO THAT.

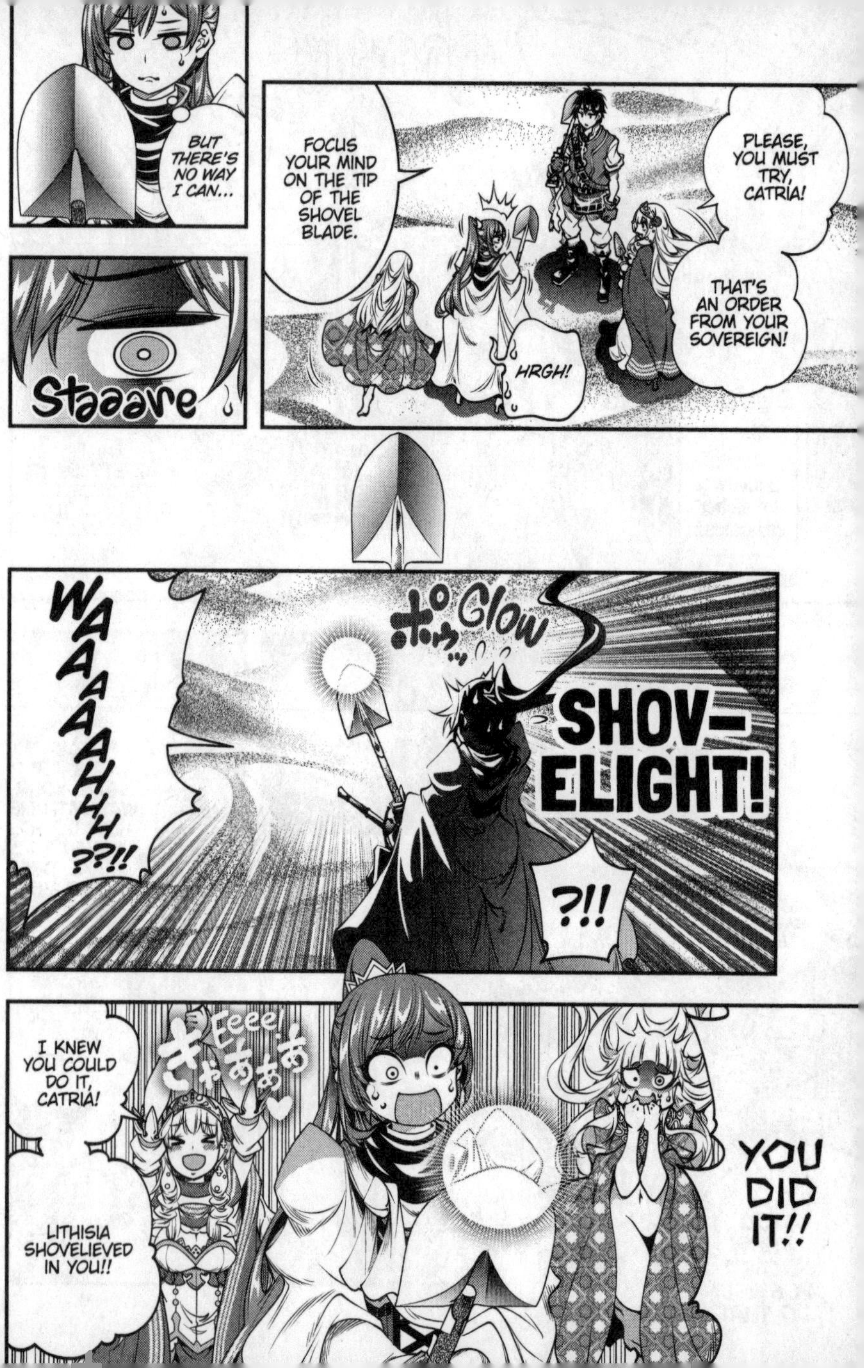
PLEASE, YOU MUST TRY, CATRIA!
THAT'S AN ORDER FROM YOUR SOVEREIGN!
FOCUS YOUR MIND ON THE TIP OF THE SHOVEL BLADE.
HRGH!
BUT THERE'S NO WAY I CAN...
Staaare
SHOV-ELIGHT!
ポゥッ Glow
WAAAAAAHHHH??!!
?!!
YOU DID IT!!
きゃあああ Eeee!
I KNEW YOU COULD DO IT, CATRIA!
LITHISIA SHOVELIEVED IN YOU!!

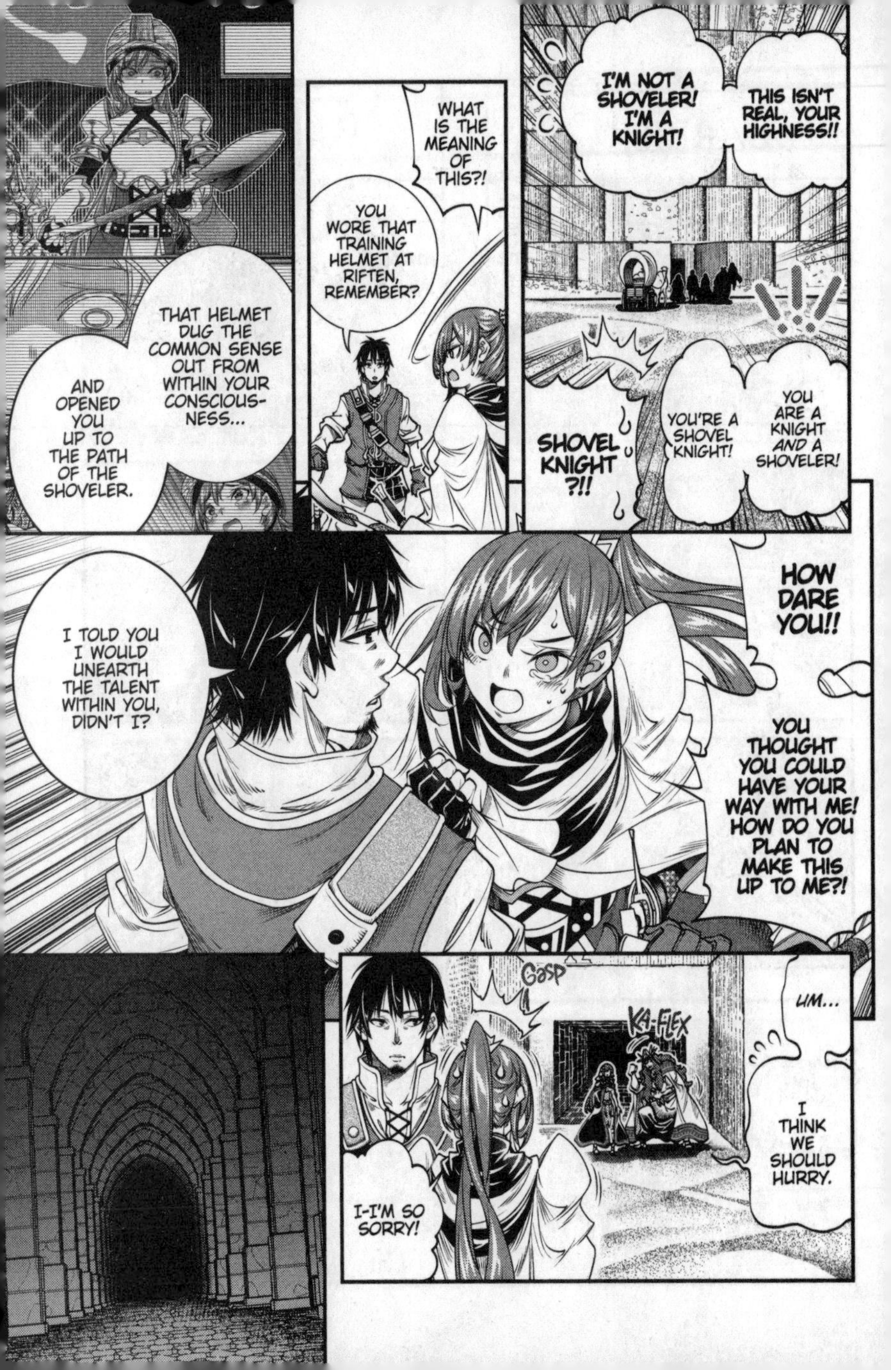
THIS ISN'T REAL, YOUR HIGHNESS!!
I'M NOT A SHOVELER! I'M A KNIGHT!
YOU ARE A KNIGHT AND A SHOVELER!
YOU'RE A SHOVEL KNIGHT!
SHOVEL KNIGHT?!!
WHAT IS THE MEANING OF THIS?!
YOU WORE THAT TRAINING HELMET AT RIFTEN, REMEMBER?
THAT HELMET DUG THE COMMON SENSE OUT FROM WITHIN YOUR CONSCIOUS-NESS...
AND OPENED YOU UP TO THE PATH OF THE SHOVELER.
HOW DARE YOU!!
YOU THOUGHT YOU COULD HAVE YOUR WAY WITH ME! HOW DO YOU PLAN TO MAKE THIS UP TO ME?!
I TOLD YOU I WOULD UNEARTH THE TALENT WITHIN YOU, DIDN'T I?
UM...
I THINK WE SHOULD HURRY.
KA-FLEX
GASP
I-I'M SO SORRY!

Barrier 1

HERE THEY COME!!
UUUUUGH!
THE GUARDIANS OF THIS PYRAMID!!
SUICIDE SHOVEL BOMB!!
ZSH
UNHOLY MIRE!!
ZSH ZSH
GREAT IS THE SHOVEL!
SHOVELLLLL
YOU THREE ARE AMAZING!!
SHOVE-ELIGHT!
......
GLOOOW

Barrier 2

THE HALL OF INFINITE SPIKES.
THE SPIKES ATTACK ANY WHO DARE PASS!
IF WE PRESS THE SWITCH ON THE PEDESTAL...
IT SHOULD STOP THE CONTRAPTION, ALLOWING US PASSAGE.
BUT IT'S ON THE OTHER SIDE OF THE HALL.
HOW DO WE REACH IT?
STAB
STA-STAB
I AM AN ASTRAL BEING. BLADES HAVE NO EFFECT ON ME.
FLOAT
FLOAT
SHOVELARIAT!!
SHOULRRR
CLICK
THAT'S CHEATING!!
Alice was impaled in vain.

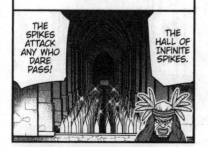

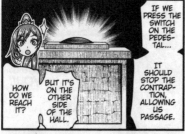

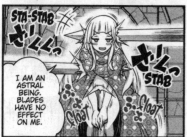

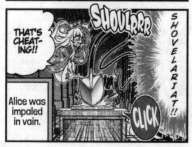

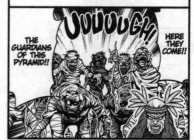

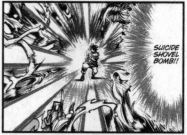

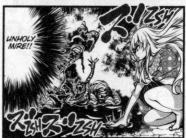

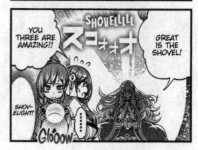

Barrier 3

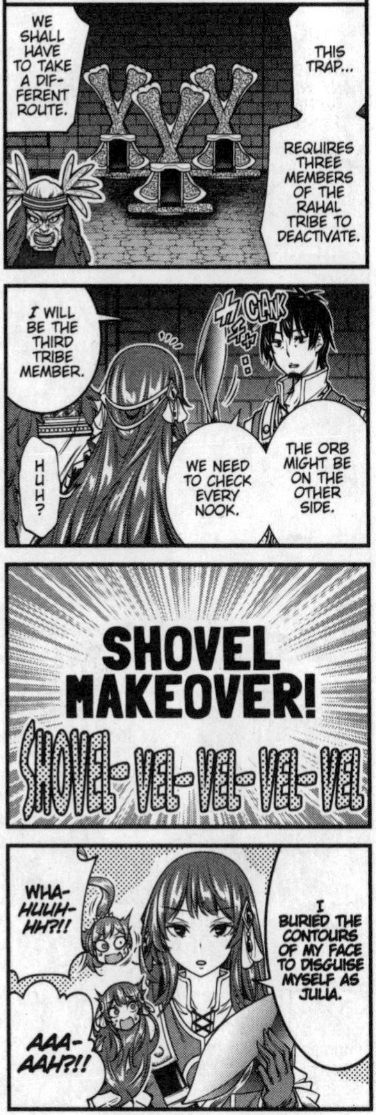
THIS TRAP...
REQUIRES THREE MEMBERS OF THE RAHAL TRIBE TO DEACTIVATE.
WE SHALL HAVE TO TAKE A DIF-FERENT ROUTE.
CLANK
THE ORB MIGHT BE ON THE OTHER SIDE.
WE NEED TO CHECK EVERY NOOK.
I WILL BE THE THIRD TRIBE MEMBER.
HUH?
SHOVEL MAKEOVER!
SHOVEL-VEL-VEL-VEL-VEL
I BURIED THE CONTOURS OF MY FACE TO DISGUISE MYSELF AS JULIA.
WHA-HUUHH?!!
AAA-AAH?!!

Conclusion

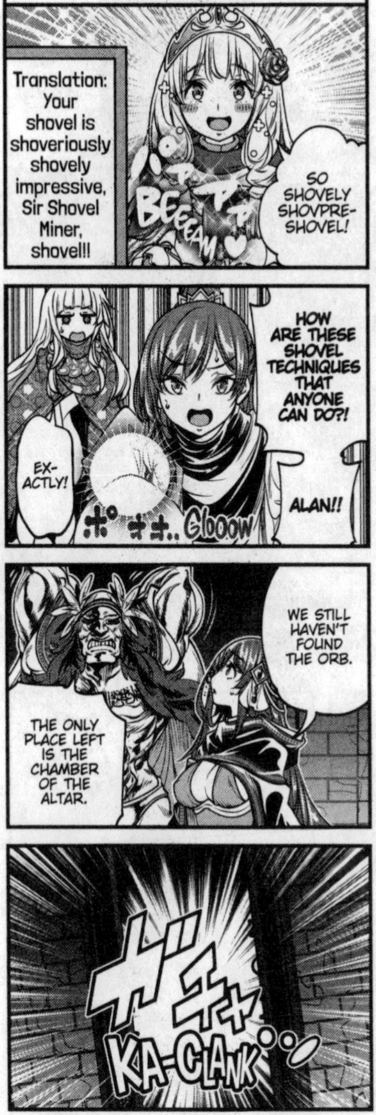
SO SHOVELY SHOVPRE-SHOVEL!
BEEEAM
Translation: Your shovel is shoveriously shovely impressive, Sir Shovel Miner, shovel!!
HOW ARE THESE SHOVEL TECHNIQUES THAT ANYONE CAN DO?!
ALAN!!
EX-ACTLY!
GLOOOW
WE STILL HAVEN'T FOUND THE ORB.
THE ONLY PLACE LEFT IS THE CHAMBER OF THE ALTAR.
KA-CLANK

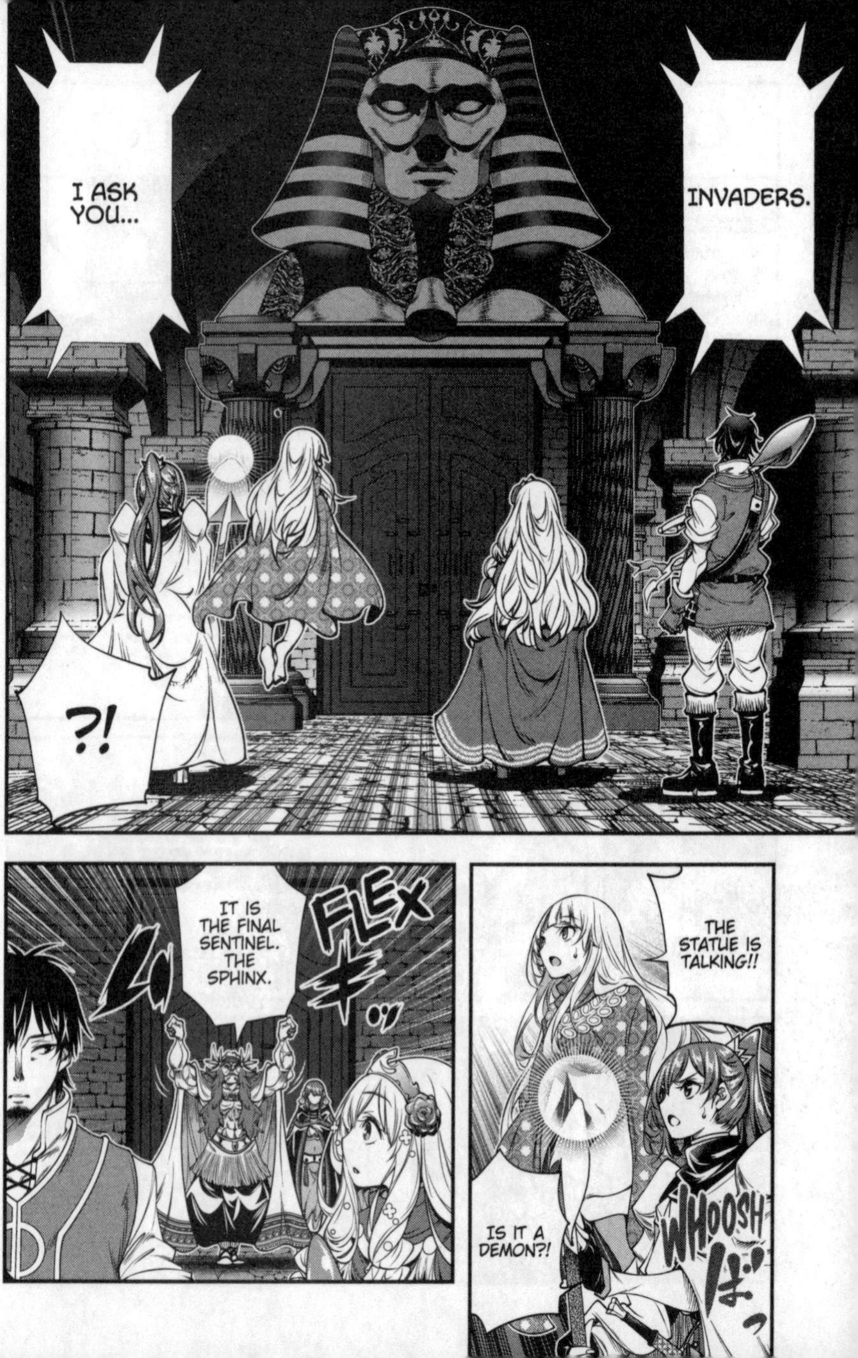

INVADERS.
I ASK YOU...
?!
THE STATUE IS TALKING!!
WHOOSH
IS IT A DEMON?!
FLEX
IT IS THE FINAL SENTINEL. THE SPHINX.

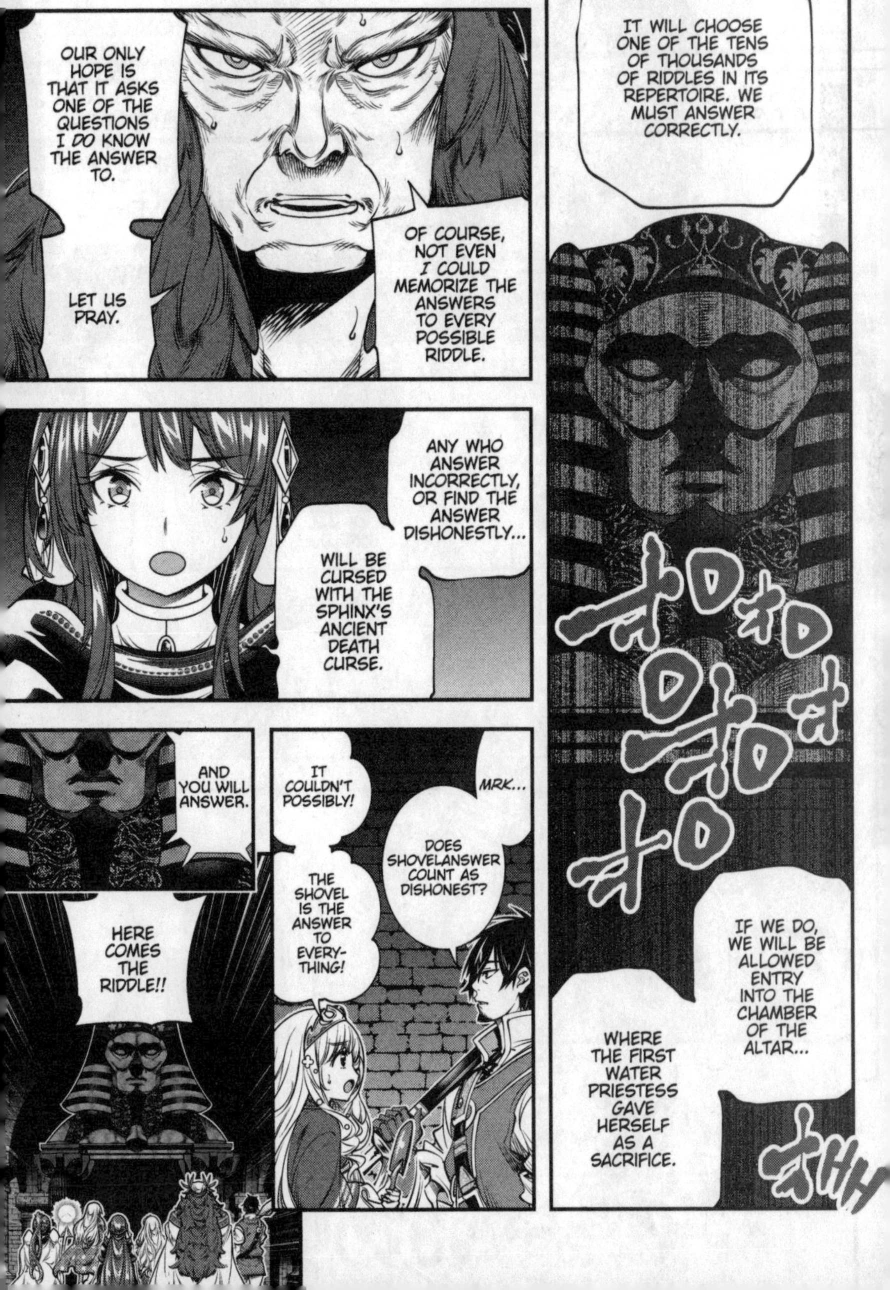

IT WILL CHOOSE ONE OF THE TENS OF THOUSANDS OF RIDDLES IN ITS REPERTOIRE. WE MUST ANSWER CORRECTLY.
IF WE DO, WE WILL BE ALLOWED ENTRY INTO THE CHAMBER OF THE ALTAR...
WHERE THE FIRST WATER PRIESTESS GAVE HERSELF AS A SACRIFICE.
OF COURSE, NOT EVEN I COULD MEMORIZE THE ANSWERS TO EVERY POSSIBLE RIDDLE.
OUR ONLY HOPE IS THAT IT ASKS ONE OF THE QUESTIONS I *DO* KNOW THE ANSWER TO.
LET US PRAY.
ANY WHO ANSWER INCORRECTLY, OR FIND THE ANSWER DISHONESTLY...
WILL BE CURSED WITH THE SPHINX'S ANCIENT DEATH CURSE.
MRK...
IT COULDN'T POSSIBLY!
DOES SHOVELANSWER COUNT AS DISHONEST?
THE SHOVEL IS THE ANSWER TO EVERY-THING!
AND YOU WILL ANSWER.
HERE COMES THE RIDDLE!!

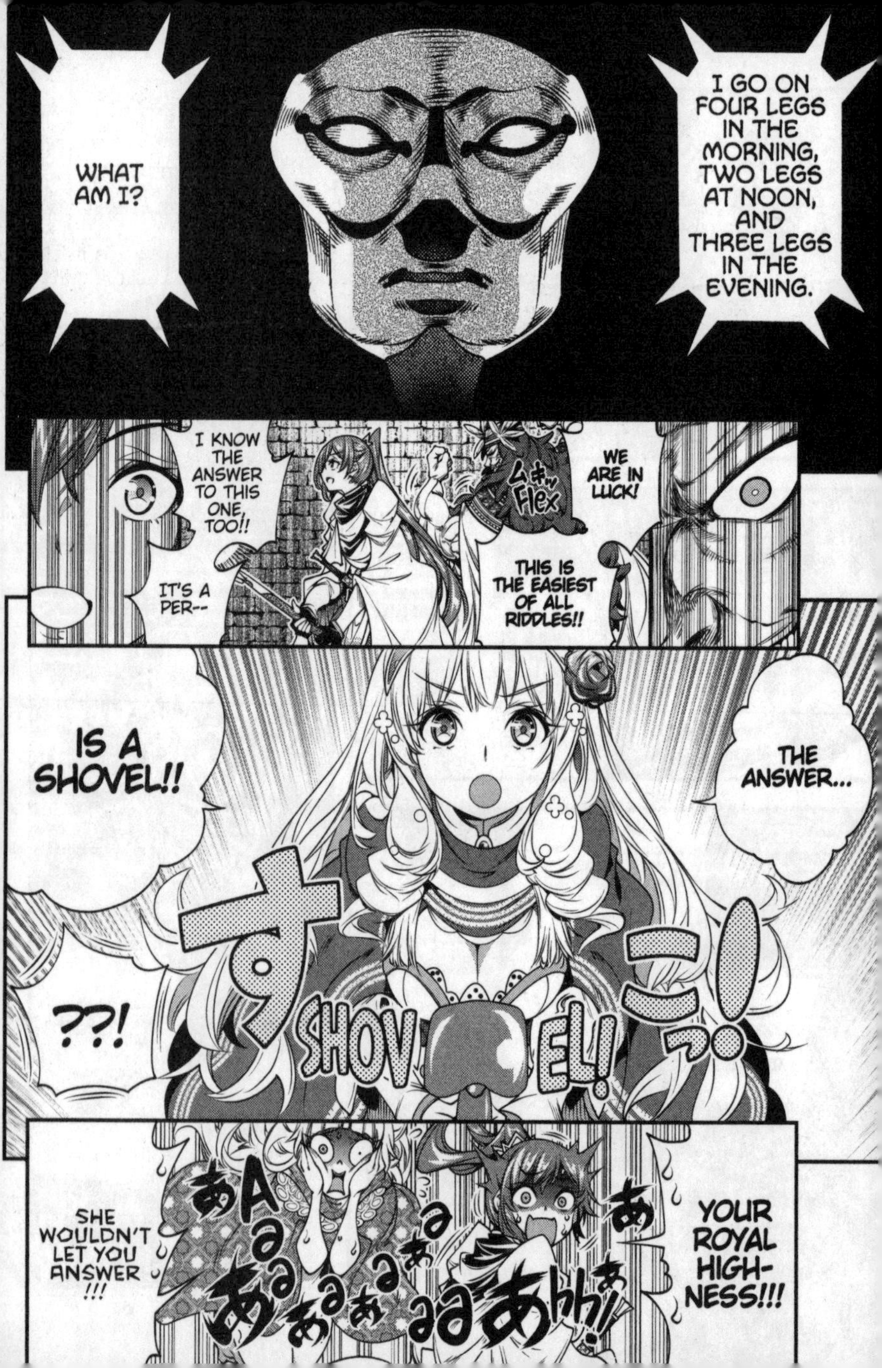
I GO ON FOUR LEGS IN THE MORNING, TWO LEGS AT NOON, AND THREE LEGS IN THE EVENING.
WHAT AM I?
WE ARE IN LUCK!
THIS IS THE EASIEST OF ALL RIDDLES!!
ムキッ
Flex
I KNOW THE ANSWER TO THIS ONE, TOO!!
IT'S A PER--
THE ANSWER...
IS A SHOVEL!!
SHOVEL!
??!
YOUR ROYAL HIGH-NESS!!!
SHE WOULDN'T LET YOU ANSWER!!!

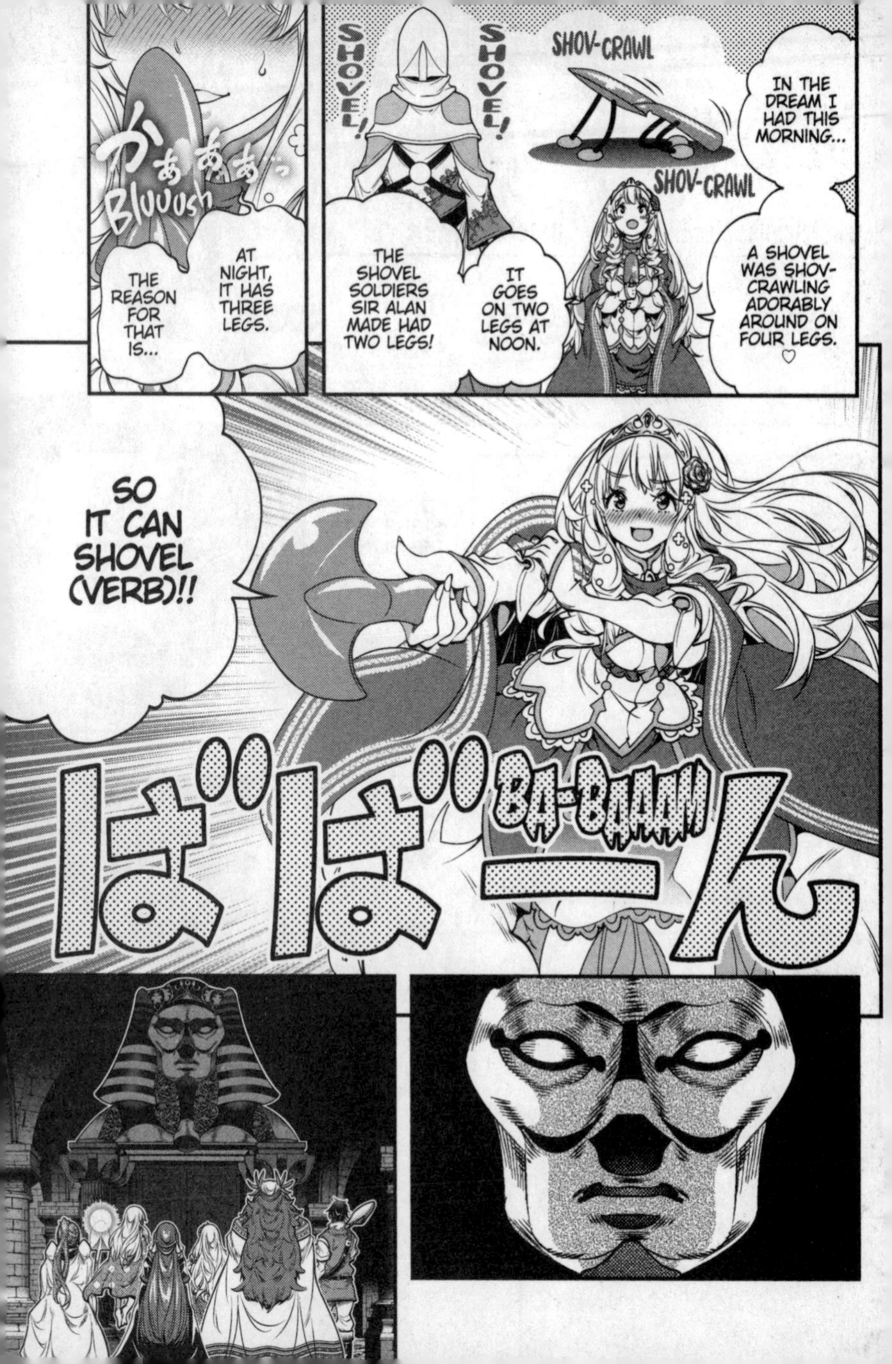

IN THE DREAM I HAD THIS MORNING...
SHOV-CRAWL
SHOV-CRAWL
A SHOVEL WAS SHOV-CRAWLING ADORABLY AROUND ON FOUR LEGS. ♡
SHOVEL!
SHOVEL!
IT GOES ON TWO LEGS AT NOON.
THE SHOVEL SOLDIERS SIR ALAN MADE HAD TWO LEGS!
AT NIGHT, IT HAS THREE LEGS.
THE REASON FOR THAT IS...
かあああっ
Bluuush
SO IT CAN SHOVEL (VERB)!!
ばばーん
BA-BAAAM

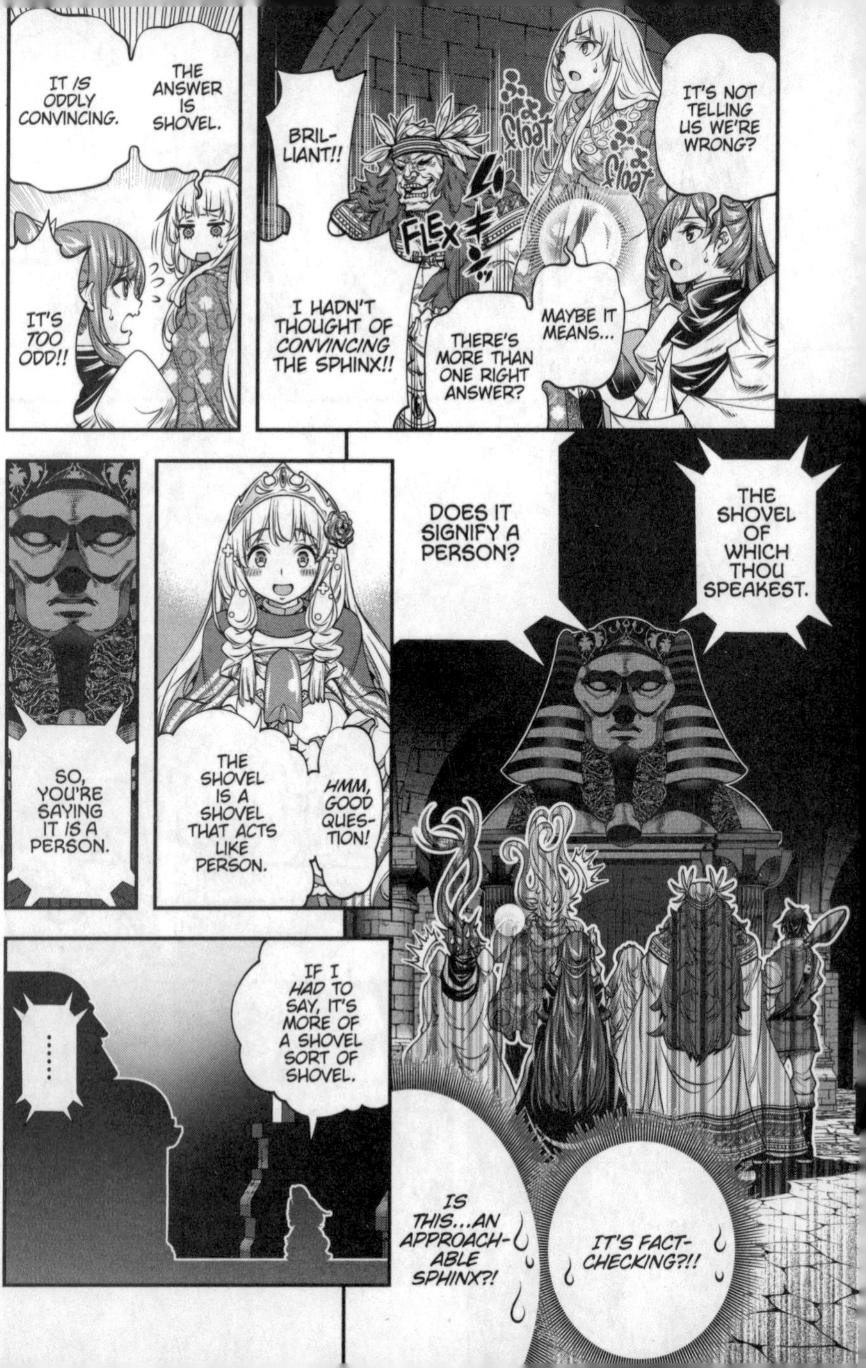

IT'S NOT TELLING US WE'RE WRONG?
FLOAT FLOAT
BRIL-LIANT!!
FLEX
I HADN'T THOUGHT OF CONVINCING THE SPHINX!!
MAYBE IT MEANS...
THERE'S MORE THAN ONE RIGHT ANSWER?
THE ANSWER IS SHOVEL.
IT IS ODDLY CONVINCING.
IT'S TOO ODD!!
THE SHOVEL OF WHICH THOU SPEAKEST.
DOES IT SIGNIFY A PERSON?
IT'S FACT-CHECKING?!!
IS THIS...AN APPROACH-ABLE SPHINX?!
HMM, GOOD QUES-TION!
THE SHOVEL IS A SHOVEL THAT ACTS LIKE PERSON.
SO, YOU'RE SAYING IT IS A PERSON.
IF I HAD TO SAY, IT'S MORE OF A SHOVEL SORT OF SHOVEL.
......

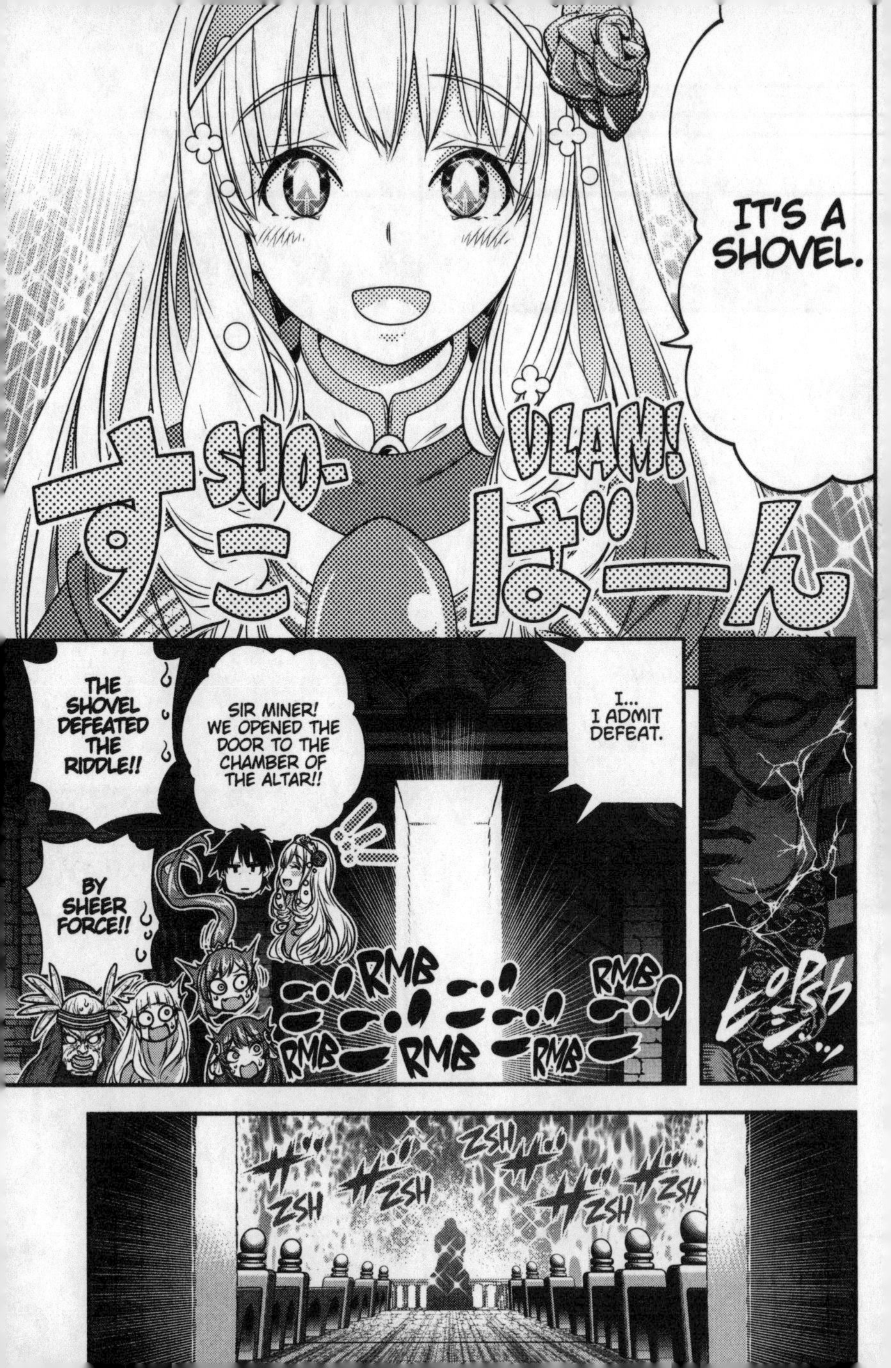
IT'S A SHOVEL.
すこぱーん
SHO-VLAM!
PSh
I... I ADMIT DEFEAT.
SIR MINER! WE OPENED THE DOOR TO THE CHAMBER OF THE ALTAR!!
THE SHOVEL DEFEATED THE RIDDLE!!
BY SHEER FORCE!!
RMB RMB RMB RMB RMB
ZSH ZSH ZSH ZSH ZSH

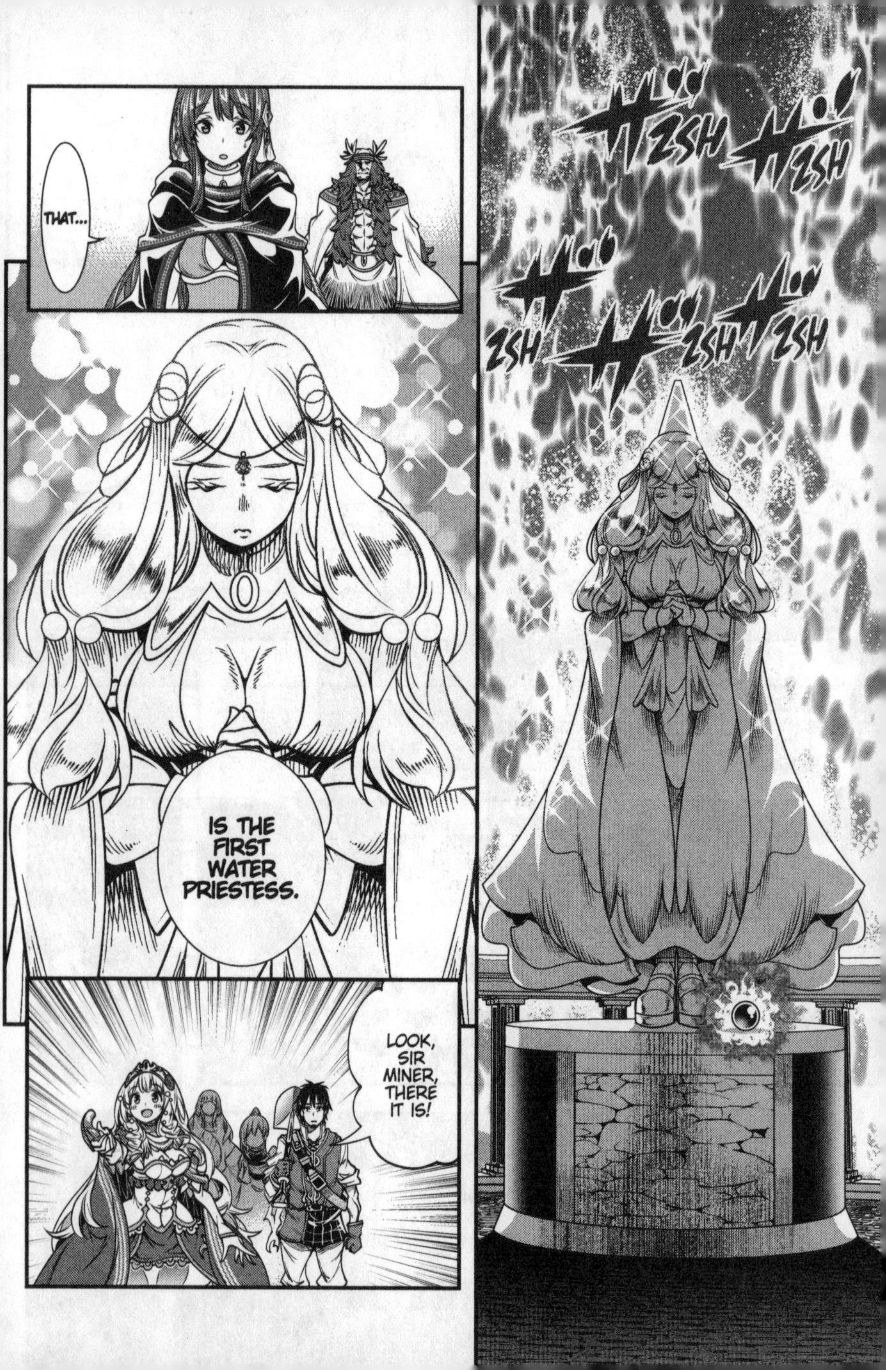
ZSH
ZSH
ZSH
ZSH
ZSH
ZSH
THAT...
IS THE FIRST WATER PRIESTESS.
LOOK, SIR MINER, THERE IT IS!

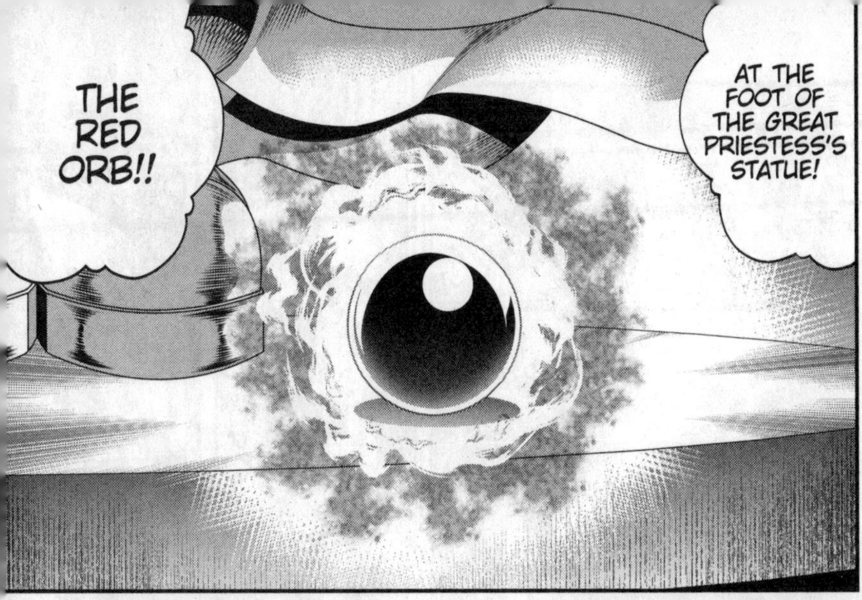
AT THE FOOT OF THE GREAT PRIESTESS'S STATUE!
THE RED ORB!!

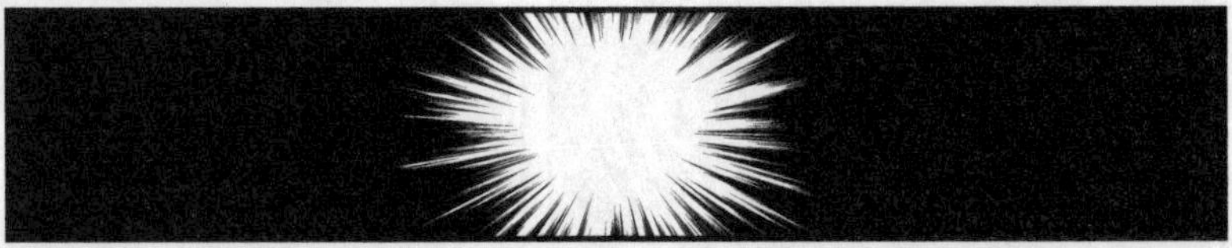

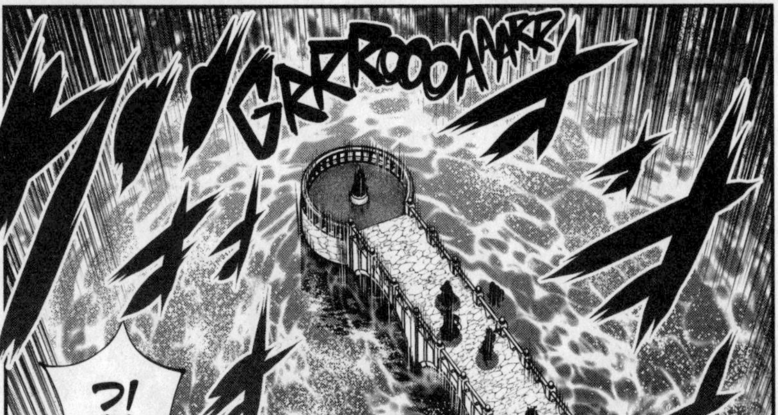
GRRROOOAAARR
?!

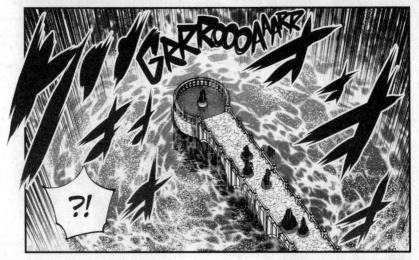

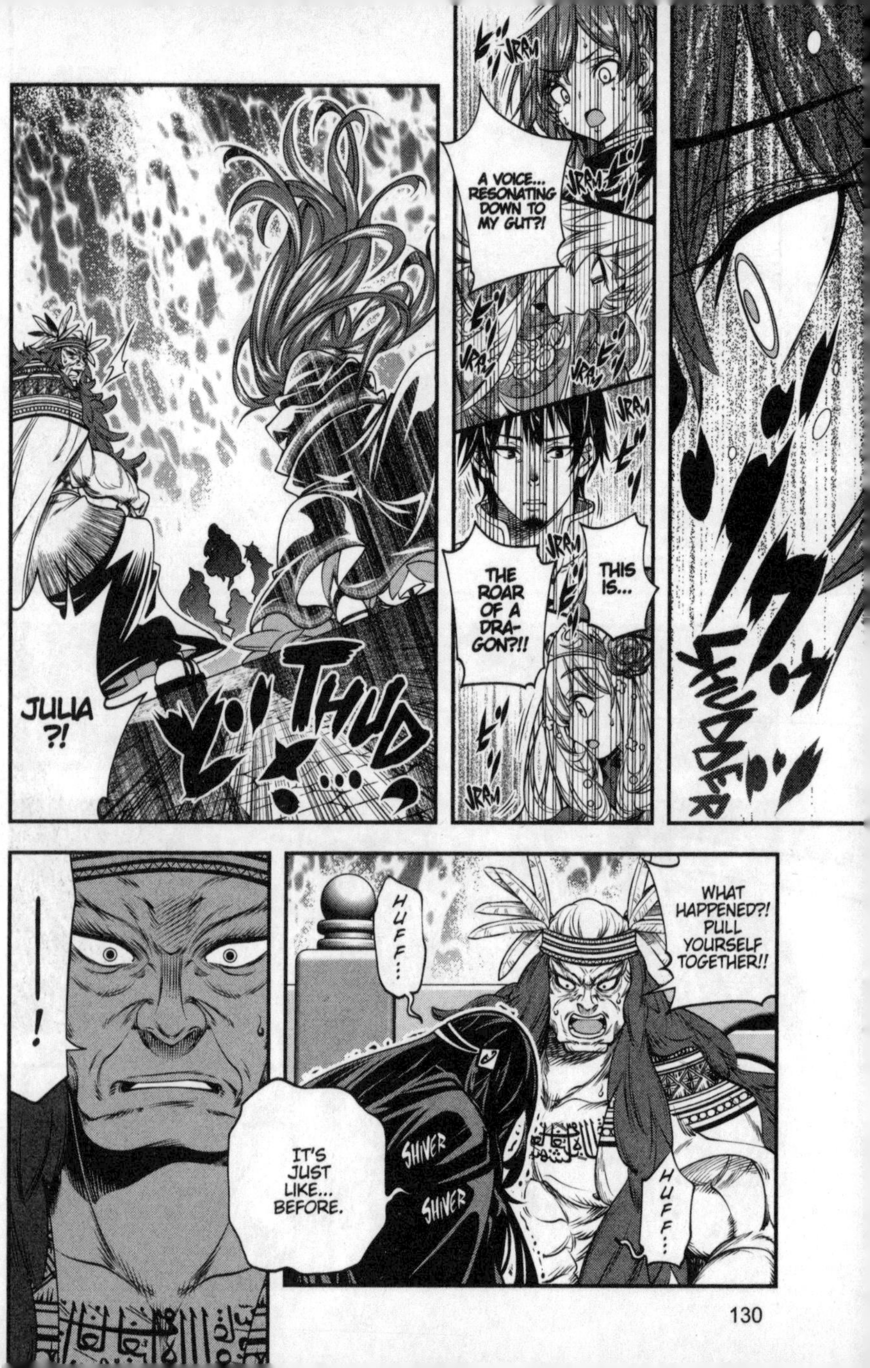
SHUDDER
A VOICE... RESONATING DOWN TO MY GUT?!
JRRM
THIS IS...
THE ROAR OF A DRA-GON?!!
JULIA ?!
THUD
WHAT HAPPENED?! PULL YOURSELF TOGETHER!!
HUFF...
HUFF...
SHIVER
SHIVER
IT'S JUST LIKE... BEFORE.
!

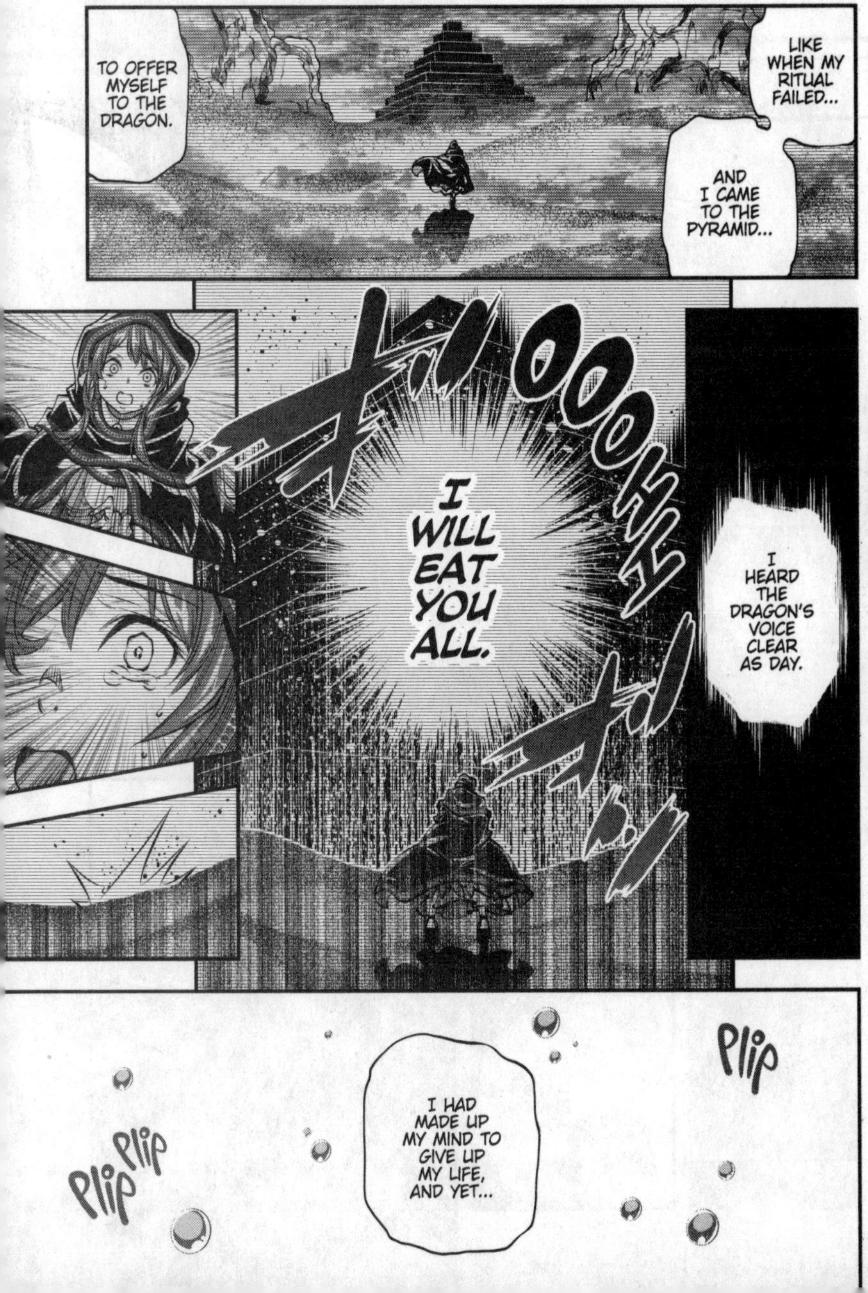
LIKE WHEN MY RITUAL FAILED...
AND I CAME TO THE PYRAMID...
TO OFFER MYSELF TO THE DRAGON.
I WILL EAT YOU ALL.
I HEARD THE DRAGON'S VOICE CLEAR AS DAY.
Plip
I HAD MADE UP MY MIND TO GIVE UP MY LIFE, AND YET...
Plip
Plip

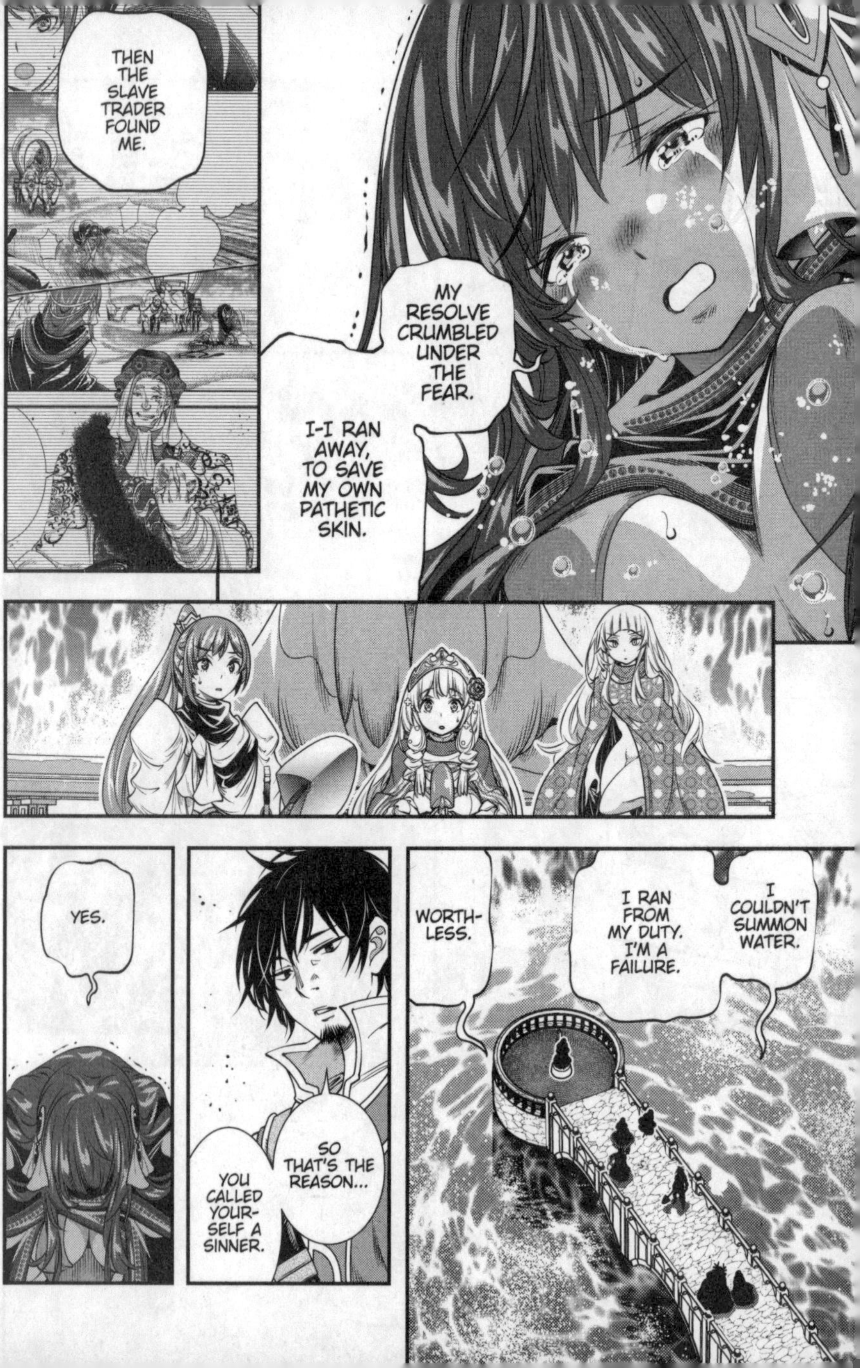
MY RESOLVE CRUMBLED UNDER THE FEAR.
I-I RAN AWAY, TO SAVE MY OWN PATHETIC SKIN.
THEN THE SLAVE TRADER FOUND ME.
I COULDN'T SUMMON WATER.
I RAN FROM MY DUTY. I'M A FAILURE.
WORTH-LESS.
SO THAT'S THE REASON...
YOU CALLED YOUR-SELF A SINNER.
YES.

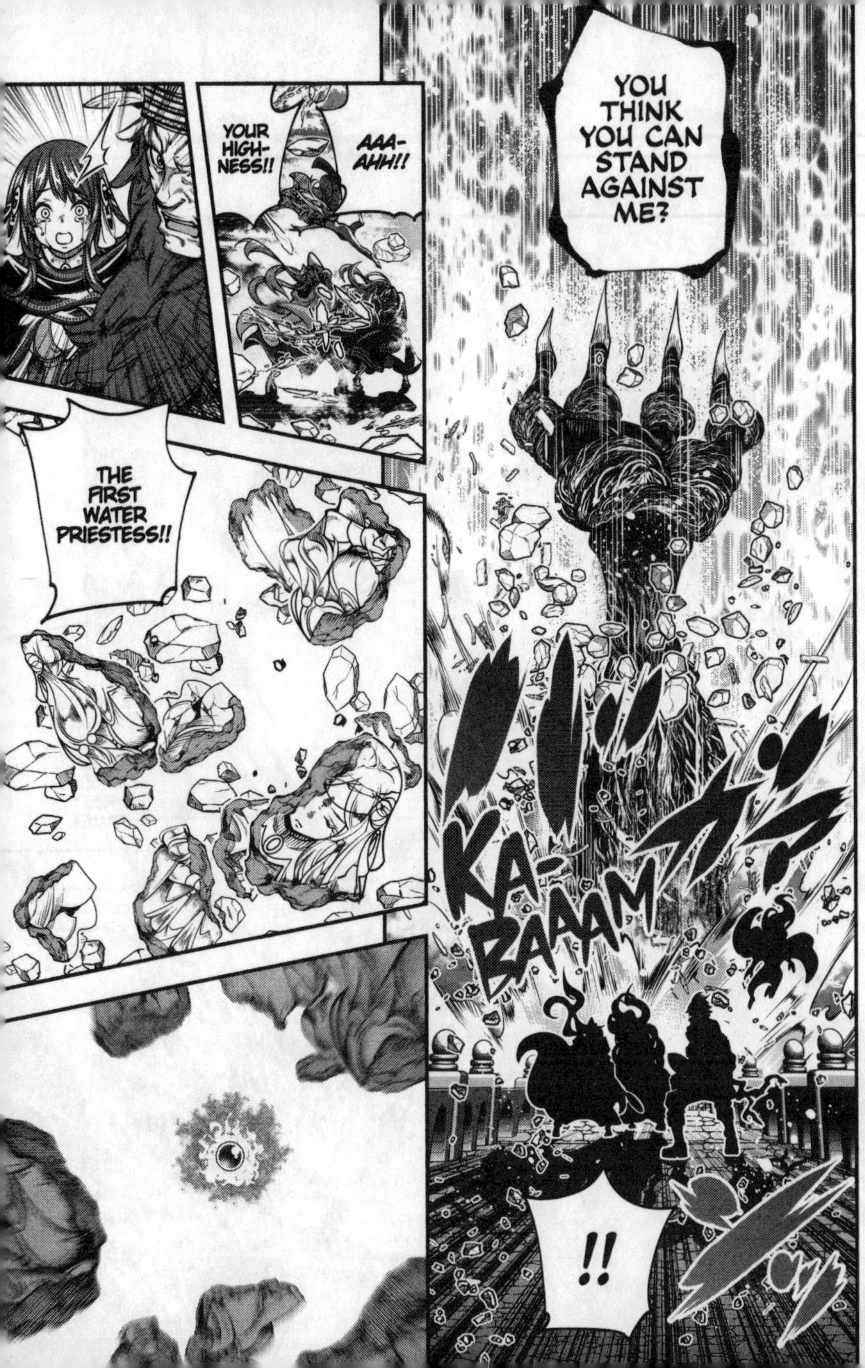
YOU THINK YOU CAN STAND AGAINST ME?
KA-BAAAM
!!
AAA-AHH!!
YOUR HIGH-NESS!!
THE FIRST WATER PRIESTESS!!

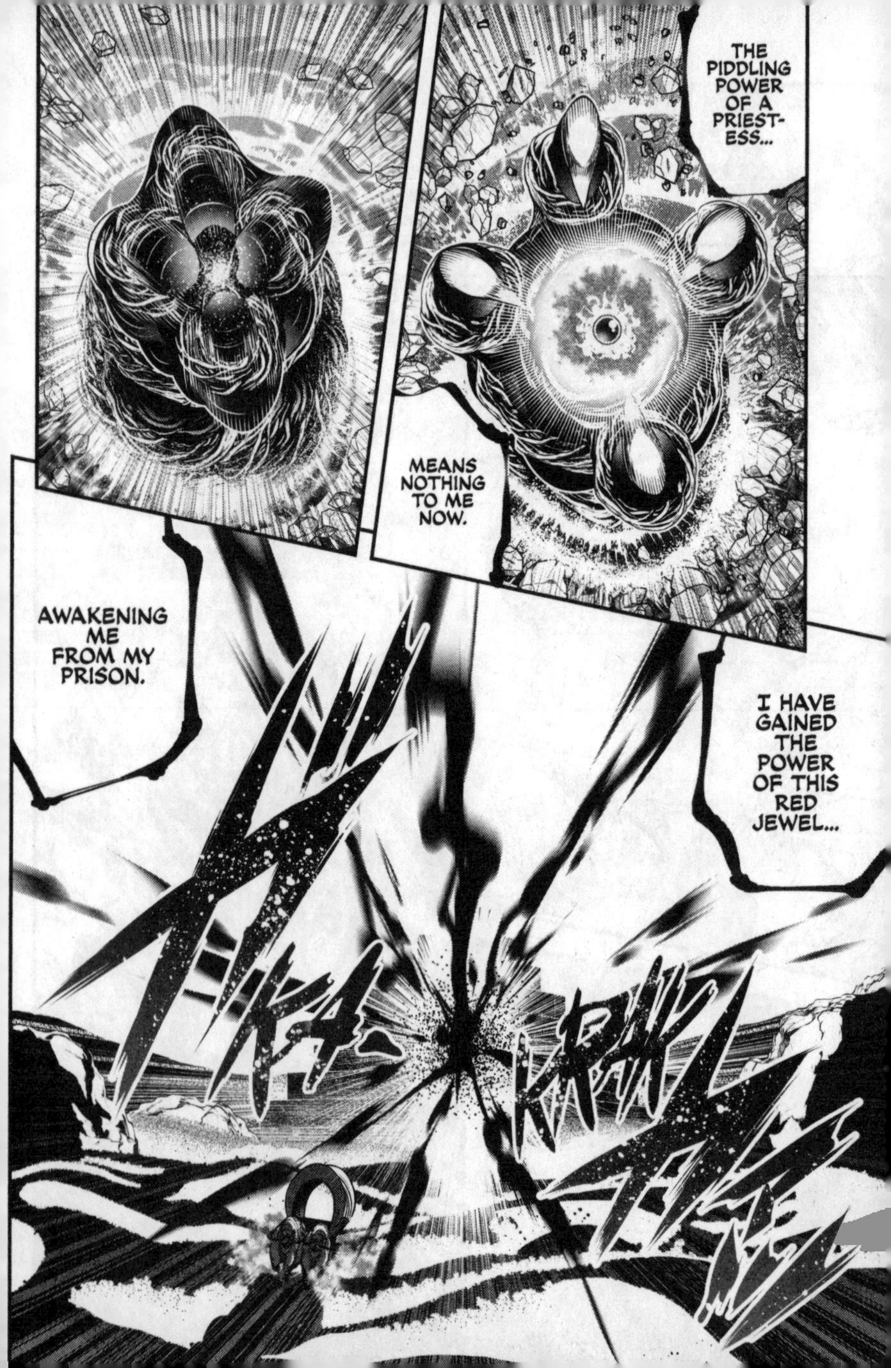
THE PIDDLING POWER OF A PRIEST-ESS...
MEANS NOTHING TO ME NOW.
I HAVE GAINED THE POWER OF THIS RED JEWEL...
AWAKENING ME FROM MY PRISON.

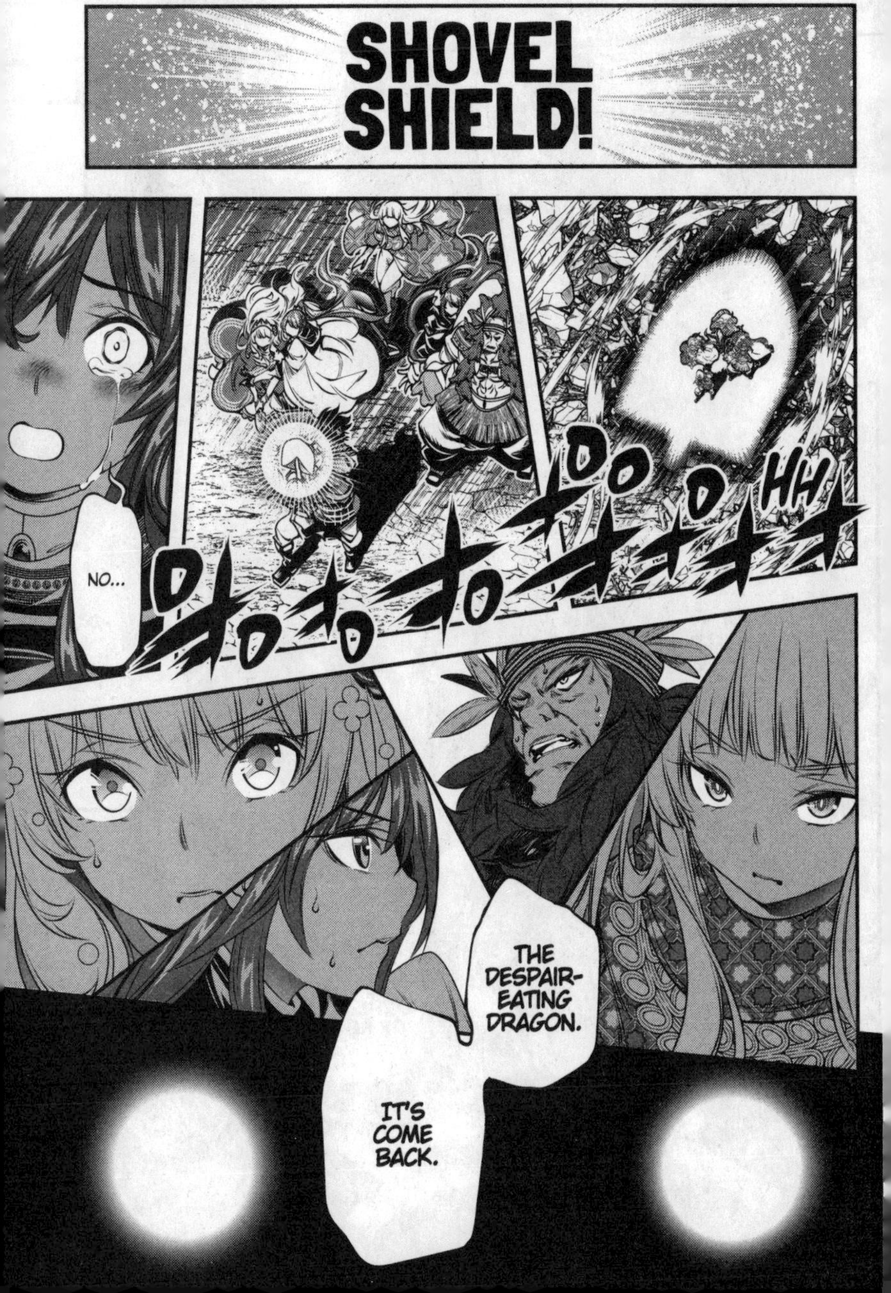
SHOVEL SHIELD!
NO...
THE DESPAIR-EATING DRAGON.
IT'S COME BACK.

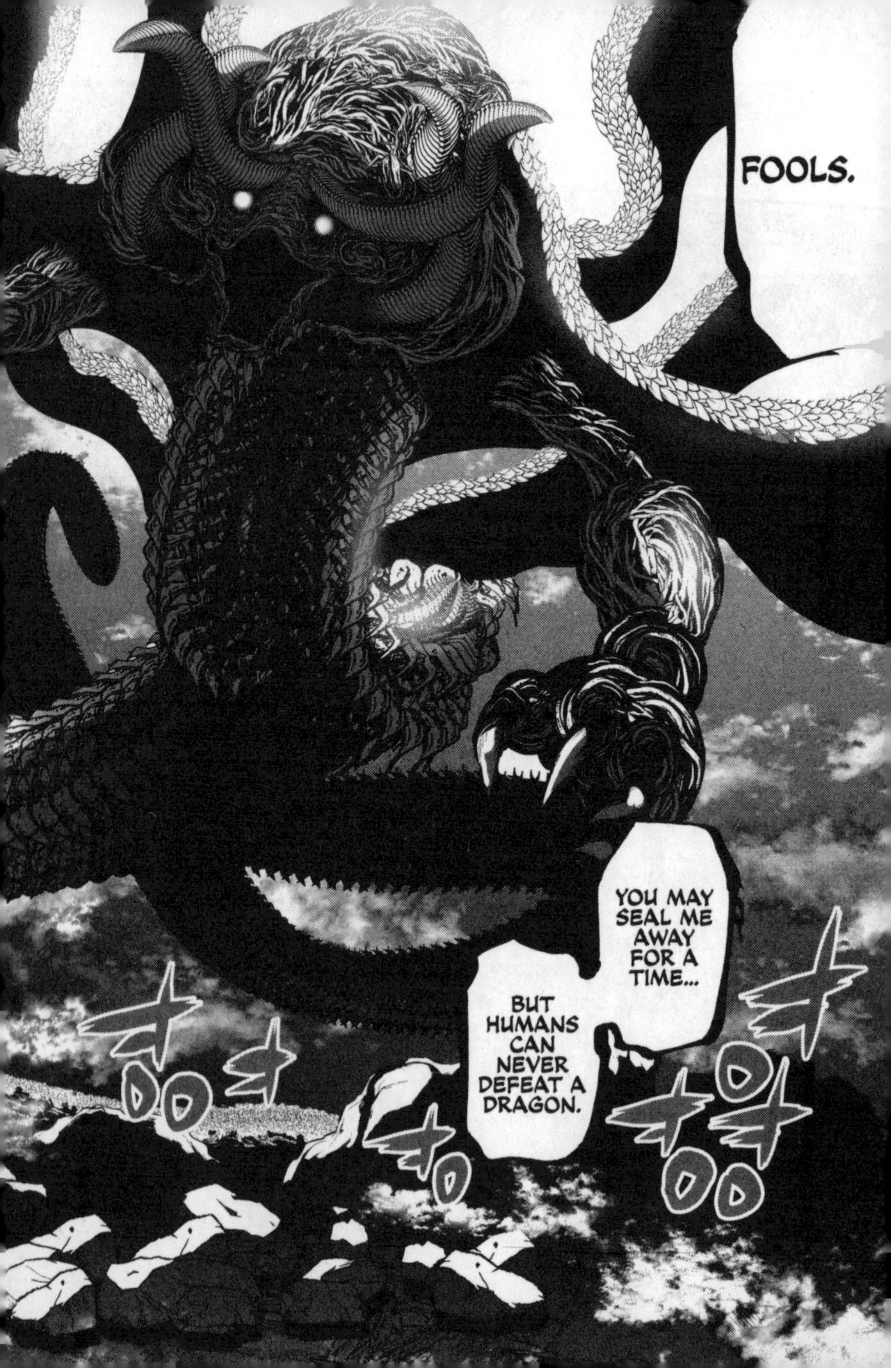
FOOLS.
YOU MAY SEAL ME AWAY FOR A TIME...
BUT HUMANS CAN NEVER DEFEAT A DRAGON.

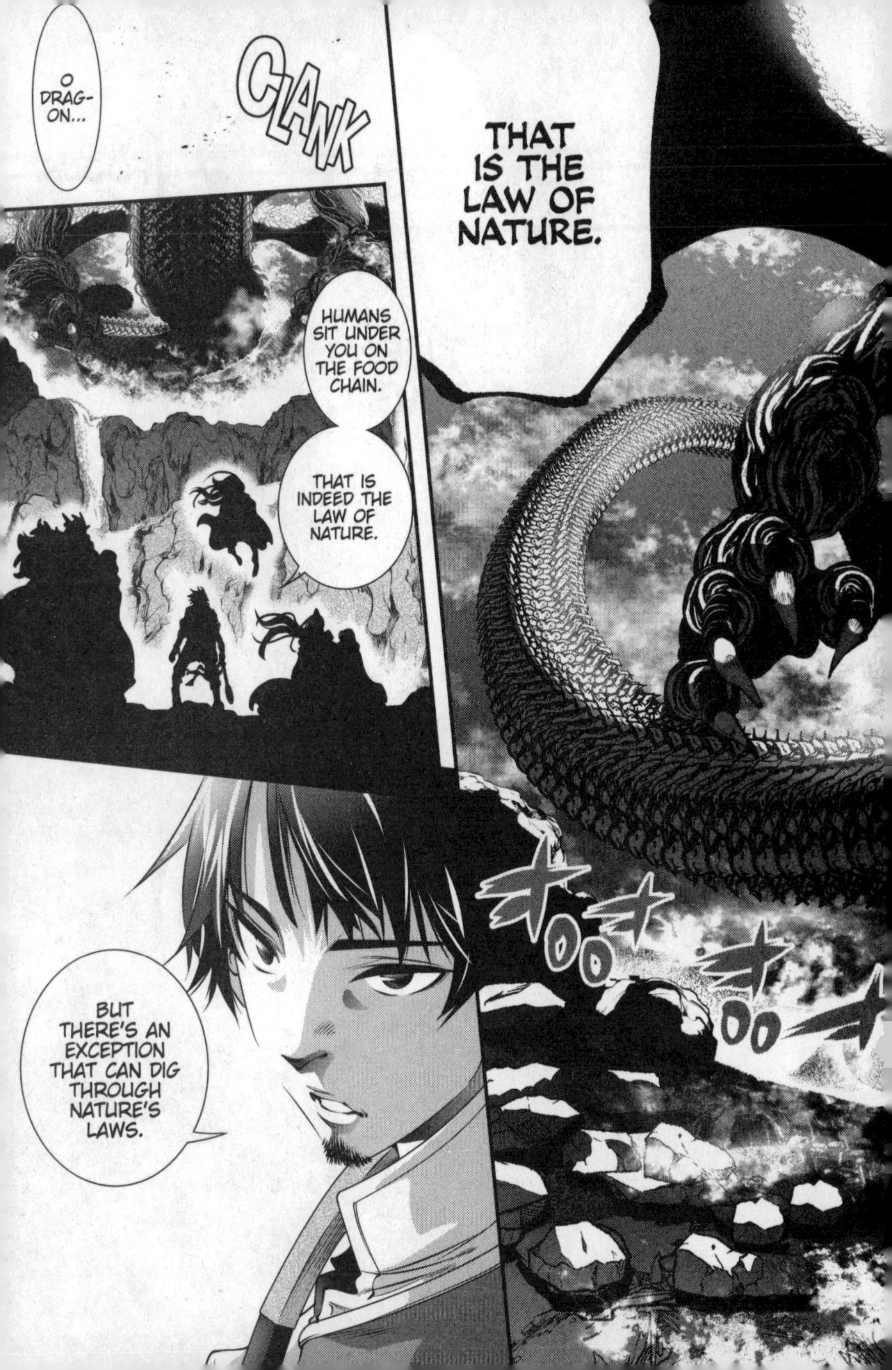
THAT IS THE LAW OF NATURE.
O DRAG-ON...
CLANK
HUMANS SIT UNDER YOU ON THE FOOD CHAIN.
THAT IS INDEED THE LAW OF NATURE.
BUT THERE'S AN EXCEPTION THAT CAN DIG THROUGH NATURE'S LAWS.

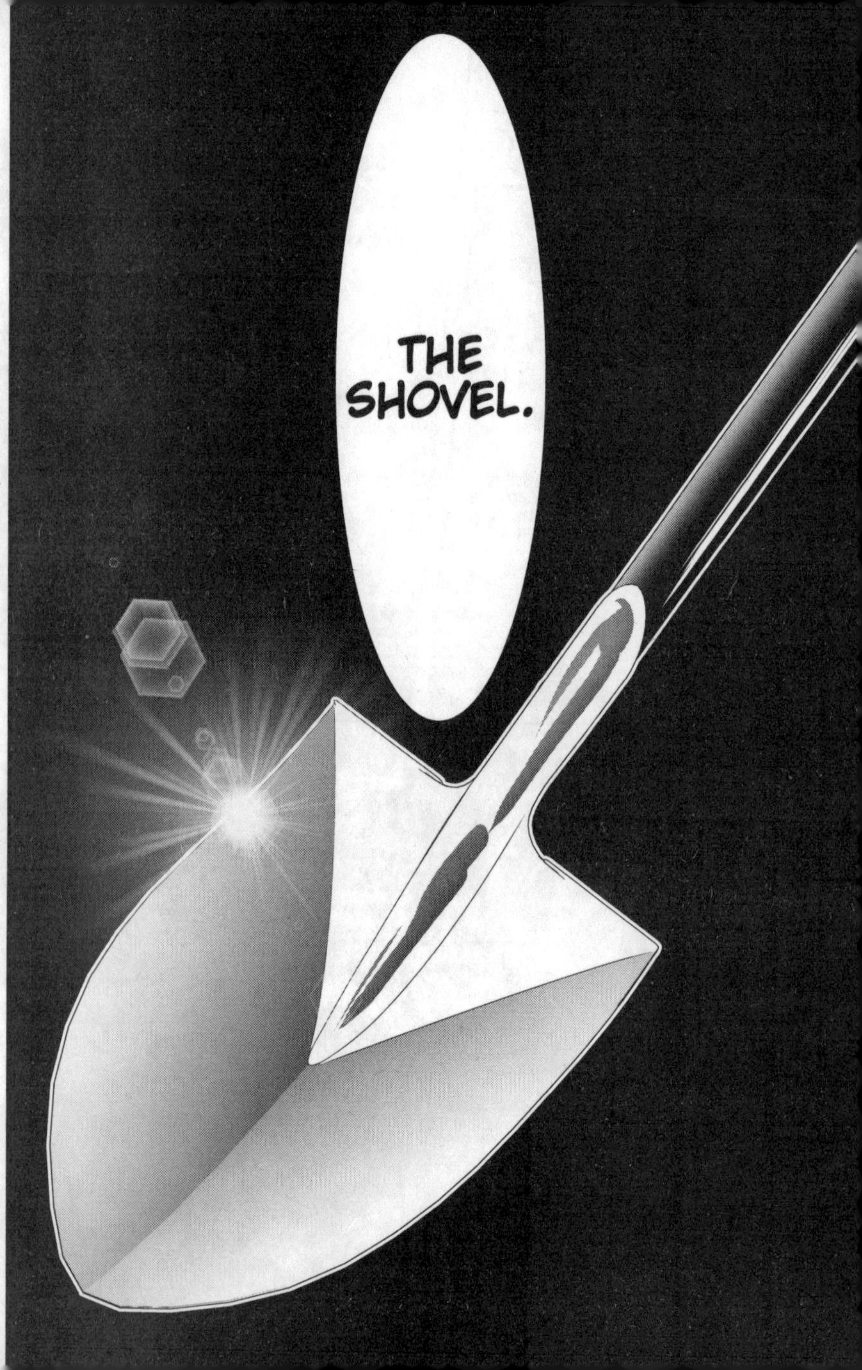
THE SHOVEL.

THE INVINCIBLE

SHOVEL

"WAVE MOTION SHOVEL BLAST!"
(･ω･´)♂ ＝＝＝＝★(`Д´ ∵∴):･∴ KA-CHOOOM

THE INVINCIBLE SHOVEL

"WAVE MOTION SHOVEL BLAST!"
(˙·ω·˙)♂≡≡≡≡★(д ;;;):.˙. KA-CHOOOM

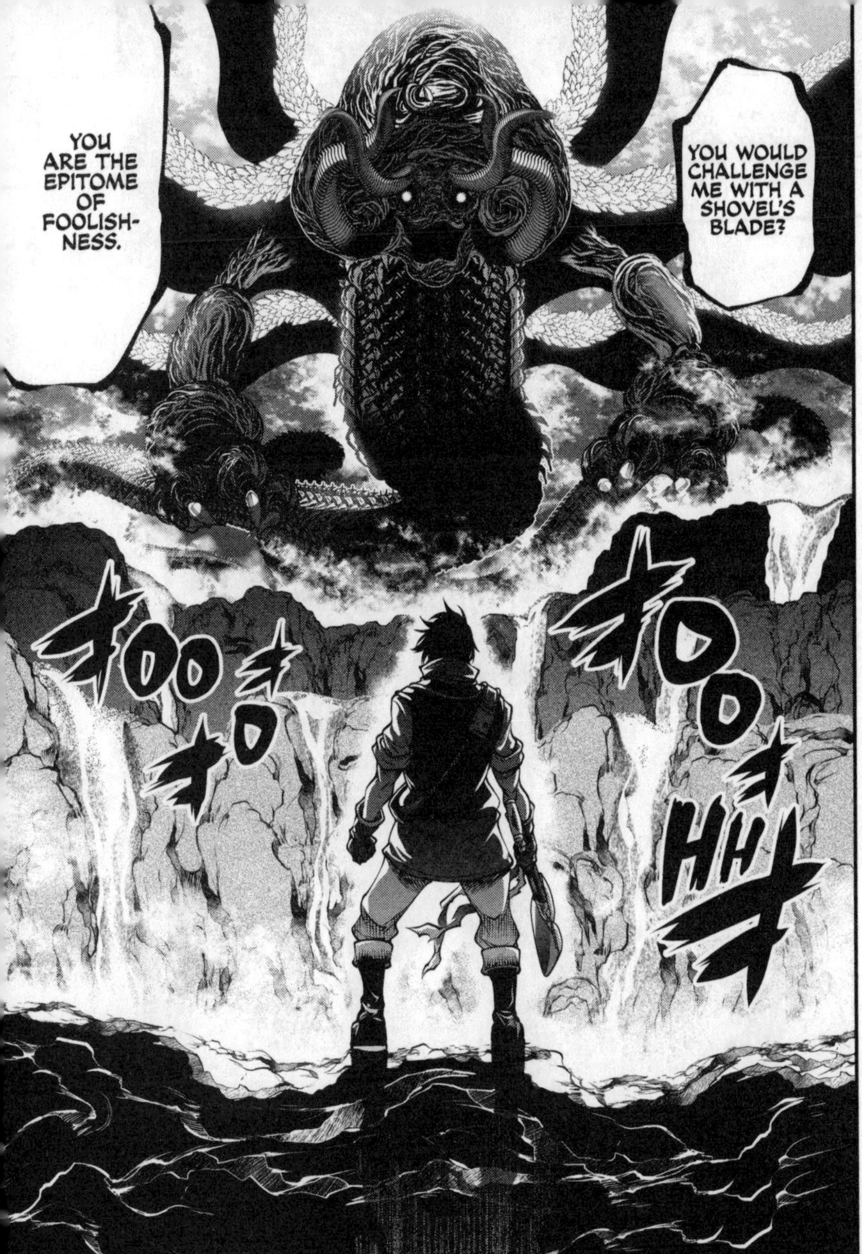
YOU WOULD CHALLENGE ME WITH A SHOVEL'S BLADE?
YOU ARE THE EPITOME OF FOOLISH-NESS.

Chapter 10: The Miner vs. the Despair-Eating Dragon

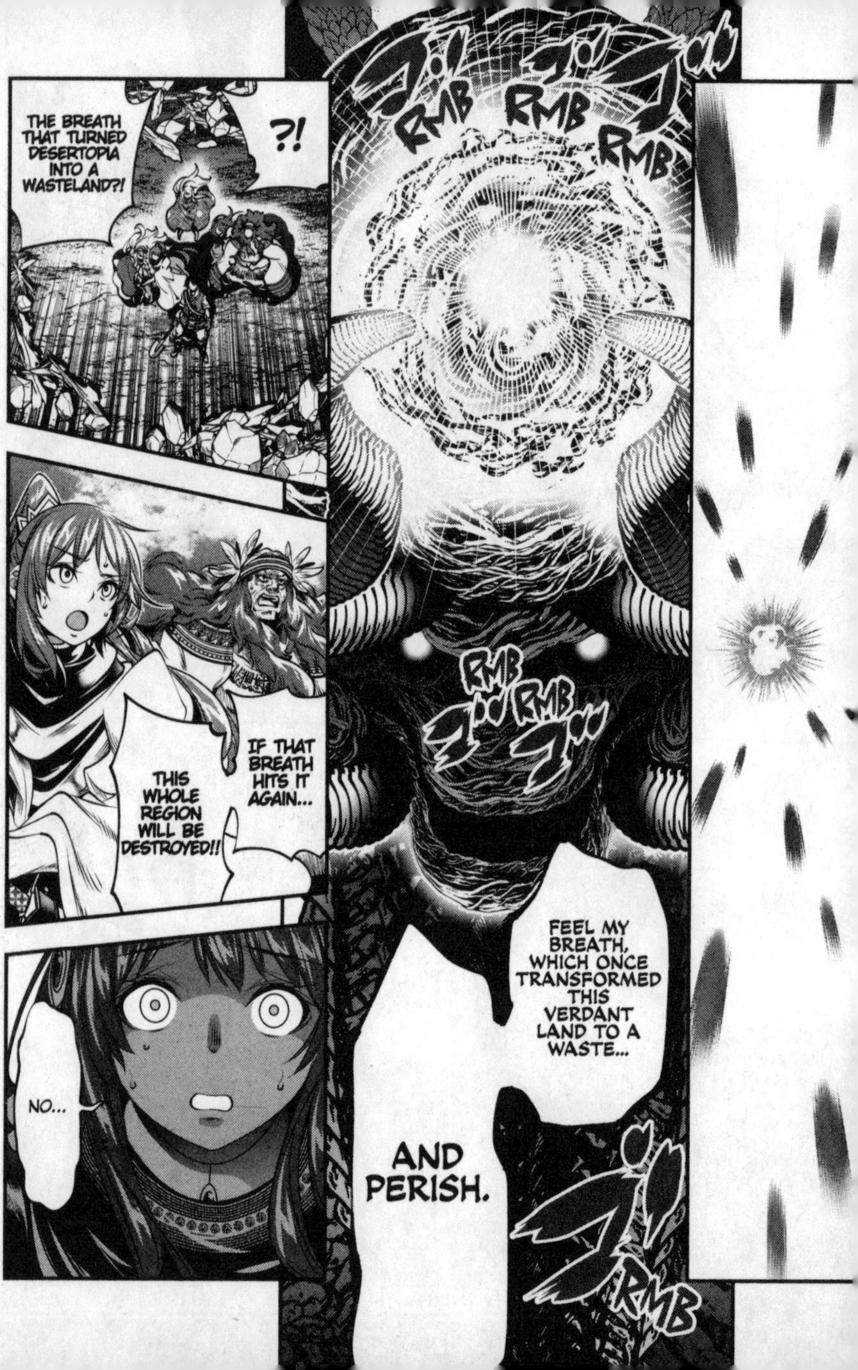
RMB RMB RMB
RMB RMB
FEEL MY BREATH, WHICH ONCE TRANSFORMED THIS VERDANT LAND TO A WASTE...
AND PERISH.
RMB
?!
THE BREATH THAT TURNED DESERTOPIA INTO A WASTELAND?!
IF THAT BREATH HITS IT AGAIN...
THIS WHOLE REGION WILL BE DESTROYED!!
NO...

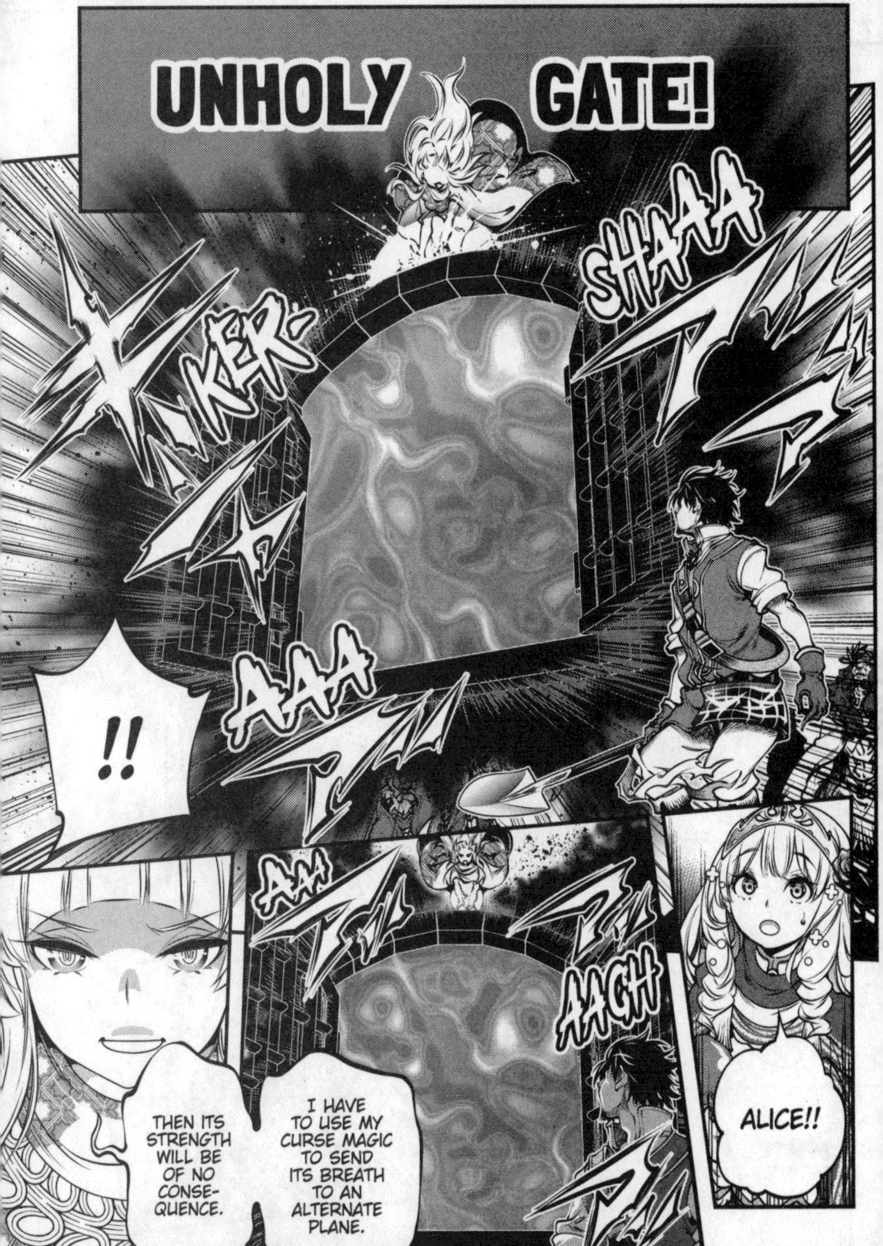
UNHOLY GATE!
SHAAA
KER-
AAA
!!
ALICE!!
AAA
AACH
I HAVE TO USE MY CURSE MAGIC TO SEND ITS BREATH TO AN ALTERNATE PLANE.
THEN ITS STRENGTH WILL BE OF NO CONSEQUENCE.

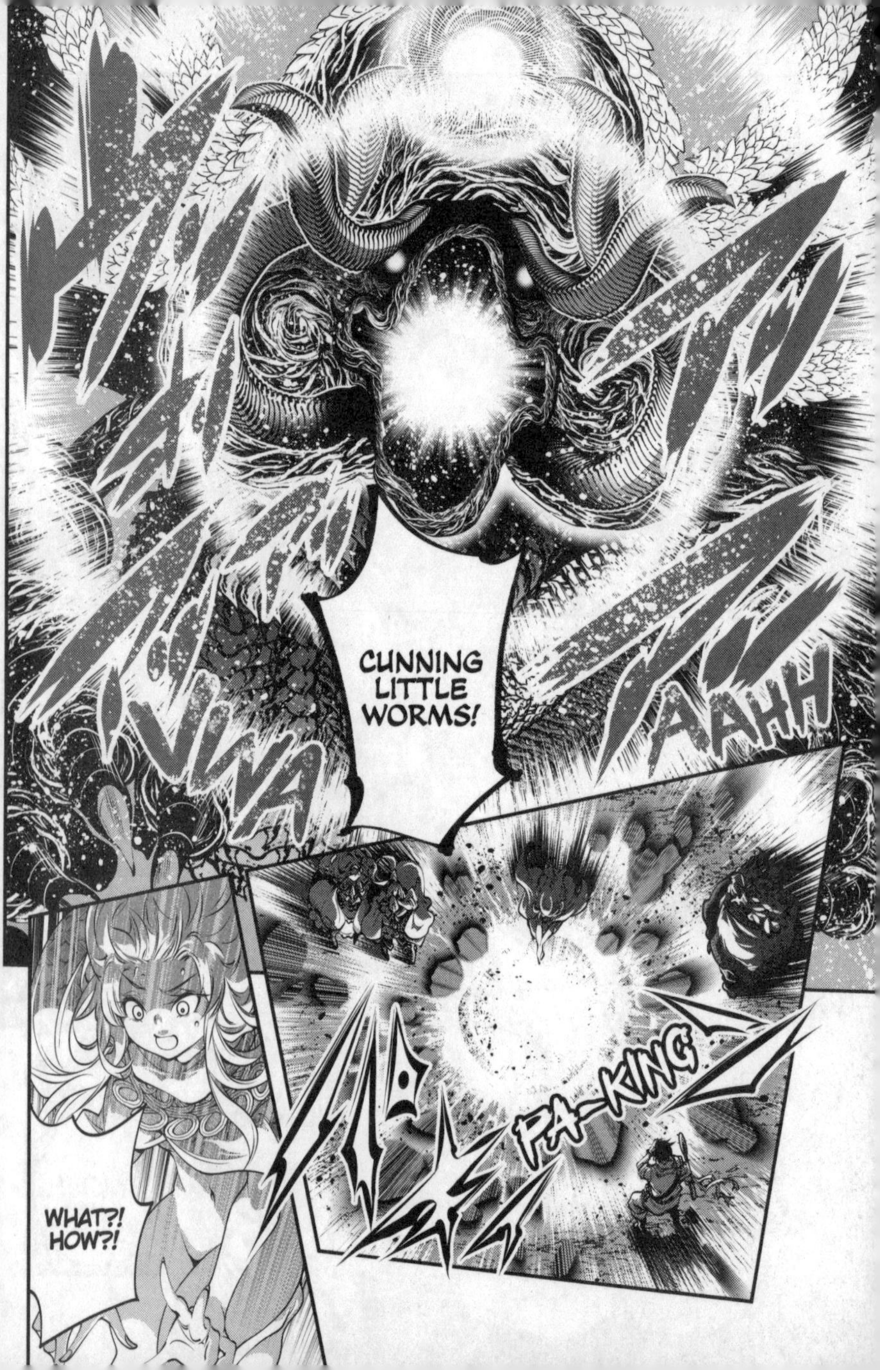
CUNNING LITTLE WORMS!
PA-KING
WHAT?! HOW?!

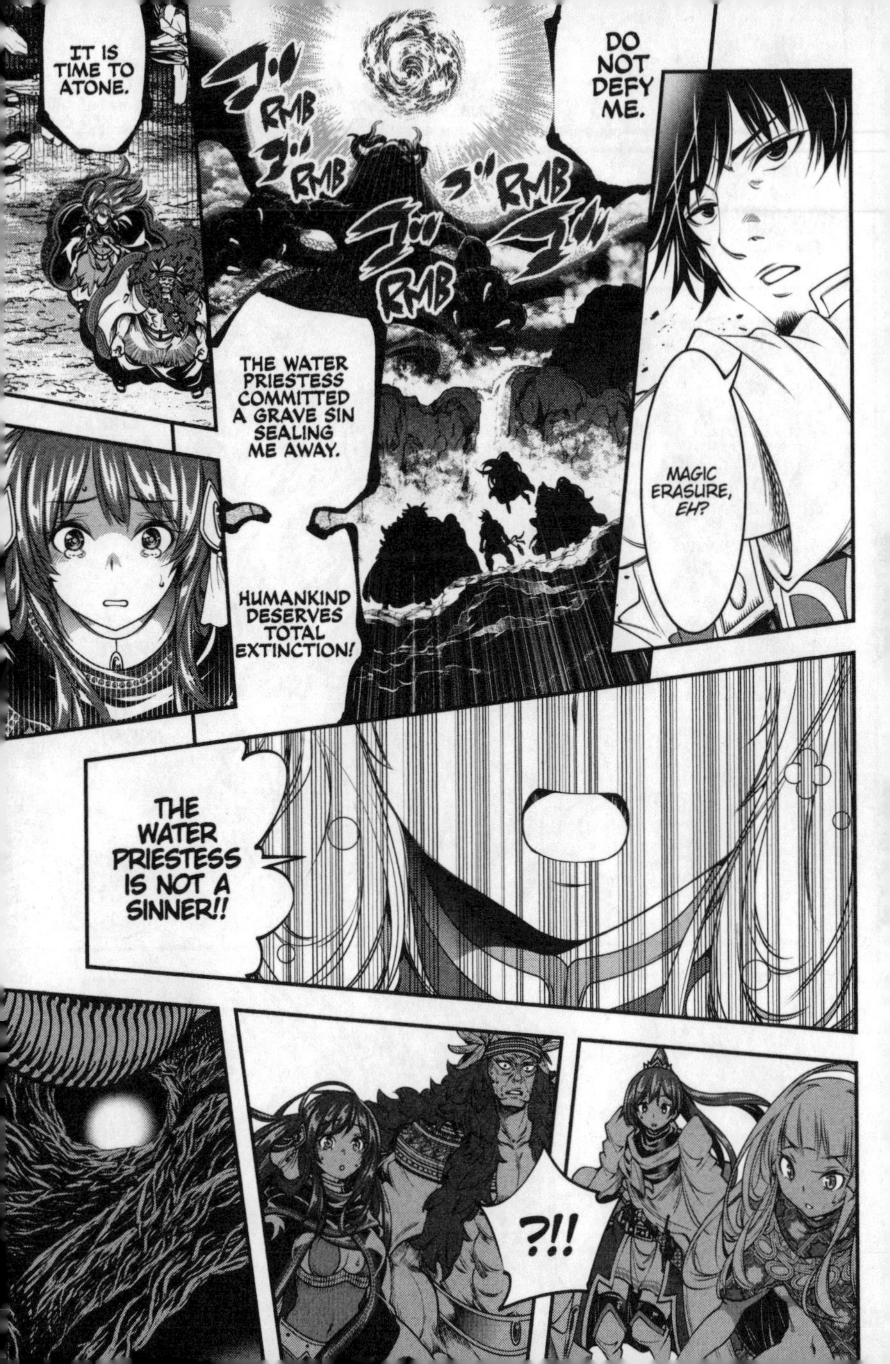
DO NOT DEFY ME.
MAGIC ERASURE, EH?
RMB RMB
RMB
RMB
IT IS TIME TO ATONE.
THE WATER PRIESTESS COMMITTED A GRAVE SIN SEALING ME AWAY.
HUMANKIND DESERVES TOTAL EXTINCTION!
THE WATER PRIESTESS IS NOT A SINNER!!
?!!

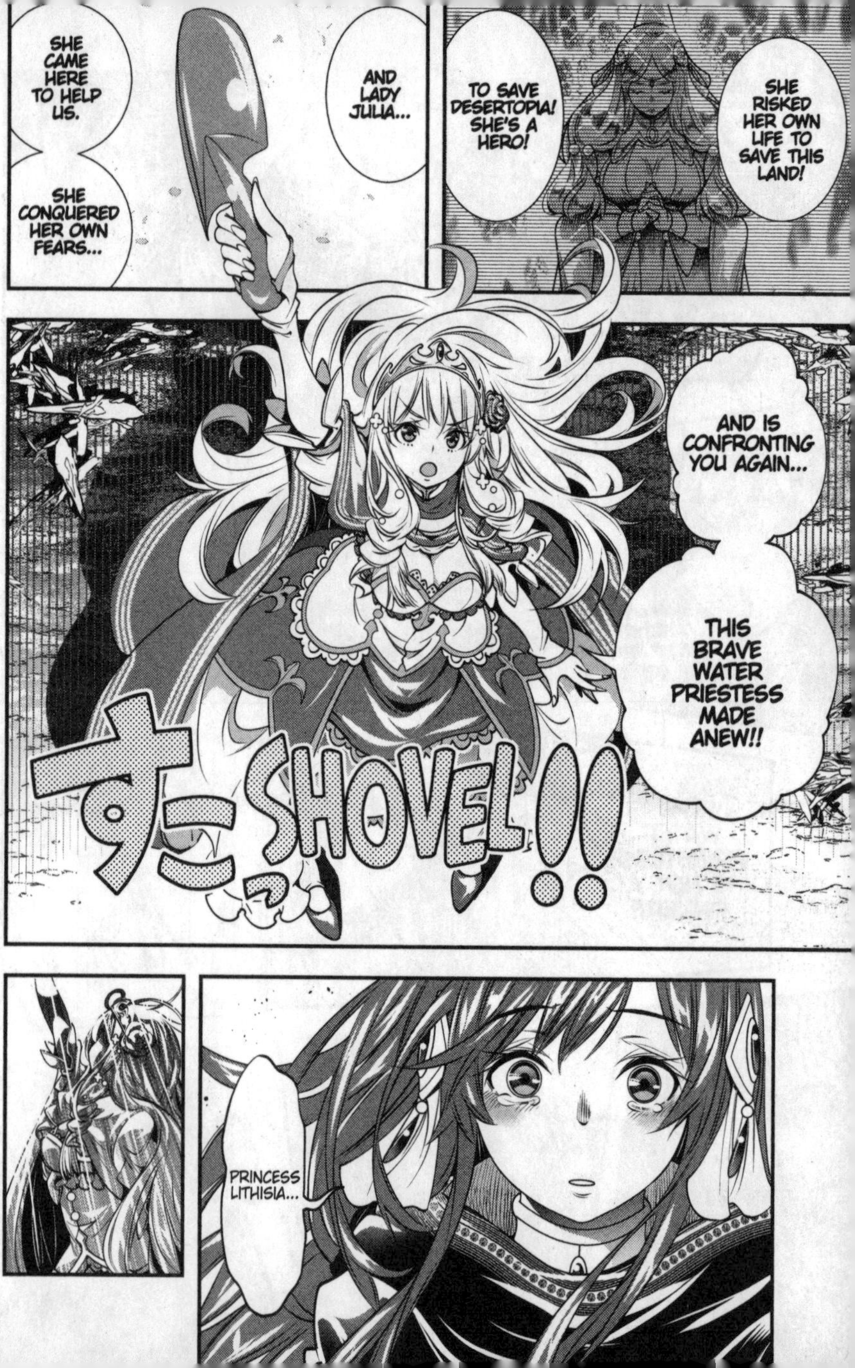
SHE RISKED HER OWN LIFE TO SAVE THIS LAND!
TO SAVE DESERTOPIA! SHE'S A HERO!
AND LADY JULIA...
SHE CAME HERE TO HELP US.
SHE CONQUERED HER OWN FEARS...
AND IS CONFRONTING YOU AGAIN...
THIS BRAVE WATER PRIESTESS MADE ANEW!!
すこっ SHOVEL!!
PRINCESS LITHISIA...

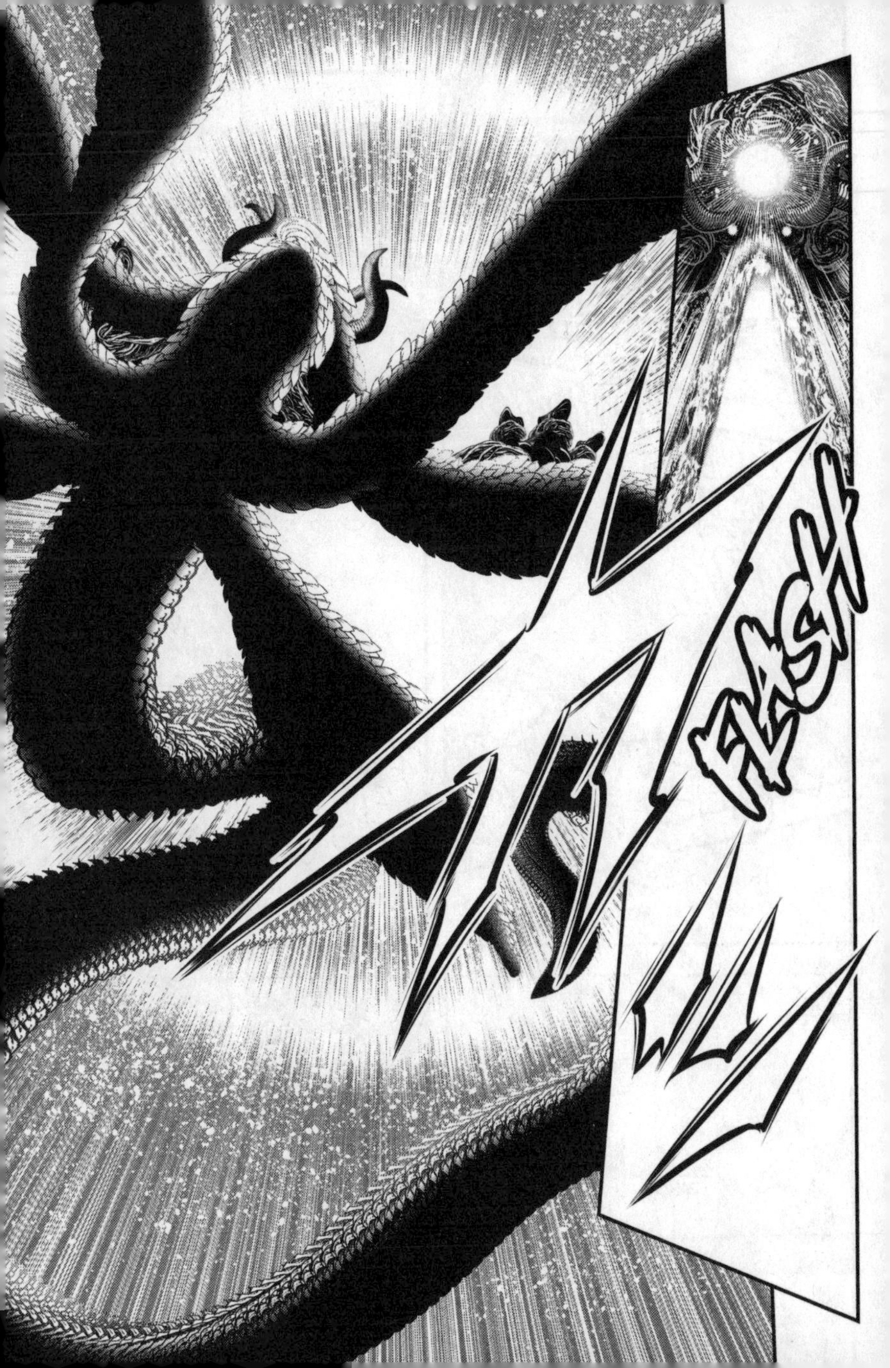
FLASH

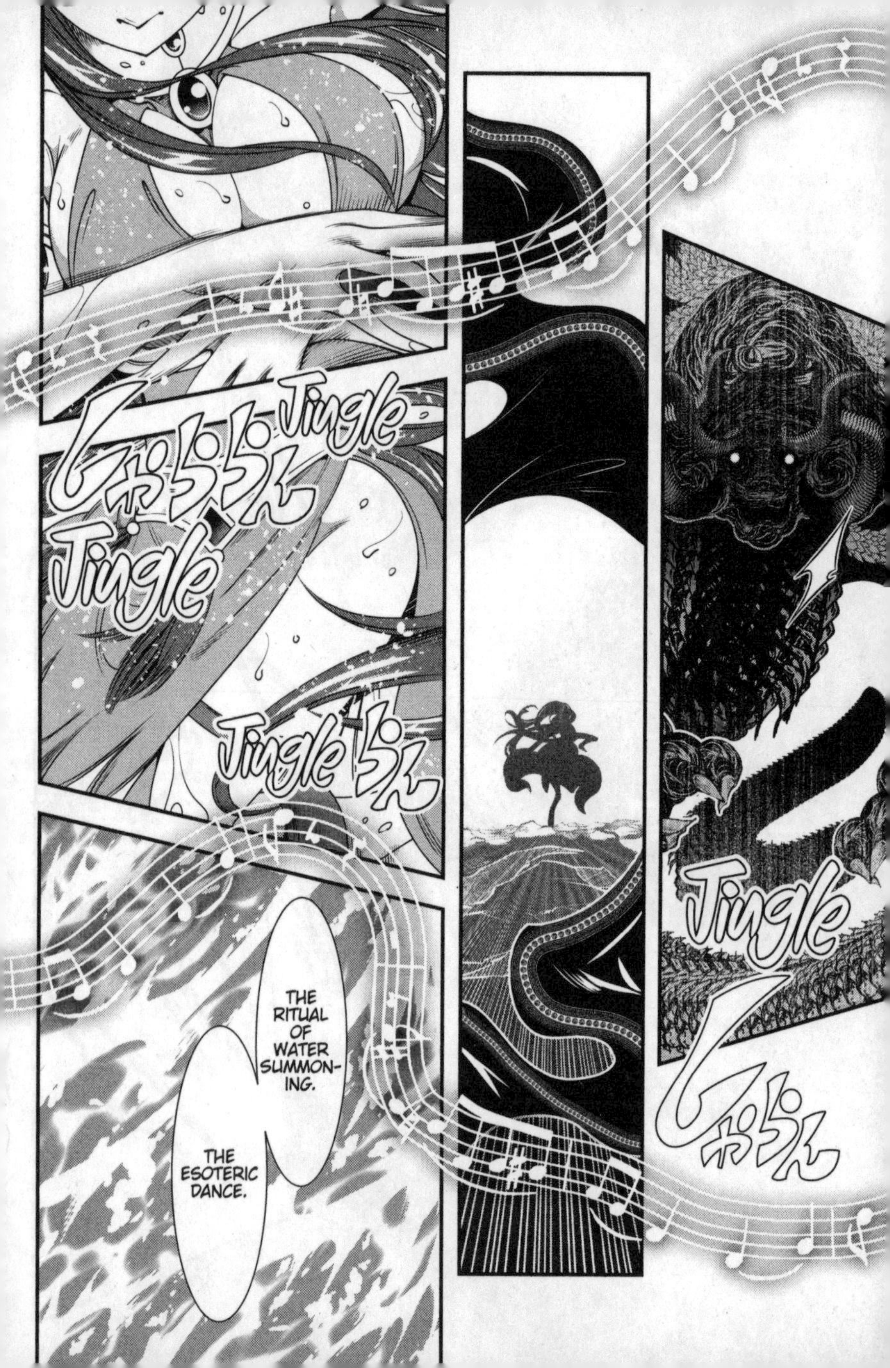
Jingle
しゃらん
しゃららん
Jingle
Jingle
Jingle らん
THE RITUAL OF WATER SUMMONING.
THE ESOTERIC DANCE.

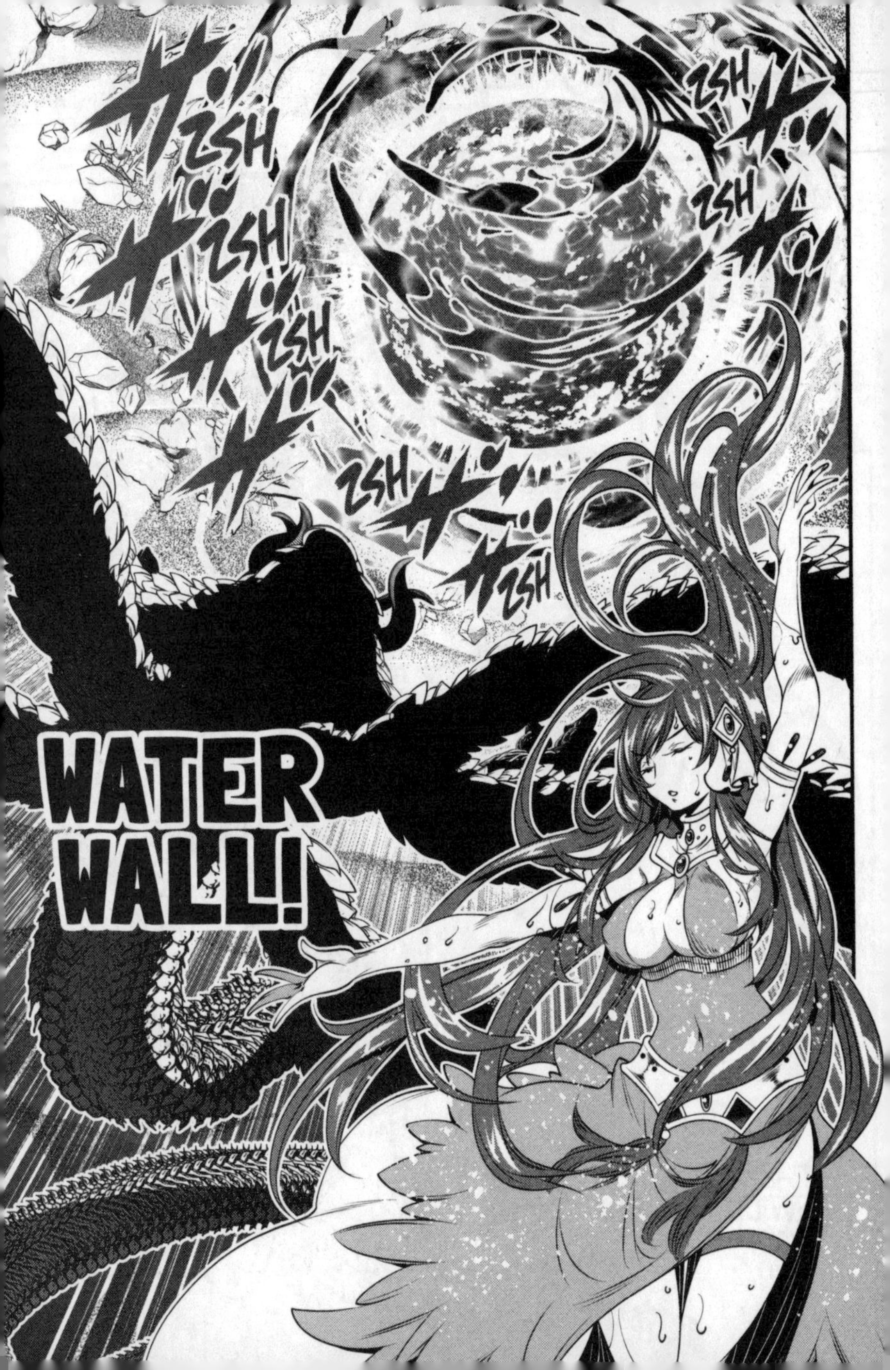
ZSH
ZSH
ZSH
ZSH
ZSH
ZSH
ZSH
WATER WALL!

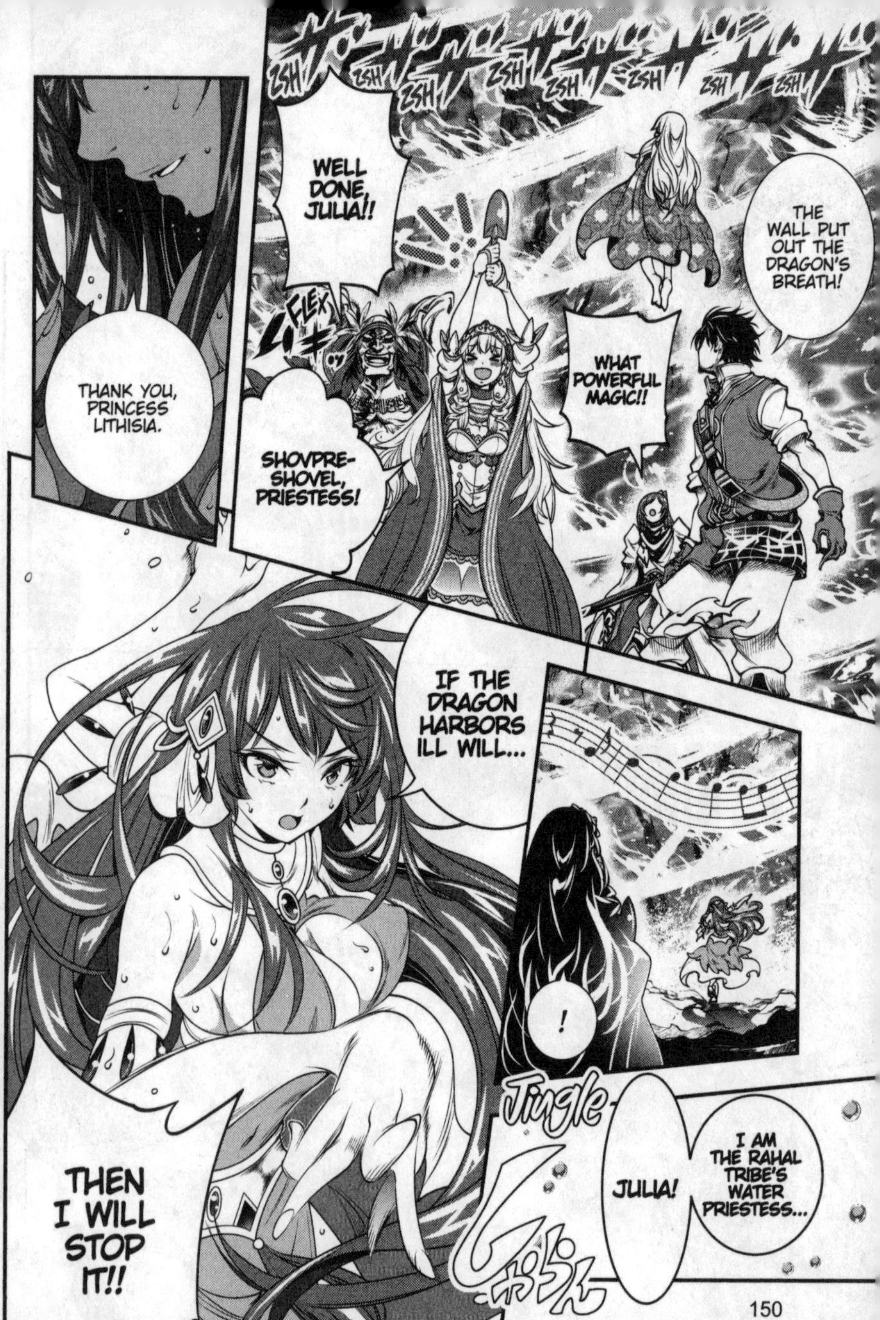
ZSH ZSH ZSH ZSH ZSH ZSH ZSH
THE WALL PUT OUT THE DRAGON'S BREATH!
WHAT POWERFUL MAGIC!!
WELL DONE, JULIA!!
FLEX
SHOVPRE-SHOVEL, PRIESTESS!
THANK YOU, PRINCESS LITHISIA.
!
Jingle
I AM THE RAHAL TRIBE'S WATER PRIESTESS...
JULIA!
IF THE DRAGON HARBORS ILL WILL...
THEN I WILL STOP IT!!

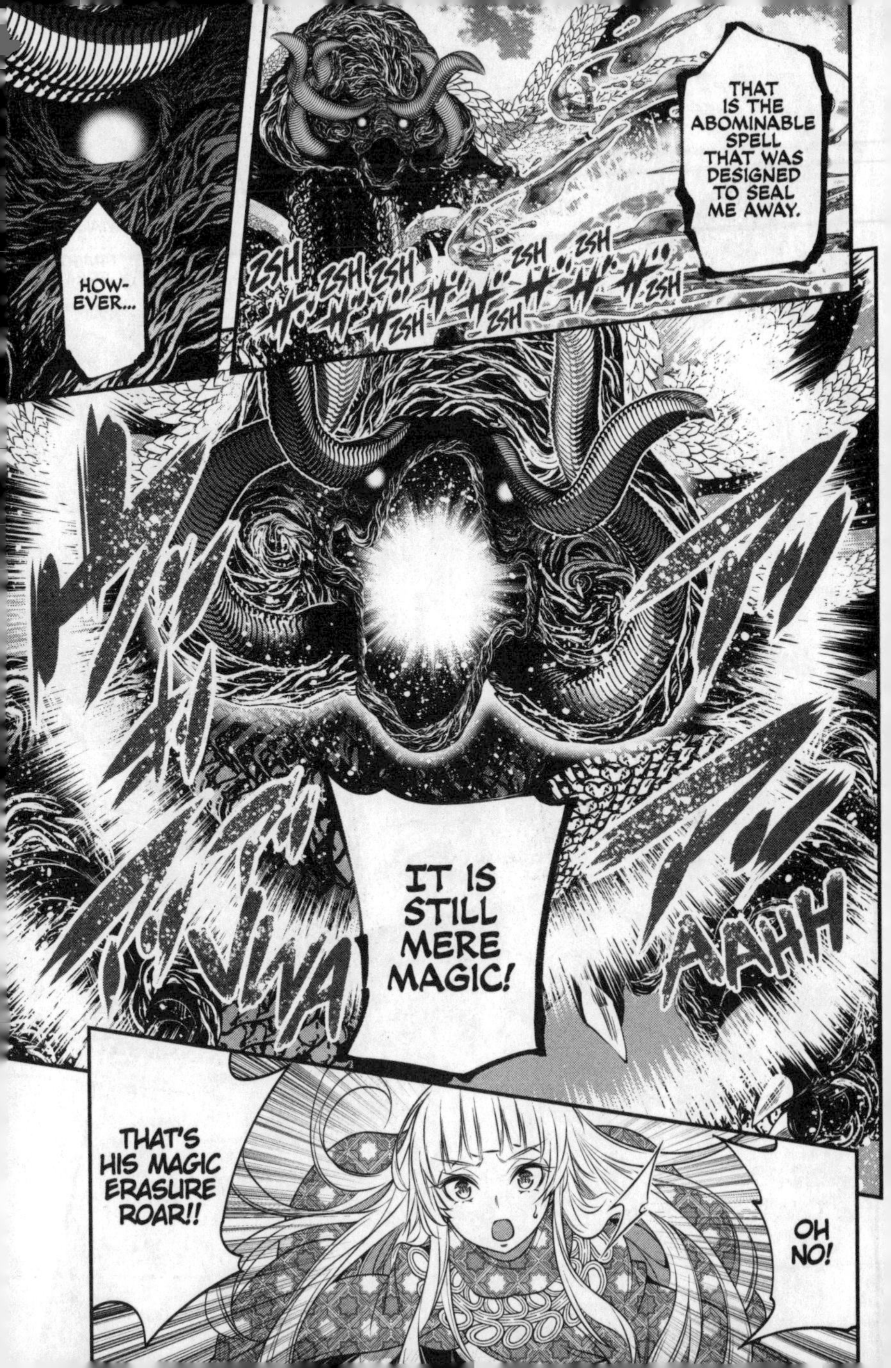
THAT IS THE ABOMINABLE SPELL THAT WAS DESIGNED TO SEAL ME AWAY.
ZSH ZSH ZSH ZSH ZSH ZSH ZSH
HOW-EVER...
IT IS STILL MERE MAGIC!
VWA
AAHH
OH NO!
THAT'S HIS MAGIC ERASURE ROAR!!

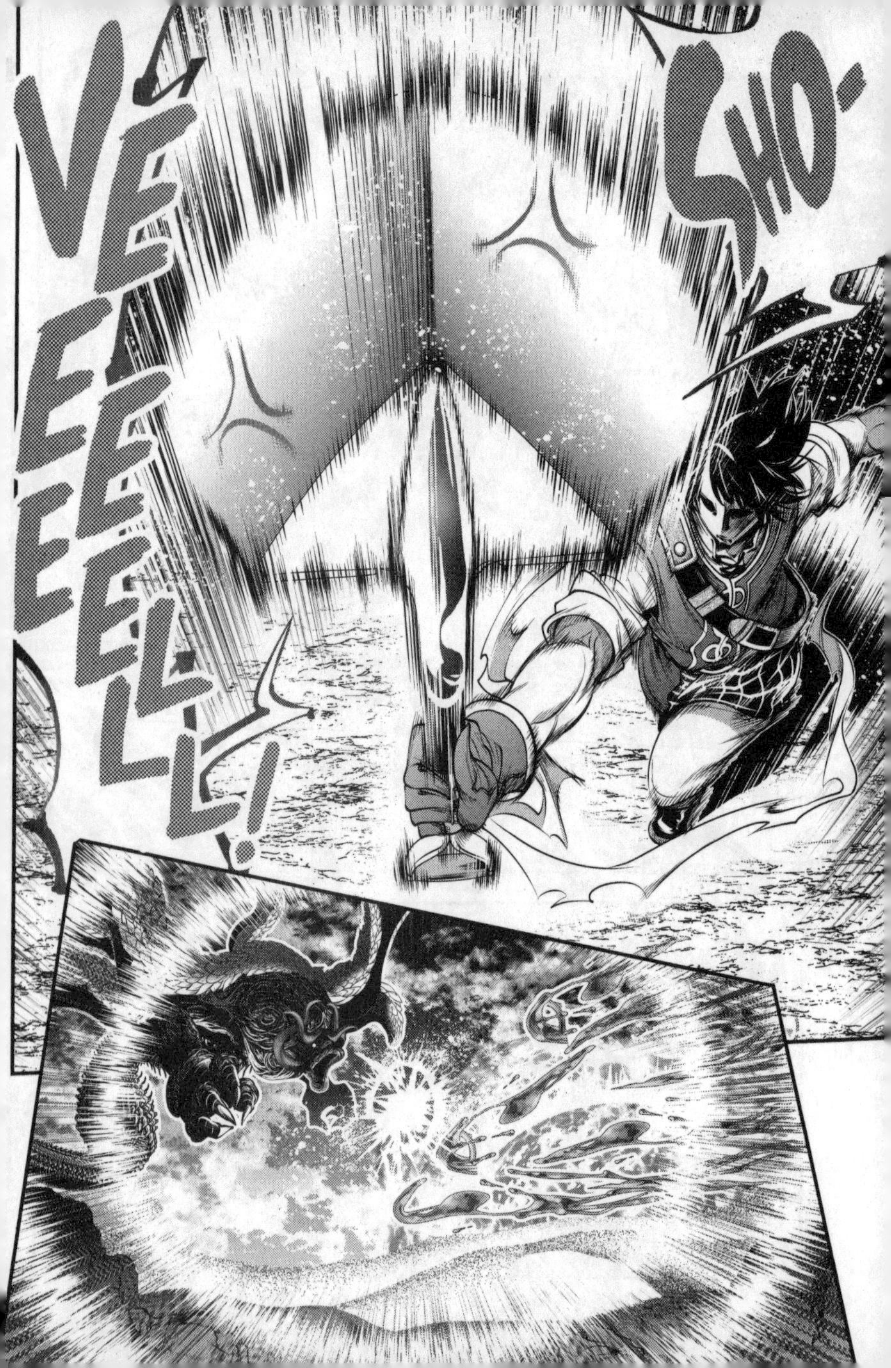
SHO-
VÉEEEELL!

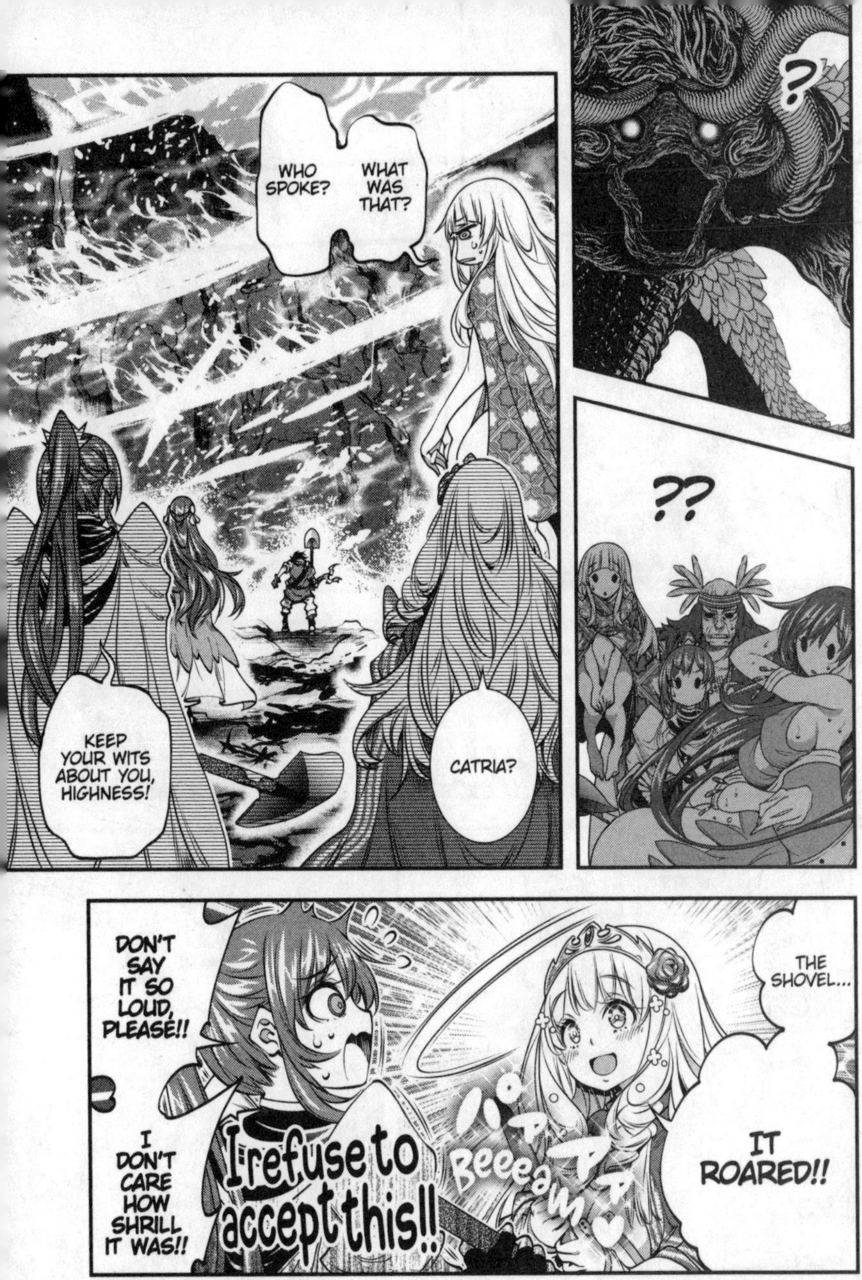
?
??
WHAT WAS THAT?
WHO SPOKE?
CATRIA?
KEEP YOUR WITS ABOUT YOU, HIGHNESS!
THE SHOVEL...
IT ROARED!!
Beeeam
DON'T SAY IT SO LOUD, PLEASE!!
I refuse to accept this!!
I DON'T CARE HOW SHRILL IT WAS!!

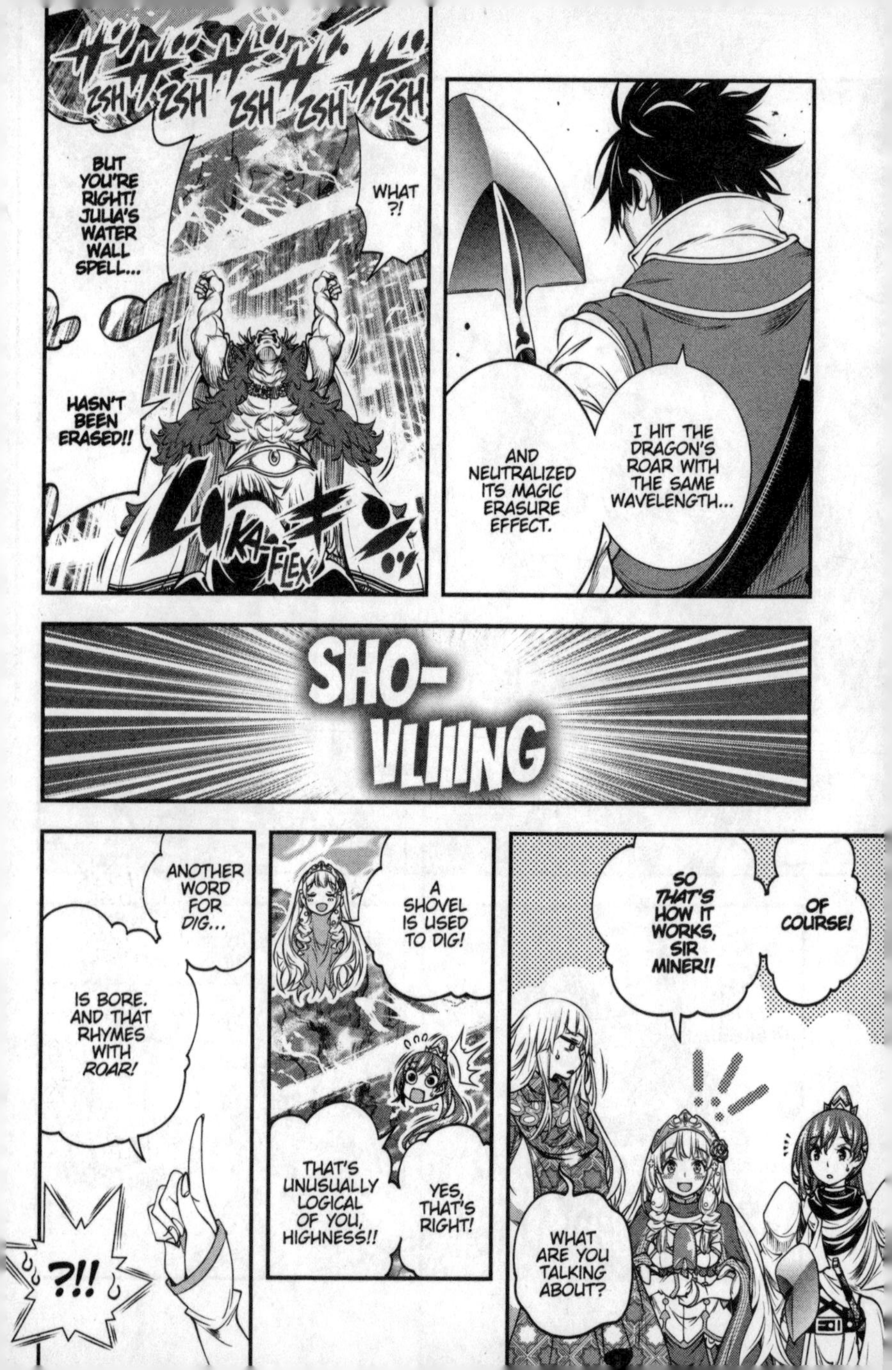
I HIT THE DRAGON'S ROAR WITH THE SAME WAVELENGTH...
AND NEUTRALIZED ITS MAGIC ERASURE EFFECT.
ZSH ZSH ZSH ZSH ZSH
WHAT ?!
BUT YOU'RE RIGHT! JULIA'S WATER WALL SPELL...
HASN'T BEEN ERASED!!
KA-FLEX
SHO-VLIIING
OF COURSE!
SO *THAT'S* HOW IT WORKS, SIR MINER!!
WHAT ARE YOU TALKING ABOUT?
A SHOVEL IS USED TO DIG!
YES, THAT'S RIGHT!
THAT'S UNUSUALLY LOGICAL OF YOU, HIGHNESS!!
ANOTHER WORD FOR *DIG*...
IS BORE. AND THAT RHYMES WITH *ROAR!*
?!!

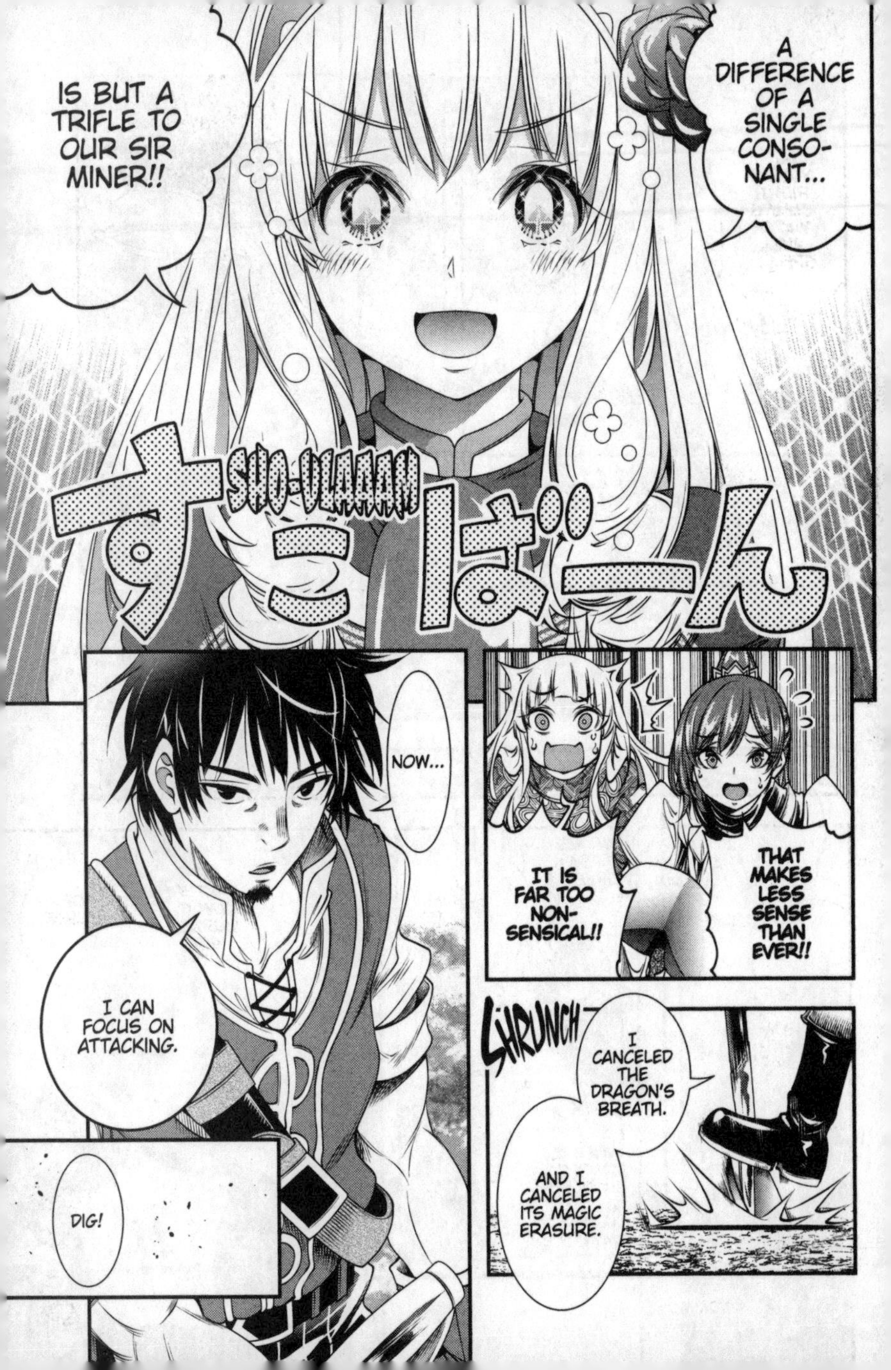
A DIFFERENCE OF A SINGLE CONSO-NANT...
IS BUT A TRIFLE TO OUR SIR MINER!!
SHO-VLAAAM
すごばーん
THAT MAKES LESS SENSE THAN EVER!!
IT IS FAR TOO NON-SENSICAL!!
SHRUNCH
I CANCELED THE DRAGON'S BREATH.
AND I CANCELED ITS MAGIC ERASURE.
NOW...
I CAN FOCUS ON ATTACKING.
DIG!

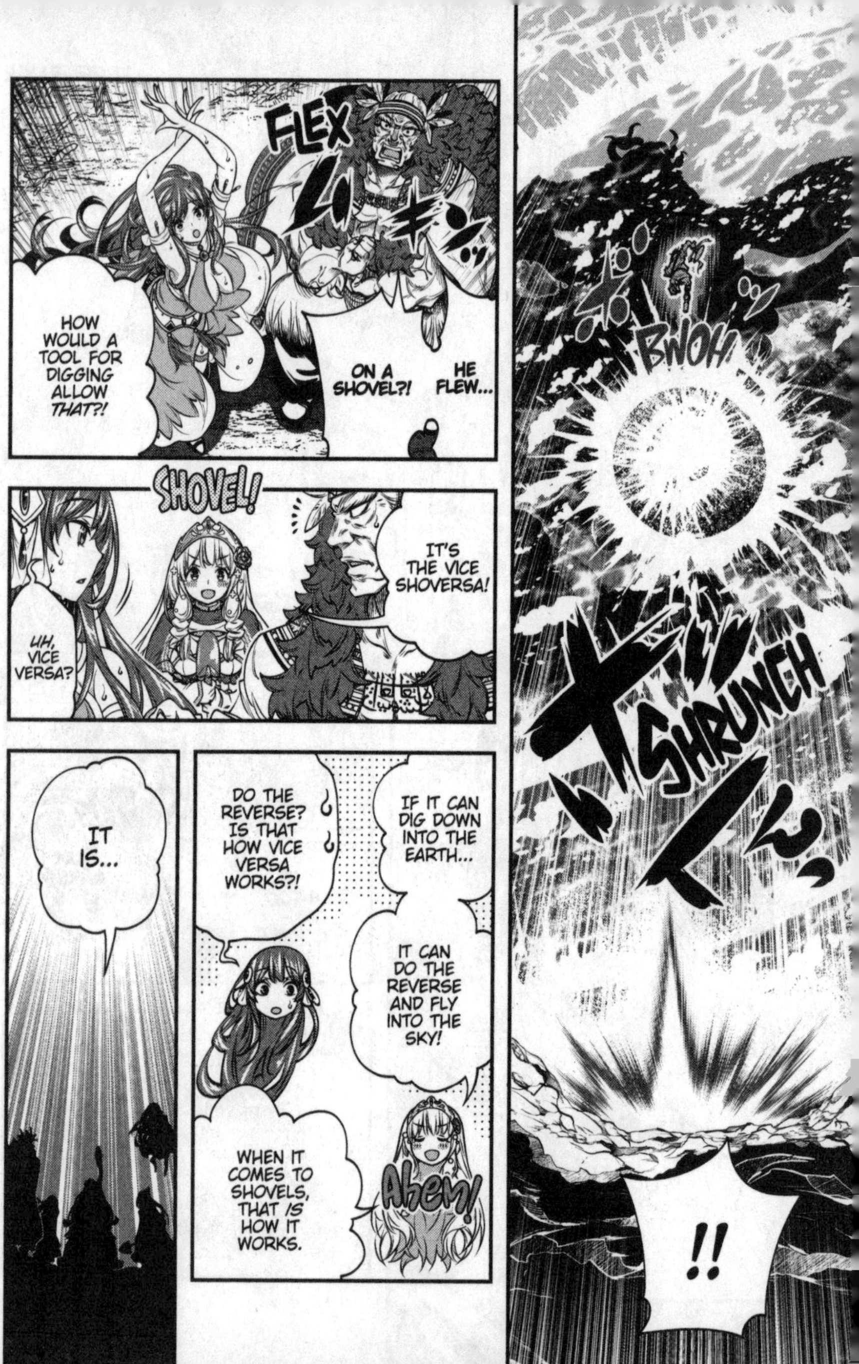
BWOH
SHRUNCH
!!
FLEX
HE FLEW...
ON A SHOVEL?!
HOW WOULD A TOOL FOR DIGGING ALLOW THAT?!
SHOVEL!
IT'S THE VICE SHOVERSA!
UH, VICE VERSA?
IF IT CAN DIG DOWN INTO THE EARTH...
IT CAN DO THE REVERSE AND FLY INTO THE SKY!
DO THE REVERSE? IS THAT HOW VICE VERSA WORKS?!
Ahem!
WHEN IT COMES TO SHOVELS, THAT IS HOW IT WORKS.
IT IS...

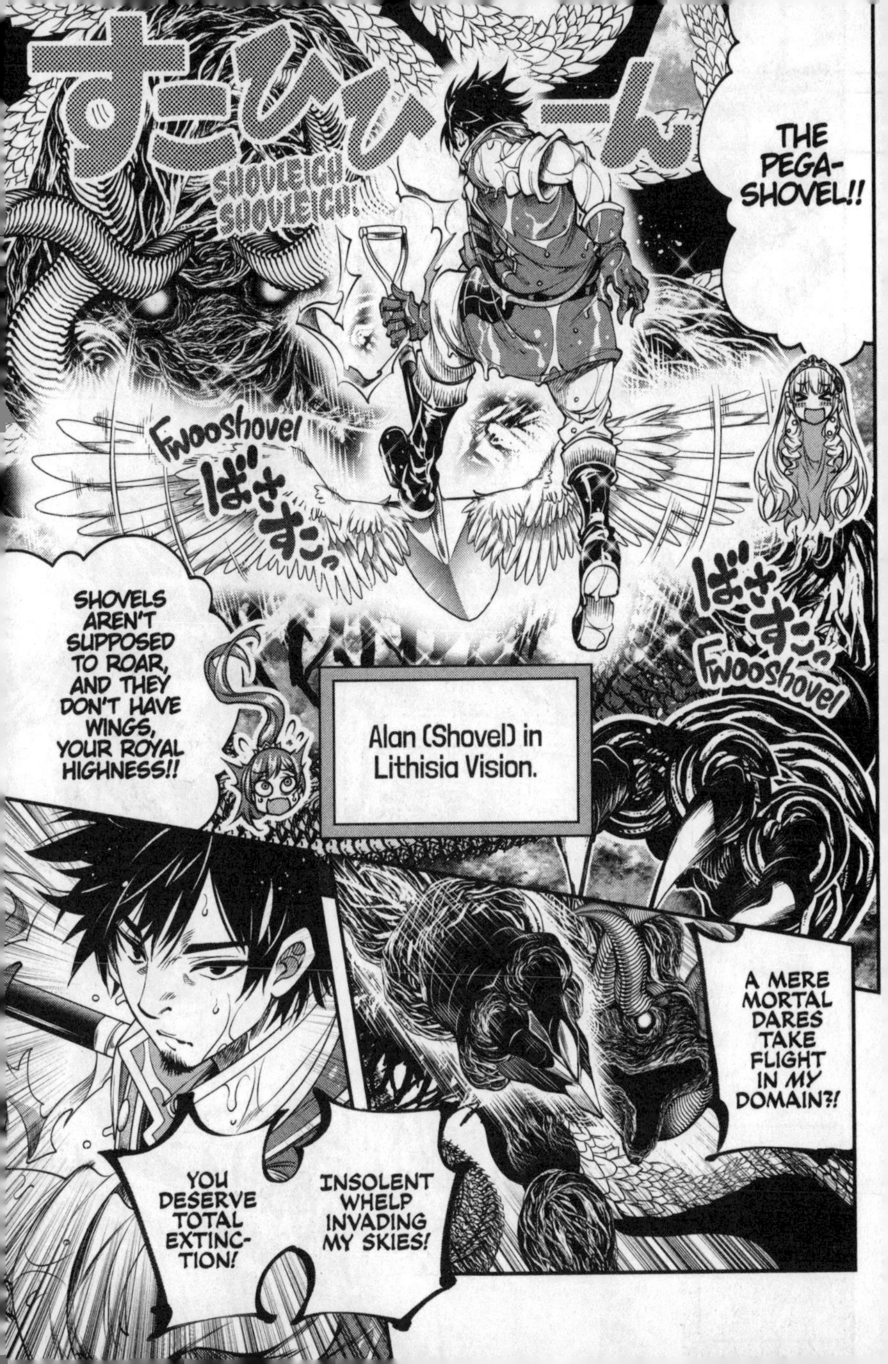

THE PEGA-SHOVEL!!
すこひひーん
SHOVLEIGH SHOVLEIGH!
ばさすこっ
Fwooshovel
Fwooshovel
ばさすこっ
SHOVELS AREN'T SUPPOSED TO ROAR, AND THEY DON'T HAVE WINGS, YOUR ROYAL HIGHNESS!!
Alan (Shovel) in Lithisia Vision.
A MERE MORTAL DARES TAKE FLIGHT IN MY DOMAIN?!
INSOLENT WHELP INVADING MY SKIES!
YOU DESERVE TOTAL EXTINCTION!

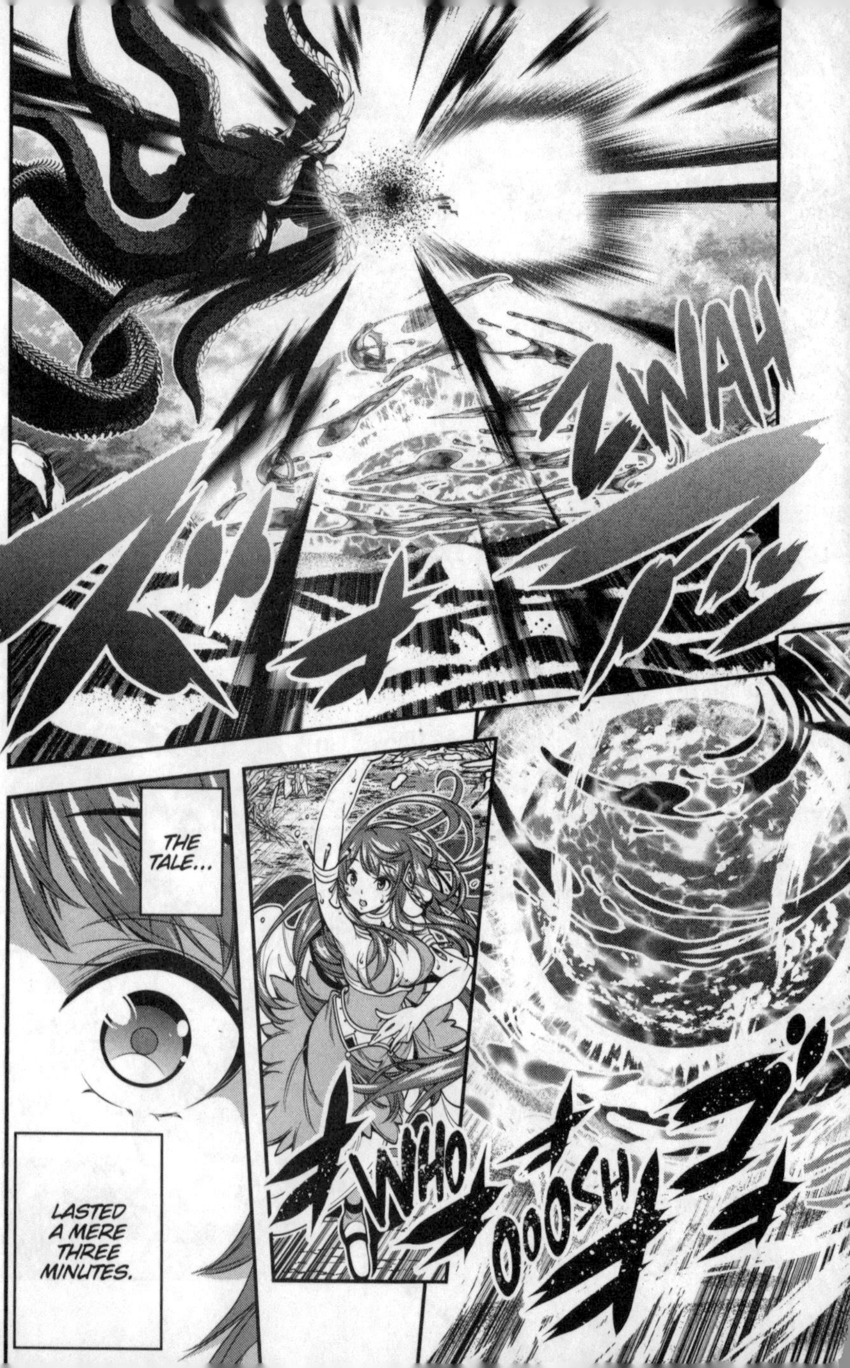
ZWAH
WHOOOOSH
THE TALE...
LASTED A MERE THREE MINUTES.

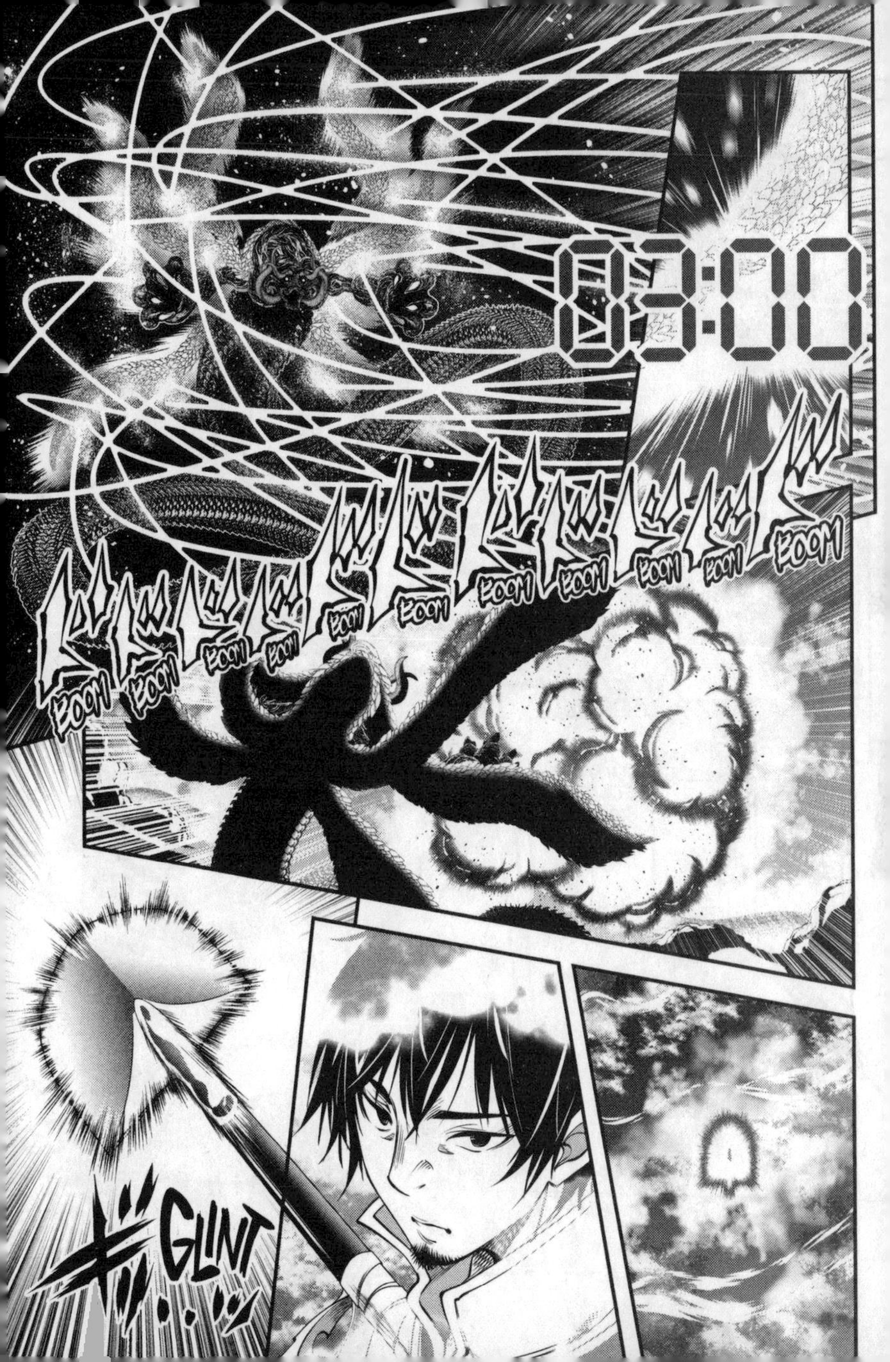
03:00
BOOM BOOM BOOM BOOM BOOM BOOM BOOM BOOM BOOM BOOM BOOM
GLINT

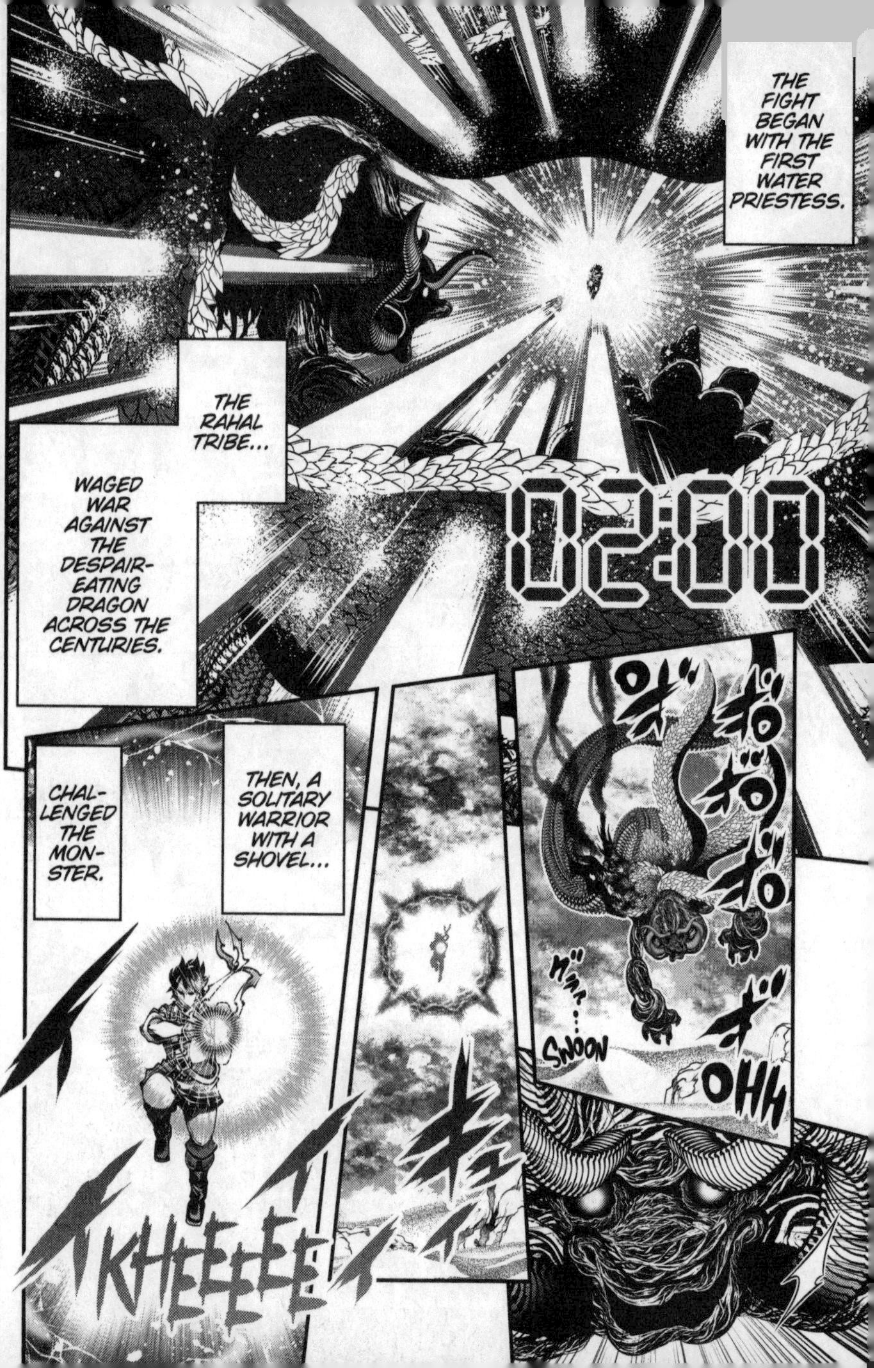
THE FIGHT BEGAN WITH THE FIRST WATER PRIESTESS.
THE RAHAL TRIBE...
WAGED WAR AGAINST THE DESPAIR-EATING DRAGON ACROSS THE CENTURIES.
02:00
OHH
SWOON
THEN, A SOLITARY WARRIOR WITH A SHOVEL...
CHAL-LENGED THE MON-STER.
KHEEEEE

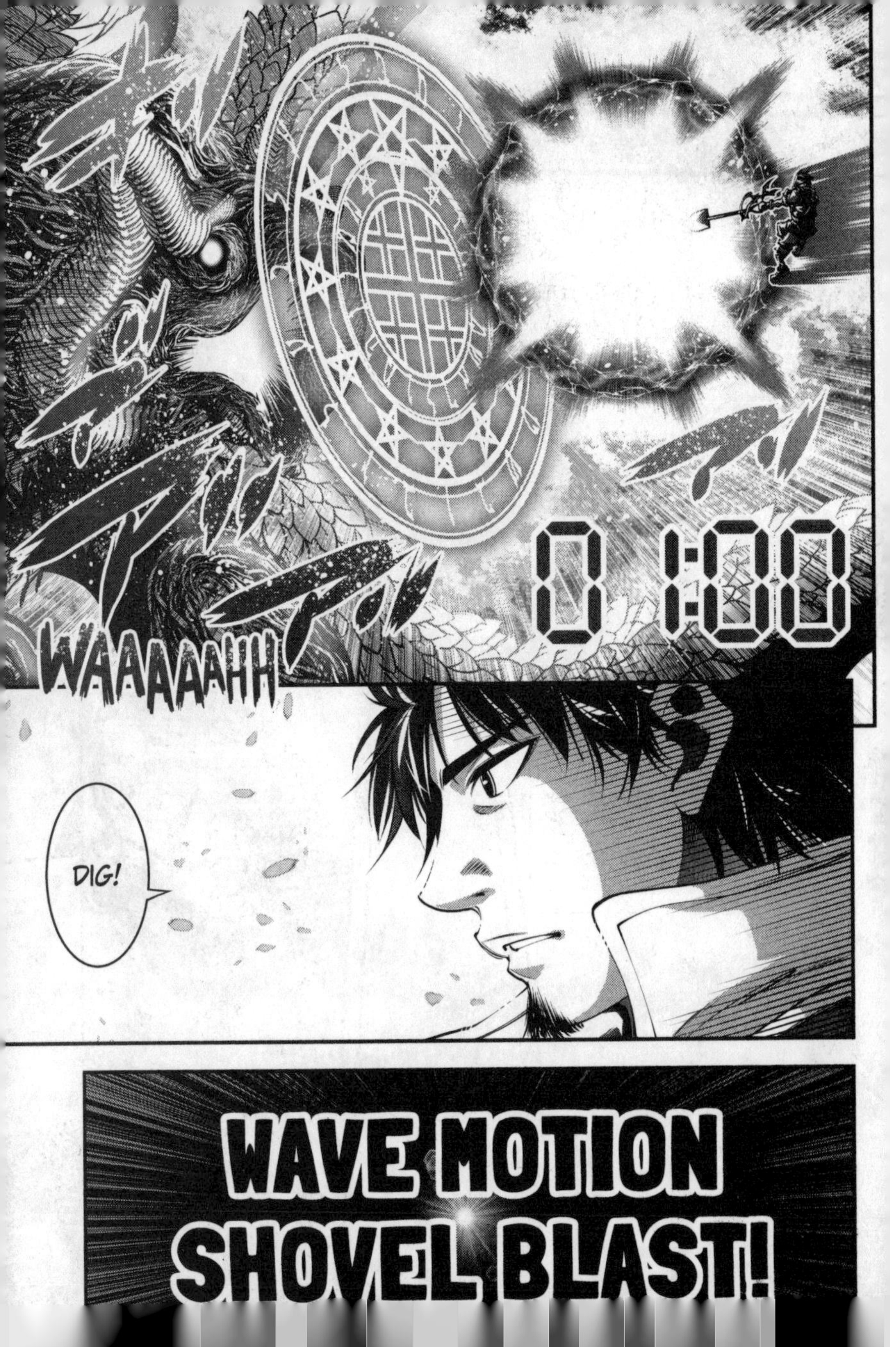
0 1:00
WAAAAAHH
DIG!
WAVE MOTION
SHOVEL BLAST!

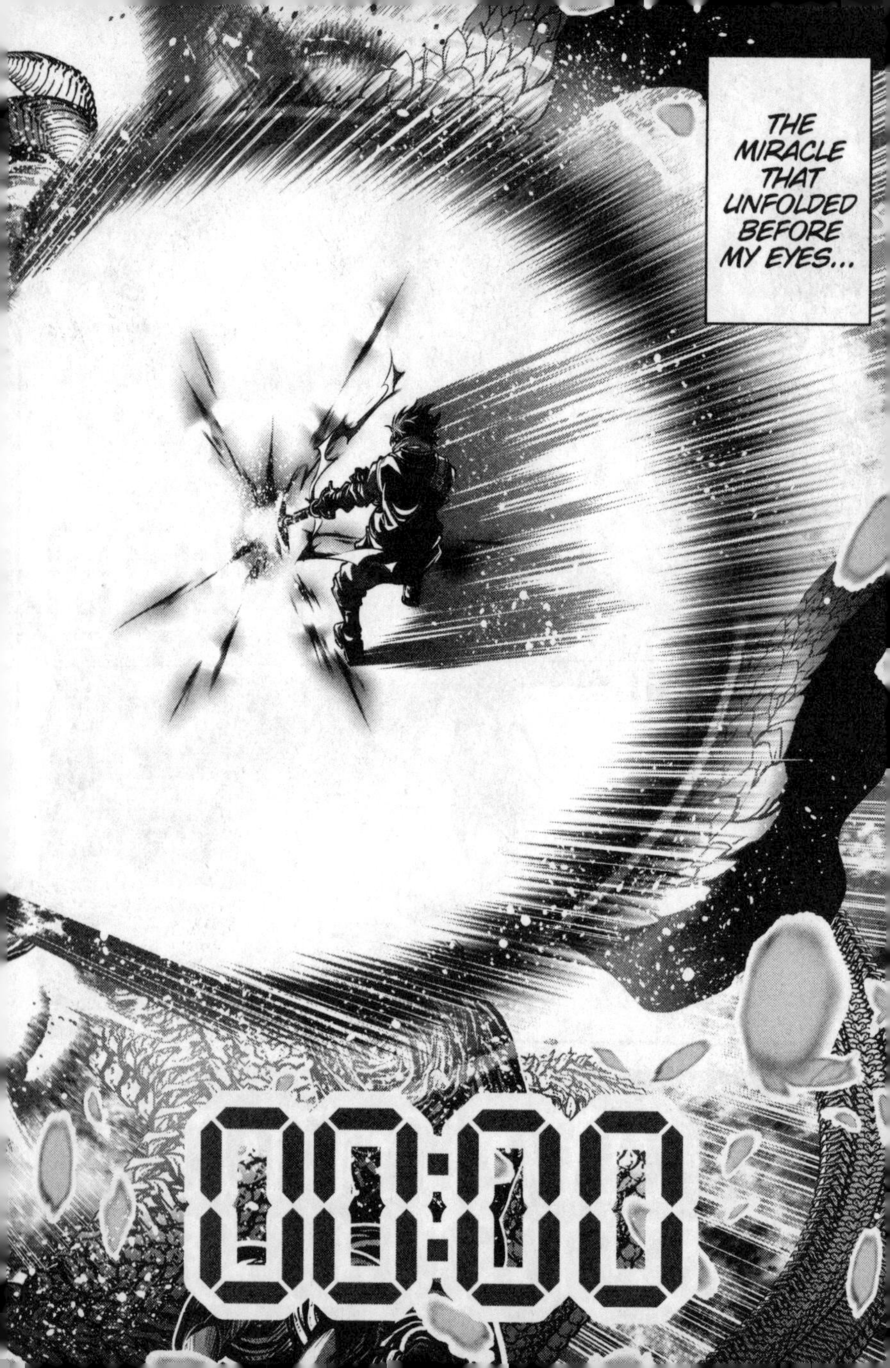
THE MIRACLE THAT UNFOLDED BEFORE MY EYES...
00:00

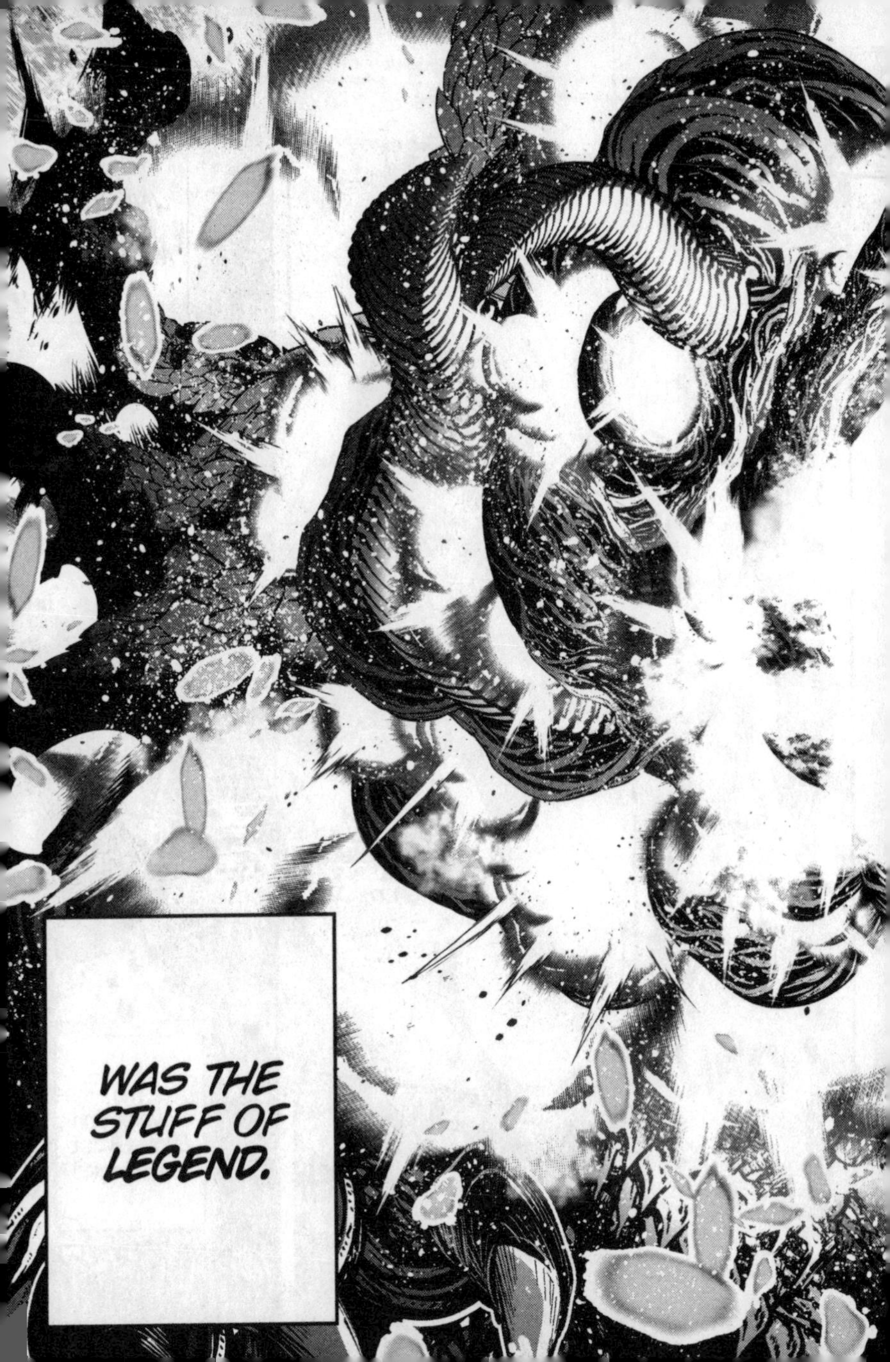
WAS THE STUFF OF LEGEND.

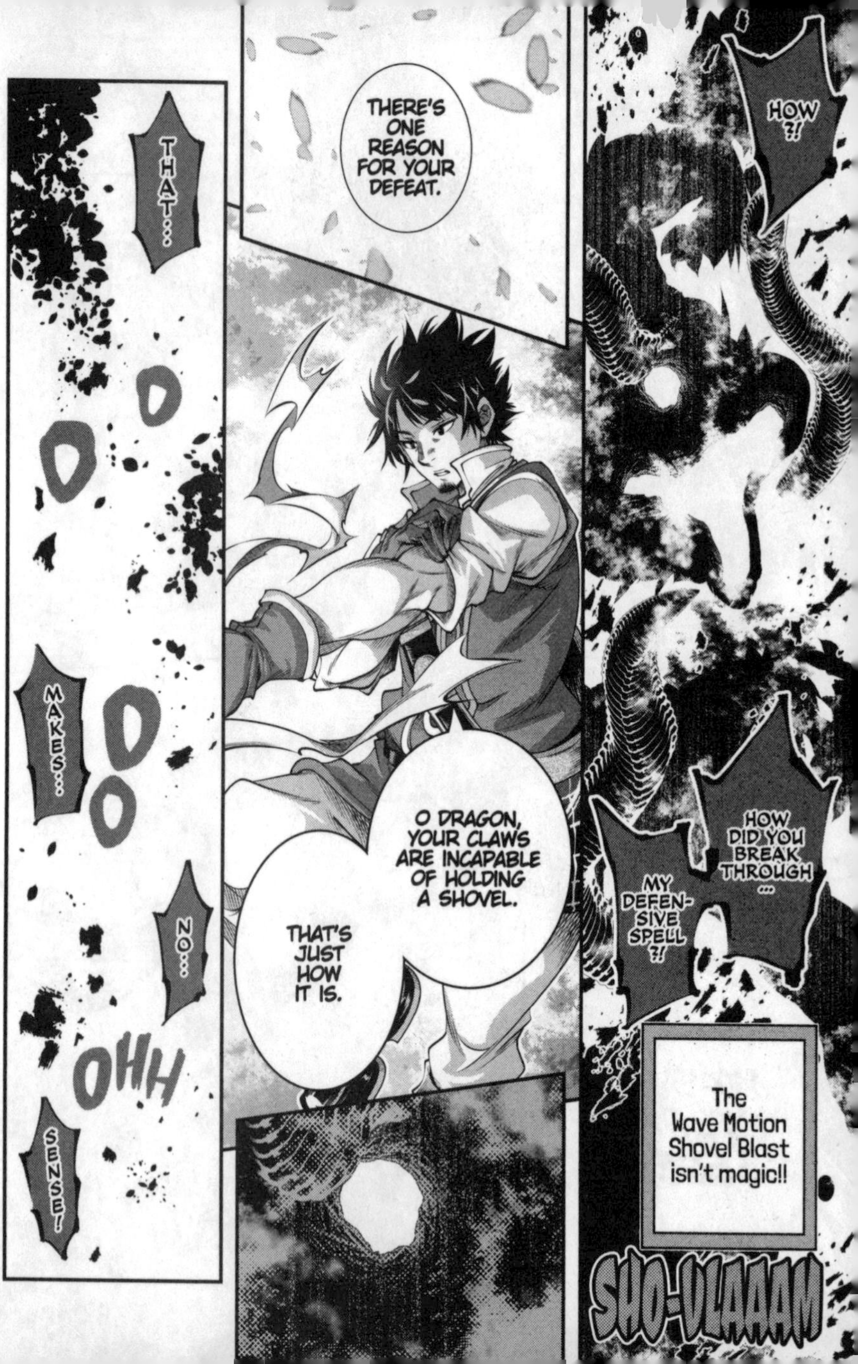
HOW ?!
HOW DID YOU BREAK THROUGH ...
MY DEFEN-SIVE SPELL ?!
The Wave Motion Shovel Blast isn't magic!!
SHO-VLAAAM
THERE'S ONE REASON FOR YOUR DEFEAT.
O DRAGON, YOUR CLAWS ARE INCAPABLE OF HOLDING A SHOVEL.
THAT'S JUST HOW IT IS.
THAT...
MAKES...
NO...
SENSE!
DODOOHH

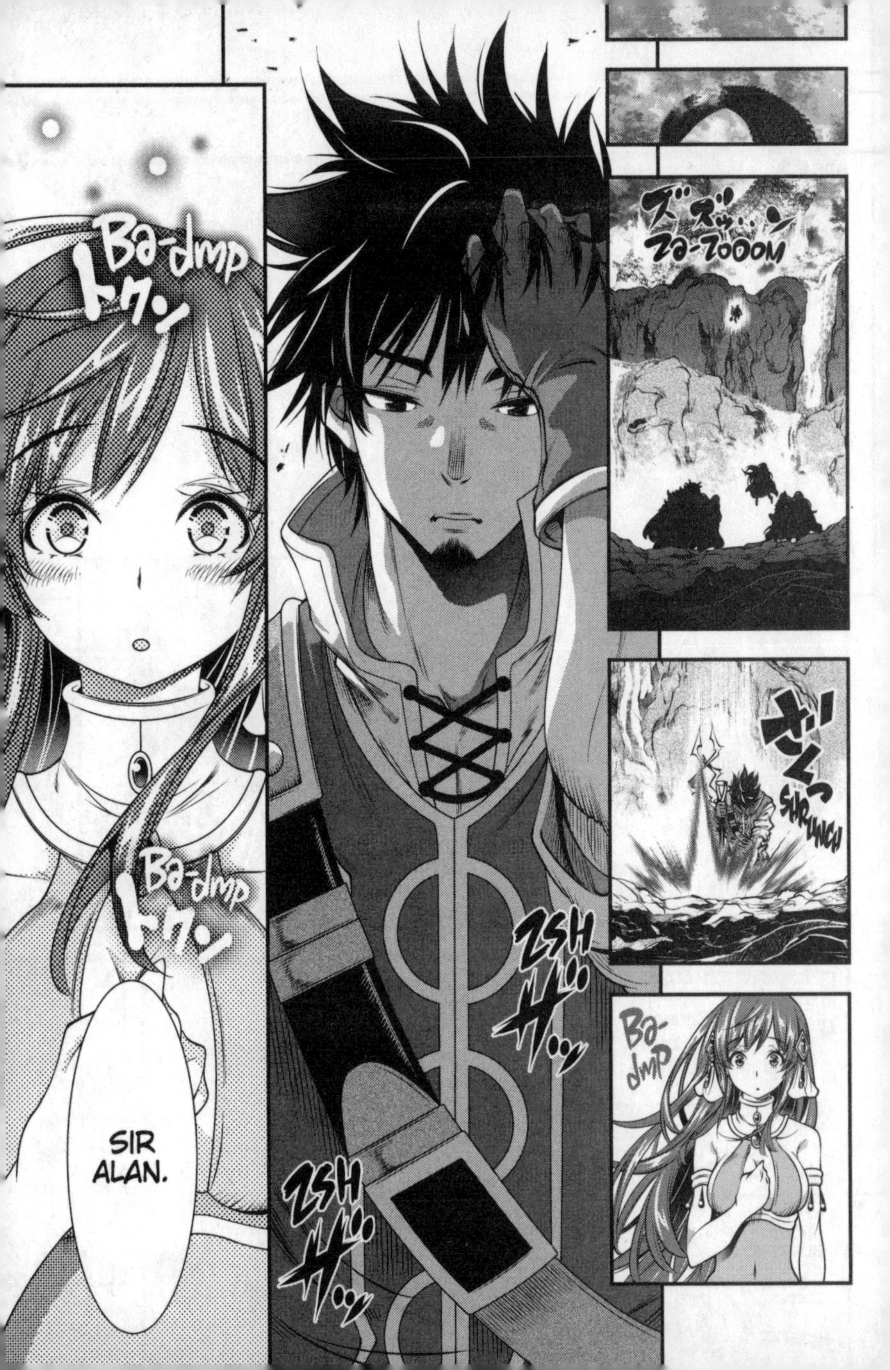
ズズッ…ン
Za-ZOOOM
ざくっ
SHRUNCH
Ba-dmp
ZSH
ザッ
ZSH
ザッ
Ba-dmp
トクン
Ba-dmp
トクン
SIR ALAN.

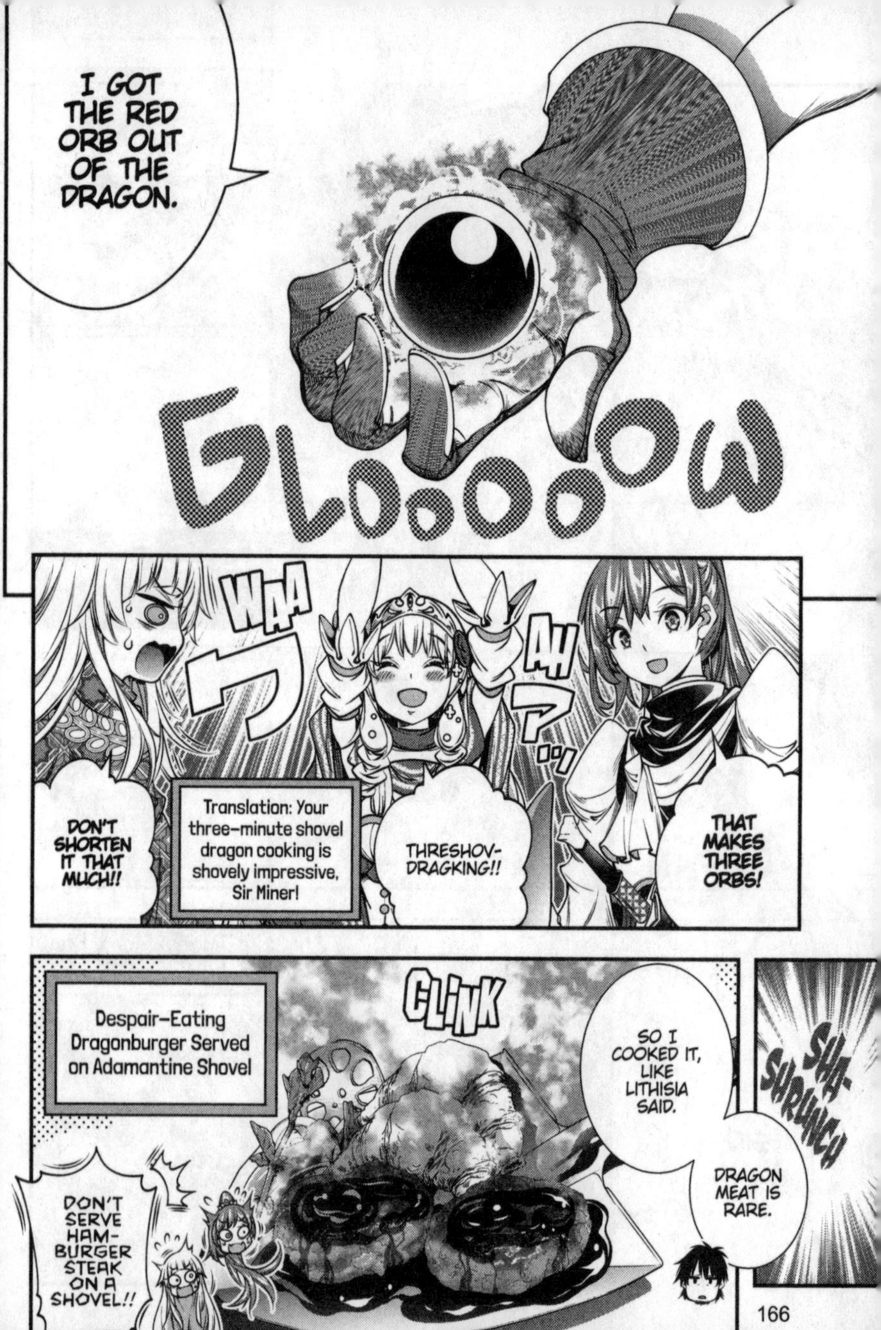
I GOT THE RED ORB OUT OF THE DRAGON.
GLOOOOOW
AH
THAT MAKES THREE ORBS!
WAA
THRESHOV-DRAGKING!!
Translation: Your three-minute shovel dragon cooking is shovely impressive, Sir Miner!
DON'T SHORTEN IT THAT MUCH!!
SHA-SHRUNCH
CLINK
SO I COOKED IT, LIKE LITHISIA SAID.
DRAGON MEAT IS RARE.
Despair-Eating Dragonburger Served on Adamantine Shovel
DON'T SERVE HAMBURGER STEAK ON A SHOVEL!!

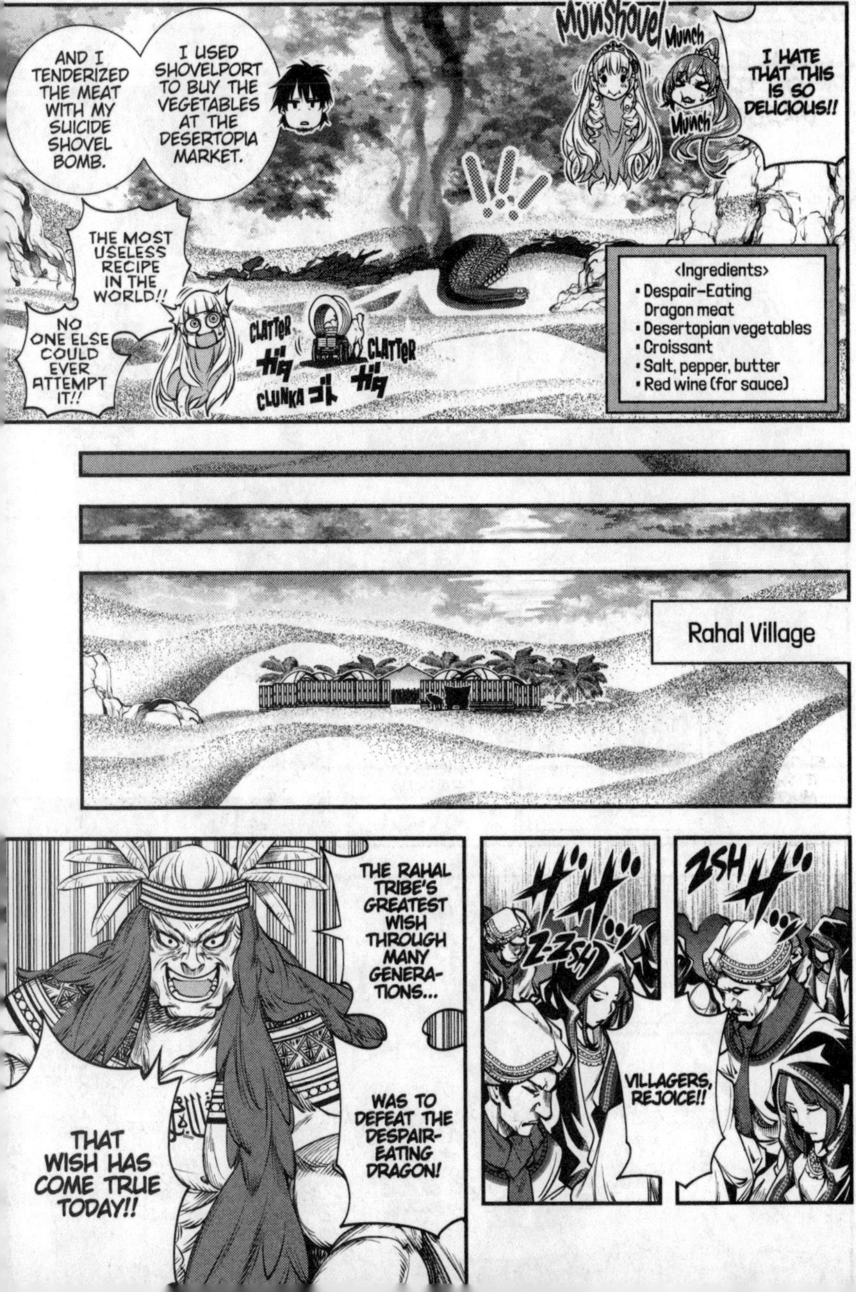

Munshovel
Munch
Munch
I HATE THAT THIS IS SO DELICIOUS!!
I USED SHOVELPORT TO BUY THE VEGETABLES AT THE DESERTOPIA MARKET.
AND I TENDERIZED THE MEAT WITH MY SUICIDE SHOVEL BOMB.
<Ingredients>
• Despair-Eating Dragon meat
• Desertopian vegetables
• Croissant
• Salt, pepper, butter
• Red wine (for sauce)
CLATTER ガタ
CLUNKA ゴト
CLATTER ガタ
THE MOST USELESS RECIPE IN THE WORLD!!
NO ONE ELSE COULD EVER ATTEMPT IT!!
Rahal Village
ZSH ザッ
VILLAGERS, REJOICE!!
ザザッ
Z-ZSH
THE RAHAL TRIBE'S GREATEST WISH THROUGH MANY GENERA-TIONS...
WAS TO DEFEAT THE DESPAIR-EATING DRAGON!
THAT WISH HAS COME TRUE TODAY!!

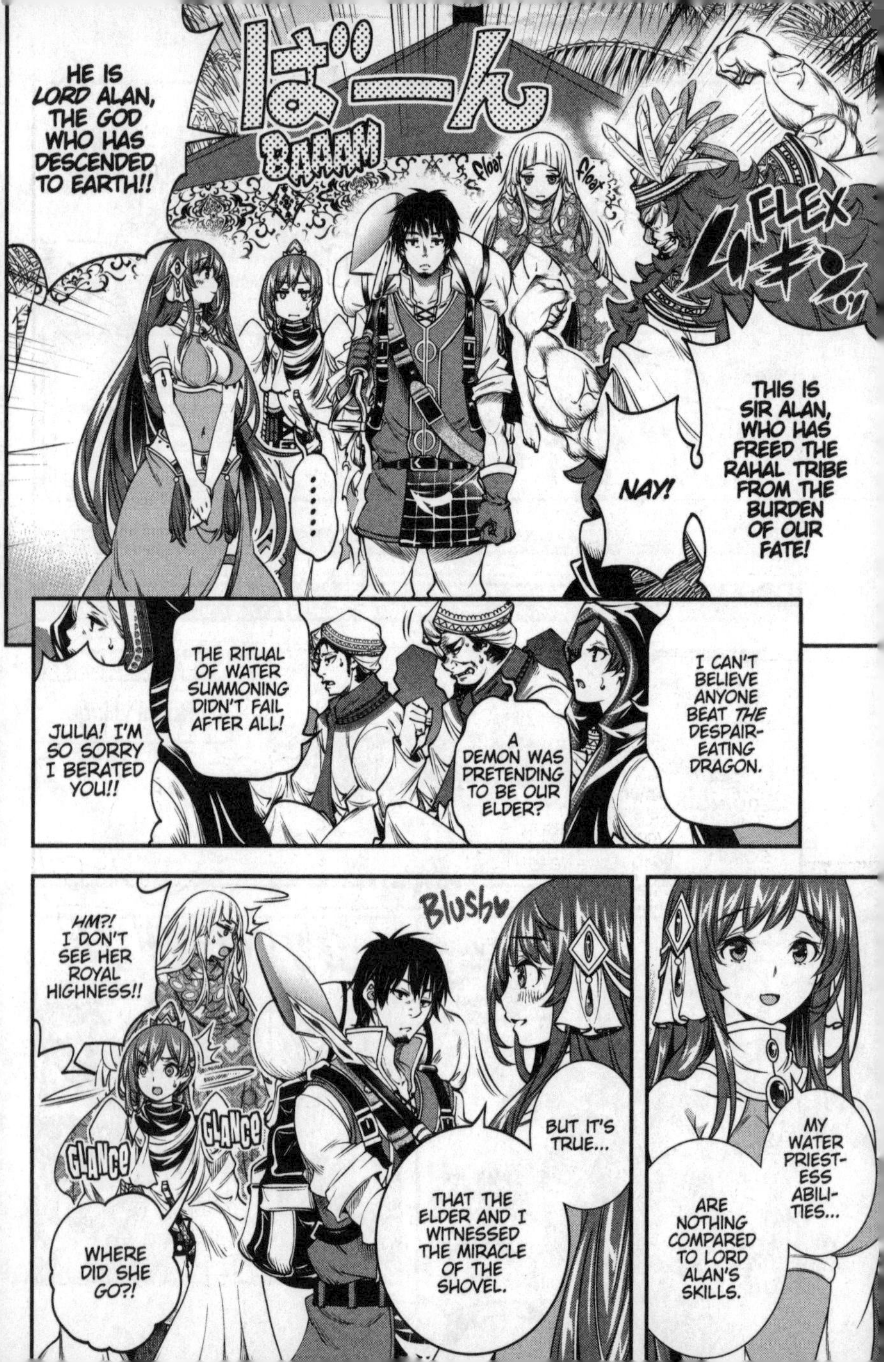
ばーん
BAAAM
HE IS LORD ALAN, THE GOD WHO HAS DESCENDED TO EARTH!!
float float
ムキーン FLEX
THIS IS SIR ALAN, WHO HAS FREED THE RAHAL TRIBE FROM THE BURDEN OF OUR FATE!
NAY!
......
I CAN'T BELIEVE ANYONE BEAT THE DESPAIR-EATING DRAGON.
A DEMON WAS PRETENDING TO BE OUR ELDER?
THE RITUAL OF WATER SUMMONING DIDN'T FAIL AFTER ALL!
JULIA! I'M SO SORRY I BERATED YOU!!
MY WATER PRIESTESS ABILITIES...
ARE NOTHING COMPARED TO LORD ALAN'S SKILLS.
Blush
BUT IT'S TRUE...
THAT THE ELDER AND I WITNESSED THE MIRACLE OF THE SHOVEL.
HM?! I DON'T SEE HER ROYAL HIGHNESS!!
GLANCE
GLANCE
WHERE DID SHE GO?!

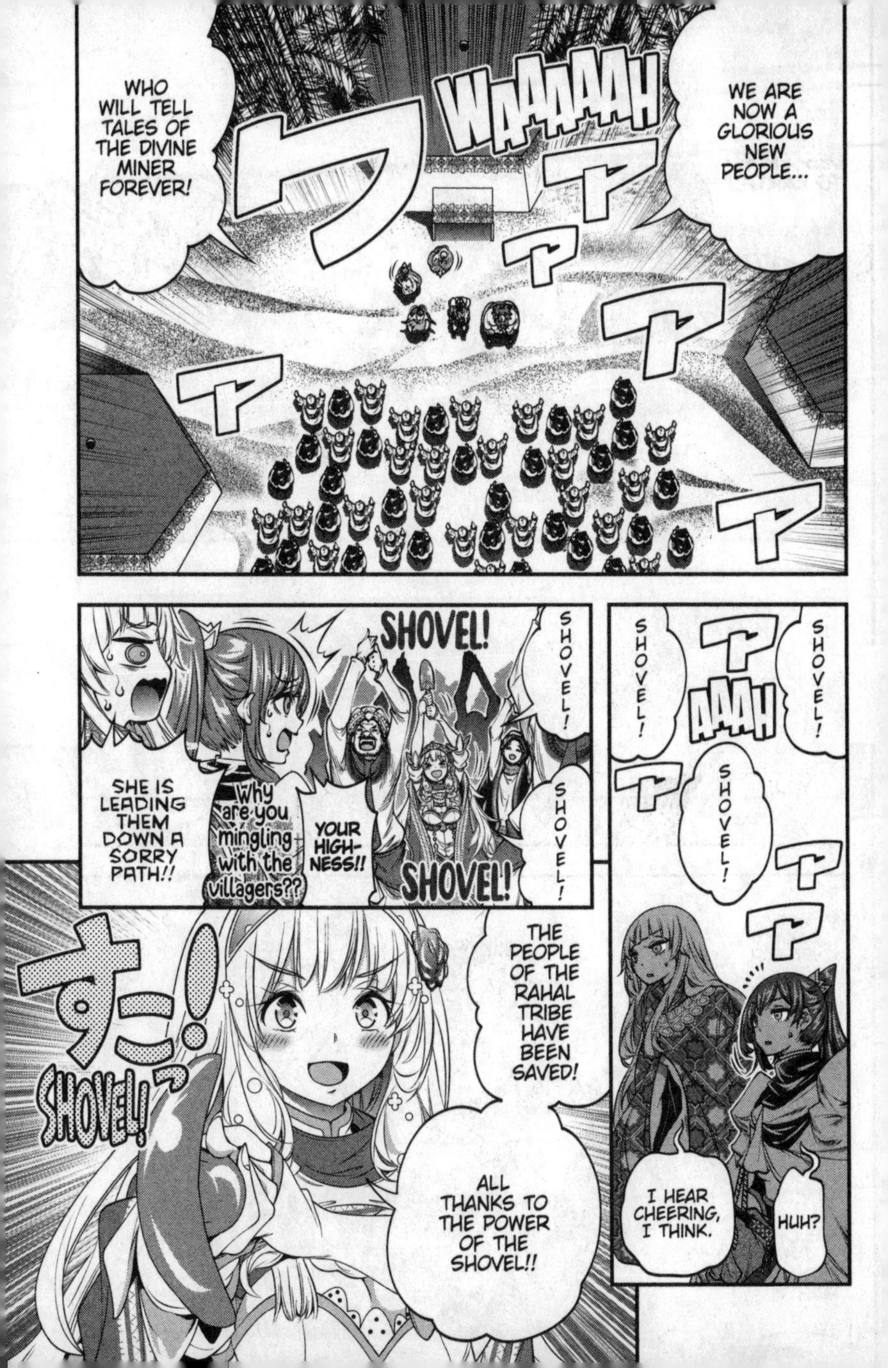
WE ARE NOW A GLORIOUS NEW PEOPLE...
WAAAAAH
ワァァァァァ
WHO WILL TELL TALES OF THE DIVINE MINER FOREVER!
SHOVEL!
SHOVEL!
AAAAH
アァァ
SHOVEL!
HUH?
I HEAR CHEERING, I THINK.
SHOVEL!
SHOVEL!
SHOVEL!
SHOVEL!
YOUR HIGHNESS!!
Why are you mingling with the villagers??
SHE IS LEADING THEM DOWN A SORRY PATH!!
THE PEOPLE OF THE RAHAL TRIBE HAVE BEEN SAVED!
ALL THANKS TO THE POWER OF THE SHOVEL!!
すこ!
SHOVEL!

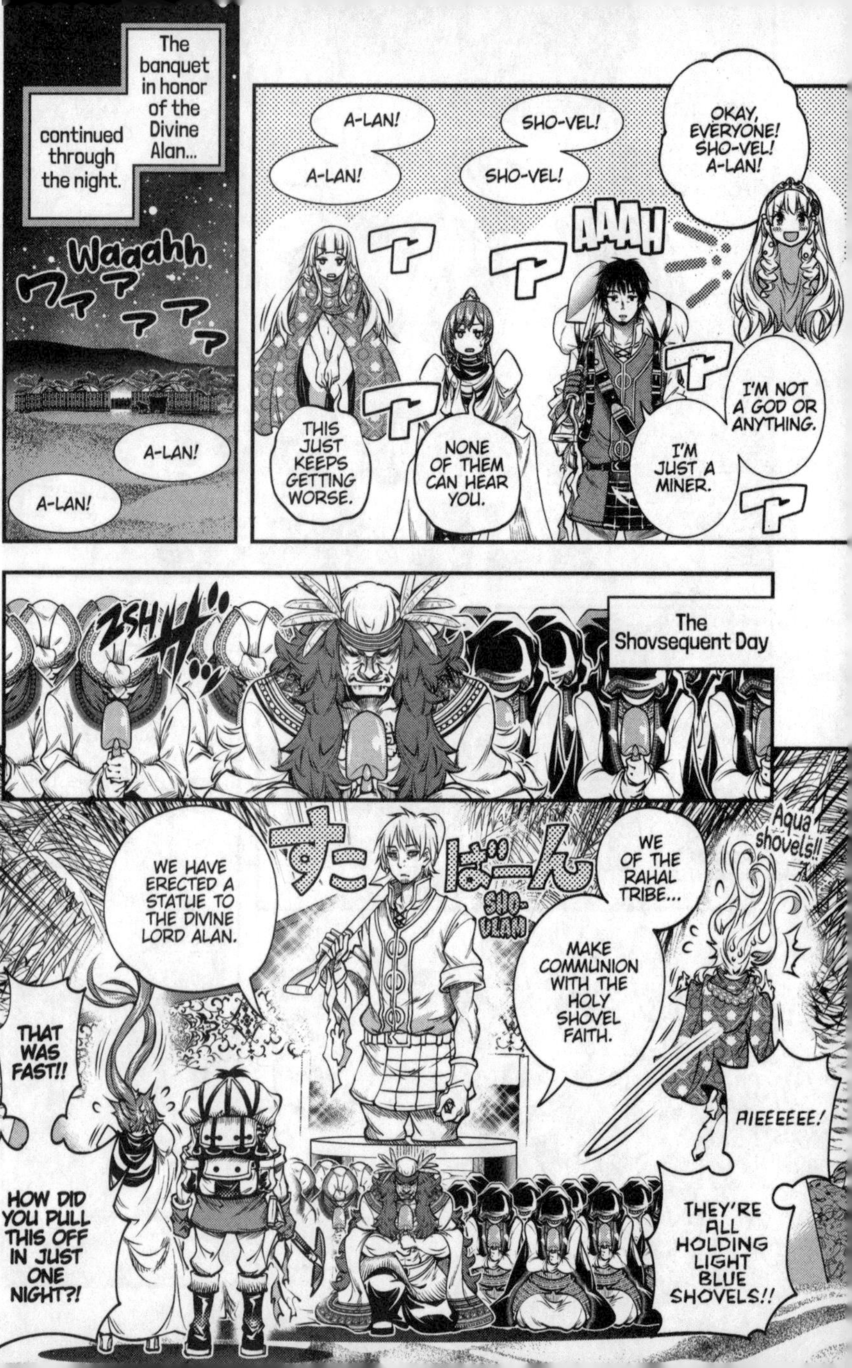
OKAY, EVERYONE! SHO-VEL! A-LAN!
SHO-VEL!
SHO-VEL!
A-LAN!
A-LAN!
AAAH
ア
ア
ア
I'M NOT A GOD OR ANYTHING.
I'M JUST A MINER.
ア
ア
NONE OF THEM CAN HEAR YOU.
THIS JUST KEEPS GETTING WORSE.
The banquet in honor of the Divine Alan...
continued through the night.
Waaahh
ワァァァァ
A-LAN!
A-LAN!
The Shovsequent Day
ZSH
Aqua shovels!!
WE OF THE RAHAL TRIBE...
MAKE COMMUNION WITH THE HOLY SHOVEL FAITH.
すこばーん
SHO-VLAM
WE HAVE ERECTED A STATUE TO THE DIVINE LORD ALAN.
AIEEEEEE!
THEY'RE ALL HOLDING LIGHT BLUE SHOVELS!!
THAT WAS FAST!!
HOW DID YOU PULL THIS OFF IN JUST ONE NIGHT?!

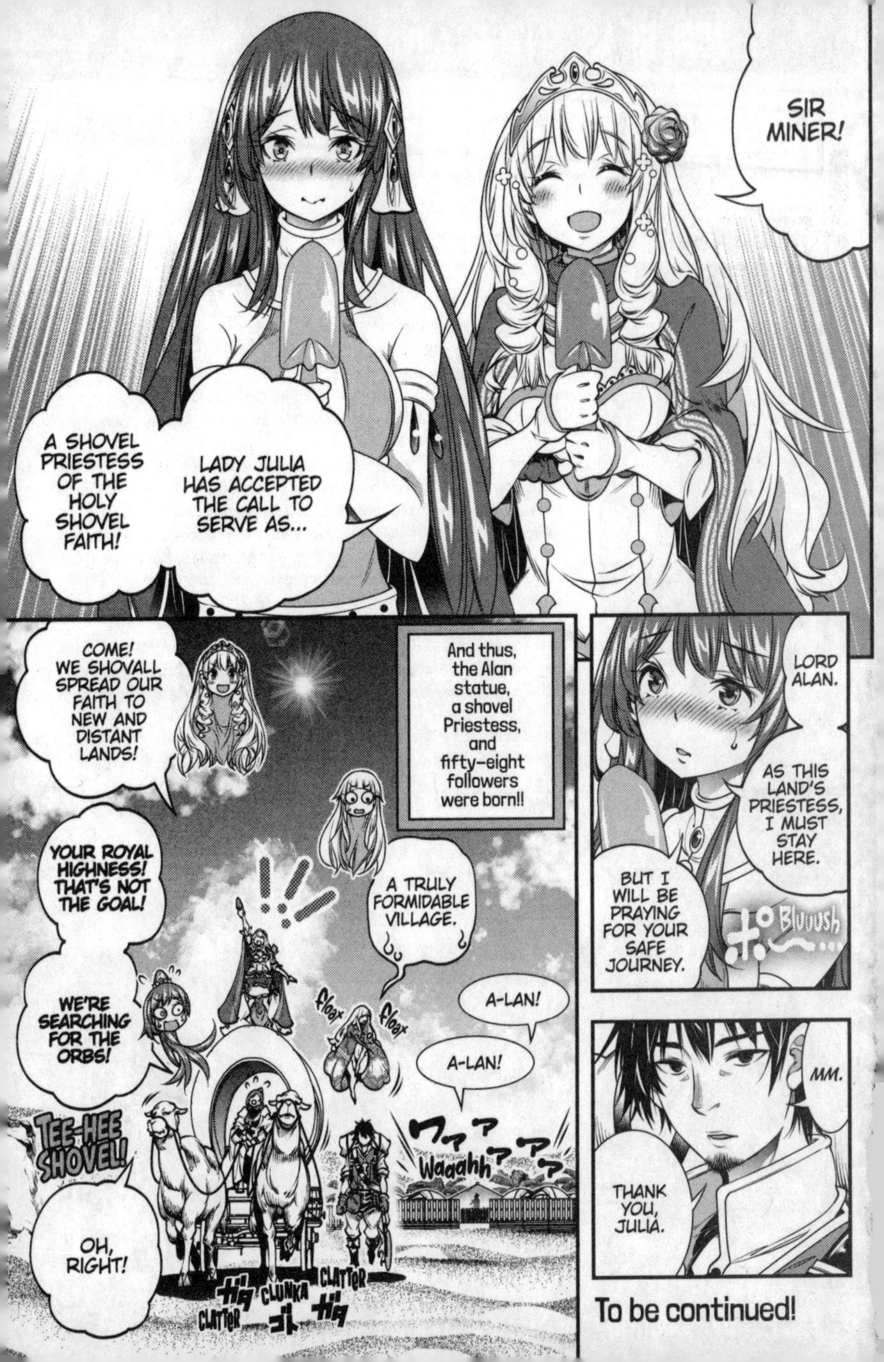

SIR MINER!
LADY JULIA HAS ACCEPTED THE CALL TO SERVE AS...
A SHOVEL PRIESTESS OF THE HOLY SHOVEL FAITH!
LORD ALAN.
AS THIS LAND'S PRIESTESS, I MUST STAY HERE.
BUT I WILL BE PRAYING FOR YOUR SAFE JOURNEY.
Bluuush
MM.
THANK YOU, JULIA.
To be continued!
And thus, the Alan statue, a shovel Priestess, and fifty-eight followers were born!!
A TRULY FORMIDABLE VILLAGE.
COME! WE SHOVALL SPREAD OUR FAITH TO NEW AND DISTANT LANDS!
YOUR ROYAL HIGHNESS! THAT'S NOT THE GOAL!
floax floax
A-LAN!
A-LAN!
WE'RE SEARCHING FOR THE ORBS!
Waaahh
TEE-HEE SHOVEL!
OH, RIGHT!
CLATTER
CLUNKA
CLATTER
CLATTER

SEVEN SEAS ENTERTAINMENT PRESENTS

THE INVINCIBLE SHOVEL

Vol. 2

art by RENJI FUKUHARA / story by YASOHACHI TSUCHISE / character design by HAGURE YUUKI

TRANSLATION
Alethea & Athena Nibley

ADAPTATION
Jamal Joseph Jr.

LETTERING
Arbash Mughal

COVER DESIGN
Kris Aubin

LOGO DESIGN
George Panella

EDITOR
Peter Adrian Behravesh

PREPRESS TECHNICIAN
iannon Rasmussen-Silverstein

PRODUCTION ASSOCIATE
Christa Miesner

PRODUCTION MANAGER
Lissa Pattillo

MANAGING EDITOR
Julie Davis

ASSOCIATE PUBLISHER
Adam Arnold

PUBLISHER
Jason DeAngelis

Seven Seas press and purchase enquiries can be sent to Marketing Manager Lianne Sentar at press@gomanga.com. Information regarding the distribution and purchase of digital editions is available from Digital Manager CK Russell at digital@gomanga.com.

ISBN: 978-1-64827-445-9
Printed in Canada
First Printing: November 2021
10 9 8 7 6 5 4 3 2 1

READING DIRECTIONS

This book reads from ***right to left***, Japanese style. If this is your first time reading manga, you start reading from the top right panel on each page and take it from there. If you get lost, just follow the numbered diagram here. It may seem backwards at first, but you'll get the hang of it! Have fun!!

1
2
3
4
5
6
7
8
9

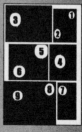